POLITICIZING MAGIC

An Anthology of Russian and Soviet Fairy Tales

EDITED BY MARINA BALINA,

HELENA GOSCILO, AND

MARK LIPOVETSKY

NORTHWESTERN UNIVERSITY PRESS

EVANSTON, ILLINOIS

Northwestern University Press

www.nupress.northwestern.edu

Copyright © 2005 by Northwestern University Press. Published 2005. All rights reserved.

Printed in the United States of America

10 9 8 7 6 5 4 3 2

ISBN-13: 978-0-8101-2031-0 (cloth)
ISBN-10: 0-8101-2031-3 (cloth)
ISBN-13: 978-0-8101-2032-7 (paper)
ISBN-10: 0-8101-2032-1 (paper)

Library of Congress Cataloging-in-Publication Data

Politicizing magic : an anthology of Russian and Soviet fairy tales / edited by Marina Balina, Helena Goscilo, and Mark Lipovetsky.

p. cm.

Includes bibliographical references.

ISBN 0-8101-2031-3 (cloth : alk. paper) — ISBN 0-8101-2032-1 (pbk. : alk. paper)

1. Fairy tales—Russian (Federation) 2. Fairy tales—Soviet Union. 3. Folk literature, Russian—Translations into English. 4. Folk literature, Soviet—Translations into English. I. Balina, Marina. II. Goscilo, Helena, 1945– III. Lipoveëtìskiæi, M. N. (Mark Naumovich)

GR203.17.P65 2005

398.2'0947—dc22

2005010140

⊛ The paper used in this publication meets the minimum requirements of the American National Standard for Information Sciences—Permanence of Paper for Printed Library Materials, ANSI Z39.48-1992.

POLITICIZING MAGIC

Barbara Landay
W177N10124 Whitetail Run
Germantown, WI 53022

For Felix J. Oinas, the supreme bogatyr of Slavic folkloristics

CONTENTS

FOREWORD

Anyone surfing the Internet in the early twenty-first century, with technology at an ambiguous peak and materialism at an all-time high, might be startled at the numerous Web sites featuring texts that recycle ageless folklore genres and, above all, fairy tales. Whether escapism or exoticized psychological landscapism, fairy tales resemble science fiction in their capacity to clothe the problematically familiar in a colorful symbolic garb that is accessible even to the intellectually challenged. Throughout the centuries, tales of happenstance and extraterrestrial heroism, inexplicable magical transformations, and narrative closures affirming eternal happiness have entranced all generations in disparate and diverse sociopolitical structures that nevertheless find common ground in folkloric modes of thought. Readers and viewers in the age of virtual reality are no exception. During an era that glorifies well-intentioned mediocrity—the ever-widening and intellectually sinking middle—Ivan the Fool in the contemporary guise of bumbling Gump remains alive and well in Hollywoodized America and, no doubt, throughout the world. Today's lottery winners are yesteryear's credulous fairy-tale protagonists. The modern Cinderella continues to toil and to toilette in virtually all cultures, from ash-filled British and Russian hearths to California's fast-dollared streets, reaping magical, logic-defying rewards in such celluloid fantasies as the Stalinist *Radiant Path* (*Svetlyi put'*,

1940, Grigory Alexandrov), the Stagnation-era blockbuster *Moscow Doesn't Believe in Tears* (*Moskva slezam ne verit,* 1979, Vladimir Menshov), Hollywood's Julia Roberts vehicle *Pretty Woman* (1990, Garry Marshall), and the recent screen adaptations of the *Harry Potter* and *Lord of the Rings* industry.

Soviet Russia, however, elaborated a very specific relationship to fantasy and wonderland, harnessing the fairy tale's teleological protagonist to socialist realist do-gooders and achievers (Gaidar's group-loyal Malchish-Kibalchish, Kataev's "consciousness-raised," petal-tearing little girl), the magic helper to benevolent older Soviet "mentors" (Kataev's anonymous kindly old woman, Lagin's ethnically suspect but politically useful Khottabych, Bazhov's rich but anticapitalist Mistress of the Copper Mountain), and the happy ending to the "radiant future" of a classless paradise (in Gaidar, Tolstoy, Lagin, and Kataev). That same politicized paradigm, though fragmented and antithetical in value, functions just as centrally in the satirized worlds of Zamyatin, Shvarts, Gorin, Shukshin, and the Strugatsky brothers. All of these works blatantly counter Vladimir Nabokov's apodictic assertion that "literature is not a dog carrying a message in its teeth." Indeed, their messages appear in oversized italics and rely on the hermeneutical drumbeat of emphatic iteration (repetition, conveniently, being a cardinal feature of fairy tales). It is no coincidence that the premier Soviet directors of fairy-tale screen adaptations, Alexander Ptushko and Alexander Rou, thrived during Stalinism—an era dominated by the brutally utopian slogan: "We were born to make fairy tales come true."[1] In accord with the vertical axis of Russian fairy tales, in 1935 Alexey Stakhanov enacted time-defying wonders in the underworld of the Donbass coal mines, and Valery Chkalov, in an unlikely synthesis of Finist and Ivan the Fool, soared high above territorial borders on his metal magic carpet—Stalin's favorite machine, the airplane.[2] Pilots renowned for their skill bore the folkloric name of "Stalin's falcons," and the populace enshrined the Leader in the thrice-tenth kingdom of the Kremlin through a "fakelore" that glorified his magical omnipotence.[3] No other era in Soviet history embraced folklore for pragmatic ends with comparable gusto and effectiveness, just as no other twentieth-century literary fairy tales have so decisively shaped an entire nation's collective unconscious. An understanding of the formative role played by Stalinist fairy tales provides its own "golden key" to Soviet culture and the mentality that credited the eventual advent of the radiant future.

The contents and structure of *Politicizing Magic* aim to spotlight the specifics of that strategic rhetorical adoption of national variations on universal collective models of human conduct. Divided into three sections, each preceded by an introduction, this collection consists of (1) Russia's most popular folkloric tales; (2) literary texts that transplant fairy-tale topoi to the realm of Soviet realia in a spirit of stirring heroism; (3) works of Soviet fiction and drama that ironically subvert the optimism of the fairy-tale paradigm while preserving its constitutive features.

PLANNED PARENTHOOD AND BIRTH

A shared passion for Russian folklore and a fascination with its manifold appropriative recastings in Soviet culture gave birth to this project à trois. Within our troika, the moving spirit behind the enterprise was Marina, who conceived of the Idea and set it in motion. Mark's dissertation at Ekaterinburg University and his subsequent publications on the genre of the fairy tale made him a "natural" collaborator. I found the role of a folkloric "third" irresistible because the enthusiasm for folklore ignited by Felix Oinas during my stint at Indiana University many moons ago redoubled in the early 1990s, when I elaborated a multimedia survey of Russian fairy tales at the University of Pittsburgh. From the outset we designated the anthology for classroom use in courses on folklore, culture, and literature—not exclusively within the framework of Russian studies.

Our omission of nineteenth-century literary fairy tales might strike readers as willfully arbitrary, particularly in light of the collection edited by N. A. Listikova, *The Russian Literary Fairy Tale*

(*Russkaia literaturnaia skazka*, 1989). The decisive difference, however, between the entries in that volume—by Karamzin, Zhukovsky, Pogorelsky, Somov, Odoevsky, Saltykov-Shchedrin, Dostoevsky, Turgenev, Tolstoy, Leskov, Remizov, Charskaya, Andreyev—and those we have anthologized is the latter's consistency of unambiguously ideological perspective. Whereas, under the influence of Herder and E. T. A. Hoffmann, nineteenth-century authors explored complex issues of art, morality, immortality, and the irrational through a modernized reassemblage of key folkloric elements, the Soviets appropriated the fairy-tale paradigm wholesale for propagandistic purposes as unproblematically as they requisitioned palaces, museums, and private estates. In that sense the freighted simplicity of the folkloric fairy tale differs radically from the nature of its orthodox Soviet literary counterpart and only slightly less from its anti-Soviet "rebuttals." In the latter two, the challenge to today's critic stems not from "decoding the message," but from analyzing the techniques of selective borrowing that on the textual level create a psychologically seductive and credible utopia—or, in its deconstructed form, dystopia. Whereas solemn exaltation presides over the Soviet utopia and its ideals, the double vision inherent in dystopia shades into irony and moments of grotesque hilarity that calmly alternate with savage cruelty and sudden death (Zamyatin, Shvarts, Gorin) so familiar to readers of folkloric fairy tales. Ultimately, the inclusion of nineteenth-century literary fairy tales would have violated the coherence of the volume.

MATURATION AND EMIGRATION

While working with available translations of the fairy tales that appear in this volume, we checked them against the originals and edited them—some lightly (*The Old Genie Khottabych*), others heavily (*The Golden Key, The Dragon*)—in the interests of accuracy, fluency, and the elimination of Briticisms and archaisms. We opted to offer fresh translations of the tales in part 1 from Alexander Afanasev's standard anthology of fairy tales only because Norbert Guterman's

excellent renditions into English sound somewhat dated to the contemporary student unfamiliar with such relics as "furbelows" and
"twain." Since the existent English version of the "Tale of the Military
Secret" proved unusable, we translated it anew as well. Translations
of the tales in part 1 from Afanasev and of "Tale of the Military Secret"
belong to Helena Goscilo. We thank Seth Graham for translating Zamyatin's ironic narratives and the folkloric "Magic Mirror," and
Christopher Hunter and Larissa Rudova for performing this metamorphosis on the works by Gorin and Kataev. A full listing of the
translators, translations, and the Russian originals of the texts in this
volume is provided in the "Translators and Sources" section at the end
of the book. Several of the selections in this volume are excerpts from
the full works; omitted passages of text are denoted by ellipses en-
closed in brackets.

ASSIMILATION/COMMUNICATION

A word about transliteration: for the primary texts we have relied on
a mixture of systems for the practical purpose of enabling Anglophone readers to approximate Russian names with reasonable pho-
netic accuracy. Our various introductions share this pragmatic goal;
however, the notes resort to Library of Congress transliteration for
Russian sources, which in any event will be meaningful only to readers with a knowledge of Russian.

Throughout we have retained the word "bogatyr" (nonitalicized),
since the original Russian struck us as preferable to its awkwardly explanatory English equivalent, "epic hero." One "verst," an antiquated
Russian measure of distance that we have preserved for flavor alone,
equals slightly more than half a mile.

DEDICATION

The study of Russian folklore would be a dramatically different, and
indisputably lesser, animal were it not for the numerous, erudite,

wide-ranging contributions to sundry aspects of that folklore by the extraordinary Felix J. Oinas. We therefore dedicate this volume to his memory, with boundless respect and admiration—and in my case with loving gratitude for some of the finest, intellectually richest, and most laughter-filled hours of my checkered graduate experience.

Helena Goscilo

NOTES

1. Ptushko completed a screen version of Aleksei Tolstoy's *The Golden Key* in 1939, and of *The Stone Flower* (from Pavel Bazhov's collection titled *The Malachite Casket*) in 1946, which are more or less the dates of Rou's most famous screen adaptations of Russian fairy tales: *Vasilisa the Beautiful* (1939) and *Koshchey the Deathless* (1944). In other words, four of Russia's best-known celluloid fairy tales emerged during Stalinism. The heavily edited, dubbed film released under Ptushko's name in the West as *The Sword and the Dragon* has the title *Il'ia Muromets* in the full Russian original; it conflates several folkloric tales about the intrepid hero, and appeared in 1956.

2. The Leader's avian romance with the skies, which Katerina Clark briefly discusses in terms of paternal-filial relations, found its way into subsequent works, such as Vasily Aksyonov's story "The Steel Bird" (1965) and the post-Soviet pop-rock group Liube's retro song, "The Little Eagles" ("Orliata," 1996). See Katerina Clark, *The Soviet Novel: History as Ritual* (Bloomington and Indianapolis: Indiana University Press, 2000), 124–29.

3. For samples and analysis of these pseudo-folkloric creations, see Frank J. Miller, *Folklore for Stalin: Russian Folklore and Pseudofolklore of the Stalin Era* (Armonk, N.Y.: M. E. Sharpe, 1990).

POLITICIZING MAGIC

PART

I

Folkloric Fairy Tales

INTRODUCTION
✃❧

HELENA GOSCILO

PERENNIAL YET MYSTERIOUS ENCHANTMENT

The abiding and universal appeal of folkloric fairy tales poses a cultural enigma: do these brief, indefatigably repeated narratives seduce the imagination through magic, fantasy, and vivid, unforgettable personae as a pleasurable mode of escapism?[1] Or do they fulfill a pragmatic function, positing practical solutions (assimilated via unconscious identification) to typical psychological dilemmas firmly grounded in everyday experience? Are fairy tales fanciful flights providing respite from, and wishful compensation for, lived reality—or are they a fundamental part of that very reality, couched in symbolic form? Whether exercising the mysterious lure of conjury, illuminating mythic origins, or functioning as paradigmatic keys to problems, to what extent do fairy tales reflect the ethos and social mores of the cultures that produce them? Whom does their presumed audience comprise? In short, what do fairy tales strive for by endlessly iterating a minuscule number of predictable plots in multiple guises? If they have a more profound and submerged agenda than mere entertainment, what is that agenda and may it be generalized across generations and cultures?

Perhaps the most striking aspect of folkloric fairy tales, and one that urges interpretation, is the complete absence of "depth" and of

even rudimentary analysis within the tales themselves.[2] Unlike literary fiction, they eschew explicit psychology and motivation; rely on a
minimal, paratactic style; usually proceed as a series of actions indifferent to logical causation yet relentless in their teleological drive;
combine supernatural, fantastic events and transformations with
banalities and mechanical repetition of set phrases and situations;
and cap dispassionately reported scenes of mayhem, inconceivable
cruelty, and violence with a formulaic happy ending—the obligatory
utopian closure that allies the genre with totalitarian scenarios of a
secular paradise. Such flagrant contradictions and heterogeneity
invite readers to elaborate some coherent hermeneutical model
capable of accounting for these glaringly incompatible extremes. Indeed, the gratifyingly ample range of approaches advocated by both
Western and Slavic scholars over many decades pays homage to the
cryptic richness of the fairy-tale genre, while simultaneously compli-
cating the most basic issues it invariably raises.[3]

INJUNCTIONS TO INTERPRETATION

By now a classic of Russian structuralism and folkloric scholarship,
Vladimir Propp's rigorously systematic *Morphology of the Folktale*
(1928) inventories the motifs that organize the fairy-tale plot and,
with impeccable logic, charts their immutable sequence. Scrupu-
lously confining himself to classification, Propp on principle ignores
the significance of the tales' contents. While invaluable for revealing
the formal consistency of tales, *Morphology* (subsequently refined
upon by E. M. Meletinsky)[4] categorically dismisses any attempt to
illuminate what fairy tales are about and why they beguile children
more potently and enduringly than any other genre.[5] Max Lüthi's for-
malist *European Folktale* (1947) extends Propp's paradigm to posit a
stylistic model of the genre, which Lüthi, however, conceives as literary. Identifying one-dimensionality, depthlessness, abstract style,
isolation, and universal interconnection, in addition to sublimation
and all-inclusiveness, as the fairy tale's constitutive features (Lüthi

4–80), Lüthi ascribes wish fulfillment to the genre on a profound spiritual level (81–106). Such an approach to the genre neatly explains the wholesale Soviet adoption of fairy-tale topoi for its portrayal of a constantly deferred "radiant future" that never eventuates in reality and therefore requires hyperbolic compensatory power in the rhetoric of its cultural texts.

Precisely where Propp and such early structuralists as A. Nikiforov fall (or stop) short, Bruno Bettelheim's *Uses of Enchantment* (1975), a famous psychoanalytical investigation mainly of French and German versions of fairy tales, offers bounties.[6] Occasionally mechanistic, arbitrary, and overdetermined, Bettelheim's study advances a content-based thesis. Fairy tales, he riskily maintains, grapple with the integration of human personality and inscribe immemorial rites of passage rooted primarily, though not exclusively, in sexuality. Controversial and recently discredited partly because of Richard Pollack's "exposé" biography of its author, *The Uses of Enchantment* nonetheless is obligatory reading for specialists in fairy tales, whatever their resistance to neo-Freudianism.[7] The Freudian concepts espoused by Bettelheim have enormous explanatory power, especially in light of the centrality accorded family and familial relations within the genre. Fairy tales, he contends, captivate children because they facilitate their maturation, subliminally furnishing ways of negotiating the ostensibly insurmountable psychological obstacles that confront them in an alienatingly adult world. How fairy tales accomplish this feat Bettelheim illustrates with copious exegetical examples. What Bettelheim fails to elucidate, and apparently finds irrelevant, is the appeal of fairy tales to adults—a blinkered omission that casts a certain naïveté over the study, which presupposes a fairy-tale readership primarily of children. In light of the sustained, large-scale Soviet co-optation of fairy-tale formulas, his perspective lacks historicity—unless, of course, one summarily concludes that Soviet culture was perpetually arrested at an infantile stage.

The conviction that fairy tales symbolically inscribe psychic phenomena likewise underpins Jungian readings, from Marie-Louise von

Franz's *Interpretation of Fairy Tales* (1970) to Clarissa Pinkola Estés's *Women Who Run with the Wolves* (1992)[8] and *The Maiden King* by Robert Bly and Marion Woodman (1998).[9] These critics, however, transfer the emphasis from sexuality to spirituality. Guided by Jung's essay "The Phenomenology of the Spirit in Fairy Tales," they focus on archetypes of the collective unconscious as manifested in the figures and patterns of the tales. This approach to the genre proves uncommonly productive for readers of Soviet texts structured around the genre's paradigms, as attested by Mark Lipovetsky's introduction to the third part of this collection.

Readers skeptical of psychological approaches to folklore have found Jack Zipes, indisputably the most prolific Western scholar of fairy tales, a more congenial explicator of the genre's import, primarily along lines of power politics. Zipes's sociohistorical analytical model takes into consideration not only cultural production and dissemination, but also gender and class. Examining the ideological components of fairy tales, Zipes, as an adherent of the Frankfurt school, unsurprisingly contends that ever since the late seventeenth century the self-serving interests of the dominant class (first aristocracy, then bourgeoisie) have undermined the subversive potential of the genuinely popular (i.e., folk) fairy tale through appropriatory revision. Zipes's neo-Marxist treatment of the genre tends to reduce consumers of fairy tales to involuntary collaborators with a political elite that is empowered to propagate class-marked values via its control of cultural production—a position consonant with the dynamics between tyrannical victimizer and victim inscribed in Yevgeny Shvarts's fairy-tale play *The Dragon*. Whereas Bettelheim (berated by Zipes for moralism and the misrepresentation of Freud) spotlights children as intuitive readers, Zipes dissects "authors" as ideologues determined to socialize children forcibly in their own image.[10] Arkady Gaidar's "Tale of the Military Secret" certainly lends credibility to such a view of authorial motivation, as noted in Marina Balina's introduction to the second part of the present volume.

Zipes's concerns overlap with those of feminists such as Marcia

Lieberman, Karen Rowe, Sandra Gilbert, Susan Gubar, and, to a lesser extent, Ruth B. Bottigheimer, who diagnose fairy tales as symptoms of their cultures' misogynistic traditions.[11] For feminists, the fairy tales favored by a given society reflect its gender biases. Accordingly, Americans' Disney-abetted passion for "Cinderella," "Sleeping Beauty," "Snow White," and "Beauty and the Beast" testifies to our culture's expediently sexist projection of women as passively compliant, self-sacrificing, beauty-obsessed creatures devoid of agency.[12] The inclusion of Russian fairy tales in Western feminists' sphere of reference would necessitate a modification of their critique, for, Russian society's notorious ageless sexism notwithstanding, some of Russia's favorite tales ("The Feather of Finist the Bright Falcon," "The Maiden Tsar," and "The Frog Princess") reverse the gender roles in the hackneyed paradigm that feminists deem generically quintessential.

Unlike the majority of their Western counterparts, contemporary Russian folklorists continue to concentrate their scholarly energies on classification, typologies, and performers/tellers of tales (*skaziteli*). Decades ago, Alexander Afanasev, Pyotr Bogatyryov, and Roman Jakobson all emphasized the collective origins of the fairy tale, the latter two conceptualizing it as an evolving entity passed from generation to generation and subject to the prophylactic strictures of each community's shared values.[13] Today, as then, such Russian specialists as Meletinsky essentially concur that a fairy tale "fulfills the role of a social utopia" (Jakobson 4:99) or, in Boris Sokolov's more mythological model, a dream compensation entailing, above all, the conquest of nature. These features of the fairy tale, of course, rendered it a genre supremely suited to the priorities of the Soviet Union's propaganda machine, which maximally exploited its miraculous and utopian attributes in virtually every cultural genre.

Anglophone scholarship on the Russian fairy tale is relatively scant. Maria Kravchenko's highly readable *World of the Russian Fairy Tale* (1987) belongs to the historical trend in folkloristics, inasmuch as it seeks above all to establish the origins of the genre, principally in ancient rituals and beliefs.[14] Jack Haney's slim monograph *An Intro-*

duction to the Russian Folktale (1999)—part of an impressive multi-volume project—privileges description over analysis, relies heavily on earlier studies, and advances no original thesis. Haney's summary of the major tendencies in Russian compilation, classification, and interpretation (chapters 1 and 2) slights the modern period and does not assess the political benefits to the Soviet state of championing genuine folklore and particularly fakelore.[15] Neither Kravchenko nor Haney grapples with the conundrum of the genre's colossal fascination for a young audience, an omission that indexes Anglophone Slavic folklorists' remoteness from current trends in Western scholarship.

THE CANON

Whereas Charles Perrault assembled the classic French collection of fairy tales in 1697, and the Grimm brothers followed suit with its German equivalent in 1812, what in modern times constitutes the standard Russian repertory appeared only in the mid-nineteenth century, compiled by Alexander Afanasev under the title of *Popular Russian Fairy Tales* (*Narodnye russkie skazki,* 1855–64).[16] The approximately 600 tales in Afanasev's three-volume anthology represent an oral tradition familiar to all Russians—a limitless source for borrowings by High Culture, in particular music and literature, ever since its publication. The impressively vulgar tales expunged from the official edition, such as "The Magic Ring," which we include in the present volume, were printed later in, of all places, Geneva, Switzerland, and restored to Russia only after glasnost.

As a living oral form, thus subject to multiple variations depending on the performance or recitation of the given work (and Afanasev's collection includes variants of individual tales), the traditional Russian fairy tale consists almost exclusively of fast-paced, plot-driven, formulaic narratives that pit mundane protagonists against apparently invincible enemies; resort to magic; incorporate proverbs, riddles, and verbal formulae; and end happily.[17] The plots, characters, and

10

motifs transcend national boundaries (i.e., the bulk of Russian tales are versions of narratives shared by western Europe), yet concrete details within fairy tales are endemic to Russia (e.g., Ivan the Fool lies on a Russian stove, the musical merchant Sadko strums the uniquely Russian *guslia,* the Russian bogatyrs [epic heroes] Ilya Muromets and Alyosha Popovich serve at Prince Vladimir's court, etc.).[18] This apparent paradox accommodates both the universalizing models of feminist and psychoanalytical criticism, on the one hand, and on the other, the empirically oriented analyses of the anthropological and sociohistorical schools, which construct their arguments on the basis of particularized conditions in specific contexts. The most tenable approach to fairy tales, in my view, is synthetic, drawing on structuralism, psychology, feminism, and sociology. Social values, including notions of gender, shape mental habits both individually and collectively, while themselves simultaneously adjusting to the aesthetics of an established, if dynamic, genre as practiced in a concrete milieu. Accordingly, the most productive reading of fairy tales requires negotiation among several interpretive models that individually are over-inclined to totalizing strategies. The portion of Sandra Gilbert and Susan Gubar's *Madwoman in the Attic* (1979) devoted to an analysis of "Snow White" stands out as an exemplar of a synthetic, multilayered reading that opens up the tale in rewardingly provocative ways.

THE PARADIGM

Russian "magical" fairy tales, like those of most nations, unfold a quest or rite of passage as a colorful, improbable adventure: slaying a dragon; creating an entire city overnight; rescuing a princess from an evil, uncanny ogre; and so forth.[19] The protagonist typically effects a watershed transition—from childhood to adolescence, from puberty to adulthood, from dependence to independence, from alienation to integration, from helplessness to control. The phenomenal effort expended on the central exploits (frequently cast as an exhausting journey) inevitably marks a new stage of life, which explains the frequency of marriage as an ultimate reward for triumph over adversity. Whether the surmounted hurdles be psychological (Bettelheim) or social (Zipes) or both (Gilbert and Gubar), fairy tales culminate in a victory over enemies and rivals achieved through a credulity-defying intermixture of ingenuity, sheer persistence, and fortuitously encountered magical resources.

Fairy-tale heroes largely divide into two contrastive types: the handsome, desirable prince, who is an object of competition among three sisters ("The Feather of Finist the Bright Falcon," "The Wicked Sisters"); or the irresponsible youngest of three sons, often signally named Ivan the Fool (Ivan Durachok), who lolls indolently on the stove or spends his days drinking in taverns until the decisive moment of action, usually undertaken in contest with his two older brothers ("The Three Kingdoms"). Both sorts of protagonists represent everyman, their generic names denoting their typological roles. Their female counterparts (both everywoman and universal ideal) appear as beautiful maidens awaiting rescue ("Tale of Prince Ivan, the Firebird, and the Gray Wolf"; Elsa in Shvarts's play) or assisting the heroes to attain their elevated status, which at the tale's conclusion they share vicariously through marriage to them. (Whereas Freudians and Jungians view these conjugal unions as a trope for desirable psychic wholeness, feminists and Marxists deplore them as female submission to repressive phallocentric institutions.) Exceptions include female warriors ("The Maiden Tsar") and wise maidens ("The Wise Maiden") distinguished by their military or intellectual and visionary prowess, and the extraordinary Swan Maiden, who, after a formidable display of magical panache, abandons her hapless husband Danilo in an eloquent flourish that would satisfy even the most exigent feminist ("Danilo the Luckless"). Tales such as "Maria Morevna," structured around a bipartite plot that casts the heroine as both imperious warrior and imprisoned victim, conflate the active-passive female paradigms.

Antagonists against whom the heroes and heroines pit their

courage and skill appear as siblings ("The Three Kingdoms"), step-parents ("The Magic Mirror," "Baba Yaga"), chance rivals ("Danilo the Luckless"), or miraculous hostile forces such as dragons, the Nightin-gale Robber, Koshchey the Deathless, and Baba Yaga. Jealousy, greed, and thirst for power most commonly operate as springboards to aggressive human enmity, though these motivations normally remain unstated, to be inferred by the reader. By contrast, supernatural fig-ures such as Koshchey the Deathless and Baba Yaga sooner incarnate eternal principles inhering in the "nature of things," their behavior a given that defies elucidation ("Maria Morevna," "Baba Yaga"). Whatever their identity, villains deploy trickery and miraculous forces whose ultimate futility is mandated by the genre's requisite happy ending, but whose pyrotechnics titillate the imagination.

Baba Yaga, by far the most popular and complex figure in Russian tales, merits special attention. A composite of contradictory traits, she encompasses the paradoxes of nature: life and death, destruction and renewal, the feminine and the masculine—the last opposition sym-bolized in the mortar and pestle that transport her through space and time ("Vasilisa the Beautiful"). As a "uroboric" entity, Baba Yaga unites fundamental polarities in a circle or ring that images the cycle of life.[20] Her dwelling on the border of the dark forest—a revolving hut mounted on chicken legs containing the symbolic life-giving and -depriving stove—testifies to her primal identity as all-embracing Nature or Mother Earth. Both villain and magic helper, in the latter hypostasis the gluttonous, time-controlling Baba Yaga ("Vasilisa the Beautiful") emerges as both practical provider and wise teacher dur-ing the young protagonist's enforced sojourn in her domain. Most fre-quently, she supplies males with a means of orientation (spools of thread, a rolling ball in "The Three Kingdoms") or modes of trans-portation (horses, eagles in "The Three Kingdoms") and through three seemingly impossible tasks teaches females the invaluable three D lessons—differentiation, duty, and domesticity.[21]

Fairy-tale magic helpers or wise counselors comprise a multifac-eted category, consisting above all of clever talking animals (from the three symbolic spheres of air, earth, and water—the birds, snakes, and fish of Shvarts's *Dragon*) whom the compassionate hero(ine) befriends or saves from death; beings such as the Great Drinker (Opivalo) and the Great Mountain (Gorynia); old men and women; and, intriguingly, Baba Yaga in her benevolent hypostasis. Enchanted maidens possessing special powers of metamorphosis likewise act as miraculous helpers, their feats of assistance crowned by marriage to the hero in a symbolic union of complementary principles.

Magic objects are a staple of the fairy tale and, given the genre's animistic nature, hardly differ from its supernatural personages. Water as a transforming entity plays a key role, especially the "water of death," which knits a dismembered body together, and "the water of life," which then animates it ("Tale of Prince Ivan, the Firebird, and the Gray Wolf"), as well as the water that increases and diminishes strength ("Ilya Muromets and the Dragon," "Maria Morevna"). Self-sufficient miraculous items include the self-spreading tablecloth, the self-playing dulcimer (*guslia*), the self-reciting psalter, the self-sewing embroidery needle ("The Feather of Finist the Bright Falcon"), and a host of implements and weapons. The flying carpet, the cap of invisibility (both in Shvarts's *Dragon*), the comb that metamorphoses into a forest, the handkerchief that turns into a river, and the like occur regularly, as do the mysteriously endowed apple, egg, seed, bone, mirror, thread, pin, ring, box, spindle, and feather. Metals function symbolically within the hierarchy of the fairy tale, with the progression from copper or brass to silver and finally to gold mapping a platonic ascent toward perfection or transcendence ("The Three Kingdoms"). Within this value system, the firebird occupies a unique niche as a symbol of illumination, of the ideal ("Tale of Prince Ivan, the Firebird, and the Gray Wolf"). Crystal mountains similarly symbolize elevated aspiration, though they tend to be plot-subordinated, installed rather unobtrusively as the magical furniture of the fairy-tale universe.

Any reader of fairy tales instantly notices the genre's relentless intercalation at all narrative levels of the number three, or what Propp calls trebling: three siblings, three stages, three helpers, three days, etc. (crucial to the Strugatsky brothers' "Tale of the Troika"). Bettelheim's explanation of the loaded numerology (3 = child and both parents, 3 = child and two rival siblings, 3 = the hero or heroine's distinguishing marks of sexual identity [penis and testicles, vagina and breasts]) minimizes the prevalence of triples in most religions and ancient rituals. As Erich Neumann astutely notes, the reason for the appearance of phenomena in threes should be sought in "the threefold articulation underlying all created things . . . most particularly . . . the three temporal stages of all growth (beginning-middle-end, birth-life-death, past-present-future)" (Neumann 228).[22] This symbolism, which recalls the Three Fates and the Sphinx's riddle, entails spinning and weaving—the occupation of countless wise maidens and other females in Russian tales. In "Vasilisa the Beautiful" the triple structure of temporality is materialized in the three riders over whom Baba Yaga as Nature has dominion.

A persuasive argument for reading fairy tales as symbolic narratives of universal rites of passage may, arguably, be found in several of the genre's formulas. The purposeful vagueness of openings ("once upon a time," "in a certain kingdom") locates the action temporally and geographically in the never-never land of anytime and anywhere—that is, always and everywhere. This generalizing tendency is reinforced by such self-erasing markers as "not near, not far," "a long time or a short time," randomly invoked fixed epithets ("beautiful maiden," "open field," "fine youth," "trusty steed"), and such "fillers" as "more beautiful than pen can describe," "quickly can a tale be spun, slowly is a real deed done," all doubling as oral techniques of retardation. Formulas likewise signal closure at tales' end, the most common being "and they lived happily ever after," but often supplemented or replaced by bravura rhymes, free-floating paronomasia, or the conventional mock insistence on reliable, sober witness-reporting: "I was there, and drank mead; it ran down my mustache but didn't go into my mouth."

CROSSING OVER AND DYING INTO LIFE

As numerous anthropologists and folklorists have remarked, in pursuing their quests the protagonists of fairy tales, like those of legends and myths, typically cross symbolically saturated boundaries. Whether in the form of flight to uncharted lands (the fabled "thrice-tenth kingdom"), descent into subterranean realms ("Three Kingdoms"), trespass into Baga Yaga's domain ("Maria Morevna"), voyage across the sea, or entry into mountains ("The Crystal Mountain"), castles, and animals' stomachs, these consequence-laden yet narratively understated traversals register initiation into a new phase of human development. The old self dies as a prerequisite for rebirth into a more mature or complete self: Vasilisa emerges from Baba Yaga's hut ready for marriage, just as Ivan the Fool exits the three kingdoms equipped to execute Baba Yaga's instructions and to make essential sacrifices—symbolized by feeding his own flesh to the eagle that carries him back to Russia, to his newly won status of happy groom and husband ("The Three Kingdoms"). In short, by eventually becoming the potential perpetuator of his family line and the guarantor of continuity, Ivan grows into the role that fulfills his social and "human" destiny.

Temporality plays an inestimable role in these scenarios, which frequently illustrate the pitfalls of premature actions and decisions (such as Ivan's precipitant incineration of the frog skin in "The Frog Princess") and the urge to postpone a psychically demanding commitment to a different mode of being. On first glance, the focus on a lack of readiness, often figured as voluntary or involuntary sleep ("The Maiden Tsar," "The Feather of Finist the Bright Falcon"), seems contradictory in a genre that embraces timelessness. Yet one of the fairy tale's salient features is precisely this sort of paradox, rooted in the inseparable oxymoronic polarities of life-death, beginning-end, high-low, inner-outer. Accordingly, timelessness tropes the universality of a rite of passage as intrinsic to the human condition, while the command that a protagonist appear at such and such a location

by a specific date and his failure to do so index the *individual's* inner
struggle, his or her temporary incapacity to assume a responsibility
that requires additional psychological preparation.
The externalization of psychological states as concrete phenomena produces the two-dimensional, object-freighted world of the fairy
tale, which teems with fantastic creatures, precious elements, and
mysterious items that appear and vanish without warning as symbols of an interior landscape. Unraveling the enigma of these colorful symbols accounts in large part for the ludic and philosophical
pleasures that the genre of fairy tales has vouchsafed generations of
spellbound readers, children and adults alike.

Notes

1. I happily acknowledge my debt to Seth Graham for his meticulous perusal of
an early draft of this introduction, which eliminated messy nails and splinters; to
Bozenka, my "always and ever" supreme editor; to the hundreds of appreciative students at the University of Pittsburgh, University of Oregon, and University of Ohio
for lively classroom discussions of Russian fairy tales; to David Birnbaum, *Volsheb-
nik* extraordinaire, for sharing the spoils; and to the teaching assistants who over the
years have aided and abetted my public passion for this genre of Russian folklore:
chronologically, Julia Sagaidak, Benjamin Sutcliffe, Petre Petrov, Dawn Seckler, and
Maria Jett.
        Throughout, I distinguish among the bona fide folk fairy tale (in Russian, *vol-
shebnaia skazka*) as a genuinely folkloric genre steeped in magic; the folktale (*skazka*),
likewise popular in origin but not necessarily infused with fantastic elements; and the
literary fairy tale, a narrative of individual authorship that has appropriated a fairy-
tale structure, personae, and motifs for specific purposes. Examples of the last range
from Aleksandr Pushkin's recasting of the traditional folktale "The Wicked Sisters"
into his "Tale of Tsar Saltan" (1831) to Andrei Siniavsky's/Abram Tertz's *The Make-
piece Experiment* (in Russian, *Liubimov*, 1963) and Liudmila Petrushevskaia's series
of short fairy tales throughout the 1990s treating everything from insects to Barbie.
        2. This phenomenon, which Max Lüthi calls "depthlessness" (11–23), corresponds
to what E. M. Forster in *Aspects of the Novel* labels "flatness" (of character), i.e., two-
dimensionality.
        3. For surveys of various "schools" among scholars of folkloric fairy tales, see
Zipes, "Might Makes Right," Dégh, Jones (119–40), and Lüthi.
        4. In English, see Meletinsky, "Structural-Typological Study of the Folktale." For
a study that focuses on the utopian-democratic aspects of the genre, see Meletinskij,
"The 'Low' Hero of the Fairy Tale."

5. Propp's other studies of the genre, such as *The Historical Roots of the Fairy Tale* and *The Fairy Tale,* contrast dramatically with his best-known work, for in addition to interpreting narratives, they readily engage in speculation.

6. Nikiforov advances the highly original (if contentious and not overly productive) notion of fairy tales having the grammatical genders of Russian nouns: masculine, feminine, and neuter.

7. Richard Pollack, *The Creation of Dr. B: A Biography of Bruno Bettelheim* (New York: Simon and Schuster, 1996). Nina Sutton's *Bettelheim: A Life and a Legacy* (New York: Basic Books, 1996) favors a more balanced and nuanced treatment of Bettelheim's personal and professional activities.

8. Estés's third chapter (74–114) blends a meandering plot summary with some keen insights into the initiatory tasks assigned the heroine of "Vasilisa the Beautiful," one of the most famous fairy tales in the Russian repertory.

9. Bly and Woodman's 264-page volume attempts to explicate the Russian fairy tale titled "The Maiden Tsar" (which the book renders as "The Maiden King") as a symbolic scenario dramatizing the reunion of the feminine and the masculine selves. The balance in their prolix discussion between extensive mini-lectures on basic Jungian principles and actual clarification of the fairy tale tilts heavily toward the former.

10. Zipes's articles and chapters treat the entire gamut of non-Slavic fairy tale collectors and adapters, from Charles Perrault and the Grimm brothers to Joanna Russ and Walt Disney. For Zipes, Disney exemplifies the self-promoting bogeyman of capitalism. The fairy tales that Zipes champions, apart from their political correctness (or because of it), tend to lack the dark imagination that lends many traditional fairy tales a frisson-inducing edge.

11. Marcia K. Lieberman, " 'Some Day My Prince Will Come': Female Acculturation through Fairy Tales" (1972); Karen Rowe, "Feminism and Fairy Tales" (1979); and Sandra M. Gilbert and Susan Gubar, "The Queen's Looking Glass" (1979) are all handily reprinted in Zipes's *Don't Bet on the Prince.* See also Ruth Bottigheimer's *Fairy Tales and Society* (1986).

12. The work of Marina Warner, though consonant with feminist values, accords incomparably more attention to historical developments than that of her colleagues in feminism.

13. As an advocate of the mythological school of folklorists, Afanas'ev sought what Yu. Sokolov calls "the deep foundations of ancestral time" (386), which encouraged the treatment of tales as a form of myth.

14. Such an orientation links Kravchenko with the mythological school of Russian folklorists, which justified mythologizing magic folktales on the grounds that they seemed to be the most ancient of all folktales.

15. For a more detailed account of the Russian folkloristic scholarly tradition, as well as its connections with western Europe, see Yu. Sokolov 40–155. For an investigation of Soviet fakelore, see Miller Howell and Dara Prescott Howell, *The Development of Slavic Folkloristics* (New York: Garland, 1992).

16. Missing from this collection were the so-called "forbidden tales" (*zavetnye skazki*), raunchy and often startlingly obscene narratives that failed to pass the Russian censor, saw first publication in Geneva, and were repatriated to Russia only after perestroika. For a commentary on these tales, see Haney, "Mr. Afanasiev's Naughty Little Secrets."

17. A small number of fairy tales constitute an exception to the rule of "a happy ending" inasmuch as they end unhappily, even tragically: for example, "Two Ivans, Soldier's Sons." For a discussion of such tales, see Kostiukhin.

18. Approximately 75 percent of Russian fairy tale subjects are international, approximately 20 percent are exclusively Russian. For more information on the relationship between Russian and western European tales, see Yu. Sokolov 397, 419–20.

19. Antii Aarne's authoritative *Types of the Folk Tale: A Classification and Bibliography* (1911, 1928) divides all tales into (1) animal tales; (2) tales, properly so called; and (3) anecdotes, and then proceeds to subdivide the second, major group into four categories of tales: (a) magical; (b) legendary; (c) romantic; and (d) about the foolish devil. My concern here is with category 2a. For an illuminating summary of taxonomical issues in this regard, see Yu. Sokolov.

20. On the uroboros, see Neumann, chap. 12.

21. For a detailed analysis of Baba Yaga, see Johns; Hubbs 36–52; and Kravchenko 184–204.

22. For an intriguing analysis of trebling in American culture, see Alan Dundes, "The Number Three in American Culture," in Dundes 134–59.

WORKS CITED AND SUGGESTED READINGS

Afanas'ev, Aleksandr. *Russian Fairy Tales.* Trans. Norbert Guterman. New York: Pantheon Books, 1945, 1973.

Bettelheim, Bruno. *The Uses of Enchantment: The Meaning and Importance of Fairy Tales.* New York: Vintage Books, 1975.

Bly, Robert, and Marion Woodman. *The Maiden King: The Reunion of Masculine and Feminine.* New York: Henry Holt, 1998.

Bogatyrev, Petr, and Roman Jakobson. "Folklore as a Special Form of Creativity." In Roman Jakobson, *Selected Writings,* 4:1–15. The Hague and Paris: Mouton. 1966.

Bottigheimer, Ruth B. *Fairy Tales and Society: Illusion, Allusion and Paradigm.* Philadelphia: University of Pennsylvania Press, 1986.

Dégh, Linda. *Folktales and Society.* Bloomington: Indiana University Press, 1969.

Dundes, Alan. *Interpreting Folklore.* Bloomington: Indiana University Press, 1980.

Eliade, Mircea. *Images and Symbols: Studies in Religious Symbolism.* Princeton, N.J.: Princeton University Press, 1991.

Estés, Clarissa Pinkola. *Women Who Run with the Wolves.* New York: Ballantine Books, 1992.

Franz, Mary-Louise von. *The Interpretation of Fairy Tales.* Boston: Shambhala Publications, Inc., 1970.

Gilbert, Sandra M., and Susan Gubar. "The Queen's Looking Glass." In *Don't Bet on the Prince,* ed. Jack Zipes, 201–8. New York: Routledge, 1987.

———. *The Madwoman in the Attic: The Nineteenth-Century Literary Imagination.* New Haven: Yale University Press, 1980.

Haney, Jack. *An Introduction to the Russian Folktale.* Armonk, N.Y.: M. E. Sharpe, 1999.

———. "Mr. Afanasiev's Naughty Little Secrets: *'Russkie zavetnye skazki.'* " *SEEFA Journal* 3, no. 2 (Fall 1998).

Hubbs, Joanna. *Mother Russia: The Feminine Myth in Russian Culture.* Bloomington: Indiana University Press, 1988, 1993.

Jakobson, Roman. "On Russian Fairy Tales." In Roman Jakobson, *Selected Writings,* vol. 4. The Hague and Paris: Mouton, 1966.

Johns, Andrea. "Baba Iaga and the Russian Mother." *Slavic and East European Journal* 42, no. 1 (Spring 1998): 21–36.

Jones, Steven Swann. *The Fairy Tale: The Magic Mirror of Imagination.* New York: Twayne, 1995.

Kostiukhin, E. A. "Magic Tales That End Badly." *SEEFA Journal* 3, no. 2 (Fall 1998).

Kravchenko, Maria. *The World of the Russian Fairy Tale.* Berne and New York: Peter Lang, 1987.

Lieberman, Marcia. " 'Some Day My Prince Will Come': Female Acculturation through Fairy Tales." *College English* 34 (1972): 383–95.

Lüthi, Max. *The European Folktale: Form and Nature.* Bloomington: Indiana University Press, 1986 (original publication in 1947).

Meletinskii, E. M. "Problems of the Structural Analysis of Fairytales." In *Soviet Structural Folkloristics,* ed. Pierre Maranda, 73–139. The Hague: Mouton, 1974.

Meletinskij, E. M. "The 'Low' Hero of the Fairy Tale." In Oinas and Soudakoff, *Study of Russian Folklore,* 235–57.

Meletinsky, Eleasar M. "Structural-Typological Study of the Folktale." Trans. Robin Dietrich. *Genre* 4 (1971): 249–79.

Miller, Frank J. *Folklore for Stalin: Russian Folklore and Pseudofolklore of the Stalin Era.* Armonk, N.Y.: M. E. Sharpe, 1990.

Neumann, Erich. *The Great Mother.* Trans. Ralph Manheim. Bollingen Series 47. Princeton, N.J.: Princeton University Press, 1955, 1963.

Nikiforov, A. I. "Towards a Morphological Study of the Folktale." In Oinas and Soudakoff, *Study of Russian Folklore,* 55–61. Translation of A. I. Nikiforov, "K voprosu o morfologicheskom izuchenii narodnoi skazki." In *Sbornik otdeleniia russkogo iazyka i solvesnosti Akademii nauk,* 3:173–78. Leningrad, 1938.

Oinas, Felix J., and Stephen Soudakoff, eds. and trans. *The Study of Russian Folklore.* The Hague and Paris: Mouton, 1975.

Propp, Vladimir. *The Morphology of the Folktale.* 2nd rev. ed. Bloomington: Indiana University Press, 1968.

Rowe, Karen. "Feminism and Fairy Tales." *Women's Studies* 6 (1979): 237–57.

Sokolov, Yu. M. *Russian Folklore*. Trans. Catherine Ruth Smith. Hatboro, Pa.: Folklore Associates, 1966.

Tatar, Maria. *Off with Their Heads: Fairy Tales and the Culture of Childhood*. Princeton, N.J.: Princeton University Press, 1992.

Warner, Marina. *From the Beast to the Blonde*. New York: Farrar, Straus and Giroux, 1994.

Zipes, Jack. *Breaking the Magic Spell: Radical Theories of Folk and Fairy Tales*. New York: Routledge, 1992.

———. *Don't Bet on the Prince*. New York: Routledge, 1989.

———. *Fairy Tale as Myth/Myth as Fairy Tale*. Lexington: University of Kentucky Press, 1994.

———. *Fairy Tales and the Art of Subversion*. New York: Methuen, 1983.

———. *Happily Ever After: Fairy Tales, Children and the Culture Industry*. New York and London: Routledge, 1997.

———. "Might Makes Right—The Politics of Folk and Fairy Tales." In Zipes, *Breaking the Magic Spell*, 20–40.

———. "On the Use and Abuse of Folk and Fairy Tales with Children: Bruno Bettelheim's Moralistic Magic Wand." In Zipes, *Breaking the Magic Spell*, 160–82.

———. *When Dreams Came True: Classical Fairy Tales and Their Tradition*. New York and London: Routledge, 1999.

THE FROG PRINCESS
꿩〵꿩

Long, long ago, in ancient times, there was a king with three sons, all of them full grown. And the king said to them, "Sons! I want each of you to make a bow for yourself and to shoot it. Whichever woman brings back your arrow will be your bride. Whoever's arrow isn't brought back is not meant to marry." The oldest son shot his arrow, which was brought back by a prince's daughter. The middle son shot his arrow, which was brought back by a general's daughter. But the arrow of the youngest, Prince Ivan, was brought back by a frog, who gripped it in her teeth. The two older brothers were happy and jubilant, but Prince Ivan grew pensive and burst into tears. "How can I live with a frog? To live one's whole life isn't like wading a river or crossing a field!" He cried and cried and cried some more, but there was nothing to be done—he married the frog. Their wedding observed traditional rites; the frog was held on a dish.

And so they lived until one day the king wanted to find out what gifts the brides could make, which one was the most skilled at sewing. He gave the order. Prince Ivan again grew pensive and cried, "What can my frog make! Everybody'll laugh!" The frog only hopped on the floor, only croaked. As soon as Prince Ivan fell asleep, she went outside, shed her skin, turned into a beautiful maiden, and cried, "Nurses-purses! Make such and such!" The nurses-purses instantly brought a shirt of the finest workmanship. She took it, folded it, and placed it beside Prince Ivan, and once again turned into a frog, as if she'd never been anything else! Prince Ivan awoke, was overjoyed, took the shirt, and brought it to the king. The king accepted it, and examined it. "Well, this is quite a shirt—made to wear on special holidays!" The middle son brought a shirt, and the king said, "The only thing it's good for is to wear in the bathhouse!" And he took the shirt the oldest brother brought and said, "The only thing it's good for is to wear in a poor peasant's hut!" The king's sons went their separate ways. The two oldest agreed. "We had no cause to laugh at Prince Ivan's wife. She's not a frog, but a cunning witch!"

Once again the king gave an order—that his daughters-in-law bake some bread and bring it to show him who could bake best. At first the other two brides laughed at the frog; but when the time came they sent the chambermaid to spy on how she baked. The frog realized this, and she went and mixed some dough, rolled it, made a hollow in the top of the stove, and tossed the dough directly into it. The chambermaid saw this and ran to tell her mistresses, the royal brides, and they did exactly the same. But the cunning frog had fooled them. She immediately dug the dough from the stove, cleaned and greased everything as though nothing had happened, went out onto the porch, shed her skin, and cried, "Nurses-purses! This very minute bake me the kind of bread that my father ate only on Sundays and holidays!" The nurses-purses instantly brought her the bread. She took it, placed it beside Prince Ivan, and turned into a frog. Prince Ivan awoke, took the bread, and brought it to his father. Just then his father was accepting the older brothers' bread: their wives had dropped theirs into the stove just as the frog had, and so it had come out any which way. The king accepted the oldest brother's bread first, looked at it, and sent it back to the kitchen; he took the middle son's, and did the same. When Ivan's turn came, he handed over the bread. His father took it, looked at it, and said, "Now, this is bread—fit to eat on special occasions! Not like the older daughters-in-law's, which is like stone!"

Next the king decided to hold a ball, to see which of his daughters-in-law danced best. All of the guests and the daughters-in-law assembled, except for Prince Ivan. He thought, "How can I turn up with a frog?" And our Prince Ivan sobbed uncontrollably. The frog said to him, "Don't cry, Prince Ivan! Go to the ball. I'll be there in an hour." Prince Ivan cheered up a little when he heard the frog's words. He left, and the frog went, shed her skin, and dressed up in wonderful clothes! She arrived at the ball. Prince Ivan was overjoyed and everyone applauded: what a beauty she was! The guests started to eat; the princess would pick a bone and toss it in her sleeve, drink something, and toss the rest in her other sleeve. The other sisters-in-law saw what she was doing and also started putting their bones in their sleeves and pouring the remnants of their drinks in their other sleeves. The time came for dancing, and the king ordered the older daughters-in-law to dance, but they let the frog go first. She instantly took Prince Ivan's arm and headed for the floor: she danced and danced, whirled and whirled, to everyone's wonder! She waved her right hand, and forests and lakes appeared; she waved her left hand, and various birds appeared in flight! Everyone was awed. When she finished dancing, everything vanished. The other sisters-in-law took their turn dancing, and tried to do the same: whenever they waved their right hands, bones came flying out right at the guests; they'd wave their left hands, and water would spray, also onto the guests. The king was displeased, and shouted, "That's enough!" The daughters-in-law stopped dancing.

The ball was over. Prince Ivan left first, found his wife's skin somewhere, took it, and burned it. She came home, looked for the skin, but it was gone, burned! She went to bed with Prince Ivan, and before morning said to him, "Well, Prince Ivan, you should have waited a bit longer. I'd have been yours, but now God knows! Good-bye! Search for me beyond the thrice-ninth lands, in the thrice-tenth kingdom." And the princess vanished.

A year passed. Prince Ivan missed his wife. During the second year he got ready, received his father's and his mother's blessing, and set off. He walked for a long time and suddenly came upon a little hut, with its front facing the forest, its back to him. And he said, "Little hut, little hut! Stand as you used to of old, the way your mother stood you—with your back to the forest, and your front facing me." The little hut turned around. He entered the hut. An old woman sat there, and said, "Fie, fie! There was no whiff of a Russian bone to be sniffed, no sight to be seen, and now a Russian bone has actually come to my house! Where are you off to, Prince Ivan?" "First give me food and drink, old woman, and then ask questions." The old woman gave him food and drink and put him to bed. Prince Ivan said to her, "Granny! I've set off to find Elena the Beautiful." "Oh, my dear child, you took so long to come! At first she often used to mention you, but now she doesn't any longer, and she hasn't visited me for a long time. Go along to my middle sister, she knows more."

Next morning Prince Ivan set off, and came to another little hut, and said, "Little hut, little hut! Stand as you used to of old, the way your mother stood you—with your back to the forest, and your front facing me." The little hut turned around. He entered, and saw an old woman sitting there, who said, "Fie, fie! There was no whiff of a Russian bone to be sniffed, no sight to be seen, and now a Russian bone has actually come to my house! Where are you off to, Prince Ivan?" "I'm here, Granny, in search of Elena the Beautiful." "Oh, Prince Ivan," said the old woman. "You took so long to come! She's started to forget you, and is marrying someone else. Their wedding is soon! She lives with my older sister now. Go there, but watch out: as soon as you come near, they'll sense it, and Elena will turn into a spindle, and her dress will become golden thread. My sister will start winding the golden thread: when she's wound it around the spindle and put it in a box and locked the box, you have to find the key, open the box, break the spindle, throw the top back over your shoulder, and the bottom in front of you. Then she'll appear before you."

Prince Ivan set off, came to the third old woman, and entered the hut. She was winding golden thread, wound it around the spindle, and put it in a box, locked it, and put the key somewhere. He took the key, opened the box, took out the spindle, and, as said and as written, broke the top and threw the top over his shoulder, and the bottom in front of him. Suddenly Elena the Beautiful appeared, and greeted

26

him. "Oh, you took so long to come, Prince Ivan! I almost married another." And the new groom was supposed to arrive soon. Elena the Beautiful took a flying carpet from the old woman, sat on it, and they took off, flew like the birds. The bridegroom suddenly appeared and found out that they'd left. He also was cunning! He followed in pursuit, and chased and chased them, and was only ten yards short of catching up with them. They flew into Russia on the carpet, and for some reason he wasn't allowed in Russia, and he returned. But they flew home, all were overjoyed, and they started to live and prosper, to everyone's glory at the end of the story.

THE THREE KINGDOMS
꽃 ₩

Once upon a time there lived an old man and old woman. They had three sons: the first was Egorushko the Strayer, the second was Misha the Pigeon-Toed, and the third was Ivashko the Stove-Sitter. The father and mother decided to marry them off. They sent the oldest to look for a bride. He walked and walked for a long time, and no matter where he checked out the girls he couldn't choose a bride for himself, for none appealed to him. Then he met a three-headed dragon on the road and was frightened, and the dragon said to him, "Where are you going, my good fellow?" Egorushko said, "I'm going so as to arrange my marriage, but I can't find a bride." The dragon said, "Come with me. I'll show you where to go and perhaps you'll get a bride."

So they walked and walked until they came to a big stone. The dragon said, "Pull up the stone. There you'll get whatever you wish." Egorushko tried to pull it up, but couldn't do a thing with it. The dragon said to him, "So there's no bride for you!" And Egorushko returned home and told his father and mother everything that had happened. The father and mother thought and thought about what to do, then sent off the middle son, Misha the Pigeon-Toed. The same thing happened with him. So the old man and woman thought and thought, not knowing what to do: if they sent Ivashko the Stove-Sitter, he wouldn't be able to do anything, for sure!

But Ivashko the Stove-Sitter himself asked to go and have a look at the dragon. At first the father and mother refused, but then let him go. And Ivashko also walked and walked, and met the three-headed dragon. The dragon asked him, "Where are you going, my good fellow?" He said, "My brothers wanted to get married, but couldn't find a bride. And now it's my turn." "Then come with me and I'll show you, and perhaps you'll be able to get a bride."

So the dragon and Ivashko set off, reached the same stone, and the dragon told him to pull the stone from its place. Ivashko gripped the stone and in a second rolled the stone away. There turned out to be a hole in the ground and some straps fastened near it.

The dragon said, "Ivashko! Sit on the straps, I'll lower you down, and there you'll walk until you get to the three kingdoms, and in each kingdom you'll see a maiden."

Ivashko was lowered and set off. He walked and walked until he reached the copper kingdom. He entered and saw a beautiful maiden. The maiden said, "Welcome, rare guest! Come and sit down wherever you see a spot. Tell me, where are you from and where are you going?" "Ah, beautiful maiden!" said Ivashko. "You've given me neither food nor drink, and you're already asking questions." And the maiden set all sorts of food and drink on the table, and Ivan ate and drank, then told her that he was searching for a bride. "If you find me appealing, please marry me." "No, my good fellow," said the maiden. "Go farther on, and you'll come to the silver kingdom. There's a maiden there even more beautiful than I!" And she gave him a silver ring as a gift.

The fine youth thanked the maiden for her hospitality, said goodbye, and set off. He walked and walked until he reached the silver kingdom. He entered and saw a maiden sitting there more beautiful than the first one. He sent up a prayer to God, and bowed humbly to her, "Greetings, beautiful maiden!" She answered, "Welcome, unknown youth! Have a seat and boast a bit: who are you, where are you from and on what business have you come here?" "Ah, beautiful maiden!" said Ivashko. "You've given me neither food nor drink, and you're already asking questions." And the maiden set all sorts of food and drink on the table, and Ivan ate and drank as much as he wanted, then told her that he'd set off in search of a bride, and he asked her to marry him. She said to him, "Go farther on, and you'll come to the golden kingdom, and in that kingdom you'll find a maiden even more beautiful than I!" And she gave him a golden ring as a gift.

Ivashko said good-bye and set off. He walked and walked until he reached the golden kingdom. He entered and saw a maiden more beautiful than the others. He sent up a prayer to God and greeted the maiden as was proper. The maiden asked him where he was from and where he was going. "Ah, beautiful maiden!" he said. "You've given me neither food nor drink, and you're already asking questions." And she set all sorts of food and drink on the table, the best one could ask for. Ivashko the Stove-Sitter treated himself generously to everything and then told her, "I set off in search of a bride for myself. If you want to marry me, then come with me." The maiden agreed and gave him a golden ball as a gift, and they set off together.

They walked and walked, and they came to the silver kingdom. They took the maiden there with them. Again they walked and walked, and came to the copper kingdom. They took the maiden there with them, and they all went to the hole through which they had to climb out and where the straps were hanging. The older brothers were already standing at the hole, about to climb down to look for Ivashko.

Ivashko seated the maiden from the copper kingdom on the straps and shook a strap. The brothers pulled, and pulled out the maiden, then lowered the straps again. Ivashko seated the maiden from the silver kingdom on the straps, and they pulled her out, and lowered the straps again. Then he seated the maiden from the golden kingdom on the straps, and they pulled her out, then lowered the straps. Finally Ivashko himself sat on the straps, and his brothers began pulling, pulled and pulled, but when they saw that it was Ivashko, they thought, "What if we pull him out and he won't give us any of the maidens?" and they cut the straps and Ivashko fell down. There was nothing he could do, he cried a bit, cried some more, and then set off. He walked and walked, and saw sitting on a tree stump an old man about an inch tall with a beard about a yard long, and he told him the whole story of what had happened. The old man instructed him to go farther. "You'll come to a little hut, and lying inside the hut is a man so long he stretches from one corner to another, and you must ask him how to get to Russia."

Ivan walked and walked until he came to a little hut, and he entered and said, "O mighty Giant Idol! Don't kill me. Tell me how to get to Russia." "Fie, fie!" said the Giant Idol. "No one summoned Russian bones, they came here of their own accord. Well, go beyond the thirty lakes, and there you'll find a little hut on chicken legs, and in that hut lives Baba Yaga. She has an eagle, and it'll take you back." The fine youth walked and walked until he came to a little hut, and he entered the hut, and Baba Yaga cried, "Fie, fie, fie! Why have Russian bones come here?" To which Ivan answered, "Well, Granny, I've come by order of the mighty Giant Idol to ask you for the mighty eagle so it can carry me back to Russia." "Go to the garden," said Baba Yaga. "There's a guard at the gates, and you must take his keys and go beyond the seventh door. When you open the last door, the eagle will flutter its wings and if you're not frightened of him, sit on him and fly off. Only take some beef with you, and when he starts looking back, give him a piece of the meat."

Ivashko did everything Baba Yaga told him to, sat on the eagle, and flew off. He flew and flew, the eagle looked back, and Ivashko gave him a piece of meat. He flew and flew, and often kept giving the eagle meat, and he'd fed him all of it, though they still had a long way to fly. The eagle looked back, but there was no meat. And the eagle tore a piece of flesh from Ivashko's shoulder, ate it, and brought him out through the same hole into Russia. When Ivashko got down from the eagle, the eagle spat out the piece of flesh and told him to put it back into his shoulder. Ivashko put it back, and the shoulder became whole. Ivashko came home, took the maiden from the golden kingdom away from his brothers, and they began to live together, and they live together till this day. I was there, I drank beer, and the beer ran down my mustache and didn't go into my mouth.

BABA YAGA
❦

Once there lived a peasant and his wife and they had a daughter. The wife died. The husband married again, and had a daughter with the new wife. The wife conceived a dislike for her stepdaughter and made the girl's life miserable. The peasant thought and thought and finally drove his daughter into the forest. As they rode through the forest he looked around and saw a little hut standing on chicken legs. And the peasant said, "Little hut, little hut! Stand with your back to the forest, and your front facing me." And the little hut turned around.

The peasant entered the little hut, and there was Baba Yaga, her head in front, a leg in one corner, and the other in another. "I smell a Russian smell!" said Yaga. The peasant bowed. "Baba Yaga the Bony-Legged! I've brought you my daughter to serve you." "Fine! Serve me. Serve me," said Yaga to the girl, "and I'll reward you for it."

The father said his farewells and drove off home. And Baba Yaga gave the girl the tasks of spinning a basketful of thread, heating the stove, and preparing everything for dinner, while she herself left. The girl bustled around the stove, crying bitterly. The mice ran out and said to her, "Maiden, maiden, why are you crying? Give us some kasha, and we'll tell you something useful." She gave them some kasha. "Here's what you should do," they said. "Stretch a thread on each spindle." Baba Yaga returned. "Well," she said, "is everything ready?" Everything was. "Now come and wash me in the bathhouse." Yaga praised the girl and gave her all sorts of beautiful outfits. Yaga left again and gave the girl even more difficult tasks. The girl cried again. The mice ran out and said, "Why are you crying, beautiful maiden? Give us some kasha, and we'll tell you something useful." She gave them some kasha, and they again told her what to do and how. Once again Baba Yaga returned and praised her and gave her some more beautiful outfits . . . Meanwhile the stepmother sent her husband to find out whether his daughter was still alive.

The peasant set off. He came and saw that his daughter had become rich, very rich. Yaga wasn't home, and he took his daughter with him. As they approached their village, their dog barked, "Woof, woof, woof! The lady's coming, the lady's coming!" The stepmother ran out and hit the dog with a rolling pin. "You're lying," she said. "Say: 'The bones are rattling in the box!' " But the dog kept barking the same thing. They arrived. The stepmother kept plaguing her husband to take her daughter to Baba Yaga. He did.

Baba Yaga gave her various tasks, and left. The girl was wild with anger and cried. The mice ran out. "Maiden, maiden! Why are you crying?" they said. But she didn't let them finish, and hit first one, then the other with a rolling-pin. She spent her time chasing them and didn't get the tasks done. Yaga returned and got angry. The same thing happened again. Yaga broke her into pieces, and put the bones in a box. And the girl's mother sent her husband to fetch their daughter. The father came and drove back with just the bones. As he approached the village, the dog on the porch once again barked, "Woof, woof, woof! The bones are rattling in the box!" The stepmother ran out with the rolling-pin. "You're lying," she said. "Say: 'The lady's coming!' " But the dog kept barking the same thing, "Woof, woof, woof! The bones are rattling in the box!" The husband arrived, and the wife wailed aloud! Here's a tale for you, for me—butter, too!

VASILISA THE BEAUTIFUL
※ ※

In a certain kingdom there lived a merchant. He and his wife lived together for twelve years, but had only one daughter, Vasilisa the Beautiful. When her mother died, the girl was eight years old. On her
deathbed, the merchant's wife called her daughter, took out a doll
from under the blanket, and gave it to her, saying, "Listen, sweet little
Vasilisa! Remember my last words, and listen. I'm dying and I'm leaving you my parental blessing and this doll. Always keep it with you
and don't show it to anyone. And if you ever come to grief, give her
something to eat and ask her for advice. She'll eat and then will tell
you how to solve your problem." Then the mother kissed the daughter and died.

After his wife's death the merchant mourned, as is proper, and then
started thinking about getting married again. He was a good man, and
there were many women who were willing, but the one he liked most
was a widow. She was no longer young and had two of her own
daughters, who were about Vasilisa's age, so she had to be an experienced housekeeper and mother. The merchant married the widow,
but he'd been fooled, and in her he didn't find a good mother for his
Vasilisa. Vasilisa was the most beautiful girl in the whole village. Her
stepmother and sisters envied her beauty, plagued her by giving her
all possible tasks so that she would grow thin from toil and dark from
the wind and sun, and made her life nothing but misery!

Vasilisa bore it all without complaint and with each day became more beautiful and plump, while the stepmother and her daughters grew thin and ugly from malice, despite always sitting and doing nothing, like ladies. How did this come about? Vasilisa's doll helped her. Without that, Vasilisa could never have coped with all the work! And Vasilisa, in turn, sometimes wouldn't eat the most tasty morsel but would save it for the doll, and in the evening, when everyone was in bed, she would lock herself in the tiny room where she lived, and would give the doll a treat, saying, "Here, little doll, have a bite as you listen to my plight! I'm living in my father's house, but I know no joy. My wicked stepmother is trying to get rid of me. Teach me how to behave, how to live, and what to do." The doll would eat, then would give her advice and comfort her, and the following morning would do all of Vasilisa's work for her. Vasilisa would rest in the cool shade and pick flowers, while the flowerbeds were weeded, the cabbage watered, the water brought in, and the stove lit. The doll even showed Vasilisa which herb would protect her from the sun's rays. She led a good life with the doll.

Several years passed. Vasilisa grew up and reached marriageable age. All of the young men in town came to court her, but no one even looked at the stepmother's daughters. The stepmother grew even nastier and told all of the young men, "I won't give away the youngest daughter until the older ones are married!" And whenever she saw them off, she'd vent her spite on Vasilisa by beating her.

One day the merchant had to go on a long trip to take care of his business. The stepmother moved to a different house. The house stood beside a dense forest, and in a clearing in the forest was a hut, and in that hut lived Baba Yaga. She didn't allow anyone to visit her, and she ate people as if they were chickens. After moving into the new house, the merchant's wife would regularly send Vasilisa, whom she hated, into the forest for one thing or another. But Vasilisa would always return home safely: the doll would tell her which path to take and didn't let her approach Baba Yaga's hut.

Autumn came. The stepmother handed out work to all three girls for the evening; she told one of them to make lace, another to knit stockings, and Vasilisa to spin. She also set them all some lessons. She extinguished the lights in the whole house, left only the one candle where the girls were working, and retired for the night. The girls worked. The candle began to sizzle, and one of the stepsisters took some small tongs to straighten the wick, but instead, following her mother's orders, she put out the candle as if accidentally. "What are we to do now?" said the girls. "There's no light at all in the house, and we haven't finished our lessons. We'll have to get some light from Baba Yaga!" "I can see by the light of my pins!" said the one who was making lace. "I won't go." "I won't either," said the one knitting stockings. "I can see by the light of my knitting needles!" "You've got to go for the light," they both cried. "Go on, hurry up to Baba Yaga's!" And they pushed Vasilisa out of the room.

Vasilisa went to her little room, placed the supper she'd prepared in front of her doll, and said, "Here, little doll, have a bite as you listen to my plight! They're sending me to Baba Yaga for light. Baba Yaga will eat me!" The doll ate, and her eyes shone like two candles. "Don't be afraid, Vasilisa!" she said. "Go where they're sending you, only keep me with you at all times. With me there, nothing will happen to you at Baba Yaga's." Vasilisa got ready, placed the doll in her pocket, and, making the sign of the cross, set off for the dense forest.

She walked and trembled. Suddenly a horseman galloped past her. He was white, dressed in white, his horse was white, and its harness was white; the sun began to rise.

Vasilisa walked all night and all day, and only toward the following evening did she come to the clearing on which stood Baba Yaga's hut. The fence around the hut was of human bones, and there were human skulls, with eyes, impaled on the fence. At the entrance there were human legs instead of doorposts, hands instead of bolts, and a mouth with sharp teeth instead of a lock. Vasilisa froze in horror and stopped dead in her tracks. And suddenly another rider appeared; he was black, dressed all in black, and on a black horse; he galloped up to Baba Yaga's door and vanished as if he'd fallen through the ground.

Night fell. But the darkness didn't last long; the eyes in all of the skulls on the fence lit up, and it became as bright as day throughout the clearing. Vasilisa trembled in terror, but, not knowing where to run, she stayed where she was.

Soon she heard a terrible noise in the forest: the trees crackled and the dry leaves rustled. Out of the forest emerged Baba Yaga, riding in a mortar, moving it along with a pestle, and sweeping the traces with a broom. She rode up to the gate, stopped, and, sniffing around her, exclaimed, "Fie, fie! I smell a Russian smell! Who's here?" Vasilisa approached the old woman in terror, and, bowing low, said, "It's me, Granny! My stepmother's daughters have sent me to get light from you." "Fine," said Baba Yaga. "I know them. Stay with me a while and work a bit, and then I'll give you the light. If not, I'll eat you!" Then she turned to the gate and cried, "Hey, my strong bolts, unlock, my wide gate, open up!" The gate opened and Baba Yaga rode in, whistling. Vasilisa followed her, and everything locked behind them. Once they entered the room, Baba Yaga stretched out and said to Vasilisa, "Bring me what there is in the stove to eat. I'm hungry."

Vasilisa lit a torch from the skulls on the fence and started taking out the food from the stove and serving it to Baba Yaga. There was enough food prepared for ten people. From the cellar she brought up kvass, mead, beer, and wine. The old woman ate everything and drank everything; she left Vasilisa only a bit of cabbage soup, a crust of bread, and a small piece of pork. Baba Yaga made ready to sleep, and said, "When I leave tomorrow, be sure to clean the yard, sweep the hut, make dinner, wash the linen, and go to the supply bin and take thirty pounds of wheat and separate it from the chaff. If all of it doesn't get done, I'll eat you!" And, having given her orders, Baba Yaga began to snore. Vasilisa placed the remains of the old woman's meal before the doll, burst into a flood of tears, and said, "Here, little doll, have a bite as you listen to my plight! Baba Yaga has given me hard tasks and threatens to eat me if I don't do all of them. Help me!" The doll answered, "Don't be afraid, Vasilisa the Beautiful! Have some supper, say your prayers, and go to bed. The morning is wiser than the evening!"

Vasilisa woke up very early, but Baba Yaga was already up. Vasilisa looked out of the window: the skulls' eyes were dimming. The white rider flashed by, and it grew light. Baba Yaga went outside, whistled, and the mortar, pestle, and broom appeared before her. A red rider flashed by and the sun rose. Baba Yaga sat in the mortar, moved it along with the pestle, and swept the traces with the broom. Vasilisa was left alone, and she looked around Baba Yaga's hut, marveled at the abundance of everything, and wondered which of the tasks she should tackle first. She looked—all the tasks were done: the doll was removing the last of the chaff from the wheat. "Ah, you're my savior!" said Vasilisa to the doll. "You've saved me from disaster!" "All that's left for you to do is prepare the dinner," replied the doll, getting into Vasilisa's pocket. "Prepare it with God's blessing, then rest to your heart's content!"

Toward evening Vasilisa set the table and waited for Baba Yaga. It began to grow dark, the black rider flashed past the gate, and darkness fell. Only the skulls' eyes shone. The trees crackled, the leaves rustled; Baba Yaga was coming. Vasilisa met her.

"Is everything done?" asked Yaga. "Please see for yourself, Granny!" said Vasilisa. Baba Yaga looked at everything, grew irritated that there was nothing to be angry about, and said, "Fine!" Then she cried, "My faithful servants, my dear friends, grind my wheat!" Three pairs of hands appeared, grabbed the wheat, and removed it. Baba Yaga ate her fill, made ready to sleep, and again ordered Vasilisa, "Do the same thing tomorrow as you did today, but in addition take the poppy seeds from the supply bin and clean them off seed by seed. Someone out of spite mixed in earth with them!" With these words, the old woman turned to the wall and began to snore, while Vasilisa got ready to feed her doll. The doll ate, and said, just as she'd done yesterday, "Say your prayers and go to bed. The morning is wiser than the evening. Everything will be done, sweet Vasilisa!"

Next morning Baba Yaga once again left in her mortar, and Vasilisa and the doll immediately got all the work done. The old woman returned, looked at everything, and cried, "My faithful servants, my dear friends, squeeze the oil out of the poppy seeds!" Three pairs of hands appeared, grabbed the poppy seeds, and removed them. Baba Yaga sat down to dinner. She ate, while Vasilisa stood there silently. "Why don't you speak to me?" said Baba Yaga. "You stand there as if dumb!" "I didn't dare speak," answered Vasilisa. "But if you allow me, I'd like to ask you something." "Ask away. Only not every question leads to something good: know a lot, age a lot!" "I only want to ask you, Granny, about what I saw: when I was coming here, a rider passed me, on a white horse, all white, and dressed in white. Who is he?" "That's my bright day," replied Baba Yaga. "Then another rider passed me, on a red horse, all red, and dressed in red. Who is he?" "That's my red sun!" replied Baba Yaga. "And what does the black rider who passed me right at your gate stand for, Granny?" "That's my dark night—they're all my faithful servants!"

Vasilisa recalled the three pairs of hands and held her peace. "Why don't you ask me anything else?" said Baba Yaga. "That'll be enough. You said yourself, Granny, know a lot, age a lot." "It's good," said Baba Yaga, "that you ask only about those things you've seen outside the house, and not inside the house! I don't like to have my dirt spread outside, and I eat those who are too curious! Now I'll ask you: how do you manage to get done all the work I assign you?" "My mother's blessing helps me," replied Vasilisa. "So that's it! Get out of here, blessed daughter! I want no blessed ones here." She dragged Vasilisa out of the room and pushed her out of the gate, took a skull with burning eyes off the fence, impaled it on a stick, gave it to her, and said, "Here's the light for your stepmother's daughters. Take it. It's what they sent you here for."

Vasilisa set off for home at a run by the light of the skull, which went out only as morning dawned, and finally, toward evening of the next day, she reached her house. As she approached the gate, she made ready to throw away the skull. "They probably no longer need a light in the house," she thought. But suddenly she heard a hollow voice from the skull: "Don't throw me away. Take me to your stepmother!"

She glanced at the stepmother's house and, not seeing a light in any of the windows, she decided to take the skull in with her. For the first time she was greeted affectionately and they told her that since she'd left they'd had no light in the house. They'd not been able to light a fire themselves, and whatever light they'd got from the neighbors had gone out as soon as they entered the room. "Perhaps your light won't go out!" said the stepmother. They carried the skull into the room, and whenever the skull's eyes fell on the stepmother and her daughters, they burned them! They tried to hide, but wherever they fled, the eyes followed them, and by morning they were burned to ashes. Only Vasilisa remained untouched.

In the morning Vasilisa buried the skull in the ground, locked up the house, went into town, and asked to stay with a childless old woman. There she remained and waited for her father. One day she said to the old lady, "I'm bored not doing any work, Granny! Go and buy me some flax, the best there is. At least I'll be able to spin." The old lady bought her some fine flax, and Vasilisa sat down to spin, working quickly and easily, and the threads came out even and as fine as hair. She soon had a lot of thread, and it was time to start weaving it, but there was no comb fine enough for her thread to be had, and no one was prepared to make one. Vasilisa asked her doll to help, and the doll said, "Bring me an old comb, an old shuttle, and a horse's mane. I'll make what you need."

Vasilisa got everything necessary and went to bed, while overnight the doll created a splendid loom. Toward the end of winter the linen was woven, and it was so fine that it could pass through the eye of a needle like a thread. In the spring they bleached the linen, and Vasilisa said to the old woman, "Sell the linen, Granny, and take the money for yourself." The old woman looked at the linen and gasped in admiration. "No, dear child! No one can wear such linen except the tsar. I shall take it to the palace." The old woman went to the tsar's palace and walked back and forth outside the windows. The tsar saw her and asked, "What do you want, old woman?" "Your Majesty," replied the old woman, "I have brought you a wondrously rare merchandise. I won't show it to anyone except you." The tsar ordered the old woman brought to him, and when he saw the linen he was awed. "What do you want for it?" asked the tsar. "It's beyond price, Tsar our father! I brought it as a gift for you!" The tsar thanked the old woman and she left with gifts from him.

The tsar ordered that shirts be made for him from the linen. It was cut, but nowhere could they find a seamstress who would take on the task. They searched for a long time, and finally the tsar summoned the old woman and said, "Since you know how to spin and weave such linen, you must know how to make shirts from it." "I'm not the one who spun and wove the linen, Your Majesty," said the old woman. "It's the work of a girl whom I've taken into my house." "So let her do the sewing!" The old lady returned home and told Vasilisa everything they'd said. "I knew I'd have to do the work myself," Vasilisa told her. She locked herself in her room and set to work. She sewed and sewed without stop, and soon a dozen shirts were ready.

The old woman took the shirts to the tsar, while Vasilisa washed, combed her hair, dressed, and sat down by the window. She sat there, waiting to see what would happen. And she saw one of the tsar's servants enter the courtyard and go to the old woman's room: "His Majesty the tsar wants to see the gifted seamstress who made the shirts for him and to reward her in person." Vasilisa went and appeared before the tsar. As soon as the tsar saw Vasilisa the Beautiful, he fell madly in love with her. "No, my beauty!" he said. "I won't let you go. You'll be my wife." And the tsar took Vasilisa by her white hands, seated her at his side, and right there and then had the wedding ceremony performed. Vasilisa's father soon returned, was overjoyed at her fate, and came to live with his daughter. Vasilisa took in the old woman, and she always carried her doll in her pocket until the end of her life.

MARIA MOREVNA
꒰ ꒱

In a certain land, in a certain kingdom, there lived Ivan the Prince. He had three sisters: one was Princess Maria, another was Princess Olga, and the third was Princess Anna. Their father and mother had died, and when dying said to their son, "Whoever asks for one of your sisters in marriage first, give her to him—don't keep them with you a long time!" The prince buried his parents and from misery went for a walk with his sisters in the green garden. Suddenly a black cloud covered the sky and a terrible storm began. "Let's go home, Sisters!" said Prince Ivan. As soon as they entered the palace, a thunderbolt struck, the ceiling split in two, and a bright falcon flew into the room. The falcon struck the floor, turned into a fine youth, and said, "Greetings, Prince Ivan! Earlier I used to visit as a guest, but this time I've come as a suitor. I want to arrange a marriage with your sister Princess Maria." "If my sister takes to you, I won't stand in the way. Let her go with God!" Princess Maria agreed, the falcon married her, and took her to his kingdom.

Day after day went by, hour raced after hour, and a whole year passed as if it had never been. Prince Ivan went for a walk with his two sisters in the green garden. Once again a dark cloud and whirlwind with lightning appeared. "Let's go home, Sisters!" said the prince. As soon as they entered the palace, a thunderbolt struck, the roof caved in, the ceiling split in two, and an eagle flew in. He struck the floor and turned into a fine youth. "Greetings, Prince Ivan! Earlier I used to visit as a guest, but this time I've come as a suitor." And he asked for Princess Olga in marriage. Prince Ivan replied, "If Princess Olga takes to you, then let her marry you. I won't go against her will." Princess Olga agreed and married the eagle. The eagle seized her and took her to his kingdom.

Another year went by. Prince Ivan said to his youngest sister, "Let's go for a walk in the green garden!" They walked a bit, and once again a dark cloud with a whirlwind and lightning appeared. "Let's go back home, Sister!" They went back home and hadn't had time to sit down when a thunderbolt struck, the ceiling split in two, and a raven flew in. The raven struck the floor and turned into a fine youth. The earlier ones had been handsome, but this one was even better. "So, Prince Ivan, earlier I used to visit as a guest, but this time I've come as a suitor. Give me Princess Anna in marriage." "I won't go against my sister's will. If she's taken to you, let her marry you." Princess Anna married the raven and he took her to his kingdom.

Prince Ivan was left alone. He lived for a whole year without his sisters, and grew bored. "I'll go and look for my sisters," he said. He made ready for the journey, and walked and walked, and saw an entire army lying defeated in a field. Prince Ivan asked, "If there's anyone alive here, please respond! Who defeated this great army?" There was a man alive, who answered, "The beautiful queen Maria Morevna defeated this great army." Prince Ivan went farther, and came upon some white tents. The beautiful queen Maria Morevna came out to meet him. "Greetings, Prince. Where is God taking you? Do you go of your own free will or by force?" Prince Ivan answered her, "Fine youths don't travel by force!" "Well, if you're not in a hurry, be my guest in these white tents." Prince Ivan was happy to do so, spent two nights in her tents, proved to Maria Morevna's liking, and married her.

The beautiful queen Maria Morevna took him with her to her kingdom. They lived there together for a while, and then the queen decided to wage war. She left all of her domestic affairs in Prince Ivan's hands and told him, "Go everywhere, take care of everything, only don't look in this closet." He couldn't resist, and no sooner had Maria Morevna left than he rushed to the closet, opened the door, and looked inside—and there was Koshchey the Deathless, hanging chained by twelve chains. Koshchey asked Prince Ivan, "Have pity on me, give me something to drink! I've been in torment here for ten years, without food or drink, and my throat's all parched!" The prince gave him a whole pail of water, and he drank it all and asked for more. "One pail won't quench my thirst. Give me more!" The prince gave him another pail. Koshchey drained it and asked for a third, and as soon as he drained the third pail he regained his former strength, shook his chains, and broke all twelve at once. "Thank you, Prince Ivan!" said Koshchey the Deathless. "Now you'll never see Maria Morevna, just as you won't see your own ears!" And in a terrible whirlwind he flew out of the window, overtook the beautiful queen Maria Morevna, seized her, and carried her off to his house. Prince Ivan cried bitterly, got ready, and set off. "Whatever happens, I'll find Maria Morevna!"

He walked for a day, he walked another, and as the third day dawned he saw a marvelous palace, an oak standing near the palace, and the bright falcon sitting on the oak. The falcon flew down from the oak, struck the earth, turned into a fine youth, and cried, "Ah, my dear brother-in-law! Has the Lord been kind to you?" Princess Maria ran out, greeted Prince Ivan joyfully, asked about his health, and told him about her own life. The prince stayed with them for three days, then said, "I can't stay with you for long. I'm on the road searching for my wife, the beautiful princess Maria Morevna." "You'll have a difficult time finding her," replied the falcon. "Leave your silver spoon here, in any case. Whenever we look at it we'll remember you." Prince Ivan left his silver spoon with the falcon and set off.

He walked for a day, walked another, and as the third day dawned he saw a palace even finer than the first, an oak standing beside the palace, and the eagle sitting on the oak. The eagle flew down from the oak, struck the earth, turned into a fine youth, and cried, "Get up, Princess Olga! Our dear brother's coming." Princess Olga instantly ran out to greet Ivan, hugged him and kissed him, asked about his health, and told him about her own life. Prince Ivan spent three days with them, then said, "I can't stay any longer. I'm on the road searching for my wife, the beautiful princess Maria Morevna." The eagle replied, "You'll have a difficult time finding her. Leave your silver fork with us. Whenever we look at it we'll remember you." He left his silver fork and set off.

He walked for a day, walked another, and as the third day dawned he saw a palace finer than the first two, an oak standing beside the palace, and the raven sitting on the oak. The raven flew down from the oak, struck the earth, turned into a fine youth, and cried, "Princess Anna! Hurry and come out here, our brother's arrived." Princess Anna ran out, greeted him joyfully, hugged him and kissed him, asked about his health, and told him about her own life. Prince Ivan spent three days with them, then said, "Good-bye! I'm off to search for my wife, the beautiful princess Maria Morevna." "You'll have a difficult time finding her. Leave your silver snuffbox with us. Whenever we look at it we'll remember you." The prince gave him the silver snuffbox, said good-bye, and went on his way.

He walked a day, walked another, and as the third day dawned he came to Maria Morevna. She saw her beloved, threw her arms around his neck, burst into a flood of tears, and said, "Ah, Prince Ivan! Why didn't you listen to me and look in the closet and let Koshschey the Deathless out?" "Forgive me, Maria Morevna! Don't recall the past, and better come with me while Koshchey the Deathless is away, or else he'll catch up with us!" They got ready and left. Koshchey was out hunting. Toward evening he returned home, and on the way his trusty steed stumbled under him. "Why are you stumbling, you greedy old nag? Do you sense something wrong?" The horse replied, "Prince Ivan was here, he's taken Maria Morevna away." "Can we catch up with them?" "We can sow wheat, wait until it grows, reap it, thresh it, turn it into flour, bake five ovenfuls of bread, eat that bread, and then give chase—and even then we'll catch up with them!" Koshchey galloped off and caught up with Prince Ivan. "Well," he said, "the first time I forgive you because of your kindness in giving me water. And I'll forgive you the next time. But the third time—watch out!—I'll cut you into pieces!" He took Maria Morevna from Ivan and carried her off. And Prince Ivan sat down on a stone and burst into tears.

He cried and cried, and went back for Maria Morevna again. Koshchey the Deathless happened to be away. "Let's go, Maria Morevna!" "Ah, Prince Ivan! He'll catch up with us." "Let him. We'll have at least an hour or two together." They got ready and left. Koshchey the Deathless returned home, and on the way his trusty steed stumbled under him. "Why are you stumbling, you greedy old nag? Do you sense something wrong?" "Prince Ivan was here, he's taken Maria Morevna with him." "Can we catch up with them?" "We can sow barley, wait until it grows, reap it and thresh it, brew some beer, drink ourselves drunk, sleep as much as we want and more, then give chase—and even then we'll catch up with them!" Koshchey galloped off and caught up with Prince Ivan. "Well, I told you that you'd never see Maria Morevna, just as you won't see your own ears!" He took her away and carried her off to his house.

Prince Ivan was left alone, cried and cried, and went back for Maria Morevna again. Koshchey the Deathless happened to be away at that moment. "Let's go, Maria Morevna!" "Ah, Prince Ivan! You know he'll catch up with us and cut you into pieces." "Let him! I can't live without you." They got ready and left. Koshchey the Deathless returned home, and on the way his noble steed stumbled under him. "Why are you stumbling? Do you sense something wrong?" "Prince Ivan was here. He's taken Maria Morevna with him." Koshchey the Deathless galloped off and caught up with Prince Ivan, cut him into tiny pieces, and put them into a tarred barrel. He took the barrel, reinforced it with iron hoops, threw it into the blue sea, and carried Maria Morevna off to his house.

At that very moment the silver Ivan had left with his brothers-in-law tarnished. "Ah," they said. "Something bad's happened!" The eagle flew off at top speed to the blue sea, seized the barrel and brought it ashore, the falcon flew to get the water of life, and the raven went for

46

the water of death. The three met at the same place, broke open the barrel, took out the pieces of Prince Ivan, and washed them and assembled them. The raven sprinkled them with the water of death, and the flesh grew together into a body. The falcon sprinkled it with the water of life, and Prince Ivan shuddered, got up, and said, "Ah, I've slept for such a long time!" "You'd have slept longer still if not for us!" replied his brothers-in-law. "Come and visit us now." "No, Brothers! I'm going to go and search for Maria Morevna."

He came to her and asked of her, "Find out from Koshchey the Deathless where he found himself such a trusty steed." Maria Morevna waited for the best moment and started questioning Koshchey. He replied, "Beyond the thrice-ninth lands, in the thrice-tenth kingdom, beyond the river of fire lives Baba Yaga. She has a mare on which she rides around the world every day. She also has a lot of other splendid mares. I served as her herdsman for three days, didn't let a single mare stray, and for that Baba Yaga gave me a colt." "And how did you manage to cross the river of fire?" "I have a handkerchief—if I wave it three times to the right, there appears a tall, tall bridge, and the fire can't reach it!" Maria Morevna listened to everything he said, passed it all on to Prince Ivan, got the handkerchief, and gave it to him.

Prince Ivan managed to cross the river of fire and set off to see Baba Yaga. He walked for a long time without food or drink. He came across an exotic bird with its young. Prince Ivan said, "I'll eat one of your fledglings." "Don't eat them, Prince Ivan!" asked the exotic bird. "I'll be useful to you someday." He went on farther and saw a beehive in the forest. "I'll take some of the honey," he said. The queen bee responded, "Don't touch my honey, Prince Ivan! I'll be useful to you someday." He didn't touch it and went farther. He came across a lioness with her young. "I'll at least eat this little lion. I'm so hungry that I feel ill!" "Don't touch him, Prince Ivan," asked the lioness. "I'll be useful to you someday." "All right, I'll do as you ask!"

He went hungrily on his way, walked and walked, and there stood Baba Yaga's house, surrounded by twelve stakes with human heads

impaled on eleven of them, and only one bare. "Greetings, Granny!"
"Greetings, Prince Ivan! Why have you come—of your own free will
or by force?" "I've come to earn a bogatyr's steed from you." "All right,
prince! I don't ask for a year's service, but for three days in all. If you
take care of my mares, I'll give you a bogatyr's steed, but if not, then
don't get angry, but your head will be stuck on the last stake." Prince
Ivan agreed. Baba Yaga gave him food and drink and ordered him to
get to work. He'd only just driven the mares into the field when the
mares raised their tails and dispersed all over different parts of the
meadow. The prince didn't have time to see where they were headed
when they all disappeared. He burst into tears and despaired, then sat
down on a stone and fell asleep. The sun was already setting when the
exotic bird flew to him and woke him. "Get up, Prince Ivan! The mares
are all back now." The prince got up and returned to the house, and
there Baba Yaga was making a fuss and shouting at her mares, "Why
have you come back?" "What choice did we have? Birds from all corners of the world descended on us, and almost pecked out our eyes."
"Well, tomorrow don't run through the meadows, but scatter all over
the dense forests."

Prince Ivan slept through the night, and the next morning Baba
Yaga said to him, "Listen, Prince, if you don't take care of the mares,
if you lose even one of them, I'll have your wild head on a stake!" He
drove the mares into the field, and they immediately raised their tails
and scattered through the dense forests. Once again the prince sat
down on a stone, cried and cried, then fell asleep. The sun was setting
behind the forest when the lioness ran up to him. "Get up, Prince
Ivan! The mares are all rounded up." Prince Ivan got up and went
home, where Baba Yaga was making a fuss and shouting at the mares
even more than before. "Why have you come back?" "What choice
did we have? Wild beasts from all corners of the world descended on
us, and almost tore us to pieces."

"Well, tomorrow run into the blue sea."

Once again Prince Ivan slept through the night, and the next
morning Baba Yaga sent him to tend the mares. "If you don't take

care of the mares, your wild head will be on that stake." He drove the mares into the field, and they immediately raised their tails, vanished from sight, and ran into the blue sea, where they stood up to their necks in the water. Prince Ivan sat down on a stone, cried, then fell asleep. The sun was setting behind the forest when the bee flew up to him and said, "Get up, Prince! The mares are all rounded up. When you get back home, don't let Baba Yaga see you, but go to the stables and hide behind the manger. There's a mangy colt wallowing in the manure. Steal him and at exactly midnight leave the house."

Prince Ivan got up, made his way to the stables, and lay down behind the manger. Baba Yaga made a fuss and shouted at the mares, "Why have you come back?" "What choice did we have? Huge swarms of bees from all corners of the world descended on us, and began stinging us until our blood ran!"

Baba Yaga fell asleep and at exactly midnight Prince Ivan stole her mangy colt, saddled it, mounted it, and galloped off toward the river of fire. When he reached it he waved the handkerchief three times to the right, and suddenly out of nowhere a tall, splendid bridge was suspended across the river. The prince crossed the bridge and waved the handkerchief just two times to the left, and the bridge left over the river was as narrow as could be! In the morning Baba Yaga woke up, and the mangy colt was nowhere to be found! She instantly gave chase, galloping in the iron mortar at full speed, urging it on with a pestle, sweeping the traces with a broom. She galloped to the river of fire, took a look, and said, "Good bridge!" She rode on the bridge and had just reached the middle when the bridge gave way and Baba Yaga tumbled into the river and suffered an excruciating death! Prince Ivan fed the colt in green meadows and he became a marvelous steed.

The prince came to Maria Morevna. She ran out and threw her arms around his neck. "How did God bring you back to life?" "In such and such a way," he said. "Let's go." "I'm afraid, Prince Ivan!! If Koshchey catches up with us, you'll be cut up into pieces again." "No, he won't catch up! I now have a splendid steed fit for a bogatyr; he flies like a bird." They mounted the horse and set off. Koshchey the Death-

49

less returned home, and on the way his steed stumbled under him. "Why are you stumbling, you greedy old nag? Do you sense something wrong?" "Prince Ivan was here, he's taken Maria Morevna away." "Can we catch up with them?" "God knows! Prince Ivan has a horse now fit for a bogatyr, better than I." "No, I won't put up with this!" said Koshchey the Deathless. "I'm going after them." After a long time or a short time he caught up with Prince Ivan, jumped to the ground, and made to swing at him with his sharp saber. At that moment Prince Ivan's steed kicked Koshchey the Deathless with all his strength and smashed his head, and the prince finished him off with his mace. Then the prince piled a heap of wood, lit a fire, burned Koshchey the Deathless in the flames, and scattered the ashes to the wind.

Maria Morevna mounted Koshchey's horse, Prince Ivan mounted his, and they rode off to visit first the raven, then the eagle, and finally the falcon. Wherever they came they were greeted joyfully. "Ah, Prince Ivan, we'd already given up hope of seeing you."

"We can see now why you went to all that trouble. You could search the whole world wide and you wouldn't find a beauty like Maria Morevna!" They visited a while, feasted, then set off for their own kingdom. They arrived, and they began to live and thrive, knew no need, and from time to time would drink some mead.

TALE OF PRINCE IVAN, THE FIREBIRD, AND THE GRAY WOLF

In a certain land, in a certain kingdom, there lived a king called Vyslav Andronovich. He had three princely sons: the first—Prince Dimitry, the second—Prince Vasily, and the third—Prince Ivan. This tsar, Vyslav Andronovich, had a garden so rich that there was none better in any other kingdom. Precious trees of all sorts grew in this garden, with fruit and without, and one apple tree was the king's particular favorite, and on this tree grew apples of pure gold. A firebird started visiting King Vyslav's orchard. It had gold feathers and eyes like oriental crystals. Each night it would fly into the garden, sit on King Vyslav's favorite apple tree, pick the gold apples from it, and fly away. King Vyslav Andronovich was most unhappy that the firebird was picking so many apples from the tree, and summoned his three sons, and said to them, "My dear children! Which one of you can catch the firebird in my garden? Whoever can take it alive, to him I'll give half of my kingdom right away, and the remainder of it after I die." In one voice his princely sons cried, "Our gracious sovereign and father, Your Majesty! We'll be most happy to try and take the firebird alive!"

The first night Prince Dimitry went to keep watch over the garden and, sitting down under the apple tree from which the firebird was picking the apples, he fell asleep and didn't hear the firebird fly into the garden and pick a lot of the gold apples. Next morning King Vyslav Andronovich summoned his son Prince Dimitry and asked,

"Well, my dear son, did you see the firebird or not?" And he answered, "No, gracious sovereign and father! It didn't come last night!" The following night Prince Vasily went to keep watch over the garden. He sat down under the same apple tree and, after sitting there for an hour, then another hour, he fell asleep so soundly that he never heard the firebird fly into the garden and pick the apples. Next morning King Vyslav summoned him and asked, "Well, my dear son, did you see the firebird or not?" "Gracious sovereign and father! It didn't come last night!"

The third night Prince Ivan went to watch over the garden and sat down under the apple tree. He sat there for an hour, another, and a third—and suddenly the entire garden became so bright, it was as if it were illuminated by many lights. The firebird came and sat on the apple tree, and started to pick the apples. Prince Ivan crept up on it so stealthily that he managed to seize its tail. But he couldn't keep a hold on the firebird, which broke free and flew away, leaving Prince Ivan with only a feather from its tail, onto which he'd held firmly. Next morning, as soon as King Vyslav awoke, Prince Ivan went to him and gave him the feather from the firebird. King Vyslav was simply overjoyed that his youngest son had at least managed to get a feather from the firebird. The feather was so wonderful and dazzling, that if placed in a dark room it would shine as brightly as if numerous candles had been lit in the room. King Vyslav placed the feather in his study as something that should be preserved forever. Thereafter the firebird never returned to the garden.

King Vyslav summoned his sons again and said, "My dear children! I give you my blessing to go and find the firebird and bring it to me alive. Whoever brings me the firebird, of course, will receive what I promised earlier." Prince Dimitry and Prince Vasily started resenting their younger brother, Prince Ivan, for having managed to pull out the feather from the firebird's tail. They accepted their father's blessing and set off together to search for the firebird. And Prince Ivan also asked his father's blessing for the same task. King Vyslav said to him, "My dear son, my dearest child! You're still young and not used to such a long and hard journey. Why must you leave me? Your brothers have already gone. And if you leave me too, what if all three of you don't come back for a long time? I'm already old and walk in the shadow of the Lord. If during your absence the Lord takes my life, who'll rule the kingdom instead of me? A rebellion could break out or a conflict among our people, and there'd be no one to ensure peace. Or an enemy could move in on us, and there'd be nobody to lead our troops." But however hard King Vyslav tried to hold Prince Ivan back, there was no way he could withhold his permission in light of his insistent pleas. Prince Ivan received his father's blessing, chose a horse, and set off, not knowing where he was going.

He rode neither near nor far, neither high nor low, for quickly can a tale be spun, but slowly is a real deed done, and he finally came to an open field, a green meadow. In the open field stood a pillar, and on this pillar were written the words, "Whoever goes straight ahead will be hungry and cold; whoever takes the right will be alive and well, but his horse will die; and whoever takes the left will be killed, but his horse will be alive and well." Prince Ivan read the inscription and turned right, keeping in mind that though his horse would be killed, he himself would stay alive and in due course could get another horse. He rode for a day, another, and a third—and suddenly met a huge gray wolf, who said, "Eh, so it's you, young Prince Ivan! Didn't you read what was written on the pillar, that your horse would die? So why did you choose this route?" Having said this, the wolf tore Prince Ivan's horse in half, and ran off.

In despair at the death of his horse, Prince Ivan burst into tears and walked on. He walked all day, was completely exhausted, and was about to sit down to rest when suddenly the gray wolf caught up with him and said, "I'm sorry, Prince Ivan, that you've exhausted yourself walking. I'm also sorry I ate your good steed. All right! Sit on me, the gray wolf, and tell me where I should take you and why." Prince Ivan told the gray wolf where he needed to go, and the gray wolf carried him along more quickly than his horse and after a certain time, right at nightfall, he brought Prince Ivan to a stone wall that wasn't too high, stopped, and said, "Get off me, the gray wolf, Prince Ivan, and climb over this stone wall. Behind the wall there's a garden and in this garden the firebird sits in a golden cage. Take the firebird, but don't touch the gold cage. If you take the cage, you won't be able to get away: you'll be captured at once!" Prince Ivan climbed over the stone wall into the garden, saw the firebird in the golden cage, and was very taken with the cage. He took the bird from the cage and started to leave, but then he changed his mind and said to himself, "Why did I take the firebird without the cage? Where will I put it?" He returned and had just taken down the golden cage when the sound of noise like thunder filled the garden, for there were strings attached to the cage. The guards instantly awoke, ran into the garden, caught Prince Ivan with the firebird, and brought him to their king, whose name was Dolmat. King Dolmat was furious with Prince Ivan and shouted at him in a loud, angry voice, "Aren't you ashamed of stealing, young man? Who are you, where do you come from, who's your father, and what's your name?" Prince Ivan said, "I'm from Vyslav's kingdom, the son of King Vyslav Andronovich, and my name's Prince Ivan. Your firebird took to flying into our garden each night and picking gold apples from my father's favorite apple tree, and practically ruined the whole tree. That's why my father sent me to find the firebird and to bring it to him." "Ah, young man, Prince Ivan," said King Dolmat. "Is it nice to behave as you have? You should have come to me and I'd have given you the firebird with honor, but now how will it be when I announce to all the lands that you behaved dishonorably in my kingdom? But, listen, Prince Ivan! If you render me a service—go beyond the thrice-ninth lands to the thrice-tenth kingdom and bring me King Afron's golden-maned horse—I'll forgive you your offense and hand over the firebird to you with great honor. But if you don't render me this service, I'll let all the lands know of you as a dishonorable thief." Deeply miserable, Prince Ivan left King Dolmat, promising to get him the golden-maned horse.

He came to the gray wolf and told him everything that King Dolmat had said. "Oh, what a young man you are, Prince Ivan!" said the gray wolf. "Why didn't you listen to what I told you and take the golden cage?" "I'm guilty before you," said Prince Ivan to the gray wolf. "Well, so be it!" said the gray wolf. "Sit on me, the gray wolf, and I'll take you where you need to go." Prince Ivan sat on the gray wolf's back and the wolf carried him as fast as an arrow, ran not a short time nor a long time, and finally at nightfall arrived at King Afron's kingdom. At the white-walled royal stables, the gray wolf said to Prince Ivan, "Go into these white-walled stables, Prince Ivan (the stable guards are all sleeping soundly now!), and take the golden-maned horse. Only don't take the golden bridle that's hanging on the wall, or there'll be trouble." Prince Ivan entered the stables, took the horse, and was about to leave, but saw the golden bridle on the wall, was very taken with it, and lifted it off the wall. As soon as he lifted it, the sound of noise like thunder filled the stables, for there were strings attached to the bridle. The stable guards instantly awoke, ran into the stables, caught Prince Ivan, and brought him to King Afron. "Oh, what a young man you are!" said King Afron, and asked, "Tell me— which kingdom are you from, who's your father, and what's your name?" Prince Ivan replied, "I'm from Vyslav's kingdom, the son of King Vyslav Andronovich, and my name's Prince Ivan!" "So, young man, Prince Ivan!" said King Afron. "Is your action that of an honorable knight? You should have come to me and I'd have given you the golden-maned horse with honor. But now how will it be if I announce to all the lands that you acted dishonorably in my kingdom? But, listen, Prince Ivan! If you render me a service and go beyond the thrice-ninth lands to the thrice-tenth kingdom and bring me Elena the Beautiful, with whom I long ago fell in love heart and soul but cannot win, then I'll forgive you your offense and will hand over the golden-maned horse and the golden bridle with honor. But if you don't render me this service, I'll let all the lands know of you as a dishonorable thief and write a record of how badly you acted in my kingdom." Prince Ivan promised King Afron to bring Elena the Beautiful, left the royal chamber, and burst into bitter tears.

He went to the gray wolf and told him everything that had happened. "Ah, what a young man you are, Prince Ivan!" the gray wolf said to him. "Why didn't you listen to what I told you and take the golden bridle?" "I'm guilty before you," Prince Ivan told the wolf. "Well, so be it!" continued the gray wolf. "Sit on me, the gray wolf, and I'll take you where you need to go." Prince Ivan sat on the gray wolf's back and the gray wolf carried him as fast as an arrow. He ran the way described in fairy tales, ran for a short time, and finally came to the kingdom of Princess Elena the Beautiful. The wolf took him as far as a golden fence that surrounded a marvelous garden, and said to Prince Ivan, "Now, Prince Ivan, get off me, the gray wolf, and go back down the road along which we came, and wait for me under the green oak in the open field." Prince Ivan went off where he was told to go. The gray wolf waited by the golden fence for Princess Elena the Beautiful to come and stroll in the garden. Toward evening, when the sun started to sink in the west, and the air grew cooler, Princess Elena the Beautiful came to stroll in the garden with her servants and ladies-in-waiting. When she came out and approached the place where the gray wolf was sitting behind the golden fence, the gray wolf suddenly leaped over the fence into the garden, seized the beautiful Princess Elena, leaped back, and ran off with her at full speed. He arrived beneath the green oak in the open field, where Prince Ivan was waiting for him, and said, "Prince Ivan, sit as fast as you can on me, the gray wolf!" Prince Ivan sat on him, and the gray wolf raced with both of them to King Afron's kingdom. The servants and all the ladies-in-waiting who'd been strolling in the garden with the beautiful Princess Elena immediately ran to the palace and sent forces after them, to chase down the gray wolf. Fast as they pursued them, however, they couldn't catch up, and came back.

Sitting on the gray wolf together with the beautiful Princess Elena, Prince Ivan fell head over heels in love with her, and she with him. And when the gray wolf arrived in King Afron's kingdom and Prince Ivan had to escort the beautiful Princess Elena to the palace and deliver her to the tsar, the prince fell into despair and started to cry. The gray wolf asked, "Why are you crying, Prince Ivan?" to which Prince

Ivan replied, "Gray wolf, my friend! How can I, a fine youth, not cry and despair? I'm head over heels in love with the beautiful Princess Elena, but now I have to deliver her to King Afron in exchange for the golden-maned horse, and if I don't deliver her, then King Afron will dishonor me throughout all the lands."

"I've rendered you many a service, Prince Ivan," said the gray wolf. "I'll render you this one, too. Listen, Prince Ivan. I'll turn into the beautiful Princess Elena, and you deliver me to King Afron and take the golden-maned horse. He'll think I'm the real princess. And when you've mounted the golden-maned horse and are already far away, then I'll persuade King Afron to let me stroll in the open field. And when he lets me go with the servants and ladies-in-waiting, and I'll be with them in the open field, remember me, and I'll be with you once again." The gray wolf said these words, struck the damp earth, and became the beautiful Princess Elena. Nobody could tell that he wasn't the real princess. Prince Ivan took the gray wolf, went to King Afron's palace, and told the beautiful Princess Elena to wait for him outside the town. When Prince Ivan appeared at King Afron's with the false Elena the Beautiful, the tsar was overjoyed that he finally had the treasure for which he'd yearned so long. He accepted the false princess and handed the golden-maned horse over to Prince Ivan. Prince Ivan mounted the horse, rode out of town, seated Elena the Beautiful beside him, and rode off, heading for King Dolmat's kingdom. The gray wolf instead of Elena the Beautiful lived at King Afron's for a day, another, and a third, and on the fourth he went to King Afron to ask that he might stroll in the open field so as to dispel his profound grief and misery. King Afron said, "Ah, my beautiful Princess Elena! I'll do anything for you, and I'll let you stroll in the open field." And he immediately ordered the servants and all the ladies-in-waiting to go and stroll with the beautiful princess in the open field.

Prince Ivan rode along with Elena the Beautiful, chatting along the way, and he forgot about his gray wolf. Then he remembered, "Ah, where's my gray wolf?" Suddenly out of nowhere the gray wolf appeared and said, "Sit on me, the gray wolf, Prince Ivan, and let the beautiful princess ride the golden-maned horse." Prince Ivan sat on the gray wolf, and they set off for King Dolmat's kingdom. They rode not for a long time or for a short time, until they reached the kingdom, and stopped three versts from the town. Prince Ivan asked the gray wolf, "Listen, my dear friend, the gray wolf! You've rendered me many a service, so render me a last one: can you turn yourself into a golden-maned horse instead of this one, for I don't want to part with this golden-maned horse?" Suddenly the gray wolf struck the damp earth and turned into a golden-maned horse. Prince Ivan left the beautiful Princess Elena in the green meadow, mounted the gray wolf, and took off for King Dolmat's palace. And as soon as he arrived, King Dolmat saw Prince Ivan riding on the golden-maned horse, was overjoyed, and at once left his royal chamber, met the prince in the spacious courtyard, kissed him on his sweet lips, took him by the right hand, and led him into his chambers of white stone. For such a joyous occasion King Dolmat ordered a feast, and they sat down at the oak tables with patterned tablecloths, and drank, ate, laughed, and made merry for two full days, and on the third day King Dolmat handed the firebird with the golden cage over to Ivan. The prince took the firebird, went outside the town, mounted the golden-maned horse together with the beautiful Princess Elena, and set off for home, for the kingdom of Vyslav Andronovich.

Next day King Dolmat decided to break in his golden-maned horse in the open field. He ordered the horse saddled, then mounted it and rode off into the open field. And as soon as he applied his spur, the horse threw off King Dolmat and, turning into the gray wolf again, ran off and caught up with Prince Ivan. "Prince Ivan!" he said. "Sit on me, the gray wolf, and let Elena the Beautiful ride the golden-maned horse." Prince Ivan sat on the gray wolf, and they went on their way. When the gray wolf brought Prince Ivan as far as the place where he'd torn apart his horse, he stopped and said, "Well, Prince Ivan, I've served you enough in faith and truth. Here's where I tore your horse in half, and here's where I've brought you. Get off me, the gray wolf.

You now have the golden-maned horse, so mount it and go where you need to. I'm no longer at your service." The faithful wolf said these words and ran off, and Prince Ivan cried bitterly at parting from the gray wolf, and then went on his way with the beautiful princess.

He rode with the beautiful Princess Elena on the golden-maned horse for a long time or a short time, and twenty versts from his own land he stopped, dismounted, and lay down with the beautiful princess under a tree to rest from the heat of the sun. He tied the golden-maned horse to the tree and set the golden cage with the fire-bird down beside him. As they lay on the soft grass murmuring sweet nothings to each other, they fell asleep. Just then Prince Ivan's brothers, Princes Dimitry and Vasily, who'd traveled through various kingdoms without finding the firebird, were returning home empty-handed, and by chance they came across their sleeping brother, Prince Ivan, with the beautiful Princess Elena. Seeing the golden-maned horse and the firebird in the golden cage on the grass, they were much taken with them and decided to kill their brother, Prince Ivan. Dimitry unsheathed his sword, stabbed Prince Ivan, and cut him up into little pieces. He then wakened the beautiful Princess Elena and asked her, "Beautiful maiden! From which kingdom do you come, who's your father, and what's your name?" The beautiful Princess Elena, seeing Prince Ivan's dead body, grew very frightened, burst into bitter tears, and tearfully said, "I'm Princess Elena the Beautiful, and Prince Ivan, whom you've killed in evil treachery, won me. If you were good knights, you'd have fought him in the open field fair and square to the death, but you killed him as he slept. What glory is there in that? A sleeping person is the same as a dead one!" Then Prince Dimitry pressed his sword against the beautiful Princess Elena's heart and told her, "Listen, Elena the Beautiful! You're in our hands now. We'll take you to our father, King Vyslav Andronovich, and you'll tell him that we found you, and the firebird, and the golden-maned horse. If you don't tell him that, I'll kill you this instant!" Frightened by the threat of death, the beautiful Princess Elena promised them, swearing by everything holy, to say what she was ordered to. Then Prince Dimitry and Prince Vasily cast lots to see who'd get the beautiful Princess Elena, and who'd get the golden-maned horse. As it turned out, Prince Vasily got the beautiful princess, while the golden-maned horse went to Prince Dimitry. Then Prince Vasily took the beautiful Princess Elena and seated her on his trusty steed, and Prince Dimitry mounted the golden-maned horse and took the firebird, so as to hand it over to his father, King Vyslav Andronovich, and they all set off.

For exactly thirty days Prince Ivan lay dead on the same spot, and then the gray wolf came upon him and recognized him by his smell. He wanted to help him, to revive him, but didn't know what to do. And just then the gray wolf noticed a raven and two young ravens flying above the dead body and intending to swoop down and eat Prince Ivan's flesh. The gray wolf hid behind a bush and as soon as the young ravens swooped down and started eating Prince Ivan's flesh, he leaped out from behind the bush, seized one of them, and made ready to tear it in half. Then the raven swooped down, settled at some distance from the gray wolf, and said to him, "Oh, you're a fine one, gray wolf! Don't touch my young child. He's done nothing to you." "Listen, Raven Ravenson!" said the gray wolf. "I won't touch your child and will release him safe and sound when you've rendered me a service: fly beyond the thrice-ninth lands to the thrice-tenth kingdom, and bring me the water of life and death." In reply to the gray wolf, Raven Ravenson said, "I'll render you this service, only don't touch my son." Having said these words, the raven flew off and soon disappeared from view. On the third day the raven returned and brought two phials with him: one with the water of life, the other—with the water of death, and he gave the phials to the gray wolf. The gray wolf took the phials, tore the young raven in half, sprinkled it with the water of death, and the young raven's body grew together. He sprinkled it with the water of life, and the young raven fluttered its wings and flew off. Then the gray wolf sprinkled Prince Ivan with the water of death, and his body grew together. He sprinkled him with the water of life, and Prince Ivan stood up and said, "Ah,

I've slept an incredibly long time!" To which the gray wolf said, "Yes, Prince Ivan, you'd have slept forever if not for me. You know, your brothers cut you up into bits and carried off the beautiful Princess Elena and the golden-maned horse and firebird with them. Now hurry home as fast as you can. Your brother, Prince Vasily, is to marry your bride, the beautiful Princess Elena, today. And to get there all the faster, you'd better sit on me, the gray wolf, and I'll get you there." Prince Ivan sat on the gray wolf, and the wolf raced off with him to King Vyslav Andronovich's kingdom, ran for a long time or a short time, until he arrived in town. Prince Ivan got off the gray wolf, went into town and, upon arriving at the palace, learned that his brother, Prince Vasily, was marrying the beautiful Princess Elena. He had just returned with her from the ceremony and was sitting at table. Prince Ivan entered the chamber, and as soon as Elena the Beautiful saw him, she instantly leaped up from behind the table, and started kissing him on his sweet lips and cried, "Here is my beloved bridegroom, Prince Ivan, and not that villain who's sitting at table!" Then King Vyslav Andronovich rose and asked the beautiful Princess Elena what she meant. Elena the Beautiful told him the whole truth about what had really happened: how Prince Ivan had won her, the golden-maned horse, and the firebird, how the older brothers had killed him in his sleep, and how they had intimidated her into saying that they'd won everything. King Vyslav was furious with Dimitry and Vasily and sent them to the dungeon. And Prince Ivan married the beautiful Princess Elena and they lived in love and such intimacy that each could not spend a single minute without the other.

THE FEATHER OF FINIST
THE BRIGHT FALCON

Once upon a time there lived an old man with three daughters. The oldest and middle ones loved fancy clothes, while the youngest only cared about household tasks. One day the father was getting ready to go to town and asked his daughters what he should buy for them. The oldest asked, "Buy me material for a dress!" The middle one said the same. "And what about you, my beloved daughter?" he asked the youngest. "Buy me a feather of Finist the Bright Falcon, Father." The father said his good-byes and left. He bought material for dresses for the older daughters, but he couldn't find a feather of Finist the Bright Falcon anywhere. He returned home, and his oldest and middle daughters were overjoyed with the material. "But I couldn't find a feather of Finist the Bright Falcon for you," he told the youngest. "If not, then not," she said. "Maybe you'll be lucky and find one another time." The older sisters cut out and sewed themselves new dresses, making fun of her, but she only kept silent.

Once again the father prepared to go to town and asked, "Well, daughters, what should I buy for you?" The oldest and middle ones asked him to buy a kerchief, while the youngest said, "Buy me a feather of Finist the Bright Falcon, Father." The father left for town, bought two kerchiefs, but didn't so much as glimpse a feather of Finist the Bright Falcon. He returned home and said, "Ah, daughter, again I couldn't find a feather of Finist the Bright Falcon." "Don't worry, Father. Maybe you'll be lucky and find one another time."

For the third time the father got ready to go to town and asked, "Tell me, Daughters, what should I buy for you?" The older ones said, "Buy us earrings," while once again the youngest said, "Buy me a feather of Finist the Bright Falcon." The father bought gold earrings, then started looking for the feather, but no one knew of such a thing. Saddened, he left town, and had just gone through the town gate when he met an old man carrying a little box. "What do you have there, old fellow?" "A feather of Finist the Bright Falcon." "What are you asking for it?" "Give me a thousand." The father paid the money and galloped home with the little box. "So, my beloved daughter," he said to the youngest, "at last I've bought a gift for you, too. Here, take it!" The youngest practically skipped with joy, took the little box, and started to kiss it and caress it, pressing it close to her heart.

After supper they all retired to their rooms, and she also went to her room, opened the little box, and the feather of Finist the Bright Falcon at once flew out, struck the floor, and a handsome prince appeared before the maiden. They exchanged sweet and loving words. The sisters heard them and asked, "Whom are you talking with, Sister?" "With myself," replied the beautiful maiden. "Oh yes? Open the door!" The prince struck the floor and turned into a feather, and she took it, placed it in the box, and opened the door. The sisters looked here, glanced there, but saw no one! As soon as they left, the beautiful maiden opened the window, took the feather out, and said, "Fly into the open field, my feather, and come back when the time is right!" The feather turned into a bright falcon and flew into the open field.

The next night Finist the Bright Falcon flew back to his beautiful maiden and they chatted merrily. The sisters heard them and instantly ran to the father. "Father! Someone comes visiting our sister at night. Even now he's sitting and chatting with her." The father rose and went to the youngest daughter. He entered her room, but the prince had turned into a feather long ago and was lying in the little box. "Ah, you spiteful girls!" the father scolded his older daughters. "Why are you telling false tales about her? You'd do better to look to yourselves!"

The next day the sisters hit upon a clever plan: in the evening when it was quite dark they put a ladder at her window, gathered some sharp knives and needles, and stuck them in the beautiful maiden's window.

That night Finist the Bright Falcon flew back, tried and tried, but couldn't get into the room, and only cut his wings. "Good-bye, beautiful maiden," he said. "If you decide to search for me, then search beyond the thrice-ninth lands, in the thrice-tenth kingdom. But before you find me—the good youth, you'll wear out three pairs of iron shoes, break three iron staffs, and swallow three stone wafers!" But the maiden slept. Even though she heard his unwelcome words through her sleep, she couldn't wake up and rise.

In the morning she awoke, looked, and saw the knives and needles stuck in the window, the blood still dripping from them. She wrung her hands, "Ah, my God! My sisters must have killed my dear friend!" At once she got ready and left the house. She ran to the smithy, had three pairs of iron shoes and three iron staffs forged for her, and supplied herself with three stone wafers, then set off to search for Finist the Bright Falcon.

She walked and walked, wore down a pair of iron shoes, broke an iron staff, and swallowed a stone wafer before coming to a hut. She knocked. "Host and hostess! Give me shelter from the dark night!" The old woman answered, "Welcome, beautiful maiden! Where are you headed, my dear?" "Ah, Granny! I'm searching for Finist the Bright Falcon." "Well, beautiful maiden, you've a long search ahead of you!" Next morning the old woman said, "Go to see my middle sister, and she'll tell you what's needed. And here's my gift to you: a silver spinning wheel and a gold spindle. You'll spin flax and pull out a gold thread." Then she took a ball, rolled it down the road, and told her to follow it, wherever the ball rolled, and not to lose track of it! The maiden thanked the old woman and followed the ball.

After a short time or a long time she wore out another pair of shoes, broke another staff, and swallowed another stone wafer. Finally the ball rolled up to a hut. She knocked. "Good hosts! Give a beautiful maiden shelter from the dark night." "Welcome!" replied an old woman. "Where are you headed, beautiful maiden?" "I'm searching for Finist the Bright Falcon, Granny." "You've a long search ahead of you!" In the morning the old woman gave her a silver dish and a gold egg and sent her to her older sister, saying, "She knows where to find Finist the Bright Falcon!"

The beautiful maiden said good-bye to the old woman and went on her way. She walked and walked, wore out the third pair of shoes, broke the third staff, and swallowed the last wafer, and then the ball rolled up to a hut. The traveler knocked and said, "Good hosts! Give a beautiful maiden shelter from the dark night." Once again an old woman came out. "Come in, dearie! Welcome! Where are you coming from and where are you headed?" "I'm searching for Finist the Bright Falcon, Granny." "Oh, it's hard, really hard to find him! He's living now in such and such a town, and he's married to the wafer-baker's daughter." The next morning the old woman said to the beautiful maiden, "Here's a gift for you: a gold embroidery frame and a needle. Just hold the frame and the needle will embroider by itself. Now, go with God and get yourself hired as the wafer-baker's servant."

No sooner said than done. The beautiful maiden went to the wafer-baker's house and got herself hired as a servant. She did everything quickly and well, heating the stove, carrying the water, and preparing the dinner. The wafer-baker looked and was pleased. "Thank God," he said to his daughter. "I've finally got an obliging and good servant. She does everything without needing to be told." And the beautiful maiden, her household tasks finished, took the silver spinning wheel and gold spindle, and sat down to spin. She spun, and from the flax she pulled out a thread, not a simple thread, but one of pure gold. The wafer-baker's daughter caught sight of it: "Ah, beautiful maiden! Won't you sell me your stuff?" "Maybe!" "What's the price?" "Let me spend a night with your husband." The wafer-baker's daughter agreed. "There's no harm!" she thought. "I can give my husband a sleeping potion, and with this spindle my mother and I can get rich!"

Finist the Bright Falcon wasn't home; he spent the entire day flying through the skies, and returned only toward evening. They sat down to supper. The beautiful maiden served the food and kept looking at him, while he, the fine youth, didn't even recognize her. The wafer-baker's daughter mixed a sleeping potion into Finist the Bright Falcon's drink, put him to bed, and said to the servant, "Go to his room and chase away the flies!" The beautiful maiden chased the flies away, weeping tears. "Wake up, do awaken, Finist the Bright Falcon! I, the beautiful maiden, have come to you. I broke three iron staffs, wore out three pairs of iron shoes, and swallowed three stone wafers while searching for you all this time, dear!" But Finist slept and heard nothing, and that's how the night passed.

The next day the servant took the silver dish and rolled the gold egg on it. She rolled many gold eggs! The wafer-baker's daughter saw her. "Sell me your stuff," she said. "Maybe." "What's the price?" "Let me spend another night with your husband." "Fine, I agree!" Meanwhile Finist the Bright Falcon again spent the entire day flying through the skies, and returned only toward evening. They sat down to supper. The beautiful maiden served the food and kept looking at him, but it was as though he'd never known her. Again the wafer-baker's daughter gave him a sleeping potion to drink, put him to bed, and sent the servant to chase away the flies. And this time, no matter how hard she cried and tried to wake him, he slept through until morning and heard nothing.

On the third day the beautiful maiden took up the embroidery frame and the needle and it began embroidering by itself, creating wonderful designs! The wafer-baker's daughter couldn't tear her eyes off them. "Sell me your stuff, beautiful maiden," she said. "Do sell it!" "Maybe." "What's the price?" "Let me spend a third night with your husband." "Fine, I agree!" In the evening Finist the Bright Falcon returned home, his wife gave him the sleeping potion to drink, put him to bed, and sent the servant to chase away the flies. The beautiful maiden sat, chasing away the flies and tearfully wailing, "Wake up, do awaken, Finist the Bright Falcon! I, the beautiful maiden, have come to you. I broke three iron staffs, wore out three pairs of iron shoes, and swallowed three stony wafers while searching for you all this time, dear!" But Finist the Bright Falcon slept soundly and heard nothing.

She cried for a long time. She tried to wake him a long time. Suddenly one of the beautiful maiden's tears fell on his cheek, and he instantly awoke. "Ah," he said, "something burned me!" "Finist the Bright Falcon," the beautiful maiden replied, "I've come to you. I broke three iron staffs, wore out three pairs of iron shoes, and swallowed three stony wafers while searching for you all this time! For the third night now I'm standing over you, while you sleep without waking, without responding to my words!" And at that moment Finist the Bright Falcon recognized her and was overjoyed beyond words. They agreed on a plan and left the wafer-baker's daughter. In the morning the wafer-baker's daughter discovered both her husband and the servant gone! She complained to her mother, who ordered that the horses be made ready, and gave chase. She drove and drove, and even went to see the three old women, but couldn't catch up with Finist the Bright Falcon, of whom there was absolutely no trace!

Finist the Bright Falcon and his wife found themselves outside her father's house. He struck the damp earth and turned into a feather. The beautiful maiden took it, hid it in her bodice, and went to see her father. "Ah, my beloved daughter! I thought you'd disappeared for good! Where were you all this time?" "I went to pray to God." It so happened that it was Holy Week. And the father and the older daughters got ready to attend morning service. "So, my dear daughter," he said to the youngest. "Get ready to come with us. It's a day of joy now." "Father, dear, I have nothing to wear." "Wear our outfits," said the older daughters. "Ah, Sisters, your dresses won't fit me! I'd better stay at home."

The father and the two daughters left for the morning service. Then the beautiful maiden took out the feather. It struck the floor and turned into a handsome prince. The prince whistled at the window, and immediately there appeared dresses, outerwear, and a gold carriage. They put on these clothes, got into the carriage, and set off. They entered the church, went to the front of the congregation, and the people wondered at the prince and princess who had deigned to come. At the end of the service they left before everyone else and drove home. The carriage disappeared, as did the dresses and outerwear, and the prince turned into a feather. The father and older daughters returned home. "Ah, Sister! You didn't come with us, and a handsome prince and exquisite princess were in church." "That's all right, Sisters! You've told me about them, which is the same as if I'd been there."

The next day the same thing happened again, but on the third day, just as the prince and the beautiful maiden were getting into the carriage, the father came out of the church and with his own eyes saw the carriage drive up to his house and then vanish. The father returned home and started asking his youngest daughter questions. And she said, "There's no other way, I've got to tell the truth!" She took out the feather; the feather struck the floor and turned into the prince. The two got married right away, and the wedding was rich! I was at the wedding and drank wine. It ran down my mustache, but didn't go into my mouth. They put a cowl on my head, and started poking me. They forced a basket on me: "Don't hang around, little man, get out of here as fast as you can."

THE MAGIC MIRROR
꽃꽃

In a certain kingdom, in a certain land, there lived a widowed merchant. He had a son, a daughter, and a brother. One day the merchant was getting ready to sail to foreign lands to sell various goods. He planned to take his son with him and leave his daughter at home. Before leaving, he summoned his brother and said to him: "I leave my entire household in your hands, dear brother, and I beg you to look after my daughter. Teach her to read and write, and don't let her misbehave!" Then the merchant bid his brother and his daughter farewell and set off on his journey. The merchant's daughter was already of age and possessed such indescribable beauty that you could not find her equal if you walked around the whole world! Her uncle began to have unclean thoughts that would not give him peace day or night. He made advances toward the maiden, telling her, "You'll either sin with me or you won't live on this earth! I'll kill you and then run away myself! . . ."

The girl ran toward the bathhouse with her uncle on her heels, and when she got there she grabbed a basin full of boiling water and soaked him from head to toe. He was laid up for three weeks and almost didn't recover. A terrible hatred gnawed at his heart and he began to think of ways he could repay the trick with one of his own. He thought and thought, and finally wrote his brother a letter: your daughter is up to no good, she gets around, never sleeps at home, and doesn't listen to me. The merchant received the letter, read it, and became very angry. He told his son, "Your sister is shaming the whole family! She deserves no mercy: I want you to go home this very minute and chop the incorrigible girl into little bits and bring me her heart on this knife. Then our family name won't be the laughing-stock of good people!"

The son took the sharp knife and headed for home. He arrived in his hometown in secret, without anyone knowing, and began to investigate: how was the merchant's daughter really living? Everyone praised her in one voice as a quiet, modest, God-fearing, obedient girl. Having heard all this, he went to see his sister. She was overjoyed and welcomed him with hugs and kisses: "Dear brother! How did the Lord bring you this way? How is our dear father?" "Oh, dear sister, don't be so quick to rejoice. My homecoming is not a happy one: father sent me with orders to chop your pale body into little pieces and bring him your heart on this knife."

The sister burst into tears. "My God," she said, "why such cruelty?" "I'll tell you why!" said her brother, and told her about their uncle's letter. "Oh, Brother, I haven't done anything wrong!" The merchant's son listened as she told him what had happened, and then he said, "Don't cry, little sister! I know that you're not at fault, and even though Father told me not to accept any excuses, I still won't punish you. Better if you pack your things, leave our father's house, and go wherever your eyes lead you. God won't abandon you!" The merchant's daughter didn't think about it for very long. She packed for her journey, bid farewell to her brother, and left. Where to, even she did not know. Meanwhile her brother killed a stray dog, cut out its heart, stuck it onto the end of the sharp knife, and took it to his father. As he handed over the dog's heart he said, "There, I've fulfilled your parental command and executed my sister." "Served her right," replied his father, "a dog like her deserved a dog's death!"

For a long time or a short time the beautiful maiden wandered the wide world, and finally she went into a thick forest. The trees were so tall she could barely see the sky. She walked through the forest and suddenly emerged into a large clearing. In the clearing was a white palace made of stone surrounded by an iron fence. "I'll pay a visit to that palace," thought the girl, "not everyone is mean, after all, so it should be all right." She entered the palace, but didn't see a human soul in the halls. She was just about to turn back when suddenly two mighty bogatyrs galloped into the courtyard and entered the palace. They saw the maiden and said, "Hello, beauty!" "Hello, honorable knights!" "Look, Brother," one of the bogatyrs said to the other, "we were bemoaning the fact that we had nobody to look after things at home, and God sent us a little sister." The bogatyrs let the merchant's daughter live with them, called her their sister, gave her the keys to the palace, and made her the mistress of the whole place. Then they took out their sharp sabers, stood chest to chest, and made a vow: "If one of us dares to encroach on our sister's honor, the other will hack him up without mercy with his saber."

So the beautiful maiden lived with the bogatyrs. Her father in the meantime finished buying goods overseas, returned home, and a short while later remarried. The new wife of the merchant was an indescribable beauty. She had a magic mirror into which you could look and find out what was happening and where. One day the bogatyrs were getting ready to go out hunting. They instructed their sister: "Make sure you don't let anyone in while we are gone!" They said good-bye and left. At that very moment the merchant's wife was gazing into her mirror, admiring her own beauty. She said, "There is none more beautiful than I in the whole world!" But the mirror replied, "You are fair, there is no doubt! But you have a stepdaughter who lives in the thick forest with two bogatyrs, and she is fairer still!"

The stepmother did not like these words at all. She summoned a mean old woman. "Here," she told the servant, "take this ring and go into the thick forest. There you will find a white stone palace. In that palace lives my stepdaughter. Bow to her and give her the ring, and tell her it is a present from her brother!" The old woman took the ring and set off for the forest. She arrived at the white stone palace, where the beautiful maiden saw her and ran out to meet her. She was keen to learn news from her native land. "Hello, Granny! How did the Lord bring you here? Is everyone alive and well?" "They live and chew bread! Your brother asked me to inquire about your health and to give you this ring as a gift. Here, put it on!" The maiden was so happy, happier than words can describe. She took the old woman inside, gave her all sorts of food and drink, and told her to give her regards to her brother. In an hour the old woman pushed off for home, and the maiden admired the ring and decided to put it on. She did, and right away fell over as if dead.

The bogatyrs returned home and entered the courtyard, but their sister did not come out to meet them. What was the matter? They went to her room and found her lying there dead, not saying a word. The bogatyrs began to grieve; death had taken the very thing that was most beautiful of all! "We must dress her in new clothes and put her in a coffin," they said. They began to prepare her and one of them noticed a ring on the maiden's hand. "We can't bury her with this ring, can we? We had better take it off and keep it as a memento." They took off the ring and immediately the fair maiden opened her eyes, gasped, and came to life. "What has happened to you, little sister? Did someone come to visit you?" the bogatyrs asked. "An old woman I know from home came and gave me a ring." "Oh, you're so disobedient! Not for nothing did we tell you not to let anyone in when we're not here. See that you don't do it again!"

A short while later the merchant's wife again looked into her mirror and found out that her stepdaughter was still alive and beautiful. She summoned the old woman and gave her a ribbon, saying, "Go to the white stone palace and give my stepdaughter this gift. Tell her it's from her brother!" The old woman came to see the maiden again, persuaded her with all sorts of clever words, and gave her the ribbon. The girl was overjoyed and tied the ribbon around her neck. Right away she fell onto the bed as if dead. The bogatyrs returned from their hunt, saw their sister lying dead, and began to dress her in new clothes. They took off the ribbon and she opened her eyes, gasped, and came to life. "What happened, little sister? Was the old woman here again?" "Yes," she said, "the old woman from home came again and brought me a ribbon." "Oh, what will we do with you, little sister? We begged you not to let anyone in when we're gone!" "Forgive me, dear brothers! I couldn't help myself! I wanted to hear news from home!"

A few days passed and again the merchant's wife looked into her mirror. Again her stepdaughter was alive. She summoned the old woman. "Here," she said, "take this strand of hair! Go to my stepdaughter and kill her once and for all!" The old woman bided her time until the bogatyrs went out hunting and again went to the white stone palace. The fair maiden saw her through the window and couldn't help herself. She jumped up to meet the old woman: "Hello, Granny! How does God find you today?" "Still alive, dearie! I've dragged myself out into the world to come see you." The fair maiden led her into the palace, gave her all sorts of food and drink, asked about her relatives, and told her to give her regards to her brother. "Alright," said the old woman, "I will. And you, dearie, you probably have nobody to search your head for lice, do you? Let me do it for you!" "Go ahead, Granny!" She began to pick at the fair maiden's head and braided the enchanted strand into her hair. The maiden fell right over as if dead. The old woman cackled and left quickly so nobody would catch her.

The bogatyrs came home and went into the palace. They saw their sister lying dead. For a long time they looked her over to see whether there was something that should not be there, but they found nothing! So they made a crystal coffin, one so magnificent that you couldn't imagine it, one that exists only in fairy tales. They adorned the merchant's daughter in a brilliant gown, like a bride on her wedding day, and laid her in the crystal coffin. They placed the coffin in the middle of the palace's great hall under a canopy of red velvet with diamond tassels and gold fringes, and hung twelve lanterns on twelve crystal columns. Then they wept bitter tears, for they were seized by a great longing. "What do we have to live for? Let's do ourselves in!" They embraced, said farewell, went up to the highest balcony, held hands, and jumped. They struck the sharp rocks below and thus ended their lives.

Many years passed. A certain prince was out hunting. He went into the thick forest, released his dogs, separated from his huntsmen, and set off alone along an overgrown path. He rode and rode and suddenly found himself in a clearing and saw in the clearing a white stone palace. The prince dismounted, went up the staircase, and looked around the palace chambers. Everywhere he looked the palace was richly adorned, but there was no sign of a mistress's hand anywhere: it had all been abandoned long ago! In one hall there stood a crystal coffin and in the coffin lay a dead maiden of indescribable beauty. There was a blush on her cheek and a smile on her lips, as if she were merely asleep.

The prince approached, looked at the maiden, and stood rooted to the spot as if held there by an unseen force. He stood from morning until late evening, unable to tear his eyes from her, with a troubled heart. He was riveted by her maidenly beauty, more wondrous than you could find anywhere on earth! His huntsmen had long been searching for him everywhere, combing the forest, blowing their horns, and shouting for him. The prince stood before the crystal coffin and did not hear a thing. The sun went down and a thick gloom set in. Only then did he come around. He kissed the dead maiden and went back. "Ah, Your Highness! Where have you been?" his huntsmen asked. "I was chasing an animal and lost my way." The next day, at first light, the prince went out hunting again. He galloped into the forest, separated from his huntsmen, and by the same path came to the white stone palace. Again he spent the entire day standing by the crystal coffin, not taking his eye off the dead maiden. Only late at night did he turn back for home. The same thing happened on the third day, and the fourth, and the rest of the week. "What's going on with our prince?" the huntsmen wondered. "Let's follow him, Brothers, and make sure he's not in any trouble."

So once again the prince went out to hunt, released his dogs in the forest, separated from his entourage, and set out for the white stone palace, this time with the huntsmen on his heels. They came to the clearing, went into the palace, saw the crystal coffin in the great hall, and their prince standing before the maiden. "Your Highness! It's no wonder you spent a week in the forest! Now we won't be able to leave until nightfall, either!" They stood in a circle around the crystal coffin looking at the maiden, admiring her beauty, and did not move an inch from morning until late evening. When it was completely dark, the prince addressed his huntsmen: "Do me a service, Brothers, a great service: take this coffin with the dead maiden, bring it to my palace, and put it in my bedroom. But do it quietly, so nobody finds out. I'll reward you handsomely, with more gold than you've ever seen." "Reward us as you will, Prince, for we are glad to serve you!" said the huntsmen. They lifted the crystal coffin, carried it into the courtyard, mounted it on the horses, and took it to the royal palace. There they put it in the prince's bedroom.

From that day on the prince thought no more about hunting. He sat at home, not setting foot from his bedroom, admiring the maiden. "What is the matter with our son?" thought the queen. "It's been so long since he's come out of his room, or even let anyone in. Has a sad longing overtaken him, or maybe some kind of illness? I should go and check on him." The queen entered his bedroom and saw the crystal coffin. What was it doing there? She asked around and gave an order immediately to bury the maiden, as custom demanded, in the damp mother earth.

The prince wept, and then went into the garden and picked some flowers. He took them to where the dead beauty lay and began to comb her light brown hair and adorn her head with the flowers. Suddenly the enchanted strand fell from her braid and the beauty opened her eyes, gasped, sat up in the crystal coffin, and said, "Oh, how long I've slept!" The prince's joy was indescribable. He took her by the hand and led her to his father and mother. "God sent her to me!" he said, "I can't live without her for a minute! Pray give us your permission to marry, dear father and mother." "Marry her, Son! We shan't go against God's will, and you won't find a greater beauty anywhere in the world!" Tsars don't waste time: on that very day there was a wedding and a great feast.

The prince married the merchant's daughter and doted on her. Some time passed and she wanted to visit her father and brother. The prince asked his father. "Alright," said the tsar, "go, my dear children! You, Prince, go by land so you can check on the state of affairs in our realm, and your wife will go by sea, a more direct route." They prepared everything for the princess's journey, equipped the sailors, and appointed a general to captain the ship. The princess went aboard and they sailed onto the open sea, while the prince set off by land.

The general saw the fair maiden, coveted her beauty, and began to make advances. What do I have to fear? he thought, since she was in his hands, and he could do whatever he pleased. "Love me," he said to the princess. "If you don't, I'll throw you into the sea!" The princess turned away without a reply, her eyes filling with tears. The general's words were overheard by a sailor, who came to the princess later that evening and told her, "Don't cry, Princess! Put on my uniform and I'll dress in your clothes. Go out onto the deck, and I'll stay in your quarters. Let the general throw me overboard, I'm not afraid. I'll just swim to shore, since we're not far from land!" They exchanged clothes and the princess went up onto the deck, while the sailor lay in her bed. At night the general appeared, seized the sailor, and threw him into the sea. The sailor swam and swam and by morning reached dry land. Meanwhile the ship docked and the sailors went ashore. The princess also disembarked, rushed to the market, bought herself a cook's outfit, put it on, and in this disguise went to work as a servant in her own father's kitchen.

A short while later the prince arrived at the merchant's house. "Hello, Father!" he said. "Accept me as your son-in-law, for I am married to your daughter. Where is she? Hasn't she arrived yet?" And then the general appeared with news: "Your Highness! A great misfortune has befallen us: the princess was standing on the deck when a storm came up and began to rock the ship. She began to swoon and was swept into the sea and drowned!" The prince began to grieve and cry, since he knew there was no return from the bottom of the sea. Her fate had been sealed! The prince stayed with his father-in-law for a few days and then ordered his entourage to prepare for the journey home. The merchant arranged a large farewell banquet. All his relatives and the local merchants and boyars gathered for the feast. His brother, the mean old woman, and the general were there, too.

They ate and drank and refreshed themselves, and one of the guests said, "Honorable friends! Why are we just eating and drinking? That's no good; let us tell tales!" "Alright! Let's!" all the guests shouted. "Who shall begin?" One guest tried but didn't know how, another was no better, and a third's memory had lapsed from the wine. What to do? One guest chimed in and said, "There is a new cook in the kitchen who has been to many foreign lands and seen many marvelous things. He's a master at telling tales!" The merchant sent for the cook. "Entertain my guests!" he said. The cook-princess replied, "What shall I tell, a fairy tale or a true story?" "Tell us a true story!" "Alright, a true story. But with one condition: if anyone interrupts me, he'll get hit on the forehead with my ladle!"

Everyone agreed. The princess began to tell the story of everything that had happened to her. "And so," she said, "there was a merchant who had a daughter, and before he went overseas he entrusted his daughter to his brother's keep. The uncle was full of desire because of her beauty and would not give her a moment's peace . . ." The uncle realized that she was speaking about him and said, "These are lies, dear people!" "Ah, so you think I'm lying? Here's a ladle to the forehead for you!" Then the story came to the episode with the stepmother and how she questioned her magic mirror, and how the mean old woman went to the white stone castle of the bogatyrs, and the stepmother and the old woman shouted in unison: "What nonsense! That's impossible!" The princess hit them on the head with the ladle and continued her story, telling about how she lay in the crystal coffin until she was found by the prince, who brought her back to life and married her, and about how she set off to visit her father.

The general knew he was in trouble and said to the prince, "I'll be going home now, if you please. I feel a headache coming on . . ." "Sit a while longer," replied the prince, "you'll be alright!" The princess began to tell the story of the general. He couldn't stand it and said, "It's all lies!" The princess whacked him on the head with the ladle. Then she cast off the cook's garments and revealed herself to the prince: "I'm not a cook, I'm your lawful wife!" The prince was overjoyed, and the merchant as well. They rushed to embrace and kiss her. Later they held a trial. The mean old woman and the uncle were shot by a firing squad. The stepmother-sorceress was tied to a stallion's tail, and the stallion galloped across a field and scattered her smashed bones over the bushes and the gullies. The general was put in prison and his place was taken by the sailor who had saved the princess. From then on, the prince, his wife, and the merchant lived a long and happy life together.

DANILO THE LUCKLESS
※※

In the city of Kiev our Prince Vladimir had many servants and peasants at court, and also the nobleman Danilo the Luckless. On Sundays Vladimir would give everyone a glass of vodka, but Danilo would get only a whack or two on the back of his neck. On big holidays some would get gifts, but he'd get nothing at all! On Saturday evening before Easter Sunday Prince Vladimir summoned Danilo the Luckless, handed him forty times forty sables, and ordered him to sew a fur coat before the holiday. The sables were not skinned, the buttons not made, and the loops not braided. He was ordered to press the shapes of forest animals into the buttons and to embroider the shapes of exotic birds into the loops.

Danilo the Luckless found the work hateful, tossed it aside, went outside the city gates, and wandered aimlessly, crying. He encountered an old, old woman going in the opposite direction. "Now, Danilo, don't split your sides with those sobs! Why are you crying, Luckless?" "Ah, you empty old bag, you silly ass, all patches and tatters, with eyes like platters! Leave me alone, I'm not in the mood!" He went on a little, and thought, "Why was I so nasty to her!" And he went back to her, and said, "Granny, dear heart! Forgive me. Here's why I'm so miserable: Prince Vladimir gave me forty times forty unskinned sables from which to make a fur coat by tomorrow morning. He wants a lot of buttons made, silk loops braided, and the buttons must have golden lions on them, and the loops must have exotic birds on them, trilling and singing! And where am I to get all this? It's easier to stand behind a counter holding a cup of vodka!"

The old woman, Patched Belly, said, "Ah, so now it's 'Granny, dear heart!' Go to the blue sea, stand by the damp oak. At exactly midnight the blue sea will swell, and Chudo-Yudo will appear, a sea monster with a gray beard, without arms and legs. Seize him by the beard and beat him until Chudo-Yudo asks, 'Why are you beating me, Danilo the Luckless?' And you answer, 'I want the beautiful Swan Maiden to appear before me, to have her body show through her feathers, her bones to show through her body, to see her marrow flow from bone to bone, like pearls being poured from cone to cone.'"

Danilo the Luckless went to the blue sea, stood by the damp oak. At exactly midnight the sea swelled, and Chudo-Yudo appeared, a sea monster without arms and legs, and nothing but a gray beard! Danilo seized him by the beard and started beating him against the damp earth. Chudo-Yudo asked, "Why are you beating me, Danilo the Luckless?" "Here's why: give me the beautiful Swan Maiden. I want her body to show through her feathers, her bones through her body, and to see her marrow flow from bone to bone, like pearls being poured from cone to cone."

In a few moments the beautiful Swan Maiden appeared, swam up to the shore, and said, "So, Danilo the Luckless, are you avoiding great deeds for fun, or are you trying to get them done?" "Ah, beautiful Swan Maiden! Sometimes I avoid, other times I try, and now I'm doubling my efforts, hoping to get by. Prince Vladimir has ordered me to make him a fur coat: the sables are not skinned, the buttons not made, the loops not braided!" "Will you take me in marriage? Then everything will be done in time!" He thought, "How can I take her in marriage?" "Well, Danilo, what do you think?" "There's nothing I can do! I'll take you!" She shook her wings, she tossed her head, and twelve sturdy men rose from the seabed. They were all carpenters, woodcutters, and masons, and they set to work immediately: a house was built in an instant! Danilo took her right hand, kissed her sweet lips, and led her to the princely chambers. They sat down at the table, ate and drank, refreshed themselves, and then and there got engaged.

"Now, Danilo, lie down and rest, don't worry about a thing! I'll get it all done."

She put him to bed, went out onto the crystal porch, shook her wings, and tossed her head. "My own dear father! Give me your crafts-men." Twelve fine fellows appeared and asked, "Beautiful Swan Maiden! What are your orders?" "Sew me a fur coat right away: the sables are not skinned, the buttons not made, the loops not braided." They set to work; some got the skins ready and did the sewing, others forged and shaped the buttons, and the rest braided the loops. In an instant a dazzling coat was made. The beautiful Swan Maiden went and awakened Danilo the Luckless. "Get up, my dear! The coat's ready and the church bells are sounding in Prince Vladimir's city of Kiev. It's time for you to get up and get ready for the morning service." Danilo got up, put on the fur coat, and left the house. She looked out of the window, stopped him, gave him a silver cane, and instructed, "As you're leaving the church, strike your chest with this: birds will start singing their song, and lions will then roar along. Take off the fur coat and without any fuss give it to Prince Vladimir, so that he won't forget about us. He'll invite you to visit and dine, and will offer a cup of wine. Don't empty the cup, though you may drink gladly, for if you empty it, things will end badly! And, above all, don't boast about me, about building a house in one night, one, two, three." Danilo took the cane and set off. She again made him come back, and gave him three eggs—two silver, one gold—and said, "Give the silver ones to the prince and princess when you offer them Easter greetings, and the gold one give to the one with whom you'll live forever."

Danilo the Luckless said good-bye to her and went to the morning service. Everyone was surprised, "What about that Danilo the Luck-less! He's managed to get the fur coat ready for the holiday." After the morning service he approached the prince and princess, offered them seasonal greetings, and accidentally took out the gold egg. Alyosha Popovich, a ladies' man, saw him do it. People started leaving the church, Danilo the Luckless struck his chest with the silver cane—and the birds sang their song, and the lions roared along. And Alyosha Popovich the ladies' man disguised himself as a crippled beggar and asked for holy alms. Everyone gave him something; only Danilo the Luckless stood there, thinking, "What can I give? I don't have anything!" And because it was a great holiday, he gave him the gold egg. Alyosha Popovich the ladies' man took the gold egg and changed back into his regular clothes. Prince Vladimir invited everyone for a bite to eat. And they ate and drank, refreshed themselves, and boasted. Danilo, who had drunk enough to be drunk, in his drunkenness began to boast of his wife. Alyosha Popovich the ladies' man started to boast about knowing Danilo's wife. But Danilo said, "If you know my wife, let my head be cut off, and if you don't know her, then you should have your head cut off!"

Alyosha went off, simply following his nose. He walked and cried. He encountered an old, old lady going in the opposite direction. "Why are you crying, Alyosha Popovich?" "Leave me in peace, you empty old bag! I'm not in the mood."

"Fine, but I can be useful to you!" And he asked her, "Granny, my dear! What did you want to tell me?" "Ah, now it's 'Granny, my dear!' " "You see, I boasted that I knew Danilo's wife . . ." "Phew! How on earth could you know her? Not even a tiny bird could get into her domain. Go to such and such a house, and ask her to dine at the prince's. She'll start bathing and getting ready, and will put her chain on the windowsill. Take this chain and show it to Danilo the Luckless." Alyosha Popovich went up to the wood-carved window and invited the beautiful Swan Maiden to dinner at the prince's. She started bathing, dressing, and getting ready for the feast. As she did so Alyosha Popovich took her chain and ran to the palace and showed it to Danilo the Luckless. "Well, Prince Vladimir," said Danilo the Luckless. "I now see that my head should be cut off. Let me go home and say good-bye to my wife."

He went home and said, "Ah, my beautiful Swan Maiden! What have I done! In my drunkenness I boasted about you, my wife, and now must pay for it with my life!" "I know all about it, Danilo the Luckless! Go and invite the prince and princess and all the citizens to our house. And if the prince tries to refuse, saying it's dusty and dirty, and the roads are poor, and the sea has risen and slippery swamps have appeared, you tell him, 'Never fear, Prince Vladimir! There are snowball-wood bridges and oak planks built over the swamps and over the rivers, with crimson cloth spread over the bridges, all fastened down with nails of cast iron. No dust will touch the fine fellows' boots, no mud will cling to their horses' hooves.'" Danilo the Luckless left so as to invite the guests, while the beautiful Swan Maiden went out onto the porch, shook her wings, tossed her head, and created a bridge from her house to Prince Vladimir's palace. It was covered with crimson cloth and fastened down with nails of cast iron. On one side of it flowers bloomed and nightingales sang, and on the other apples ripened and fruit trees flourished.

The prince and princess set out for the visit with all their brave warriors. They approached the first river—wonderful beer flowed in it, and many soldiers fell near it. They approached the second river—wonderful mead flowed in it, and more than half of the brave troops paid their respects to the mead and tumbled on their sides. They approached the third river—wonderful wine flowed in it, and the officers rushed to it and drank till they were drunk. They approached the fourth river—strong vodka flowed in it, kin to that very wine, and the prince glanced around and saw his generals flat on their backs. The prince remained with only three companions: his wife, Alyosha Popovich the ladies' man, and Danilo the Luckless. The guests arrived, entered the high-ceilinged chambers, and in the chambers stood maple tables covered by silken tablecloths, and painted chairs. They sat down at table—there were many various dishes, and foreign drinks not in bottles, not in jugs, but flowing in entire rivers! Prince Vladimir and the princess didn't drink anything, didn't eat, but simply looked, waiting to see when the beautiful Swan Maiden would appear.

They sat at table for a long time, for a long time they waited, until the time came to return home. Danilo the Luckless called her once, twice, three times—but she didn't come out to join the guests. Alyosha Popovich the ladies' man said, "If my wife did this, I'd teach her to listen to her husband!" The beautiful Swan Maiden heard this, came out onto the porch, and said, "And here's how I teach husbands!" She shook her wings, tossed her head, and flew off, and the guests were left in the mud on the hillocks: on one side was the sea, on another grief, on the third was moss, and on the fourth no relief! Prince, better put your pride aside, mount Danilo for your ride! By the time they reached home they were covered in mud from head to toe! I wanted to see the prince and princess, but it was hard because they chased me from the yard. I ducked beneath the gate, and whack!—I banged against it, hurt my back!

ILYA MUROMETS AND THE DRAGON
꩜

In a certain land, in a certain kingdom, there lived a peasant and his
dear wife. They lived amidst plenty, enjoyed enough of everything,
and had a considerable fortune in savings. Once, when they were sitting together, he said to her, "You know, Wife, we have enough of
everything, only we don't have any children. Let's pray to God. Maybe
the Lord will give us a child in our old age, during our last years." They
prayed to God, and she became pregnant, and when the time came
she gave birth. A year went by, a second, and a third, but the child's legs
didn't move properly, and after eighteen years he still couldn't walk.

The father and mother went to mow and stack hay, and the son was
left alone. A beggar-pilgrim approached the house and asked for alms.
"Little host! Give an old man of God alms for Christ's sake!" And the
son said to him, "Old man of God, I can't give you alms, for I can't
walk." The old man entered the house. "Now," he said, "rise from your
bed and fetch me a pitcher of water." The son rose and brought him
the pitcher. "Now go," the old man said, "and fetch me some water."
The son brought him some water and handed it to him. "Here you are,
old man of God!" And the old man gave it back to him. "Drink all the
water in the pitcher," the old man said, and once again sent him for
water: "Go again and fetch me another pitcher of water." As the son
went for more water he pulled out by the roots every tree he held on
to. The old man of God asked him, "Can you feel the strength in you

now?" "I can, old man of God! I've got great strength in me now. If a ring were attached to the world, I could grab it and turn the world over." When he brought another pitcher, the old man of God drank half of it, and gave him the other half to drink. His strength decreased. "That'll be enough strength for you!" he said. The old man of God prayed to the Lord and then went home. "May God be with you!"

The son was bored with lying down, and went to dig in the forest, to test his strength. And people were terrified at what he could do, at how much of the forest he dug up! His father and mother returned from mowing the hay and wondered what had happened. The entire forest was dug up. Who could have dug it up? They came closer, and the wife said to the husband, "Look, it's our Ilyushenka who's digging it up!" "You fool," he said. "Our Ilyushenka can't do something like that. What nonsense you talk!" And they approached Ilya. "Ah, holy Father! How on earth did this happen?" And Ilya said, "An old man of God came, asking for alms. I told him, 'Old man of God, I can't give you alms, for I can't walk.' And he came inside the house and said, 'Now, rise from the bed and fetch me a pitcher of water!' I got up and brought him the pitcher. He says, 'Go and fetch me some water.' I brought him some water and handed it to him. 'Drink all the water in the pitcher!' the old man says. I did, and felt enormous strength within me!"

The peasants gathered in the street and said among themselves, "Look at what a strong, mighty bogatyr he's become!" That's what the peasants called Ilya. "See how much he dug up! We need to tell people in town about him," they said. And the tsar learned of him, about his being such a strong, mighty bogatyr, and summoned him, and Ilya pleased the tsar, who supplied him with an appropriate outfit. And he pleased everybody and served well. And the tsar said, "You're a strong, mighty bogatyr! Could you lift my palace on its corner?" "Yes, Your Majesty! I can lift it even on its side, anyway one wants." The tsar had a lovely daughter, so beautiful that no mind could conceive, no word could express, no pen could describe. And she pleased Ilya and he wanted to marry her.

One day the tsar left to see a king in another kingdom. He arrived, and learned that the king also had a lovely daughter, whom a twelve-headed dragon was in the habit of visiting. He had drained her dry, and she had no energy at all! And the tsar said to the king, "I have such a strong and mighty bogatyr that he'll kill the twelve-headed dragon." The king asked, "Please send him to me." And the tsar returned home and said to the tsarina, "A twelve-headed dragon is in the habit of visiting this king's daughter. He's drained her dry, sucked her life juices." And he said, "Ilya Ivanovich! Can't you render a service and kill him?" "Yes, Your Majesty, I can. I'll kill him."

And the tsar said, "You'll go by coach and along the highway, and take such and such." "I'll go on horseback and alone. Please give me a horse." "Go into the stables," the tsar told him, "and choose any one you want." But his daughter said from the other room, "Don't go, Ilya Ivanovich. The twelve-headed dragon will kill you, you won't be able to deal with him." And he said, "Just stay here and don't worry about it. I'll come back safe and sound." He went to the stables to choose a horse for himself. He came to the first horse, laid his hand on it, and the horse stumbled. He tried out all the horses in the stables: as soon as he laid his hand on any horse it would stumble. Not one could stand firm. He went up to the very last horse, which stood neglected in a corner, and slapped it on the back. The horse merely neighed. And Ilya said, "Here's my faithful servant! He didn't stumble!" He returned to the tsar. "I've chosen my horse, my faithful servant, Your Majesty." He was sent off with prayers and due ceremony.

He mounted his trusty steed, rode for a long time or a short time, until he came to a mountain, a very steep, tall mountain, and covered with sand. He could barely ride up it. On the mountain stood a pillar, and on the pillar were indicated three roads: "If you take this road you'll be sated, but your steed will go hungry; if you take that road, your steed will be sated, but you'll go hungry; if you take the third road, you'll be killed." He took the third road, on which it said he would be killed, for he had faith in himself. He rode for a long time or a short time through dense forests, so dense he couldn't see anything! And suddenly he came upon a wide clearing in the forest, with a little hut standing on it! He rode up to the hut and said, "Little hut, little hut! Stand with your back to the forest, and your front facing me." The hut turned around, and stood with its back to the forest and its front facing him. He dismounted from his trusty steed and tied him to a post. And Baba Yaga heard him, and said, "Who's that lout? My grandfather and great-grandfather never had a whiff of a Russian, but now I'm about to see a Russian with my own eyes."

She struck the door with a staff, and the door opened. And she had a curved scythe in her hands, and made ready to take the bogatyr by the throat and cut off his head. "Wait, Baba Yaga!" he said. "I'll set you straight." He went and tore the scythe out of her hands, seized her by the hair, struck her, and said, "You should have asked me first what my name was, what's my lineage and disposition, and where I'm going." And she asked, "What's your name, what's your lineage, and where are you going?" "My name's Ilya Muromets, and I'm going to such and such a place." "Please come in, Ilya Muromets," she said. And he went in. She seated him at table, and placed food and all sorts of drink on the table, and sent her maid to heat the bathhouse for him. He ate and he steamed himself, and stayed with her for a full day and night, and then made ready to set off again. "Let me write a letter to my sister," said Baba Yaga, "so that she won't harm you, but will receive you with fitting honors . . . Otherwise she'll kill you as soon as she sees you!" She gave him the letter and saw him off with fitting honors.

And the bogatyr mounted his trusty steed and set off through the dense forest. He rode a long time or a short time. The forest was so dense he couldn't see anything!

And he came to a clearing, a wide clearing with a little hut standing on it. He rode up to the hut, dismounted from his trusty steed, and tied his trusty steed to the post. Baba Yaga heard him tying his horse to the post and cried, "What's this? My grandfather and my great-grandfather never had a whiff of a Russian, but now I'm about to see a Russian with my own eyes." And she struck the door with a staff, and the door opened. And she seized him, swinging a saber at his neck. And he said, "You can't fight with me! Here's a letter for you sent by your sister." She read it, and invited him inside with honor. "Please, do come in!" He entered the hut. She seated him at table and placed food and all sorts of drink on the table and sent her maid to heat the bathhouse for him. He ate, then went to the bathhouse and steamed himself. He stayed with her for two days and nights, rested, and had his trusty steed rest. He mounted his trusty steed, and she saw him off with honor. "Well, Ilya Muromets," she said, "you won't be able to make any headway now. Nightingale the Robber's waiting. He's built his nest on seven oaks, and he won't let you come within thrice-ten versts of him. He'll deafen you with his whistling!"

He rode on, for a long time or a short time, until he came to a place where he heard Nightingale the Robber's whistling, and when he was halfway to Nightingale the Robber, his horse stumbled. He said, "Don't stumble, trusty steed, but serve me." He approached Nightingale the Robber, who continued to whistle. Ilya rode close to the nest, took an arrow, drew his bow, and shot the arrow at him— and Nightingale the Robber fell from the nest. When he was on the ground Ilya struck him, but made sure not to kill him, and placed him in his saddlebag and rode on to the palace. He was seen from the palace, and the word got around, "Nightingale the Robber is bringing someone here in his saddlebags!" The bogatyr rode up to the palace and handed over a piece of paper. The paper was passed on to the king, who read it and ordered that he be admitted inside. And the king said to Ilya Ivanovich, "Order Nightingale the Robber to whistle." And Nightingale the Robber said, "You should give Nightingale the Robber food and drink: my mouth is parched." And they brought him some wine, and he said, "What's a jugful for me! You should bring me a regular barrelful." They brought him a barrel of wine and poured it into a bucket. He drained it at once and said, "If you brought Nightingale the Robber two more buckets, he could drink those too!" But they didn't give him any more. And the king requested, "Now, order him to whistle." Ilya ordered him to whistle, but placed the king and his family against his own body, under his arms. "Otherwise he'll deafen you!" he said. When Nightingale the Robber began to whistle, Ilya Ivanovich could barely stop him. He hit him with a staff, and he stopped whistling. Otherwise everybody would have fallen down!

And the king said to Ilya Ivanovich, "Will you render me a service if I ask you to? There's a twelve-headed dragon that keeps visiting my daughter. Could you kill him?" "Certainly, Your Majesty! Anything you need. I'll do everything." "If you will, Ilya Ivanovich. The dragon comes flying to my daughter at such and such a time. Do try to do it then!" "Certainly, Your Majesty!" The princess was lying down in her room, and at twelve o'clock the dragon came flying to her. And the dragon and Ilya started to fight: Ilya would strike a blow, and a head would roll. With each blow, another head off! They fought for a long time or a short time, and only one head remained. And Ilya knocked off the last head; he hit it with the staff and shattered it. The happy princess rose, came to Ilya, and thanked him. She told her father and mother that the dragon was dead, all of his heads had been knocked off! And the king said, "I thank you. Stay here a while in my service." "No," said Ilya. "I'm going to my kingdom." The king let him go with fitting honors. And he set off again, taking the same route. When he arrived to spend the night at the first Baba Yaga's, she received him with honor; and he came to the second Baba Yaga, and she also received him with all honors. He arrived in his kingdom and gave the tsar a paper from the king he had helped. The tsar received him with honor, and his daughter could barely contain her impatience. "Now, Father, please let me marry him." Her father did not oppose her will. "Well, if you want to, go ahead!" They married and live together till this day.

THE MAIDEN TSAR

In a certain land, in a certain kingdom, there was a merchant. His wife died, and he was left with a son, Ivan. He put a tutor in charge of the son, and after a certain while he himself married another woman. When Ivan the merchant's son grew of age and was very handsome, his stepmother fell in love with him. One day Ivan the merchant's son was on a raft at sea fishing with the tutor, when suddenly they saw thirty ships sailing toward them. On these ships was sailing a maiden tsar, with thirty maidens whom she called her sisters. When the raft drew close to the ships, all thirty ships dropped anchor. Ivan the merchant's son and the tutor were invited aboard the best ship, and there the maiden tsar, accompanied by the thirty maidens she called her sisters, greeted them and told Ivan the merchant's son that she'd fallen deeply in love with him and had come to see him. They became engaged on the spot.

The maiden tsar told Ivan the merchant's son to be in the same place at the same time the following day, and she said good-bye to him and sailed off. And Ivan the merchant's son returned home, had supper, and went to bed. The stepmother summoned the tutor to her room, got him drunk, and started asking him whether anything had happened while they'd been fishing. The tutor told her everything. She listened to the end, then gave him a pin, and said, "Tomorrow, when the ships approach, stick this pin into Ivan the merchant's son's clothes." The tutor promised to carry out her order.

The next morning Ivan the merchant's son got up and went fishing. As soon as the tutor saw the ships sailing in the distance, he instantly stuck the pin in Ivan's clothes. "Ah, I'm so sleepy!" said the merchant's son. "Listen, tutor, I'll lie down and sleep a bit, and as soon as the ships come close, please wake me up." "Fine! Of course I'll wake you." The ships drew close and dropped anchor. The maiden tsar sent for Ivan the merchant's son, asking that he hurry to see her, but he was dead to the world. They started trying to get him up, shook him, poked him, but no matter what they did they couldn't wake him, and so they gave up.

The maiden tsar told the tutor to have Ivan the merchant's son come to the same place again the next day, and ordered the crew to lift anchor and set sail. As soon as the ships left, the tutor took out the pin and Ivan the merchant's son awoke, leaped to his feet, and began shouting for the maiden tsar to come back. But she was already far away and didn't hear him. He came home sad and disappointed. The stepmother led the tutor to her room, got him drunk, asked him about everything that had happened, and ordered him to stick the pin into Ivan again the following day. Next day Ivan the merchant's son went fishing, again slept through the visit, and didn't see the maiden tsar. She told the tutor that he should turn up once more.

On the third day Ivan set off fishing with the tutor. As they approached the usual place and saw the ships sailing in the distance, the tutor immediately stuck the pin in, and Ivan the merchant's son fell into a deep sleep. The ships arrived and dropped anchor. The maiden tsar sent for her fiancé, inviting him to come aboard her ship. They tried everything they could to wake him, but no matter what they did he slept on. The maiden tsar learned of the stepmother's trickery and the tutor's disloyalty, and she wrote to Ivan the merchant's son that he had to cut off the tutor's head and, if he loved his fiancée, to seek her beyond the thrice-ninth lands in the thrice-tenth kingdom.

As soon as the ship set sail and made for the open sea, the tutor took the pin out of Ivan the merchant's son's clothes and he awoke, began shouting loudly and calling to the maiden tsar, but she was far away and didn't hear him. The tutor handed him the maiden tsar's letter. Ivan the merchant's son read it, drew his sharp sword, cut off the tutor's head, made with all haste for the shore, went home, said goodbye to his father, and set off to search for the thrice-tenth kingdom.

He walked where his eyes led, for a long time or a short time, for quickly can a tale be spun, but slowly is a real deed done, and he came to a hut, a hut standing in an open field, turning around on chicken legs. He entered the hut, and there found Baba Yaga the bony-legged. "Fie, fie!" she said. "There wasn't sight or sound of a Russian smell before, and now here he is. Are you here of your own free will or by force, fine youth?" "A bit of free will, and twice as much by force! Do you know the thrice-tenth kingdom, Baba Yaga?" "No, I don't!" said Yaga and told him to go to her middle sister and ask her.

Ivan the merchant's son thanked her and went on. He walked and walked, not near and not far, not a long time or a short time, and came to an identical hut. He entered and found Baba Yaga. "Fie, fie!" she said. "There wasn't sight or sound of a Russian smell before, and now here he is. Are you here of your own free will or by force, fine youth?" "A bit of free will, and twice as much by force! Do you know where to find the thrice-tenth kingdom?" "No, I don't!" replied Yaga and told him to see her younger sister, who might know. "If she gets angry at you and wants to eat you, take the three trumpets she has and ask to play them. Play the first softly, the second louder, and the third loudest of all." Ivan the merchant's son thanked Yaga and went on.

He walked and walked, for a short time or a long time, neither near nor far, and finally saw a hut standing in an open field, turning around on chicken legs. He entered and found Baba Yaga. "Fie, fie! There wasn't sight or sound of a Russian smell before, and now here he is!" said Yaga and rushed to sharpen her teeth so as to eat her uninvited guest. Ivan the merchant's son asked her for the three trumpets, and played the first softly, the second louder, and the third loudest of all. Suddenly all kinds of birds came swooping down from all directions, the firebird among them. "Sit on me quickly," said the firebird, "and we'll fly wherever you need to go, or else Baba Yaga will eat you!" No sooner had he sat on it than Baba Yaga rushed back, seized the firebird by the tail, and pulled out quite a few feathers.

The firebird flew off with Ivan the merchant's son, and for a long time it soared high in the skies, until finally it arrived at the broad sea. "Well, Ivan the merchant's son, the thrice-tenth kingdom lies beyond this sea. I'm not strong enough to carry you over to the other side. Try to get there as best you can!" Ivan the merchant's son got down from the firebird, thanked it, and went off along the shore.

He walked and walked, came upon a hut, and entered. An old, old woman greeted him, gave him food and drink, and asked where he was going, why he was journeying so far. He told her that he was going to the thrice-tenth kingdom in search of the maiden tsar, his true love. "Ah!" said the old woman. "She no longer loves you. If she catches sight of you, the maiden tsar will tear you apart. Her love is hidden far, far away!" "How can I get it?" "Wait a bit! My daughter is living at the maiden tsar's and today she promised to visit me. Maybe we can find out from her." And the old woman changed Ivan the merchant's son into a pin and stuck him in the wall. In the evening her daughter flew in. Her mother asked whether she knew where the maiden tsar's love was hidden. "I don't know," replied the daughter and promised to find out from the maiden tsar herself. Next day she flew in again and told her mother, "On the other side of the sea there's an oak, and in the oak there's a chest, and in the chest there's a hare, and in the hare there's a duck, and in the duck there's an egg, and in the egg is the maiden tsar's love!"

Ivan the merchant's son took some bread and set off for the place she'd described. He found the oak, took the chest from it, pulled the hare out of the chest, the duck out of the hare, the egg out of the duck, and returned with the egg to the old woman. It was the old woman's name day soon, and she invited the maiden tsar and her thirty maidens whom she called sisters. She baked the egg, decked Ivan the merchant's son in holiday finery, and hid him.

At noon the maiden tsar and her thirty maidens suddenly flew in, sat down at table, and started to eat dinner. After dinner the old woman gave each of them a regular egg, but gave the maiden tsar the one that Ivan the merchant's son had obtained. The maiden tsar ate it and instantly fell passionately in love with Ivan the merchant's son. The old woman led him out from his hiding place. What joy there was, what happy celebration! The maiden tsar left with her fiancé, the merchant's son, for her kingdom. They married and really started to thrive, and prospered while they were both alive.

THE MAGIC RING

In a certain kingdom, in a certain land, there lived three peasant brothers. They quarreled among themselves and started to divide their property. They didn't divide it equally: the older brothers got a lot, while the third, the youngest, got little. All three were unmarried. They met in the yard and decided among themselves, "It's time we got married!"

"That's fine for you two!" said the youngest brother. "You're rich and you'll marry into rich families. But what can I do? I'm poor. I've got neither wood nor brick, all I've got is a knee-length prick!"

Just then a merchant's daughter was passing by and overheard this conversation. She thought, "Ah, would I like to marry this fellow, with a prick to his knees!"

And the older brothers got married, while the youngest one stayed a bachelor. From the time the merchant's daughter came home all she could think about was how to marry the young brother. Various rich merchants courted her, but she refused all of them.

"I'll marry no one," she said, "but this young stud!"

Her father and mother kept trying to persuade her:

"What's got into you, you fool? Come to your senses! How can you marry a poor peasant?"

She replied, "What do you care? You won't be living with him!"

"Fine! Do what you want, Daughter! Such, it seems, is your fate!"

So the merchant's daughter got a matchmaker and sent her to the young fellow, so that he'd come courting. The matchmaker came to him and said, "Listen, my dear! Why are you wasting your time? Get going and court the merchant's daughter. She's been waiting for you a long time and will gladly marry you."

The fine young fellow got ready at once, put on his new coat, took his new cap, and went directly to the merchant's house to court his daughter. As soon as the merchant's daughter saw him and recognized him as the one with the prick to his knees, she didn't even bother speaking to him, but started asking her father and mother to bless their marriage immediately and forever. And so they married her to the poor peasant. On their wedding night she lay down to sleep with her husband and saw that his little prick was nothing special, no bigger than a finger.

"Ah, you scoundrel!" she shouted at him. "You boasted that you have a prick down to your knees. Where did you put it?"

"Ah, my wife, my queen, you know I was real poor as a bachelor. I had no money to pay for the wedding, nothing to offer, and I pawned my prick."

"How much did you pawn it for?"

"Not much, fifty rubles in all."

"Fine. Tomorrow I'll go see my mother and ask her for the money, and you go at once and buy your prick back—or else don't bother coming home!"

Next morning right away she ran to her mother and said, "Mother, do me a favor! Give me fifty rubles, I really need them!"

"But what do you need them for?"

"Well, Mother, here's how it is. My husband had a prick down to his knees, but for the wedding he had nothing to offer and so he pawned it for fifty rubles. Now my husband's little prick is nothing special, smaller than a finger, so we need to buy his old prick back as soon as possible!"

Her mother saw the problem, took out fifty rubles, and gave them to her daughter.

The daughter ran home, gave her husband the money, and said, "So, run as fast as you can now and buy your old prick back. Don't let other people use it!"

The young fellow took the money and off he went. He walked and thought, "What can I do now? Where can I get such a prick for my wife? I'll simply follow my eyes."

He walked neither a short way nor a long way, neither quickly nor slowly, and met an old woman.

"Hello, Granny!"

"Hello, my good man! Where are you off to?"

"Ah, Granny! If you only knew the mess I'm in, where I'm going!"

"Tell me about your mess, dearie, maybe I can help you."

"I'm too ashamed to say!"

"Don't be ashamed, just tell me straight out!"

"Well, Granny, here's how it is! I bragged that I have a prick down to my knees, the merchant's daughter heard me and married me, but on our wedding night she saw that my little prick was nothing special, smaller than a finger—and she got real mad and started asking, 'Where did you put the big prick?' And I told her I'd pawned it for fifty rubles. And she gave me the money and said I had to buy it back at once. And if I don't buy it back, I needn't show myself back home. I don't know what to do, I can't think!"

The old woman said, "Give me your money and I'll get you out of your mess!"

He at once took out the money and gave all fifty rubles to her, and the old woman gave him a ring. "Here," she said, "take this ring, but put it on only as far as your fingertip."

The fellow took the ring and put it on. As soon as he put it on his fingertip his prick grew as long as his forearm.

"So," asked the old woman, "is your prick down to your knees?"

"Yes, Granny, even lower than the knees."

"So, dearie, move the ring all the way down onto your finger."

He moved the ring down onto his finger, and his prick extended to almost five miles.

"Hey, Granny, where can I put it? I'm going to have trouble with it, you know!"

And the old woman said, "Move the ring back onto your fingertip and it'll be just as long as your forearm." He moved the ring back onto his fingertip and his prick shrank to the length of a forearm. "All right, that's enough! Just be sure you always move the ring no farther than your fingertip."

He thanked the old woman and headed back home. As he walked along, he was happy that he wouldn't return to his wife empty-handed. He walked and walked, and suddenly grew hungry. He turned off the road, sat by the roadside near a burdock, took some crackers from his knapsack, dipped them in some water, and ate the snack. He suddenly wanted to rest, and immediately lay down, belly up, and admired the ring: he moved it to his fingertip, and his prick extended to the length of a forearm; he moved it down his finger, and his prick rose up almost five miles long. He took off the ring, and his little prick grew small, just as before. He looked and looked at the ring, and then fell asleep, forgetting to hide the ring. It lay on his chest. A nobleman was driving by in a carriage with his wife and saw a peasant sleeping nearby, a ring glittering on his chest, just like heat glimmering in the sun. The nobleman stopped the horses and said to his servant, "Go over to that peasant, take his ring, and bring it to me."

The servant immediately rushed over and brought the ring to the nobleman. And then they rode on. Meanwhile, the nobleman admired the ring.

"Look, sweetheart," he said to his wife, "what a wonderful ring. I'll try it on."

And he put it all the way onto his finger, and his prick extended so far that it knocked the driver off his seat and nudged the mare under her tail. It began ramming into the mare and propelling the carriage forward. The noblewoman saw that they were in trouble, became really alarmed, and yelled to the servant, "Run back to that peasant, and bring him here, fast!"

The servant raced to the peasant, woke him, and said, "You'd better get to my master as fast as you can!"

But the peasant looked around for his ring. "Fuck it! Did you take the ring?"

"Don't bother looking for the ring," said the servant. "Hurry along to my master, he's got the ring. It's got us into a lot of trouble."

The peasant rushed over to the carriage. The nobleman said to him, "Forgive me! Get me out of this mess!"

"And what'll you give me, sir?"

"Here's a hundred rubles!"

"Give me two hundred, then I'll help!"

The nobleman pulled out two hundred rubles, the peasant took the money, and tugged the ring off the nobleman's finger—and the prick instantly disappeared! The nobleman was left with his regular little prick. The nobleman drove off, and the peasant went home with his ring.

His wife saw him from the window and ran out to meet him.

"Well," she asked, "did you buy it back?"

"I sure did."

"So, show it to me!"

"Let's go inside, I'm not about to show it to you here!"

They went inside, and the wife kept repeating, "Come on, show it!"

He put the ring on as far as his fingertip and his prick extended to the length of a forearm. He took it out of his pants and said, "All right, Wife, have a look!"

She started kissing him.

"Husband, dear! Better that we keep such a treasure here than let other people use it. Let's have dinner quickly, then we'll go to bed and try it out!"

She quickly laid out various food and drink on the table, and took care of him. They had dinner and went to rest. He fucked his wife with his prick so long and hard that for a full three days she kept looking under her skirt, imagining that it was still sticking there between her legs!

She went to visit her mother, while her husband went out into the garden and lay down under an apple tree.

"So," the mother asked her daughter, "did he buy his prick back?"

"He sure did, Mother!"

And the merchant's wife began thinking of only one thing: how to get to her son-in-law while her daughter was there, so as to try out his big prick. While the daughter chattered away unawares, the mother-in-law made off to her son-in-law's. She ran to the garden, looked, and saw the son-in-law sleeping, the ring on the tip of his finger, his prick as long as his forearm.

"I'll climb onto his prick," thought the mother-in-law, climbed onto it, and started rocking on the prick. It was her bad luck that the ring slipped all the way down the sleeping son-in-law's finger, and the prick lifted the mother-in-law up almost five miles in the air.

The daughter noticed that her mother had disappeared, she figured out where, and raced home. There was no one in the house, but in the garden she saw her husband sleeping, his prick sticking high up in the air, with his mother-in-law, barely visible, on top of it. Whenever the wind blew, she would spin on the prick as if on a spear. How was she to get her mother down off the prick? A huge crowd of people had gathered by now, and they tried to figure out what to do. One fellow said, "The only thing to do is take an ax and chop the prick down."

Others said, "No, that's not the answer! Why kill two people? If we chop down the prick the woman'll fall and kill herself. Better we all pray together quick, maybe a miracle will get her off the prick!"

Just then the son-in-law awoke, saw that the ring was all the way down his finger, with his prick sticking almost five miles up in the air and weighing him down on the ground, so that he couldn't even turn on his side! Slowly he moved the ring up his finger, and his prick began to shrink. He moved it to his fingertip, and his prick became a forearm in length, and the son-in-law saw his mother-in-law impaled on it.

"Mother, how did you land up there?"

"I'm sorry, I'll never do it again!"

PART

II

Fairy Tales of Socialist Realism

INTRODUCTION
✵

MARINA BALINA

The utopianism that P. Bogatyryov and Roman Jakobson attributed to folk fairy tales likewise informs socialist realist literature and, above all, the Soviet fairy tale. Soviet literature's efforts in the 1930s to subordinate the fairy tale genre to ideological purposes were neither startling nor unprecedented. In the 1920s the highly political proletarian writers of the Weimar Republic in Germany insisted on creating a new type of fairy tale (the "proletarian tale") "in which workers' struggles, their lives and their ideas are reflected" (Hoernle 237). The major task of proletarian fairy tales was "to instill a sense of hope that a new, more egalitarian society could be realized if people recognized who the true enemy was—namely, capitalism in various disguised forms—and learned to work together to defeat that enemy" (Zipes, *Fairy Tales and Fables* 20). The similarities in the approach to the genre between the proletarian writers of the Weimar period and their Soviet counterparts are striking. Why, though, did it take Soviet authors an additional decade to realize the suitability of the fairy tale as a didactic tool for influencing future generations?

A major reason for the delay was a collectively authored volume, *We Are Against the Fairy Tale,* which appeared in Kharkov in 1928. It was edited by leading Soviet pedologists, who also contributed some of the articles. Pedology represented a new approach in education intended to replace the old pedagogy (*pedagogika*) and was proclaimed an "empirical, scientific discipline" (*Pedagogicheskaia entsiklopediia* 91). Intent on establishing standards and applying measurements to every child's activities, pedology strived to create rules and regulations that also could be applied to children's literature, which the Soviet establishment viewed as a useful tool rather than a means of influencing children's imagination. Pedologists demanded that children's literature have "class-oriented content"—the only true measure of a literary work's value for children. One might ask what kind of "class-oriented content" could be provided by a genre that spotlights princes and princesses, kings and queens, and beautiful palaces into which the fairy-tale simpleton moves after successfully completing difficult tasks. Yet pedologists found strong support among party leaders and government institutions. According to Felix J. Oinas, in the early 1920s "the belief that folklore reflected the ideology of the ruling classes gave rise to a strongly negative attitude toward it . . . A special Children's Proletkult sought to eradicate folktales on the basis that they glorified tsars and tsareviches, corrupted and instigated sickly fantasies in children, developed the kulak attitude, and strengthened bourgeois ideals" (Oinas 77). Among the "enemies" of the fairy tale was the powerful Nadezhda Krupskaya, Lenin's widow, as well as a leading authority on education and library science in the new Soviet state. In 1924 Krupskaya (then the chair of the Central Committee on Political Education, or Glavpolitprosvet) was instrumental in putting together an influential manual that led to the exclusion of fairy tales from library shelves (Dobrenko 173).[1] Four years later she launched a campaign against Korney Chukovsky's literary fairy tales with an article in the leading governmental newspaper *Pravda* titled "On Crocodile," denouncing his famous fairy tale as "bourgeois nonsense" (*burzhuaznaia mut*'). This attack was supported by K. Sverdlova (wife of the late Yakov Sverdlov), whose own article, "On Chukovshina," accused Chukovsky of neglecting recent developments in children's education, particularly collectivism. As a result, Chukovsky's best and most famous fairy tales, "Moidodyr" (1923), "The Cockroachiad" (1923), "Wonder-Tree" (1924), "Telephone" (1925), and "Mukha-Shchekotukha" (1924), had no chance of publication until much later, in the 1930s.[2]

Such attitudes, which enjoyed official endorsement, effectively prevented the fairy tale during the 1920s from performing its major function: the "socialization of children" (Zipes, *Happily Ever After* 3). The genre's form and structure were perceived as "directly opposed to the task of fostering communist values," and therefore "even if [the tale . . .] did contain revolutionary content" (Rybnikov 119), it was considered "bourgeois" by its very nature. Fairy-tale features such as magic, fantasy, animism, and anthropomorphism—all the devices that compose the essence of the genre—were condemned as "idealism." Just as "bourgeois" culture was supposed to have disappeared after the October Revolution, so the fairy-tale tradition should have been eliminated from the new Soviet literature.[3] But, as Hermann Bausinger demonstrates in his study of folk culture in the world of technology, "although man's environment changes, the dynamics of tradition may be transformed but . . . do not disappear" (Bausinger 88).

Even in its transformed state, however, tradition still needs someone to bring it back to life. The task of revitalization fell to Maxim Gorky, the father of socialist realism, whose speech at the First Soviet Writers' Congress in August 1934 signaled the fairy tale's ideological rehabilitation. Of this famous opening speech, Oinas has written, "Gor'kii's insistence that folklore belonged, first of all, to working people had far-reaching implications. As if by magic, it opened the eyes of the party leaders to the possibilities that folklore would have for the advancement of communism. And from that time on, we can follow the conscious use of folklore for social and political use" (Oinas 78). In his speech, Gorky pronounced such folktale characters as Vasilisa the Wise and "the ironically lucky Ivan the Simple" to be meritorious individuals and praised both folklore and the folktale for their lack of pessimism and their participation in the struggle for "the renovation of life" (Gorkii 36). This rediscovery of positive forces in the folk tradition enabled folktales to find their way back to Soviet readers.

However, this was only the first step. Samuil Marshak, who delivered his speech immediately after Gorky's, made the next important statement. The topic of his presentation was children's literature, and the importance given to this subject indicates the special significance the party assigned to literature of the new generation. Marshak's speech outlined key moments in the development of children's literature. While Gorky carefully confined himself to general statements about folklore, Marshak did not hesitate to use the word "fairy tale" (*skazka*). In the Soviet Union, he insisted, "We have everything necessary for the development of an outstanding and unique literature for children, for the creation of such fairy tales . . . as have never existed anywhere else" (Marshak 14).

Thus, the fairy tale returned to the arsenal of Soviet literary genres, but not as a free agent. It came back to fulfill an important ideological function in the education of the future; fairy tales became "builders of communism." As Katerina Clark argues, "In order to describe *homo extraordinarius*, one needed more fabulous forms, such as fairy tales" (Clark 147). Indeed, many prominent Soviet writers, such as Alexey Tolstoy, Arkady Gaidar, Mikhail Prishvin, and Konstantin Paustovsky, started to explore the fairy tale as one of their favorite literary genres. Three different directions were identified for Soviet fairy-tale writing: creative revision of folktales, creation of poetic fairy tales about nature, and fairy tales/jokes that found "their roots in the depths of the folk tradition" (Polevoi 52).

The five fairy tales included in this part of the volume treat the peculiar relationship between everyday reality and the extraordinary reality of the fairy-tale world in diverse ways. What links them is the same ideological message—the triumph of Soviet reality over any fantasy. To make this point, all five tales rely on the traditional features of the folk genre: their major characters are ordinary people who resemble the simpletons of folktales. Every folkloric fairy tale starts with a conflict, and its protagonist has to overcome a series of obstacles on the way to his or her ultimate goal, which is "the restoration of natural order" (Röhrich 208). What distinguishes these literary fairy tales from their folkloric models is the equation of "natural order" with Soviet everyday reality. Moreover, the motif of wandering, which is a crucial element of the fairy-tale narrative, here brings the protagonists back home, but does not result in a changed social status, as in genuine folktales. Instead, protagonists become wiser, more experienced, and therefore more appreciative of the Soviet reality in which they live.

The five fairy tales provide examples of the three directions established for the Soviet fairy tale mentioned earlier: Bazhov's "Malachite Casket" combines revision of the folktale tradition with poetic representation of nature. Tolstoy's *Golden Key* approximates the fairy tale/joke that extends its folk roots via earlier works of literature. Both Kataev's "Flower of Seven Colors" and Lagin's *Old Genie Khottabych* transfer the action into the actual world of contemporary Soviet life, yet preserve a loose connection to the folk tradition by focusing on moral transformation. The most ideologically charged fairy tale, Gaidar's "Tale of the Military Secret," is a purely metaphorical construction, lacking any indicators of specific time or place.

The world of Gaidar's fairy tale, "Tale of the Military Secret, Malchish-Kibalchish and His Solemn Word" ("Skazka o voennoi taine, o Mal'chishe i ego tverdom slove"), published in 1935, is built on references to the historical facts of the recent past: the Civil War of 1918 to 1921 is cast as "the Big War," and the enemies of the revolution are "bourgeouins." Gaidar preserves the major referential divider between the worlds of the Red and the White armies, and this division serves a dual purpose: it establishes the binary opposition of good and evil inherent in the fairy-tale genre, while also marking the class division already accepted in Soviet society. Thus, the world of Soviet reality subsumes the fairy-tale plot, making it a vessel for its ideology.

Though Gaidar retains many traditional fairy-tale elements, he reworks or reconfigures them in line with Soviet ideals: for instance, tripling is employed to show how each generation continues the revolutionary struggle waged by the previous one. No magic helpers or magic objects appear in the tale, for Malchish's leadership qualities and organizational skills, as well as his dedication to the true cause, are what guarantee victory of the children's army. The protagonist undergoes no magical transformation, but his strength seems to increase hyperbolically because he chooses the right cause for his struggle— support of the Red Army. It is precisely his "right choice" that entitles him to acquire knowledge of the "military secret" of the Red Army's invincibility, which he proceeds to protect with his life.

Gaidar frames the traditional fairy-tale juxtaposition of hero and villain within the larger diegesis of class consciousness–raising. The reprehensible Malchish-Plokhish sells out his friends for "a barrel of jam and a basket of cookies" with which he sits, "stuffing himself and rejoicing." His gluttony (traditionally presented in the Soviet context as the sin of the rich) has led him to commit the worst possible crime, treason. This particular type of villain is the focus of the political awareness that Gaidar attempts to quicken among his young readers.

However, the tale's focus on betrayal *from within* undermines the utopian solidarity of the Young Pioneer camp, where (in the full version of Gaidar's text) this tale is told to an international group of children. The fairy tale replaces brotherly love, which transcends national and cultural boundaries, with "a watchful eye" (*nedremliushchee oko*) that enables one to detect the traitor hiding in the collective midst. In this way, the tale conveys the message of suspicion and mistrust dominating Stalinist culture of the 1930s.

At first glance, Tolstoy's *Golden Key* seems to move away from the ideology of the 1930s by transporting the young audience into a real fairy-tale land. Yet no matter how far removed geographically, the wooden puppet Buratino, who is the tale's protagonist, clearly is rooted in socialist reality, and the tale's didactic features bring its readers back to their homeland. Based on *The Adventures of Pinocchio*, the famous Italian literary fairy tale by Carlo Collodi, Tolstoy's *The Golden Key, or The Adventures of Buratino* (*Zolotoi kliuchik, ili prikliucheniia Buratino*) was first published in the Young Pioneers' newspaper *Pioneers' Truth* in 1936. Two years later it was reworked into a play for the Central Children's Theater and staged by Natalia Satz. In 1939 it appeared in a film version by Alexander Ptushko. A remarkable addition to the movie was the song written by Mikhail Froman, which bears an interesting resemblance to the famous "Somewhere, over the rainbow, way up high . . ." from the 1939 Hollywood film *The Wizard of Oz*. Although both songs cast the beautiful land where the dreams "that you dare to dream really come true" as a utopian landscape without any specific geographical markers, multiple references in the song from *The Golden Key*—for example, the huge size of the land located "far away beyond the sea" (*daleko, daleko za morem*)— make it easy to identify utopia's coordinates with those of Soviet Russia.[4]

The Golden Key underwent a series of different media adaptations: Tolstoy was asked to write a play for the puppet theater and a libretto for a children's opera; a board game titled *The Golden Key* was also produced. In the course of this proliferation, the fairy tale's ideological message became more and more direct. Thus its stage version explicitly replaces the mysterious dreamland for which the protagonists are searching with a concrete location: the U.S.S.R. Papa Carlo speaks about only one country in the world "where old people live in prosperity and comfort" (Tolstoi, *Zolotoi kliuchik* 8:307), and the poodle Artemon firmly plants this politically loaded "discovery" in the Soviet Union. Looking from the stage directly into the audience, he says to Buratino, "Look, Buratino, I recognize it. It's the country of happy children—the U.S.S.R." (Tolstoi, *Zolotoi kliuchik* 8:314).

Tolstoy creates a highly class-conscious world in his story. The Doctor of Puppetry, Signor Karabas Barabas, is a genuine villain whose degeneracy is attested not only by his wealth, but by his having amassed it through exploiting poor little dolls that fear and therefore never resist him. The class struggle generates longing for a strong leader who will come and inspire everybody to unite their forces for the right cause: happiness for the poor and the end of exploitation. To make Buratino into such a leader, Tolstoy empowers him with special knowledge of a secret. As in the case of Gaidar's Malchish-

Kibalchish, this secret knowledge enables him to lead others. Malchish, a simple boy, is an equal among his peers and proves to be extraordinary because he knows the true cause of revolutionary struggle. Buratino, however, in many respects is worse than his fellow puppets: he is a lazy liar, who sells the ABC blocks that Papa Carlo made for him so as to buy a theater ticket. Buratino is a considerably more complicated character than Malchish, who merely accepts the truth when it is given to him. By contrast, Buratino actively seeks truth, and the process of his search brings the fairy tale closer to its primary purpose of educating its audience, while also making its didactic message less blunt and direct.

The Golden Key employs many traditional fairy-tale motifs. Its very title refers to a magic object—here, the golden key that is supposed to open the door to a dreamland of justice and equality. Absent from the Collodi tale, the prized object is the key to happiness, and Buratino has already seen the door that it will unlock. The search for the magic key forms the core of his journey. Whereas Collodi's fairy tale focuses on the magical transformation of a puppet into a boy, for Tolstoy the protagonist's moral transformation is primary. At tale's end Buratino does not need to become human, for he already behaves like a Soviet citizen.

Buratino differs from both Pinocchio and the fairy-tale simpleton in the nature of the happiness he pursues. Both the folktale hero and Pinocchio selfishly seek rewarding solutions for themselves alone, whereas Buratino from the outset aims to achieve universal paradise, happiness for everyone. His goal is a world where not only his social status will improve, but the needs of the communal utopian fantasy will be met. Pinocchio's transformation into a human realizes the central principle of the bourgeois work ethic: hard work finally brings rewards. On his way to join the human race he becomes an animal (a donkey), who toils and suffers cruel beatings. For every mistake he makes, he pays with personal losses and physical pain. The moral transformation of Buratino, however, results from collective effort. Through his encounters with Pierrot, Malvina, and the other puppets, he becomes a better person. He is courageous but somewhat restless and ill-behaved, and finds the magic door only with the help of friends. Needless to say, the equivalent of the Fairy with the Blue Hair who grants Pinocchio's wish to become a boy never appears in the group-oriented socialist realist narrative. Magic power is replaced by the power of the collective, which is capable of bringing out the best in an individual. In this respect *The Golden Key* resembles the most celebrated socialist realist *Erziehungsroman* (novel of education), Anton Makarenko's *Road to Life* (*Pedagogicheskaia poema*, 1939). Makarenko shows the power of collective work toward a common goal as the perfect tool for the transformation of delinquents (*besprizorniki*) into New Soviet Men. Buratino, similarly, illustrates how a simple piece of wood, with no appropriate heritage, and, moreover, affiliated with thieves (Alice the Fox and Basilio the Cat), may be changed through proper collective endeavor and the support of his peers.

Lagin's *The Old Genie Khottabych* (*Starik Khottabych*) likewise evidences the infusion of socialist didacticism into the literary fairy tale. First published in 1938 in the ideologically charged literary journal for children *The Young Pioneer*, this tale, like *The Golden Key*, belongs to the category of poetic revisions of the folktale. Like Tolstoy, Lagin bypassed Russian folk tradition, borrowing a plot from *One Thousand and One Nights* for his adaptation. *The Old Genie Khottabych* offers an excellent example of symbiosis within a single text between the world of Soviet reality and fairy-tale fantasy. Lagin's reworking of the famous Aladdin story builds the narrative around the acquisition of a magic object: the mysterious vessel at the bottom of which an old genie has been imprisoned for centuries. The genie makes every effort to thank his new master for his liberation by employing traditional "genie" magic: when the boy expresses a wish, the old genie tries to fulfill it. Although the traditional folktale theme of wish fulfillment is incorporated into the plot, the old, "backward" genie always fails in his attempts, since he operates with the outmoded assumption that riches are the key to happiness. The irrelevance of these old values to the new Soviet way of life requires that he constantly be rescued by his new master, Volka Korostylev, the ordinary thirteen-year-old Moscow schoolboy. Lagin's fairy tale destabilizes the relationship between the characters (Röhrich 8), for the magic helper normally destined to assist the protagonist himself needs help from the schoolboy. This reverse dependence textually implants the main ideological concept of the socialist realist fairy tale: residents of Soviet reality need no magic, for their reality is, in fact, the fulfilled utopian dream. Even the old genie finally understands that the fairy tale has come true, and he abandons his magic tricks in order to embrace the new "magic" of the Soviet world. If one views this fairy tale in the context of the cultural revolution of 1920 to 1940 (with its central goal of creating a new revolutionary culture to replace the values of the old capitalist society), the ideological import of a plot that converts an old genie to the new socialist way of life cannot be clearer.

Bazhov's "The Malachite Casket" ("Malakhitovaia shkatulka"), also the title of his collection of fourteen tales, was published in 1939. By 1942 the first four of these tales had appeared in the literary magazine *Red Virgin Soil,* and Bazhov insisted that they belonged to the genre of the tale (*skaz*), not the fairy tale (*skazka*). *The Russian Literary Encyclopedia*'s definition of *skaz* points out its emphasis on history and its closeness to the historical song or *bylina*—an epic form of Russian oral folklore (*Literaturnaia entsiklopediia* 382). Bazhov's choice of genre for his tales underscores their connection to folk traditions. If the cultural policies of the 1920s were intended to create a new revolutionary culture divorced from its past, the 1930s marked a significant change in ideology. Bazhov's tales describe the history of working people in the Urals, a region famous for its rich natural resources, various minerals, and precious stones. Bazhov's characters are factory serfs, representatives of the underprivileged, oppressed class in tales that focus on their hardships and exploitation. The majority of Bazhov's plots dramatize class conflicts between poor, deprived workers and the evil masters on whom their lives completely depend. Here traditional fairy-tale binarism emerges along class lines: positive characters belong to the world of the oppressed, while villains consist of factory owners and their cohorts.

Bazhov's tales widely employ the traditional fairy-tale motif of magic helpers who embody various natural entities. These include the Mistress of Copper Mountain, Great Poloz the snake, and Silver Hoof the deer, among others. This traditionalism is directly related to two of the three major currents in socialist realist fairy tales: the creation of poetic fairy tales about nature and the creative revision of existent folktales. Magical helpers in Bazhov's narratives reconfigure their traditional roles by unequivocally siding with the oppressed elements within the binary power structure. This dual model is reinforced by the figure of the storyteller, Grandpa Slyshko, whose language consists of a regional dialect infused with endearing archaic sayings. Part eyewitness (*slyshat'* = "to hear"), part safekeeper of traditions, Slyshko acts as an ideological bridge between past and present: he constantly refers to the fact that life in the "old days" (before the Revolution) was harder for working people, thereby reminding his young audience that times have changed for the better. While the complex interrelationship between reality and fantasy is a prominent and quite natural feature of Bazhov's fairy tales, the past-present dichotomy emerges as a forced attempt to impose an ideological doctrine upon the reader.

The tendencies described above are, perhaps, best illustrated by the characters in "The Malachite Casket." In the fluid interplay between reality and fantasy, the main character, Tanyushka, inhabits both worlds simultaneously. In the empirical world she is the pious daughter of a peasant, while in the realm of fantasy she is a double of the Mistress of Copper Mountain (a major regional magic force). The Mistress herself also exists in both worlds, as the magical ruler of all natural resources, and as a poor beggar woman who visits Tanyushka's home. The magical object binding the two worlds and the two characters is the malachite box that contains precious jewelry. The narrative is woven around various schemes to take the box away from its rightful owner. Given to Tanyushka's father, Stepan, for his service to the Mistress, it is sought after by many "wrongful" owners. Rich merchants, the factory owner's lover, and the factory owner himself all try to buy this gift, only to discover that they are unable to keep it. The magical object, which in fairy-tale tradition always finds its true owner, functions as a signifier of class in "The Malachite Casket." It eludes the rich and deceitful and is restored to the poor and honest. It defines Tanyushka's navigation in the world of binary opposites; she abandons the "real" world, full of betrayal and false promise, for the realm of fantasy, ruled by truth and equality. The reader is constantly reminded that such an escape was a viable choice in prerevolutionary days but has become superfluous, since contemporary Soviet society has righted all the wrongs of fairy-tale "reality."

Kataev's "The Flower of Seven Colors" ("Tsvetik-semitsvetik") represents a later development in the socialist realist fairy tale. Published in 1940, the tale abandons the direct ideological discourse of the earlier texts discussed above. "The Flower of Seven Colors" embodies two parallel processes developed simultaneously within the narrative. While continuing to work on the formation of moral values of the new socialist society, this tale also revives the depiction of universal human values as part of the folktale's persistent function as an "educator of mankind." The binary opposition of past and present (Bazhov), of communist and capitalist societies (Gaidar, Lagin), the conflict between the oppressed and their oppressors (Tolstoy, Gaidar, Bazhov, and Lagin) cease to be of primary importance. The class struggle between the hero and the villain so characteristic of Soviet fairy tales of the 1930s becomes a moral struggle within oneself. "The Flower of Seven Colors" presents its young audience with several moral dilemmas. Magic teaches the child protagonist, Zhenya, to make right moral decisions and fight her own worst enemy: herself and her greed.

The evolution of this fairy-tale character from the protagonists of the 1930s is remarkable, for Zhenya is highly individualized. Gaidar's Malchish *knows* true values because they are given to him with his class origin. Buratino's "moral conversion" takes place under the direct influence of his friends, but he is also a priori entitled to secret knowledge. Lagin's Volka Korostylev occasionally succumbs to selfish acts and employs his magic helper, Khottabych, to fulfill his "wrong" desires, but it is the old genie who takes these wishes to an extreme and, by doing so, spotlights Volka's flaws. In Kataev's fairy tale, little Zhenya is left alone to fight her moral battles, without even the benefit of a counterpart villain to show her what wrongdoings are possible. The image of the enemy *within our midst* is transformed in this narrative into the enemy *within*—the selfish promptings and wishes that every human being has to overcome. Moreover, Kataev deprives his protagonist of all forms of external moral support (friends and family in *The Golden Key*, attributes of the Soviet system in *The Old Genie Khottabych*, magic forces in "The Malachite Casket") that earlier guaranteed protagonists victory in their struggles with antagonists. Here the responsibility and power of moral choice reside within, and it is exclusively the goodness of Zhenya's heart that wins her independence, converting her into a magic helper figure.

The didactic message of Kataev's fairy tale is all too clear: the tale teaches young readers answerability for *their* wishes and desires. In congruence with the folktale tradition, misguided selfish desires are punished: wishing for too many toys creates disaster, and boasting results in near-death. A selfless wish to help a sick boy, on the other hand, brings the protagonist happiness. "She carefully removed the last blue petal of the flower and started to sing the magic spell at the top of her voice, which was trembling with happiness." This is how Kataev describes the magic transformation of his character, whose impulse to help the needy differs from the "goodness" of early socialist realist fairy-tale protagonists. Class consciousness–raising elements play no role in Kataev's tale, for Zhenya helps a boy suffering not from social deprivation, but from illness. The narrative represents a major departure from the socialist realist fairy-tale canon. Fairy-tale "genre memory," with its predilection for humanist values, rescues "The Flower of Seven Colors" from the rigidity of the earlier paradigm.

Although Kataev's fairy tale focuses on universal values, its Soviet reality is, nonetheless, easily identifiable as such. The boys with whom Zhenya wants to play prepare for an expedition to the North Pole—a widely celebrated event of Soviet life in the late 1930s; the toys with which Zhenya wishes to impress her girlfriends come from the toy stores of Moscow, Leningrad, and Kharkov.[5] By making the "real" world of the fairy tale so recognizably Soviet, Kataev grounds his didactic message about the universal human values of kindness and selfishness in Soviet reality. Without explicitly linking goodness and Sovietdom, he implicitly establishes their connection. Zipes's notion that fairy-tale didacticism strives to create a social code of universal values must be modified in the context of Kataev's tale, which promotes a specifically Soviet societal code. Such encodings became a major focus of the "education by fairy tale" in socialist realist literature.

Dmitry Likhachev wrote: "Fairy-tale time never spills beyond the boundaries of a fairy tale. It is hermetically sealed in the plot. It does not exist before the beginning of the fairy tale and it ceases at the tale's conclusion. When the plot ends, so does fairy-tale time" (Likhachev 232). The fairy tale of socialist realism, however, breached the boundaries of time and extended the limits of fairy-tale temporality to include a contemporary Soviet reality. Clark states that in Stalinist culture of the 1930s, "the distinction between ordinary reality and fiction lost the crucial importance it has in other philosophical systems" (Clark 146). In Soviet fairy tales the world of magic is easily interchanged with the world of real-life events. Fantastic characters mingle with Soviet citizens and learn true moral values from them. The fluidity of this interplay makes magic or miracle a natural and expected part of Soviet life. The traditional magical transformation of a single fairy-tale protagonist is replaced, in the Soviet context, by the magical transformation of the whole country. In keeping with the Stalinist formula, Soviet life becomes the embodiment of the fairy-tale utopian dream that finally comes true.

Notes

1. Among those publications were the folktale collections by A. Afanas'ev, the famous fairy tale "Scarlet Flower" by S. Aksakov, collections of fairy tales by Klavdiia Lukashevich, and *Russian Fairy Tales for Little Ones* by Ol'ga Rogova. Both the folktales and the literary fairy tales were denigrated as works that "negatively influenced children's conscience, which still had to be developed," and destroyed "their ability to comprehend material images of the world."

2. Kornei Chukovskii was not the only one under attack. Samuil Marshak, Boris Zhitkov, and Vitalii Bianki—all canonical names in Soviet children's literature—were subjected to constant criticism for their attempts to employ the fairy-tale genre in their writings. This criticism was sometimes paradoxical: the highly ideological yet cruel "Fairy Tale about Petia, a Fat Child, and Sima, a Skinny One" (1925) by Vladimir Maiakovskii was considered "unacceptable, ideologically wrong, and full of nonsense," since it referred to Young Pioneers "collecting and eating the leftovers from greedy Petia, who bursts after stuffing himself with an enormous quantity of goods" (Petrovskii 61).

3. In 1925 A. Kozhevnikova wrote the play *Hey, Fairy Tale, Come to the Young Pioneers' Court* for the express purpose of having it staged in school theaters. The plot of this anti–fairy-tale play was based on a fairy tale. It was overpopulated with devils and fairies, angels and Baba Yaga, princes and cruel magicians. Toying with the basic concept of magical transformation, the author brought standard fairy-tale characters into real life so as to be destroyed. Despite the author's "right" intentions, the magic characters appeared to be much more appealing and real than their judges—the Young Pioneers.

4. Miron Petrovskii and Elena Tolstaia in their analyses offer a different reading of this fairy tale. Both scholars consider the tale to be geared more toward adult readers rather than a young audience, so their discussions present Tolstoi's narrative as a polemical text that satirizes literary and cultural traditions of the Silver Age.

5. Here the author makes a direct reference to real-life events. The Arctic expedition on the ship *Cheluskin* (1933–34), led by Otto Schmidt, was a revolutionary attempt to make a nonstop voyage from Murmansk to Vladivostok. The effort failed, and stranded members of the expedition had to be rescued from the ice by Soviet pilots, who were awarded the first Hero of the Soviet Union medals.

Works Cited

Bausinger, Hermann. *Folk Culture in a World of Technology.* Trans. Elke Dettmer. Bloomington: Indiana University Press, 1990.

Bazhov, P. P. *Malachite Casket: Tales from the Urals.* Trans. Eve Manning. Moscow: Foreign Language Publishing House, 1949.

Bogatyrev, Petr, and Roman Jakobson. "Folklore as a Special Form of Creativity." In Roman Jakobson, *Selected Writings,* 4:1–15. The Hague: Mouton. 1966.

Clark, Katerina. *The Soviet Novel: History as Ritual.* Chicago: University of Chicago Press, 1981.

Dobrenko, Evgenii. *Formirovka sovetskogo chitatelia.* St. Petersburg: Akademicheskii proekt, 1997.

Gorkii, Maxim. "Speech at the First Soviet Writers' Congress." In *Problems of Soviet Literature,* ed. H. G. Scott. Westport, Conn.: Hyperion, 1975.

Hoernle, Edwin. "Die Arbeit in den kommunistischen Kindergruppen." Quoted in Jack Zipes, "Marxists and the Illumination of Folk and Fairy Tale." In *Fairy Tales and Society: Illusion, Allusion and Paradigm,* ed. Ruth B. Bottigheimer. Philadelphia: University of Pennsylvania Press, 1986.

Ianovskaia, E. "Nuzhna li skazka proletarskomu rebenku." In *My protov skazki,* ed. I. Sokolianskii, V. Popov, and P. Zaluzhnyi. Kharkov, 1928. Quoted in *Pedagogicheskaia entsiklopediia,* 2:91. Moscow: Rabotnik prosveshcheniia, 1928.

Kataev, V. P. "Tsvetik-semitsvetik." In *Sobranie sochinenii.* Vol. 1. Moscow: Khudozhestvennaia literatura, 1968.

Lagin, L. I. *The Old Genie Hottabych.* Trans. Faina Solasko. Moscow: Foreign Language Publishing House, 1973.

Likhachev, D. *Poetika drevnerusskoi literatury.* Leningrad: Khudozhestvennaia literatura, 1971.

Literaturnaia entsiklopediia. Moscow: Sovetskaia entsiklopediia, 1987.

Makarenko, A. S. *The Road to Life: An Epic of Education.* Moscow: Progress Publishers, 1951.

Marshak, S. Ia. "O bol'shoi literature dlia malen'kikh: Doklad na pervom s"ezde sovetskikh pisatelei." In *Schast'e literatury. Gosudarstvo i pisateli. 1925–1938 gg. Dokumenty,* comp. D. L. Babichenko. Moscow: ROSSPEN, 1997.

Oinas, Felix J. "The Political Uses and Themes of Folklore in the Soviet Union." In *Folklore, Nationalism and Politics,* ed. Felix J. Oinas, 77–97. Columbus, Ohio: Slavica, 1978.

Pedagogicheskaia entsiklopediia. Vol. 2. Moscow: Rabotnik prosveshcheniia, 1928.

Petrovskii, Miron. *Knigi nashego detstva.* Moscow: Kniga, 1986.

Polevoi, Boris. "Doklad na vtorom vserosiiskom s"ezde sovetskikh pisatelei." In *Sbornik,* 52–67. Moscow: Sovetskii pisatel', 1956.

Putilova, E. *O tvorchestve A. P. Gaidara.* Leningrad, 1960.

Röhrich, Lutz. *Folktales and Reality.* Trans. Peter Tokofsky. Bloomington: Indiana University Press, 1991.

Rybnikov, N. *Skazka i rebenok: Sbornik statei.* Moscow and Leningrad: Gosudarstvennoe izdatel'stvo, 1928.

Stites, Richard. "Stalinism and the Restructuring of Revolutionary Utopianism." In *The Culture of the Stalin Period,* ed. Hans Guenther. New York: St. Martin's, 1990.

Sverdlova, K. "O 'chukovshchine.'" In K. Chukovskii, *Dnevnik: 1901–1929,* 126. Moscow: Sovremennyi pisatel', 1997.

Tolstaia, E. D. "Buratino i podteksty Alekseia Tolstogo." *Isvestiia akademii nauk: Seriia literatury i jazyka* 56, no. 2 (1997): 28–47.

Tolstoi, A. N. *Zolotoi kliuchik* (*Skazka dlia detei*). In *Sobranie sochinenii v 10-ti tomakh*, 8: 263–319. Moscow: Khudozhestvennaia literatura, 1960.

Tolstoy, Aleksey. *The Golden Key, or The Adventures of Buratino.* Trans. Eric Hartley. London: Hutchinson's Books for Young People, 1947.

Zipes, Jack. *Fairy Tales and Fables from Weimar Days.* Hanover, N.H., and London: University Press of New England, 1989.

———. *Happily Ever After: Fairy Tales, Children and the Culture Industry.* New York and London: Routledge, 1997.

———. *When Dreams Came True: Classical Fairy Tales and Their Tradition.* New York and London: Routledge, 1999.

TALE OF THE MILITARY SECRET, MALCHISH-KIBALCHISH AND HIS SOLEMN WORD

꙳

ARKADY GAIDAR

Long, long ago, right after the Big War ended, there lived a boy called Malchish-Kibalchish.

By then the Red Army had driven out the cursed bourgeouins' White troops and there was peace in the wide fields, in the green meadows where the rye grew, where the buckwheat flourished, where amid dense orchards and raspberry bushes stood the little house in which lived Malchish, nicknamed Kibalchish, and his father and his brother, but without a mother.

The father worked, mowing hay; the brother worked, carting hay. And Malchish helped, first his father, then his brother, or simply played with other boys and got into mischief.

Ahhhhh! How good life was! No whining bullets, no bursting shells, no burning villages. No need to get down on the floor to avoid bullets, no need to hide in the cellar from shells, no need to run into the forest to escape fires. No need to fear the bourgeouins. No one to bow down to. All you had to do was live and work—a good life!

And then one day—it was close to evening—Malchish-Kibalchish went out onto the porch. He looked around: the sky was clear, the wind warm, and the sun about to set behind the Black Mountains. And everything would have been fine, but something was wrong. And

Malchish thought he heard something booming, something pounding. It seemed to Malchish as if the wind smelled not of orchard flowers, not of honey from the meadows, but either of smoke from fires or of powder from exploding shells. He told his father, but his father had come home tired.

"What're you talking about?" he said to Malchish. "That's the sound of a thunderstorm on the other side of the Black Mountains. That's the herdsmen's fires smoking behind the Blue River—they're tending their herds and cooking supper. You go to bed, Malchish, and sleep well."

Malchish left the room. He went to bed. But he couldn't sleep, no matter how he tried.

Suddenly he heard the sound of hoofs outside, then a knock at the window. Malchish-Kibalchish looked out and saw a rider by the window. The horse was coal black, the man's saber was shiny, his fur hat was gray, and the star on it was red.

"Hey! Get up!" the horseman shouted. "We've got trouble from where we least expected it. The cursed bourgeouins have attacked us from across the Black Mountains. It's flying bullets, exploding shells once again. Our units are fighting the bourgeouins, and our fastest messengers have galloped off to get help from the Red Army, which is far off."

His alarming announcement made, the horseman with the red star galloped off. And Malchish's father snatched his rifle from the wall, threw his bag over his shoulder, and put on his ammunition belt.

"Well," he told his older son, "I planted the rye thick, you'll clearly have a lot to harvest. Well," he told Malchish, "I've lived life under constant threat, and clearly you'll have to live it peacefully in my stead, Malchish."

With these words he soundly kissed Malchish and went off. And he had little time to spare for kissing, because by now everyone could hear and see how shells were bursting beyond the meadows and the dawn sky was burning from the glow of smoking fires beyond the mountains . . .

A day went by, then another. Malchish went out onto the porch; no, no sign yet of the Red Army. Malchish climbed up onto the roof. He sat there all day. But there was nothing to see. Toward night he went to bed. Suddenly he heard hoofs again, a knock at the window. Malchish looked out: the same horseman was at the window. Only his horse was thin and tired, his saber bent and dark, his fur hat bullet-ridden, the star all torn, and his head bandaged.

"Get up!" shouted the horseman. "If it was a disaster before, it's now total disaster. There's a lot of bourgeouins, there are few of us. Nonstop bullets in the field, thousands of shells among the units. Hey, get up, you gotta help!"

The older brother got up and said to Malchish: "Good-bye, Malchish . . . You're on your own now. There's cabbage soup in the pot, bread on the table, water in the spring, and your head on your shoulders. Live as best you can and don't wait for me."

A day went by, then another. Malchish sat on the roof by the chimney and in the distance saw a horseman racing toward him.

The horseman galloped up, leaped from his horse, and said:

"Give me a drink of water, good Malchish. I've not drunk for three days, not slept for three nights, and ridden three horses to death. The Red Army knows of our disaster. All the trumpets have sounded as loud as loud can be. All the drums have sounded as loud as loud can be. All the war banners have been unfurled as far as far can be. All the Red Army is racing and galloping to help us. All we need, Malchish, is to hold out until tomorrow night."

Malchish climbed down from the roof, brought him water to drink. The messenger drank his fill and cantered off.

Evening arrived, and Malchish went to bed. But Malchish couldn't fall asleep—how could he possibly sleep?

Suddenly he heard footsteps on the street, rustling at the window. Malchish looked out and saw the same man standing at the window.

The same, yet not the same: he had no horse—his horse was dead; no saber—his saber was broken; no fur hat—his hat had blown off; and he staggered where he stood.

"Hey, get up!" he shouted for the last time. "We've got shells, but the gunners have had it. We've got rifles, but few fighting men. And help is near, but we've no strength. Hey, whoever's left, get up! All we need is to make it through the night and hold out a day."

Malchish-Kibalchish looked down the street: the street was empty. The shutters weren't banging, the gates weren't creaking—there was no one to get up. The fathers had gone off, and the brothers had gone off—and no one was left.

All Malchish could see was an old man a hundred years old come out from behind a gate. The old man tried to lift a rifle, but he was so old he couldn't lift it. He tried to buckle on a saber, but he was so weak he couldn't buckle it. And the old man sat down on the ground, his head drooping, and he wept.

And it pained Malchish to see him. Malchish-Kibalchish went out into the street and shouted loud—loud enough for everyone to hear:

"Hey, you boys, boys big and small! Are we boys just to go on playing with wooden swords and skipping rope? Our fathers have gone, our brothers have gone. Are we boys just going to sit around waiting for the bourgeouins to come and carry us off to their cursed bourgeouinland?"

When they heard these words, boys big and small raised a great shout! Some ran out the door, some climbed out the window, and others jumped over the fence.

They all wanted to go and help fight. Only the bad boy called Malchish-Plokhish wanted to go to bourgeouinland. But he was so cunning, this Plokhish, that he didn't say anything; he only pulled up his breeches and ran off with the others, as though he intended to help.

And the boys fought through the dark night to the bright dawn. Only Plokhish didn't fight, but walked about looking for some way to help the bourgeouins. And behind a small hill Plokhish saw a pile of boxes, and in the boxes were hidden black bombs, white shells, and yellow cartridges. "Uh-uh," thought Plokhish. "This is just what I need."

Just then the Head Bourgeouin asked his bourgeouins: "So, bourgeouins, have you won the victory yet?" "No," the bourgeouins replied. "We trounced the fathers and the brothers, and we'd have been completely victorious, but Malchish-Kibalchish came to help them, and we can't beat him for the life of us."

The Head Bourgeouin was startled, grew furious, and shouted in a threatening voice: "How's it possible you can't beat Malchish? Akh, you useless yellow-belly bourgeois-nellies! How's it possible you can't trounce a kid like that? Get back there fast, and don't come back until you're victorious."

And the bourgeouins sat wondering what on earth they could do to defeat Malchish-Kibalchish. Suddenly they saw Malchish-Plokhish come crawling out of the bushes and making straight for them.

"Rejoice!" he shouted. "I, Plokhish, did it all myself. I chopped some logs, I got some hay, and set fire to all the boxes with the black bombs, the white shells, and the yellow cartridges. It'll all go up any minute!"

The bourgeouins were overjoyed at the news, enrolled Malchish-Plokhish instantly in their bourgeouin ranks, and gave him a whole barrel of jam and a whole basket of cookies.

Malchish-Plokhish sat there, stuffing himself and rejoicing.

All of a sudden the boxes he'd lit exploded! And the bang sounded like a thousand thunderbolts striking in one spot, and a thousand flashes of lightning bursting from a single cloud.

"Treason!" cried Malchish-Kibalchish.

"Treason!" cried all his faithful boys.

Then out of the smoke and fire poured the bourgeouin forces, and they overcame and seized Malchish-Kibalchish.

They put Malchish in heavy chains. They imprisoned Malchish in a stone tower. And they hurried off to ask what the Head Bourgeouin wanted to do with the captured Malchish.

The Head Bourgeouin thought long and hard, then he got an idea, and said:

"We'll kill this Malchish. But first we'll make him tell us their Military Secret. You go to him, bourgeouins, and ask him: 'How is it that forty Tsars and forty Kings fought the Red Army, fought and fought, but only got trounced? How is it, Malchish, that all the prisons are full, that all the penal colonies are packed, and all the police are at their posts, and all our armies are on the go, yet we have no peace during the light of day or the dark of night? How is it, Malchish, cursed Kibalchish, that in my High Bourgeouinland, and in the Plains Kingdom, and in the Snow Realm, and in the Sultry State, everywhere on the same day in early spring and on the same day in late fall, they sing the same songs, though in different languages, carry the same banners, though in different hands, make the same speeches, think the same thoughts, and do the same things?' You ask him, bourgeouins, 'Does the Red Army, Malchish, have a military secret?' And have him tell you the secret. 'Do your workers have foreign aid?' And let him tell you where that aid comes from. 'Is there a secret passageway, Malchish, from your country to all the countries in the world, along which as soon as you call, our people here immediately respond; any time you burst into song, ours join in; anything you say, ours start to ponder?' "

The bourgeouins went off, but soon returned:

"No, Head Bourgeouin, Malchish-Kibalchish didn't reveal the Military Secret to us. He laughed right in our faces. 'The strong Red Army does have a powerful secret,' he said. 'And no matter when you attack, you'll not gain a victory.' He said, 'We have help beyond calculation, and however many people you throw in prison, you still won't succeed, and you'll have no peace during the light of day or the dark of night. There are profound secret passageways,' he said. 'But however hard you look, you won't find them. And even if you do find them, you won't be able to block them, close them, cover them. And that's all I'll tell you, and you cursed bourgeouins will never figure it out yourselves.' "

The Head Bourgeouin frowned at this and said:

"Put this secretive Malchish-Kibalchish to the most terrible torture known to man, and get the Military Secret from him, for we'll have neither life nor peace without this important Secret."

The bourgeouins left and this time returned after a long while, shaking their heads. "No," they said. "It didn't work, chief Head Bourgeouin. He stood pale, did Malchish, but proud, and he didn't tell us the Military Secret because he'd given his solemn word. And when we were leaving he got down and put his ear to the heavy stone of the cold floor, and, would you believe it, Head Bourgeouin, he smiled in such a way that all of us bourgeouins shuddered in fear, wondering if he'd heard our inevitable destruction marching along those secret passageways . . ."

"What kind of country is this?" exclaimed the Head Bourgeouin in amazement. "What an inexplicable country, where even boys like this know the Military Secret and keep their solemn word so faithfully! Move quickly, bourgeouins, and kill this proud Malchish. Load the cannons, unsheathe your sabers, unfurl our bourgeouin banners, because I hear our signalmen sounding the alarm and our standard-bearers waving the flags. Looks like it'll be no light skirmish, but a heavy battle."

And Malchish-Kibalchish perished.

It was like a storm. Military guns rumbled like a peal of thunder. Exploding shells flashed like a streak of lightning. Men on horses swept in like the wind. And red banners sailed past like storm clouds. That's how the Red Army attacked.

Just as streams flowing down a dusty mountain unite in turbulent, foamy torrents, so at the first violent sound of war uprisings started seething in Mountainous Bourgeouinland, and thousands of angry voices joined them in the Plains Kingdom, and the Snow Realm, and the Sultry State.

And the defeated Head Bourgeouin fled in fear, loudly cursing the country with its amazing people, its invincible Red Army, and its undiscovered Military Secret.

They buried Malchish-Kibalchish on the green knoll by the Blue River. And they placed a big red flag above his grave.

Steamships sailing by hail Malchish!

Pilots flying by hail Malchish!

Locomotives racing by hail Malchish!

And Pioneers passing by salute him!

1935

THE GOLDEN KEY, OR
THE ADVENTURES OF BURATINO
❧❧

EXCERPTS

ALEXEY TOLSTOY

When I was a little boy, very, very long ago, I had a book called *Pinocchio, or The Adventures of the Little Wooden Puppet* (in Italian, a wooden puppet is "buratino").

I often used to tell my playmates, boys and girls, all about Buratino's exciting adventures. But the book got lost, and so each time I would tell the story differently and invent all kinds of adventures that were never actually in the book at all.

And now, children, after many, many years, my memory harks back to my old friend Buratino, and I have made up my mind to tell you all about the little wooden puppet's extraordinary adventures.

[*The old cabinet master Giuseppe finds a talking log. After a series of funny misadventures he decides to present this log to his old friend, the carpenter Carlo.—Editors*]

CARLO MAKES A WOODEN PUPPET AND CALLS IT BURATINO

Carlo lived in a tiny little room under the stairs where all he had was a beautiful fireplace on the wall facing the door. But the beautiful fireplace and the fire blazing in it, and the pot boiling on the fire, were not real. They were drawn on a piece of old canvas.

Carlo entered the little room, sat down by a rickety table on the

131

only chair there was, and, turning the log round this way and that, began to carve a puppet out of it.

"Whatever shall I call it?" reflected Carlo. "Why, I'll call it Buratino! It'll bring me good luck. I knew a family and all of them were called Buratino; the father was Buratino, the mother Buratino, and the children Buratino, too. And they all lived happy, carefree lives."

First of all he carved the hair on the end of the log, then the forehead, then the eyes—but suddenly the eyes opened and stared at him.

Carlo gave not the slightest sign of fear, but asked in a kindly voice:

"Why do you look at me so strangely, wooden eyes?"

But the puppet said nothing—probably because it had no mouth yet. Carlo planed the cheeks and fashioned a nose—just an ordinary one. But suddenly the nose began to stretch out and grow, and became so long and pointed that Carlo gasped, "It's not nice so long," and started to cut off the tip. But it was no use. The nose twiddled itself round, wriggled out of the way, and simply stayed as it was—an incredibly long, peculiar, pointed nose.

Carlo set to work on the mouth. But hardly had he managed to cut out some lips than the mouth opened and laughed:

"Ha-ha-ha! Hee-hee-hee!"

And a little red tongue stuck out teasingly.

Carlo no longer paid any attention to these pranks, but went on with his planing, carving, and tinkering. He made the puppet a chin, a neck, shoulders, a body, and arms.

But hardly had he finished fashioning the last little finger, when Buratino began pummeling Carlo on his bald pate with his fists, and pinched and tickled him.

"Look here," said Carlo severely. "I haven't finished making you yet, you know, and you've already started being naughty. Whatever's going to happen later on, eh?"

And he gave Buratino an uncompromisingly stern look. And Buratino gazed at Papa Carlo with his round eyes, like a mouse.

Carlo made him some long legs out of laths that could take great big steps. Thereupon, his work done, he put the little wooden fellow on the floor to teach him to walk.

Buratino swayed and tottered on his slender little legs, took one pace, then another, and a hop, skip, and jump straight to the door. Over the threshold he went, and out into the street.

Carlo, getting anxious, went after him.

"Hey, you little rogue! Come back!"

But what was the use! Buratino ran down the street like a hare, and all you could hear was his wooden soles going clip-clop, clip-clop as they struck the cobbles.

"Stop him!" cried Carlo.

The passersby laughed and pointed with their fingers at Buratino as he ran. An enormous policeman with turned-up mustachios and a three-cornered hat was standing at the crossroads.

Seeing the little wooden fellow running along, he planted his legs widely apart so that he blocked the whole street with them. Buratino was just going to slip through his legs, but the policeman grabbed him by his nose and just held on until Daddy Carlo came up.

"Just you wait, I'll get even with you all right!" said Carlo, panting, and was just going to shove Buratino into his jacket pocket.

Buratino did not feel at all like sticking his legs up out of a jacket pocket on such a nice day, with everybody looking on. He nimbly wriggled out of the way and flopped onto the pavement, pretending to be dead.

"Ho!" said the policeman. "This is a nasty business, it seems."

The people in the street began to gather round. They shook their heads as they looked at Buratino lying there. "Poor little chap," said some of them. "He must have been starved."

"Carlo's beaten him to death," said the others. "The old organ-grinder!—he only pretends he's a good sort. He's a horrid brute really."

When he heard this the policeman with the mustachios seized the unfortunate Carlo by the collar and dragged him to the police station.

Carlo's shoes stirred up the dust and he groaned:

"Oh, dear! I did myself a bad turn when I made that wooden puppet!"

But when the street had emptied Buratino stuck up his nose, looked around, and skipped off home.

[*Papa Carlo sells his only jacket to buy a set of ABC blocks for his troublesome but beloved Buratino. Buratino, touched by Carlo's sacrifice, promises to "learn ever such a lot and grow up and buy Carlo a thousand new jackets." Inspired by this dream, he plans to take the alphabet blocks to school.—Editors*]

BURATINO SELLS HIS ABC BLOCKS AND BUYS A TICKET FOR THE PUPPET THEATER

Early in the morning Buratino put his ABC set in a little bag and, skipping along, ran off to school.

On the way he didn't so much as look at the sweets displayed in the shops—three-cornered honey cakes with poppy seeds, sweet cookies, and lollipops in the shape of cockerels stuck upon sticks.

He didn't even want to watch the little boys flying kites.

Basilio, the tabby cat, crossed the street. Buratino could have caught him by the tail. But he refrained.

As he got nearer the school he could hear the sound of some gay music getting louder and louder, not far off on the shore of the Mediterranean Sea.

"Fee-fee-fee!" whistled the flute.

"La-la-la-la!" sang the violin.

"Jin-jin-jin!" tinkled the cymbals.

"Boom!" went the drum.

He had to turn right to go to school; the music sounded from the left. Buratino stumbled—and his legs turned of their own accord toward the seashore from which the sounds of music came:

"Fee-fee-feeee!"

"Jin-la-la, jin-la-la!"

"Boom!"

"Well, anyway, the school won't run away," Buratino told himself in a loud voice. "I'll just have a look and a listen, and then I'll run back there."

He set off as fast as he could to run to the seashore, and there he saw a marquee decorated with many-colored flags flapping in the sea breeze.

Up on the marquee four musicians were dancing and playing. Beneath them an old lady of ample proportions and wreathed in smiles was selling tickets.

Around the entrance a large crowd was gathered—boys and girls, soldiers and lemonade vendors, nurses with infants, firemen and postmen—all of them reading a great big poster:

PUPPET THEATER

POSITIVELY ONLY ONE PERFORMANCE

Hurry!

Hurry!

Hurry!

Buratino tugged a little boy by the sleeve.

"Please, can you tell me how much it costs to go in?"

The boy was not quick to reply.

"Four kopeks, wooden puppet," he muttered through his teeth.

"I say, I left my purse at home. You can't lend me four kopeks, can you, boy?"

The boy gave a scornful whistle.

"Here's a simpleton!"

"I'm simply *dying* to see the Puppet Show," said Buratino through his tears. "Buy my lovely jacket from me! You can have it for four kopeks."

"What! A paper jacket for four kopeks? Go on with you, you fool!"

"Well, then, what about my little cap?"

"Your cap! It's not fit for catching tadpoles! Go on. Stupid!"

Buratino began to itch all over, he was so eager to get into that theater.

"Then take my new ABC for four kopeks, boy!"

"Has it got pictures?"

"*Wonderful* pictures and large letters."

"All right, give it here," said the boy. He took the ABC and reluctantly counted four kopeks.

Buratino ran up to the ample old lady wreathed in smiles.

"I say," he squeaked, "give me a ticket for the front row at the only performance of the Puppet Theater!"

BURATINO IS RECOGNIZED BY THE PUPPETS DURING THE PERFORMANCE

Buratino sat down in the front row and gazed delightedly at the curtain, which was down.

On it were drawn dancing puppets, little girls in black masks, terrible bearded folk with pointed caps and stars on them, the sun, looking like a pancake with nose and eyes, and other exciting pictures.

There were three bell rings, and the curtain rose. To the right and left of the little stage were cardboard trees. Above them hung a lantern in the shape of the moon, and it was reflected in a piece of mirror on which swam two swans made out of cotton wool with golden beaks.

From behind a cardboard tree appeared a little puppet in a long white shirt with long sleeves. His face was powdered all over as white as tooth powder.

He bowed most respectfully to the audience and said in a sad voice:

"How do you do! My name is Pierrot. We are about to present a show titled 'The Little Girl with Blue Hair, or Thirty-three Cuffs on the Head.' I'm going to be thrashed with a stick, slapped in the face, and cuffed. It's a very funny show!"

Then out jumped another fellow from behind the other cardboard tree, his outfit all checkered like a chessboard.

He bowed most respectfully to the audience.

"How do you do! I'm Harlequin."

Then he turned on Pierrot and let go at him with two slaps in the face so resounding that the powder flew off his cheeks in all directions.

"What are you sniveling for, you fool?"

"I'm feeling sad because I want to get married," answered Pierrot.

"So why don't you marry?"

"Because my girl's run away from me—"

"Ha, ha, ha!" Harlequin rocked with laughter. "There's a fool for you!"

Then he seized a stick and gave Pierrot a thorough whacking.

"What's your girl's name?"

"You won't beat me anymore?"

"Come on, I've only just begun."

"In that case her name's Malvina, or the Little Girl with Blue Hair."

"Ha, ha, ha!" Harlequin rocked with laughter again and gave Pierrot three cuffs on his head. "Just listen, ladies and gentlemen; have you ever heard of little girls having blue hair?"

But just then, as he turned to the audience, he suddenly caught sight of the wooden puppet on the front bench, with his long nose and his pointed cap, grinning from ear to ear.

"Look! It's Buratino!" cried Harlequin, pointing his finger at him.

"It's Buratino himself!" bawled Pierrot, waving his long sleeves.

A crowd of puppets jumped out from behind the cardboard trees—little girls in black masks, terrible bearded men in pointed caps, shaggy dogs with buttons instead of eyes, and hunchbacks with noses like cucumbers.

They all ran up to the candles standing along the footlights to look at him and started to chatter:

"Buratino! It's Buratino! Come on, come up to us, Buratino, you fun little scamp!"

Buratino jumped from the bench to the prompter's box, and from there onto the stage. The puppets seized hold of him and began to hug and kiss and pinch him. And then they all struck up the "Polka Bird":

> *O! A birdie danced the polka*
> *In a meadow at break of day—*
> *Beak to the left,*
> *Tail to the right—*
> *That's the Karabas polka way!*
> *Two beetles beat the big brass drum,*
> *A toad did the double-bass play.*
> *Beak to the left,*
> *Tail to the right—*
> *That's the Barabas polka way!*
> *A birdie danced the polka,*
> *For he felt so bright and gay.*
> *Beak to the left,*
> *Tail to the right—*
> *That's how he danced away.*

The spectators were deeply touched. A nurse even shed a tear, and a fireman began to sob.

The little boys on the back benches, however, were annoyed and stamped their feet.

"That's enough sob-stuff!" they yelled. "Don't be babies. Get on with the show!"

At all this uproar there came out from behind the curtain a fellow of such dreadful appearance that you would have been frozen stiff with terror at the mere sight of him.

His thick, uncombed beard dragged along the floor and his protruding eyes rolled, and he ground his teeth in his enormous mouth as though he were a crocodile and not a man. In his hand he carried a seven-tailed whip.

This was the proprietor of the Puppet Theater, Doctor of Puppetry Signor Karabas Barabas.

"Ha, ha, ha! Ho, ho, ho!" he roared at Buratino. "So it's you who've spoiled my magnificent show?"

He grabbed Buratino and carried him off to the lumber room of the theater, where he hung him up on a hook. Then back he came and threatened the puppets with his seven-tailed whip to make them go on with the performance.

Somehow or other they got through the show, then the curtain fell and the audience dispersed.

Doctor of Puppetry Signor Karabas Barabas went to the kitchen to have supper.

He tucked the lower part of his beard into his pocket so that it would not get in the way and sat down in front of the fireplace, where a whole rabbit and two pullets were roasting on the spit. Licking his fingers, he felt the roast and seemed to think it was not yet done. There was not much wood on the hearth, so he clapped his hands three times. In ran Harlequin and Pierrot.

"Fetch me that good-for-nothing Buratino!" said Signor Karabas Barabas. "He's made of dry wood; I'm going to throw him on the fire and then my roast'll get done quickly."

Harlequin and Pierrot fell on their knees and begged him to have mercy on poor little Buratino.

"Where's my whip?" snorted Karabas Barabas.

So off they went, sobbing, to the lumber room, took Buratino down from the nail, and hauled him to the kitchen.

INSTEAD OF BURNING BURATINO, SIGNOR KARABAS BARABAS
GIVES HIM FIVE GOLD RUBLES AND LETS HIM GO HOME

When the dolls dragged Buratino in and threw him on the floor by the fender, Signor Karabas Barabas was snorting most alarmingly through his nose and stirring the coals with a poker.

Suddenly his eyes became bloodshot, while his nose, and then his whole face, contracted into a maze of wrinkles. A speck of coal dust must have gone up his nostrils.

"Hup-hup-hu-up!" gasped Karabas Barabas, rolling his eyes. "Hup-hup-a-tshooo!"

He sneezed so hard that the ashes in the hearth rose straight up in a column.

Now, whenever the Doctor of Puppetry began to sneeze he could never stop, but would sneeze fifty and sometimes a hundred times in a row. Such an extraordinary fit of sneezing would quite exhaust him and put him in a better frame of mind.

"Try and start talking to him in between the sneezes," whispered Pierrot surreptitiously to Buratino.

"Hup-a-tshoo! Hup-a-tshoo!" Mouth gaping, Karabas Barabas drew breath and sneezed with a roar, shaking his topknot and stamping his feet.

Everything in the kitchen trembled, the glasses rattled, and the frying pans and saucepans swung on their hooks.

Between these sneezes Buratino began to howl in a pitiful little voice:

"Oh, dear, poor wretched me! Nobody's sorry for me!"

"Stop blubbering!" cried Karabas Barabas. "You're stopping me . . . Hup-hup-hu-up-a-tshoo!"

"Bless you, Signor!" sobbed Buratino.

"Thanks . . . Tell me, are your parents living? Hup-a-tshoo!"

"I never ever had a mommy, Signor. Oh, oh, I'm so unhappy!" And Buratino began to cry so shrilly that it seemed to Karabas Barabas as if needles were piercing his eardrums.

He stamped his feet on the floor.

"Stop screaming, I tell you! Hup-a-tshoo! Tell me, is your father alive?"

"Yes, Signor, he is. Poor Father!"

"I can just picture how he'll take the news that I've used you to roast a rabbit and two pullets. Hup-a-tshoo!"

"My poor father'll soon die of hunger and cold, anyway. I'm his only support in his old age. Have pity, let me go, Signor!"

"Ten thousand devils!" shouted Karabas Barabas at the top of his voice. "There can be no question of pity whatsoever. The rabbit and the pullets have got to be done. Get into the fireplace!"

"Signor, I can't do it!"

"Why not?" asked Karabas Barabas, but only for the sake of getting Buratino to go on talking, instead of screeching in his ears.

"I've already tried to stick my nose into a fireplace once, Signor, and all I did was to make a hole in it."

"What nonsense!" Karabas Barabas was surprised. "How could you make a hole in a fireplace with your nose?"

"Because the fireplace and the pot over the fire, Signor, had been drawn on a piece of old canvas."

"Hup-a-tshoo!" sneezed Karabas Barabas, and made such a noise that Pierrot flew off to the left, Harlequin to the right, while Buratino spun round like a spinning top.

"Where've you seen a fireplace and a fire and a pot drawn on a piece of old canvas?"

"In my Papa Carlo's little room."

"Carlo—your father!" Karabas Barabas jumped from his chair, waved his hands, and his beard flew out all over the place. "So you mean to say, in old Carlo's little room there's a secret—"

But here Karabas Barabas jammed both his fists in his mouth. He evidently did not wish to finish what he had to say about the secret something or other. He sat like that for some time, gazing goggle-eyed into the dying fire.

"Good!" said he at last. "I'll sup off underdone rabbit and raw pullets. I'll make you a present of your life, Buratino. That's not all, though—"

He felt under his beard in his waistcoat pocket and drew out five gold rubles, which he held out to Buratino.

"That's not all. Take this money and give it to Carlo. Give him my greetings and say that I beg of him under no circumstances to die of hunger and cold, and, most important of all, not to leave his little room with the fireplace drawn on the piece of old canvas. Off with you! Sleep, then run home first thing in the morning."

Buratino put the five gold rubles in his pocket and, bowing politely, replied:

"Thank you, Signor. You couldn't have entrusted the money to more reliable hands."

Harlequin and Pierrot took Buratino away to the puppets' dormitory, where the puppets once more began to hug and kiss and pinch and shove him, and then to hug him again—Buratino, who had so inexplicably escaped such a terrible fate in the fireplace.

"There's something mysterious going on here," he said to the puppets in a whisper.

[*On his way home next day Buratino meets two beggars—Basilio the Cat and Alice the Fox. They have learned of the money given to Buratino by Karabas Barabas. Masked, they attack him at night and try to steal his money, but Buratino has put the coins in his mouth. The angry robbers leave him hanging upside down until morning. Fortunately, Buratino is found and saved by Malvina, the Little Girl with Blue Hair, and her faithful servant-poodle, Artemon. The most beautiful marionette in Karabas Barabas's Puppet Theater, Malvina could no longer endure the proprietor's cruelty. She ran away and settled down at a lonely little cottage in the forest glade. With the help of the animals who are very fond of her, Malvina brings the unconscious Buratino back to life, and determines to educate him.—Editors*]

THE LITTLE GIRL WITH BLUE HAIR TRIES TO TEACH BURATINO MANNERS AND ARITHMETIC

In the morning Buratino woke up, happy and healthy, just as if nothing at all had happened.

The Little Girl with Blue Hair was waiting for him in the garden, sitting at a little table set with doll's china. Her face was freshly washed; and her cheeks and her little turned-up nose were powdered with pollen. She was getting tired of the butterflies, and as she waited for Buratino she waved her arms in vexation to get rid of them.

"Now, really, you are the limit!" she said.

She looked the little wooden puppet up and down from head to foot and frowned. She told him to sit down at the table and poured him out some cocoa into a teeny-weeny cup.

Buratino sat down and tucked one of his legs under him. Into his mouth he began to stuff whole almond pastries, which he swallowed without chewing. His fingers found their way into the jam jar and he sucked them with great relish.

When the little girl turned round to throw a few crumbs to an elderly beetle, he grabbed hold of the jug and drank up all the cocoa through the spout. It went down the wrong way, though, and he sputtered it all over the tablecloth.

"Sit up properly," said the girl severely. "And put both your legs under the table. And don't eat with your hands. The spoons and forks are there for that." Her eyelashes quivered with indignation. "Who, may I ask, has been looking after your education?"

"Papa Carlo sometimes—sometimes no one."

"Well, from now on I'm going to take your education in hand, rest assured!"

"Now I'm in for it!" thought Buratino.

On the grass near the house Artemon the poodle was chasing little birds. As they flew up into the trees he would crane his neck and jump up with an eager, whining bark.

"My! He sure knows how to chase birds!" thought Buratino enviously.

As he sat respectably at the table, the ants kept crawling up from the seat and all over his body.

At length the painful breakfast came to an end. The little girl told him to wipe the cocoa off his nose. She put the pleats and ribbons on her dress in order, took Buratino by the hand, and led him indoors—to see to his education.

But Artemon, the frisky poodle, still ran about the lawn barking, while the birds, who were not in the least afraid of him, warbled happily, and a gentle breeze blew merrily over the treetops.

"Take off your rags. You'll be given a respectable jacket and breeches," said the little girl.

Four tailors—Mr. Pinchum, a morose old crawfish, who was a master craftsman, Mr. Woodpecker, all in grey with a little topknot, big Mr. Stag Beetle, and Lisette, the mouse—made him a beautiful little-boy's suit out of the little girl's cast-off dresses.

Mr. Pinchum did the cutting, Mr. Woodpecker poked the holes through with his bill and sewed, Mr. Stag Beetle twisted the thread with his hind legs, and Lisette gnawed it off with her teeth.

Buratino was ashamed to put on the little girl's castoffs; nevertheless, he had to change. He gave a loud sniff and hid his four gold pieces in the pocket of his new jacket.

"Now sit down, put your hands in front of you, and don't talk," said the little girl, picking up a piece of chalk. "We're going to do arithmetic. In your pocket you have two apples—"

Buratino gave a sly wink.

"Wrong," he said. "I've none at all."

"I mean," the little girl repeated patiently, "let's *suppose* that you have two apples in your pocket. Somebody takes one of them away from you. How many apples have you left?"

"Two."

"Think carefully."

Buratino knitted his brows and thought hard.

"Two."

"Why?"

"Huh! I'd never give nobody an apple, I can tell you, even if he fought me for it!"

"You're absolutely no ability in math." She was quite upset. "Let's try dictation."

Her pretty little eyes gazed up at the ceiling.

"Write down, 'Esora saw Anna was a rose.' Have you finished? Now read it to me backwards. It's a magic sentence."

As you and I are quite aware, Buratino had never before so much as seen a pen or an inkpot. When the little girl said, "Write," he at once stuck his nose in the inkwell and was terribly scared when the ink dripped off it and made blotches on the paper.

The little girl threw up her hands in dismay and tears started from her eyes.

"You horrid, mischievous thing, you! You should be punished for this!"

She leaned out of the window.

"Artemon," she called. "Take Buratino away and shut him up in the dark cupboard."

The good dog Artemon appeared in the doorway and his teeth flashed. He caught hold of Buratino by his jacket and dragged him along backward to the lumber room, where spiders' webs, with great big spiders in them, hung in all the corners. He locked him in there, gave a snort to frighten him properly, and hurried off again to chase the little birds.

The little girl lay down upon her little lace doll's bed and sobbed and sobbed because she had had to treat the little wooden puppet so cruelly. But, having once begun his education, she felt she had to go through with it.

Meanwhile Buratino grumbled away in the dark lumber room. "What a stupid little girl . . . A governess! Huh, just fancy! And she's only got a china head and a body stuffed with cotton wool!"

There was a faint squeak in the dark room, as though someone with very tiny teeth were grinding them together.

"Hullo, hullo!"

Buratino raised his inky nose and through the gloom made out a bat hanging upside down from the ceiling.

"What is it?"

"Shhh, shhh!" rustled the spiders in their corners. "Don't shake our webs—you'll frighten away the flies."

Buratino sat down on a broken pot, his head in his hands. He was in a fix and no mistake, and the injustice of it made him indignant.

"Is that how they bring children up?" he thought. "It's agony, not education . . . You can't sit, you can't eat like that . . . *Every* child hasn't learned the alphabet, anyway—and she goes and gets hold of an inkpot straightaway . . . I bet that dog's chasing the birds! It's all right for him."

Again the bat squeaked.

"Just wait till nightfall, Buratino," it said, "and I'll take you to Fool Land. Your friends are waiting for you there—the cat and the fox, and gaiety and happiness. Just wait till dark."

BURATINO COMES TO FOOL LAND

The Little Girl with Blue Hair went up to the door of the lumber room.

"Buratino, dear, are you sorry now for what you did?"

Buratino was very indignant; besides, his mind was altogether elsewhere.

"I've got nothing to be sorry for! Don't expect—"

"Very well. You'll have to sit in the lumber room till the morning, then!"

With a bitter sigh she turned and left.

Night fell. Up in the loft an owl hooted. A toad crawled out of the cellar to go and splash its stomach in the puddles that reflected the moon.

The little girl retired to her lacy bed and bitterly sobbed and sobbed until she fell asleep. Artemon, his head tucked under his tail, slept by her bedroom door.

The pendulum clock in the cottage struck twelve. The bat flew down from the ceiling.

"In the corner of the room there's a rat hole—it leads down to the cellar. I'll be waiting for you on the lawn."

It flew out through the dormer window. Buratino rushed to the corner of the lumber room, getting all tangled in the spiders' webs. The spiders hissed balefully after him. He climbed down the rat hole that led to the cellar. It got narrower and narrower as he went, until he could scarcely squeeze his way through. Then suddenly he pitched down head first into the cellar.

He nearly fell into a rattrap, trod on the tail of a grass snake that had just finished drinking some milk from the jug in the dining room, and scrambled out through a passage, used by the cats, onto the lawn.

The bat was fluttering noiselessly above the blue flowers.

"Follow me, Buratino! To Fool Land!"

A bat has no tail. For this reason it does not fly straight, like a bird, but up and down, up and down, for all the world like a little devil. It keeps its mouth open all the time, ready to snap at and swallow alive the gnats and moths on its way.

Buratino ran after it, up to his neck in grass, the wet blades slapping against his cheeks.

Suddenly the bat swept high up toward the round moon.

"Here he is!" it called out to someone below.

At that very moment Buratino tumbled head over heels, hurtling over a steep slope, and rolled over and over, coming to an abrupt halt in a bed of burdock.

He sat up and opened his mouth wide. He was scratched all over and his mouth was full of grit.

"Oh, so it's you!"

In front of him stood Basilio the Cat and Alice the Fox.

"Brave, courageous little Buratino! He must have fallen from the moon."

"Amazing he's still alive," said the cat in a glum voice.

Buratino was delighted to find his old acquaintances again, though he thought it rather strange that the cat should have its right paw bandaged up with a rag and that the fox's tail was all soiled with bog mud.

"Every cloud has a silver lining," said the fox. "You've got to Fool Land, anyway."

She pointed a paw toward a broken-down bridge over a dried-up stream. On the far side, among some garbage dumps, could be seen some semi-dilapidated cottages, withered trees with broken branches, and bell towers leaning untidily this way and that.

"They sell those famous hareskin jackets in this town," trilled the fox, licking her chops. "Just the thing for Papa Carlo! ABC blocks, too, with colored pictures. Oh, and you can buy such lovely cream pastries and lollipops in the shape of cockerels! I suppose you haven't lost your money yet, you little wonder of a Buratino, have you?"

Alice the Fox helped him to his feet, spat on her paw, and cleaned his jacket, then took him across the broken-down bridge. Basilio the Cat hobbled sullenly behind.

It was midnight already, but everyone in Fool Land was awake.

Scraggy dogs, covered in burrs, were wandering along the dirty, winding street, their mouths gaping with hunger.

"Gr-r-r-r-rrrrim!"

Goats with mangy sides munched at the dusty grass growing by the pavement and shook their stumpy tails.

"Mi-i-i-i-isery!" they bleated.

A cow was standing with its head hanging down and its bones sticking out beneath its hide.

"Muuuuurder!" she mooed ruminatively.

Molting sparrows were sitting around on little mounds of dirt. They did not fly away, even if trampled on.

Hens with bedraggled tails staggered about from exhaustion.

At the crossroads, however, fierce bulldog police, dressed in three-cornered hats and spiked dog collars, were standing to attention.

"Moooooove along there! Keep to the rrrrright! Keep moving!" they shouted at the hungry, mangy inhabitants.

The fox pulled Buratino farther along the street. In the moonlight they could see well-fed tomcats in gold spectacles strolling along, arm in arm with she-cats in mob caps.

A great fat fox—the Governor of the City—with his nose in the air and looking very important, sauntered by. With him was a haughty-looking vixen with a sprig of damewort in her hand.

"The people taking a stroll are the ones who've planted their money in the Field of Miracles," whispered the fox. "Tonight's the last night for doing it. You'll pick up a pile of money in the morning and be able to buy yourself all sorts of nice things. Hurry up!"

The fox and the cat brought Buratino to a piece of waste ground where broken pots, torn shoes, rags, and galoshes with holes in them were lying around untidily.

There they started to jabber at him, interrupting each other:

"Scrape a hole out."

"Put in your rubles."

"Sprinkle some salt on."

"Water it well—scoop it from a puddle."

"And don't forget to say 'Krex, Phex, Pex.'"

Buratino scratched his inky nose.

"You might at least keep back a little," he said.

"Good heavens! We don't want to watch where you're putting your money," said the fox.

"Good heavens, no!" said the cat.

They drew a little to one side and hid behind a pile of garbage.

Buratino dug a hole and put in the four gold coins. "Krex, Phex, Pex," he whispered three times, filled the hole up, took a pinch of salt from his pocket, and sprinkled it on top. He scooped up some water from a puddle, poured it over the spot, then sat down to wait for a tree to grow.

ARRESTED BY THE POLICE, BURATINO IS NOT ALLOWED TO SAY A SINGLE WORD IN HIS OWN DEFENSE

Alice the Fox had thought that Buratino would go away to sleep somewhere, but he kept sitting on the garbage heap, his nose sticking patiently out in front of him.

So Alice told the cat to stay guard while she ran off to the nearest police station.

There, in a smoke-filled room, snoring away heavily behind an ink-bespattered desk, was the bulldog on duty.

"Mr. Duty Officer," said the fox in her most ingratiating tone of voice, "you're so manly—could you arrest a homeless pickpocket? He's a dreadful menace to all the rich, worthy citizens of the town."

The bulldog on duty, befuddled with sleep, gave such a loud bellow that a puddle appeared underneath the frightened fox.

"Pickpocket! Rrrrrah!"

Alice explained that the dangerous pickpocket—Buratino—had been seen in the abandoned lot.

Still snorting, the Police Officer on duty rang a bell. Two Doberman pinscher sleuth-hounds burst into the room, detectives who never slept, believed no one, and even suspected themselves of harboring criminal intentions.

The Police Officer on duty instructed them to bring back the dangerous criminal to the police station, dead or alive.

"Wooff!" replied the detectives laconically, and off they dashed to the abandoned lot at a clever lope, their hind legs tilting to one side.

The last hundred paces they crawled on their bellies and, both at once, flung themselves on Buratino, seized him beneath the arms, and dragged him off to the police station.

Buratino, legs dangling, begged them to tell him what he had done.

"They'll clear it all up once we get there," the detectives replied.

The fox and the cat lost no time in digging out the four gold coins. So astutely did the fox divide the money that the cat was left with one piece, while she herself had three.

Without a word, the cat clawed the fox in the mouth. The fox firmly seized hold of the cat with her paws and they both rolled around all over the abandoned lot, while tufts of cat and fox fur flew about in the moonlight.

When they had both given each other a thorough drubbing, they divided the money equally and, that very night, disappeared from the town.

Meanwhile the detectives brought Buratino to the police station. The bulldog on duty extricated himself from behind the table and searched the puppet's pockets himself. Finding nothing but a lump of sugar and some crumbs of almond pastry, the Duty Officer gave a bloodthirsty snort:

"You've committed three crimes, you scoundrel! You've no home, no identity card, and no work. Take him out of town and drown him in the pond."

"Wooff!" answered the detectives.

Buratino tried to tell him about Papa Carlo and about his own adventures. But all in vain! The detectives grabbed hold of him and at full speed loped off, out of the town, dragging him with them; they threw him off the bridge into a deep, dirty pool, full of frogs, leeches, and water beetle grubs.

Buratino plopped into the water and the green duckweed closed over him.

BURATINO BECOMES ACQUAINTED WITH THE INHABITANTS
OF THE POND, LEARNS OF THE LOSS OF HIS FOUR GOLD
PIECES, AND IS GIVEN THE GOLDEN KEY BY CHERRYBACK
THE TURTLE

It must not be forgotten that Buratino was made of wood and therefore could not drown.

All the same, he got so frightened that he lay still on the water for a long time, with the duckweed clinging to him all over.

The inhabitants of the pond gathered around him: black, bloated tadpoles, well known for their stupidity, water boatmen with hind legs like oars, leeches and grubs that ate everything they came across, even one another, and, last of all, various tiny infusoria.

The tadpoles tickled him with their stiff lips and seemed to enjoy nibbling the tassel on his cap. The leeches crawled into his jacket pocket. One of the water boatmen climbed several times up to his nose and took swallow dives off it.

The tiny infusoria wriggled about, frantically shaking the little hairs that serve them as hands and feet, trying to catch something good to eat, but instead landing up in the mouths of the water boatmen's grubs.

Buratino eventually became bored with this and he splashed his heels in the water.

"Go away! What do you think I am? A dead cat?"

The denizens of the pond scattered in different directions, while he turned over onto his stomach and swam off.

On the round leaves of the water lilies, wide-mouthed frogs sat staring at him with their goggle-eyes.

"Must be some sort of cuttlefish swimming about," croaked one of them.

"It's got a nose like a stork's bill," croaked a second.

"It's a sea frog," croaked a third.

Buratino climbed out onto a large water lily leaf to get his breath. He sat down on it, clasped his little knees tightly, and said through chattering teeth:

"Every little boy and girl's had a drink of milk and is asleep in a nice warm bed. I'm the only one sitting on a wet leaf . . . Oh, frogs, give me a bite to eat!"

As everyone knows, frogs are very cold-blooded. It's quite wrong, however, to think that they have no heart. When Buratino, his teeth chattering hard, began to tell them about his unfortunate adventures, the frogs hopped up one by one and, with a flash of their hind legs, dived to the bottom of the pond.

They brought him back a dead beetle, a dragonfly wing, a small portion of slime, a tiny bit of crawfish roe, and a few rotten roots.

They placed all these eatables in front of Buratino and jumped up back onto the water lily leaves, where they sat as if made of stone, their wide-mouthed, goggle-eyed heads in the air.

Buratino sniffed the frogs' fare and sampled it.

"Ugh! It makes me ill," he said. "What horrid stuff!"

At that, with one accord, the frogs plopped into the water again.

The green duckweed shook on the surface of the pool; a frightful, large snakelike head appeared and swam toward the leaf on which Buratino was sitting.

The tassel on the end of his cap stood up on end. He was so frightened that he nearly tumbled into the water.

But it was no snake. It was a perfectly harmless, elderly, shortsighted turtle called Cherryback.

"Oh, you brainless, gullible child!" said Cherryback. "You've no sense at all! You ought to be at home, learning your lessons like a good boy . . . and instead you landed in Fool Land."

"Yes, but I wanted to get some more gold pieces for Papa Carlo, and I'm a verrrry good, sensible boy . . ."

"The cat and the fox stole your money," said the turtle. "They were running past the pond and stopped for a drink, and I heard them boasting how they'd dug up your money and how they'd fought over it. Oh, you brainless, credulous, silly little fool! You've got no sense at all!"

"Being told off isn't what I need," muttered Buratino. "This is where a fellow could use some help. What am I going to do now? Oh dear, oh dear, oh dear! However shall I get back to Papa Carlo? Oh-oh-oh!"

He rubbed his eyes with his fists and whimpered so pitifully that suddenly all the frogs sighed in unison:

"A-a-h! Cherryback, do help the fellow!"

The turtle gazed up at the moon for some time, then remembered something . . .

"Once upon a time," she said, "I did help a certain fellow, but afterward he went and turned my grandmother and grandfather into tortoiseshell combs." Again she fixed her eyes on the moon for a while. "Tell you what, little fellow, you sit here, and I'll go for a crawl on the bottom—maybe I'll find a certain little something that'll be of use."

She pulled in her snakelike head and slowly descended beneath the water.

"Cherryback the Turtle has got a great secret," whispered the frogs.

A long, long time went by. The moon was already sinking behind the hills when the green duckweed trembled again and the turtle appeared, holding a little golden key in her mouth.

She placed it on the leaf at Buratino's feet.

"There, you brainless, credulous, silly little fool, with no sense at all," said the turtle. "Don't be upset that the fox and the cat stole your gold coins. I'm giving you this little key. It was dropped into the pond by a man who had such a long beard that he used to tuck it into his pocket, so it wouldn't get in his way when he walked. Ah! How he begged me to find his key at the bottom of the pond for him!"

The turtle sighed, was silent for a while, then sighed again so heavily that little bubbles gurgled out of the water . . .

"But I didn't help him. I was very angry with people at that time, on account of my grandfather and grandmother having been turned into tortoiseshell combs. The bearded fellow told me a lot about this little key, but I've forgotten it all. I only remember that you have to unlock some door or other with it, and that that will bring you happiness."

Buratino's heart started to thump and his eyes grew bright. He at once forgot all his misfortunes. Pulling the leeches out of his pocket, he put the little key inside. He politely thanked Cherryback the Turtle and the frogs, plunged into the water, and swam off toward the bank. When he became visible as a black shadow on the bank of the pond, the frogs croaked after him:

"Buratino! Don't lose the key!"

[*Buratino and Pierrot overhear Karabas's conversation with his associate. Pierrot learns that the golden key opens the door behind the canvas with a boiling pot painted on it in Papa Carlo's little room. After many adventures Buratino, Pierrot, and Malvina are reunited. Papa Carlo has saved them from the police dogs, and now they all rush home. In the meantime, Karabas Barabas had learned that Buratino now possesses the Golden Key.—Editors*]

KARABAS BARABAS BREAKS INTO THE LITTLE ROOM UNDER THE STAIRS

As we know, Karabas Barabas took great pains to try and persuade the sleepy policeman to arrest Carlo. But, unable to get his way, Karabas Barabas ran off down the street.

His beard flew out in all directions and got caught in the buttons and parasols of passersby. He jostled them and gnashed his teeth. The little boys whistled shrilly after him and let fly rotten apples at his back.

Karabas Barabas ran in to see the town Mayor. At this hot hour of the day the Mayor was sitting in his garden near a fountain, in nothing but a little pair of shorts, drinking lemonade.

The Mayor had six chins and his nose, so to speak, drowned in his pink cheeks. Behind him, beneath a lime tree, four glum-faced policemen from time to time would uncork bottles of lemonade.

Karabas Barabas dashed up and fell on his knees before him.

"I'm a poor little orphan," he howled, smearing tears all over his face with his beard. "I've been insulted, robbed, and beaten up—"

"Who's insulted you, orphan?" asked the Mayor, panting as he spoke.

"A most nasty enemy, the old organ-grinder Carlo. He's stolen my three best puppets and he wants to burn down my famous theater, and he'll plunder and set fire to the whole town if you don't arrest him on the spot."

To add force to his words, Karabas Barabas brought out a fistful of gold coins and placed them in the Mayor's shoe.

To cut a long story short, he slandered and lied so much that the Mayor took fright.

"Go along with this worthy orphan," he instructed the policemen beneath the lime tree, "and take the necessary steps in the name of the law."

Karabas Barabas ran off with the four policemen to Carlo's little room.

"In the name of the King of Mumbo-Jumbo," he cried, "arrest this thief and scoundrel!"

But the doors were shut. Nobody responded within.

"In the name of the King of Mumbo-Jumbo," ordered Karabas Barabas, "break in the door!"

The policemen heaved and the leaves of the double doors, which were rotten, broke away from the hinges and the four policemen, rattling their sabers, tumbled with a crash into the little room beneath the stairs.

This happened just at the moment when Carlo, scrunching up, left through the little secret door. He was the last to disappear.

"Bang!" went the little door. The soft music ceased to play. The dirty bandages and ripped canvas with the picture of the fireplace were all that was left, lying on the floor of the little room beneath the stairs.

Karabas Barabas bounded up to the secret door and hammered at it with his fists and heels.

"Rat-tat-tat-tat!"

But the little door was shut fast.

Karabas Barabas took a run at the door, striking it hard. But it would not give.

"Break in the cursed door, in the name of the King of Mumbo-Jumbo!"

The policemen felt each other's bumps—one had a bang on his nose, the other a lump on his head.

"No! This here's a very difficult job," they replied, and set off to tell the town Mayor that they had done everything required by the law, but it seemed that the devil himself was helping the old organgrinder, for he had disappeared through the wall.

Karabas Barabas tore his beard, threw himself on the floor, and began to roll, howl, and roar like a madman all around the little room under the staircase.

WHAT THEY FOUND BEHIND THE SECRET DOOR

While Karabas Barabas was rolling about like a madman and tearing his beard, the group—with Buratino in front, Malvina, Pierrot, and Artemon behind him, and Papa Carlo bringing up the rear—was going down a steep stone staircase leading to an underground vault.

Papa Carlo was holding a candle end. Its flickering flame cast great shadows, now from Artemon's shaggy head, now from Pierrot's outstretched hand, but could not illuminate the darkness into which the stairs descended.

Malvina pinched her ears to prevent herself from crying out with fright.

Pierrot, as usual given to irrelevancies, was muttering verses to himself:

> The shadows dance upon the wall,
> But nothing frightens me at all.
> What matter if the stairs are steep,
> Let danger from the darkness leap!
> This subterranean path must go
> Somewhere or other down below.

Buratino had got ahead of the others; his white pointed cap could be made out with difficulty far below.

Suddenly there was a hissing noise down there as something fell and rolled over.

"Help! Come here!" his pitiful voice could be heard.

Instantly, Artemon, forgetting his wounds and his hunger, dashed like a black whirlwind down the steps, knocking down Malvina and Pierrot on the way.

His teeth snapped. Some kind of creature gave a verminous squeal.

A broad stream of light from below struck the stairs. The flame of the candle held by Papa Carlo paled to a faint yellow.

"Look, look, quick!" called Buratino at the top of his voice.

Malvina, back to front, began hurriedly clambering step by step; behind her Pierrot started jumping down. Last of all, bending forward, came Carlo, his wooden shoes slipping off every now and then.

Below, where the stairs came to an end, Artemon was sitting on the stone-flagged landing. He was licking his chops. At his feet Scruffy, the rat, lay dead.

Buratino was holding up with both hands a rotten felt hanging that covered a gap in the stone wall. It was from here that a stream of blue light was pouring.

The first thing they saw when they had crawled through the opening was the sunlight falling with spreading rays from a round window in the vaulted roof.

The broad rays, in which the dust was dancing, lit up a round chamber, all of yellow marble. In the middle of it stood a Puppet Theater of wondrous beauty. On its curtains gleamed a golden zigzag of lightning.

On either side of the curtains loomed two square towers, painted to look as though they were built of little bricks. The high roof, made of green metal, shone brightly.

On the left-hand tower was a clock with bronze hands. Opposite each figure on the dial were drawn the laughing little faces of a boy and a girl.

On the right-hand tower was a little round window with multicolored panes.

Above this window, on the green metal roof, perched the Talking Cricket.

"I warned you, Buratino, that there were awful dangers and terrible adventures waiting for you," said the cricket in a slow, deliberate voice, as they all stood there, mouths gaping, in front of the wonderful theater. "It's a good thing everything's ended all right. It might not have. Well, well—"

The cricket's aged voice had a note of grievance in it, for the Talking Cricket, after all, had once had his head hit with a mallet, and in spite of his hundred years and his natural kindliness he could not forget an undeserved injury. He therefore added no more to what he had said, twitched his whiskers as though he were shaking the dust off them, and slowly crept away into some lonely chink far from all turmoil and bustle.

"I did think," said Papa Carlo when he had gone, "that we'd at least find a heap of gold and silver here. But all we've found is an old toy."

He went up to the clock set in the little tower and tapped on the dial with his fingernail. As there was a little key hanging on a brass hook at the side of the clock, he took it and wound it up.

There was a loud ticking sound. The hands moved. The big hand was close to twelve o'clock, the little one was almost at six. From inside the tower came a whirring and a wheezing. The clock melodiously struck six.

As it did so the little window with the multicolored panes in the right-hand tower opened wide. Out jumped a mottled little clockwork bird.

"Come along, come along, come along, come along, come along, come along!" it sang six times over, fluttering its wings.

The bird disappeared, the little window shut with a bang, and some hurdy-gurdy music began to play. The curtain rose.

No one, not even Papa Carlo, had ever set eyes on such a lovely scene.

On the stage was a garden. There were little trees with gold and silver leaves and, singing on them, starlings the size of a thumbnail. On one tree hung apples, each no bigger than a grain of maize. Beneath the trees peacocks strutted, stretching up on tiptoe to peck at the apples. Two little goats were frisking and butting in a paddock, and butterflies, scarcely visible to the naked eye, fluttered about in the air.

This scene lasted a minute. Then the starlings grew quiet, and the peacocks and goats withdrew backstage. The trees dropped down through the secret trapdoors beneath the stage.

Fluffy clouds began to spread over the background. A red sun appeared over a sandy desert. From backstage, both left and right, were thrown out drooping trails of liana that looked like snakes—and on one of them there actually hung a boa constrictor. From another a family of monkeys were swinging by their tails.

This was Africa.

Across the sandy desert, beneath the red sun, passed the wild beasts.

A lion with a great mane bounded past in three leaps—and though he was no bigger than a cat, he looked terrifying.

A plush bear with a parasol waddled across on his hind paws with a rolling gait.

A revolting crocodile crawled by. His small, villainous eyes pretended to look kind. Even so, Artemon did not believe them and growled at him.

A rhinoceros thundered past, with a rubber ball over his horn for safety's sake.

A giraffe, looking like a striped camel with horns, raced by, its neck stretched out as far as it would go.

Then came an elephant, the children's friend, clever and kind-hearted—and he waved his trunk, which held a soybean candy.

Last of all, a terrible, dirty, wild jackal came skulking sideways. Artemon rushed at it, barking—Papa Carlo only just succeeded in dragging him away from the stage by his tail.

The wild animals had gone. Suddenly the sun was extinguished. In the darkness unseen objects were lowered from above, while others were moved out from the sides. A sound like a bow upon strings was heard.

Some frosted street-lamps lit up. The scene was a city square. The doors of the houses opened and little people ran out of them and got onto a toy tramcar. The conductor rang the bell, the tram driver turned a handle, a little boy nimbly seized hold of the coupling, a policeman blew his whistle—and the tram drove off down a side turning between tall buildings.

A cyclist rode past. The wheels of his bike were no bigger than the rim of a jam dish. A newspaper delivery boy ran by, his papers the size of a tear-off calendar sheet folded in four.

An ice-cream man pushed his ice-cream cart across the square, and little girls ran out onto the balconies of the houses and waved to him, but the ice-cream man spread out his hands, saying, "All gone. You'll have to come another time."

Then the curtain fell and the golden zigzag of lightning gleamed upon it again.

Papa Carlo, Malvina, and Pierrot could not get over their delight. Buratino, however, stuck his hands in his pockets and his nose in the air.

"Well, you see?" he said boastfully. "It's clearly not for nothing I got soaked through in Aunt Cherryback's bog. We'll put on a show in this theater—and you know what we'll call it? 'The Golden Key, or The Extraordinary Adventures of Buratino and His Friends.' Karabas Barabas'll burst with vexation."

Pierrot rubbed his fists across his furrowed forehead.

"I'll write the words in sumptuous rhyme!"

"I'll sell ice creams and tickets!" said Malvina. "And if you find I have any talent I'll try and play the parts of good little girls."

"Not so fast, children," said Papa Carlo. "When are you going to do your lessons?"

"We'll do our lessons in the morning," they all answered in unison. "And in the evening we'll act in the theater."

"Well, that's all right then, my dears," said Papa Carlo. "And I, my dears, shall grind the organ to entertain the worthy public and, if we're going to journey about Italy from town to town, I'll drive the horse and cook the mutton broth with garlic."

Artemon listened, pricking up one ear, then turned his head, his shining eyes gazing at his friends with the question: and what was he to do?

"Artemon shall look after the props and stage costumes," said Buratino. "We'll give him the key to the wardrobe. During the performance he can imitate the roar of the lion from backstage, the thud of the rhinoceros, the grinding of the crocodile's teeth, and the wailing of the wind—by swishing his tail quickly—and the other sound effects that we need."

"And you, what about you, Buratino?" they all asked. "What's your role in the theater going to be?"

"What a question!" he answered. "Why, I'll act myself in the show and become famous throughout the world!"

THE NEW PUPPET THEATER GIVES ITS FIRST PERFORMANCE

Karabas Barabas was sitting in front of the fire in a vile mood. The damp wood was barely smoldering. Outside, the rain was pouring down. The roof of the Puppet Theater was full of holes and leaked. The puppets' arms and legs had grown all damp and nobody wanted to work during rehearsals, even under the threat of the seven-tailed lash. For three days now the puppets had eaten nothing, and they whispered ominously among themselves as they hung on their hooks in the storeroom.

Not a single ticket had been sold for the theater that morning. Indeed, who'd want to go and watch Karabas Barabas's boring plays and hungry, ragged actors?

The clock on the town-hall tower struck twelve. Karabas Barabas wandered gloomily into the auditorium. It was empty.

"Devil take the 'worthy public'!" he muttered, and went outside. As he came out he glanced around, blinked, and opened his mouth so wide that a crow could have flown in without any difficulty.

Opposite his theater, paying no attention to the damp sea wind, a crowd had gathered in front of a big new marquee.

On a dais above the entrance stood a long-nosed puppet in a pointed hat, blowing at a blaring trumpet and shouting something. The people were laughing and clapping their hands, and many of them were going inside the theater.

As Karabas Barabas stood there, Foolchump came up to him; he smelled of slime worse than ever.

"Ah, dear me!" he said, puckering his face into a maze of sour wrinkles. "This medical leech business is getting me nowhere. I want to join them now." Foolchump pointed toward the new marquee. "I want to ask them for a job lighting candles or sweeping the floor."

"Whose theater is it? Where's it come from?" growled Karabas Barabas.

"It's the puppets themselves. They've opened their own puppet theater, 'The Lightning Theater.' They're writing their own plays in verse and acting on their own."

Karabas Barabas ground his teeth, tore at his beard, and strode over to the new marquee.

"First performance of an exciting, interesting comedy from the life of wooden puppets!" Buratino was shouting. "The true story of how we beat our enemies by means of sharp wits, daring, and presence of mind!"

At the entrance to the Puppet Theater sat Malvina in a little glass box, a lovely ribbon in her blue hair. She could not give out the tickets fast enough to the people who wanted to see the lively comedy all about puppet life.

Papa Carlo, in a new velvet jacket, was grinding the organ and winking merrily at the worthy public.

Artemon was dragging Alice the Fox, who'd sneaked in without a ticket, out of the tent by her tail.

Basilio the Cat, who also had entered without a ticket, had managed to get away and was sitting up a tree in the rain, looking down with baleful eyes.

Buratino puffed out his cheeks and blew his blaring trumpet:

"The performance is about to begin!"

And he ran down the little ladder to take part in the first scene of the comedy, which showed poor Papa Carlo chiseling a little wooden puppet out of a log, without the slightest idea that it was going to bring him happiness.

The last one to crawl into the theater was Cherryback the Turtle, with a complimentary ticket printed on parchment paper with gold edgings in her mouth.

The performance had begun. Karabas Barabas returned gloomily to his empty theater. He picked up his seven-tailed whip and unlocked the storeroom door.

"I'll teach you to be lazy, you mangy wretches!" he snarled fiercely. "I'll teach you to lure the public here!"

He cracked his whip. But no one answered. The storeroom was empty. All that was left on the hooks were some remnants of string.

All the puppets—Harlequin, the little girls in black masks, the wizards in high pointed caps with stars, the hunchbacks with noses like cucumbers, the blackamoors and the little dogs—all, all, all of them had fled from Karabas Barabas.

With a dreadful howl he bounded out of his theater into the street. He was just in time to see the last of his actors scampering over a puddle into the new theater, where music was gaily playing and from where laughter and applause could be heard.

All Karabas Barabas managed to grab was a little fustian dog with buttons for eyes. But, as if from nowhere, Artemon flew at him, knocked him over, seized the little dog from his grasp, and sped off into the tent, where backstage some hot mutton broth with garlic had been prepared for the hungry actors.

And Karabas Barabas was left sitting in a puddle in the rain.

1936

THE OLD GENIE KHOTTABYCH:
A STORY OF MAKE-BELIEVE
ᗡᖇ

EXCERPTS

LAZAR LAGIN

AN UNUSUAL MORNING

At 7:32 a.m. a cheerful patch of sun slipped through a hole in the curtain and settled on the nose of Volka Kostylkov, a sixth-grade pupil. Volka sneezed and woke up.

Just then, he heard his mother in the next room say:

"Don't rush, Alyosha. Let the child sleep in a bit longer. He's got exams today."

Volka winced. When, oh when, would his mother stop calling him a child!

"Nonsense!" he heard his father answer. "The boy's nearly thirteen. He might as well get up and help us pack. Before you know it, this child of yours will be using a razor."

The packing! How could he have forgotten about it!

Volka threw off the blankets and hurriedly started pulling on his pants. How could he ever have forgotten such a day!

This was the day the Kostylkov family was moving to a different apartment in a new six-floor house. Most of their belongings had been packed the night before. Mother and Grandma had packed the dishes in a little tin tub in which once, very long ago, when Volka was a baby, they had bathed him. His father had rolled up his sleeves and, with a mouthful of nails, just like a shoemaker, spent the evening hammering down the lids on crates of books.

Then they had all argued as to the best place to put the things so as to have them handy when the truck arrived in the morning. Then they had had their tea on an uncovered table—as if they were on the march. And deciding that their heads would be clearer after a good night's sleep, they'd all gone to bed.

In a word, there was just no explaining how on earth he could have forgotten that this was the morning they were moving to a new apartment.

The movers barged in before breakfast was quite over. The first thing they did was to open wide both halves of the door and ask in loud voices, "Well, can we begin?"

"Yes, please do," both Mother and Grandma answered and began to bustle about.

Volka marched downstairs, solemnly carrying the sofa pillows to the waiting truck.

"Are you moving?" the boy from next door asked.

"Yes," Volka answered indifferently, as though he were used to moving from one apartment to another every week and there was nothing very special about it.

The janitor, Stepanych, walked over, slowly rolled a cigarette, and began an unhurried conversation as one adult talking to another. The boy felt dizzy with pride and happiness. He gathered his courage and invited Stepanych to visit them at their new home. The janitor said, "With pleasure." A serious, important, man-to-man conversation was beginning, when all at once Volka's mother's voice came through the open window:

"Volka! Volka! Where can that awful child be?"

Volka raced up to the strangely large and empty apartment in which shreds of old newspapers and old medicine bottles were lying forlornly about the floor.

"Finally!" his mother said. "Take your precious aquarium and get right into the truck. I want you to sit on the sofa and hold the aquarium on your lap. There's no other place for it. But be sure the water doesn't splash on the sofa."

It's really strange the way parents worry when they're moving to a new apartment.

THE STRANGE VESSEL

Well, the truck finally choked exhaustedly and stopped at the attractive entrance of Volka's new house. The movers quickly carried everything upstairs and soon were gone.

Volka's father opened a few crates and said, "We'll do the rest in the evening." Then he left for the factory.

Mother and Grandma began unpacking the pots and pans, while Volka decided to run down to the river nearby. His father had warned him not to go swimming without him, because the river was very deep, but Volka soon found an excuse: "I have to go in for a dip to clear my head. How can I take an exam with a fuzzy brain!"

It's wonderful the way Volka was always able to think of an excuse when he was about to do something he was not allowed to do.

How convenient it is to have a river near your house! Volka told his mother he'd go sit on the bank and study his geography. And he really and truly intended to spend about ten minutes leafing through the textbook. The minute he reached the river, however, he got undressed and jumped into the water. It was still early, and there wasn't a soul on the bank. This had its good and bad points. It was nice, because no one could stop him from swimming as much as he liked. It was bad, because there was no one to admire what a good swimmer and especially what an extraordinary diver he was.

Volka swam and dived until he became blue. Finally, he realized that he had had enough. He was ready to climb out when he suddenly changed his mind and decided to dive into the clear water one last time.

As he was about to come up for air, his hand hit a long hard object on the bottom. He grabbed it and surfaced near the shore, holding a strange-looking, slippery, moss-covered clay vessel. It resembled an ancient type of Greek vase called an amphora. The neck was tightly sealed with a green substance and was imprinted on top with what looked like a seal.

Volka weighed the vessel in his hand. It was very heavy. He caught his breath.

A treasure! An ancient treasure of great scientific value! How wonderful!

He dressed quickly and dashed home to open it in the privacy of his room.

As he ran along, he could visualize the notice that would certainly appear in all the papers the next morning. He even thought of a heading: "A Pioneer Aids Science."

> Yesterday, a Pioneer named Vladimir Kostylkov appeared at his district militia station and handed the officer on duty a treasure consisting of antique gold objects that he had found on the bottom of the river, in a very deep place. The treasure has been handed over to the Historical Museum. According to reliable sources, Vladimir Kostylkov is an excellent diver.

Volka slipped by the kitchen, where his mother was cooking dinner. He dashed into his room, nearly breaking his leg as he stumbled on a chandelier lying on the floor. It was Grandma's famous chandelier. Very long ago, before the Revolution, his deceased grandfather had converted it from a hanging oil lamp. Grandma would not part with it for anything in the world, because it was a treasured memory of Grandfather. Since it was not elegant enough to be hung in the dining room, they had decided to hang it in Volka's room. That is why a huge iron hook had been screwed into the ceiling.

Volka rubbed his sore knee, locked the door, took his penknife from his pocket, and, trembling from excitement, scraped the seal off the bottle.

The room immediately filled with choking black smoke, while a noiseless explosion of great force threw him up to the ceiling, where he remained suspended from the hook by the seat of his pants.

THE OLD GENIE

While Volka was swaying back and forth on the hook, trying to understand what had happened, the smoke began to clear. Suddenly, he realized there was someone else in the room besides him. It was a skinny, sunburnt old man with a beard down to his waist and dressed in an elegant turban, a white coat of fine wool richly embroidered in silver and gold, gleaming white silk puffed trousers, and petal-pink morocco slippers with upturned toes.

"*Hachoo!*" the old man sneezed loudly and prostrated himself. "I greet you, O wonderful and wise youth!"

Volka shut his eyes tight and then opened them again. No, he was not seeing things. The amazing old man was still there. Kneeling and rubbing his hands, he stared at the furnishings of Volka's room with shrewd, lively eyes, as if it were all goodness knows what sort of a miracle.

"Where did you come from?" Volka inquired cautiously, swaying back and forth under the ceiling like a pendulum. "Are you . . . from an amateur troupe?"

"Oh, no, my young lord," the old man replied grandly, though he remained in the same uncomfortable pose and continued to sneeze. "I am not from the strange country of Anamateur Troupe you mentioned. I come from this most horrible vessel."

With these words he scrambled to his feet and began jumping on the vessel, from which a wisp of smoke was still curling upward, until there was nothing left but a small pile of clay chips. Then, with a sound like tinkling crystalware, he yanked a hair from his beard and tore it in two. The bits of clay flared up with a weird green flame until soon there was not a trace of them left on the floor.

Still, Volka was dubious. You must agree, it's not easy to accept the fact that a live person can crawl out of a vessel no bigger than a decanter.

"You don't believe me, O despicable one?!" the old man shouted angrily, but immediately calmed down. Once again he fell to his knees, hitting the floor with his forehead so strongly that the water shook in the aquarium and the sleepy fish began to dart back and forth in alarm. "Forgive me, my young savior, but I am not used to having my words doubted. Know ye, most blessed of all young men, that I am none other than the mighty Genie Hassan Abdurrakhman ibn Khottab—that is, the son of Khottab, famed in all four corners of the world."

All this was so interesting it made Volka forget he was hanging under the ceiling on a chandelier hook.

"A 'gin-e'? Isn't that some kind of drink?"

"I am not a drink, O inquisitive youth!" the old man flared up again, then took himself in hand once more and calmed down. "I am not a beverage, but a mighty, unconquerable spirit. There is no magic in the world that I cannot perform, and my name, as I have already had the pleasure of conveying to your great and extremely respected attention, is Hassan Abdurrakhman ibn Khottab, or, as you would say in Russian, Hassan Abdurrakhman Khottabych. If you mention it to the first Ifrit or Genie you meet, you'll see him tremble, and his mouth will go dry from fear," the old man continued boastfully.

"My story—*hachoo!*—is strange, indeed. And if it were written with needles in the corners of your eyes, it would be a good lesson for all those who seek learning. I, most unfortunate Genie that I am, disobeyed Sulayman, son of David (on the twain be peace!)—I, and my brother, Omar Asaf Khottabych. Then Sulayman sent his Vizer Asaf, son of Barakhiya, to seize us, and he brought us back against our will. Sulayman, David's son (on the twain be peace!), ordered two bottles brought to him: a copper one and a clay one. He put me in the clay vessel and my brother Omar Khottabych in the copper one. He sealed both vessels and imprinted the greatest of all names of Allah on them and then ordered his Genies to carry us off and throw my brother into the sea and me into the river, from which you, O my blessed savior—*hachoo, hachoo!*—have fished me. May your days be prolonged. O . . . Begging your pardon, I would be indescribably happy to know your name, most beautiful of all youths."

"My name's Volka," our hero replied as he swayed softly to and fro under the ceiling.

"And what is your fortunate father's name, may he be blessed for eternity? Tell me the most gentle of all his names as he is certainly deserving of great love and gratitude for presenting the world with such an outstanding offspring."

"His name's Alexei. And his most gentle . . . most gentle name is Alyosha."

"Then know ye, most deserving of all youths, the star of my heart, Volka ibn Alyosha, that I will henceforth fulfill all your wishes, since you have saved me from the most horrible imprisonment. *Hachoo!*"

"Why do you keep on sneezing so?" Volka asked, as though everything else was quite clear.

"The many thousand years I spent in dampness, deprived of the beneficial rays of the sun, in a cold vessel lying on the bottom of a river have given me, your undeserving servant, a most tiresome running nose. *Hachoo! Hachoo!* But all this is of no importance at all and unworthy of your most treasured attention. Order me as you wish, O young master!" Hassan Abdurrakhman ibn Khottab concluded heatedly with his head raised, but still kneeling.

"First of all, won't you please rise," Volka said.

"Your every word is my command," the old man replied obediently and rose. "I await your further orders."

"And now," Volka mumbled uncertainly, "if it's not too much trouble . . . would you be kind enough . . . of course, if it's not too much trouble . . . What I mean is, I'd really like to be back on the floor again."

That very moment he found himself standing beside the old man Khottabych, as we shall call our new acquaintance for short. The first thing Volka did was to grab the seat of his pants. There was no hole at all.

Miracles were beginning to happen.

[*Khottabych's efforts to serve Volka in his own fashion result in a long series of extraordinary misadventures.—Editors*]

WHO'S THE RICHEST?

"Let's go for a walk, O crystal of my soul," Khottabych said the next day.

"On one condition only, and that's that you won't shy away from every bus like a village horse. But I'm insulting village horses for nothing. They haven't shied away from cars in a long, long time. And it's about time *you* got used to the idea that these aren't any Jirjises, but honest-to-goodness Russian internal combustion engines."

"I hear and I obey, O Volka ibn Alyosha," the old man answered timidly.

"Then repeat after me: I will never again be afraid of . . ."

"I will never again be afraid of . . ."

". . . buses, trolleybuses, trolley cars, trucks, helicopters . . ."

". . . buses, trolleybuses, trolley cars, trucks, helicopters . . ."

". . . automobiles, searchlights, excavators, typewriters . . ."

". . . automobiles, searchlights, excavators, typewriters . . ."

". . . gramophones, loudspeakers, vacuum cleaners . . ."

". . . gramophones, loudspeakers, vacuum cleaners . . ."

". . . electric plugs, TV sets, fans, and rubber toys that squeak."

". . . electric plugs, TV sets, fans, and rubber toys that squeak."

"Well, I guess that takes care of everything," Volka said.

"Well, I guess that takes care of everything," Khottabych repeated automatically, and they both burst out laughing.

In order to harden the old man's nerves, they crossed the busiest streets at least twenty times. Then they rode on a trolley car for a long while and, finally, tired but content, they boarded a bus.

They rode off, bouncing softly on the leather-upholstered seats.

Volka was engrossed in a copy of *Pioneers' Truth*, the children's newspaper. The old man was lost in thought and kept glancing at his young companion kindly from time to time. Then his face broke into a smile, evidently reflecting some pleasant idea he had conceived.

The bus took them to the doorstep. Soon they were back in Volka's room.

"Do you know what, O most honorable of secondary school pupils?" Khottabych began the minute the door closed behind them. "I think you should be more aloof and reserved in your relations with the young inhabitants of your house. Believe it or not, my heart was ready to break when I heard them shouting: 'Hey, Volka!' 'Hello, Volka!' and so forth, all of which is obviously unworthy of you. Forgive me for being so outspoken, O blessed one, but you have slackened the reins unnecessarily. How can they be your equals when you are the richest of the rich, to say nothing of your other innumerable qualities?"

"Huh! They certainly are my equals. One boy is even a grade ahead of me, and we're all equally rich."

"No, you are mistaken here, O treasure of my souls!" Khottabych cried delightedly and led Volka to the window. "Look, and be convinced of the truth of my words."

A strange sight met Volka's eyes.

A few moments before, the left half of their tremendous yard had been occupied by a volleyball pitch, a big pile of fresh sand for the toddlers, "giant steps" and swings for the daring, exercise bars and rings for athletics fans, and one long and two round bright flower beds for all the inhabitants to enjoy.

Now, instead of all this, there towered in glittering magnificence three marble palaces in ancient Asiatic style. Great columns adorned the facades. Shady gardens crowned the flat roofs, and strange red, yellow, and blue flowers grew in the flower beds. The spray issuing from exotic fountains sparkled like precious stones in the sunlight. Beside the entrance of each palace stood two giants holding huge curved swords. Volka and Khottabych went down to the yard. At the sight of Volka, the giants fell to their knees as one and greeted him in thunderous voices, while terrible flames escaped their mouths. Volka shuddered.

"May my young master not fear these beings, for these are peaceful Ifrits whom I have placed at the entrance to glorify your name."

The giants again fell to their knees and, spitting flames, obediently thundered, "Order us as you wish, O mighty master!"

"Please get up! I do wish you'd get up," Volka said in great embarrassment. "Why do you keep falling on your knees all the time? It's just like feudalism. Get up this minute, and don't you ever let me catch you crawling like this. Shame on you! Shame on both of you!"

Looking at each other in dismay, the Ifrits rose and silently resumed their previous stance of "attention."

"Well, now!" Volka mumbled. "Come on, Khottabych, let's have a look at your palaces." He skipped up the steps lightly and entered the first palace.

"These are not my palaces, they are your palaces," the old man objected respectfully as he followed Volka in.

The boy, however, paid no attention to his words.

The first palace was made entirely of rare pink marble. Its heavy carved sandalwood doors were studded with silver nails and adorned with silver stars and bright red rubies.

The second palace was made of light blue marble and had ten doors of rare ebony studded with gold nails and adorned with diamonds, sapphires, and emeralds.

In the middle of the second palace was the mirrorlike surface of a large pool, the home of goldfish the size of sturgeon.

"That's instead of your little aquarium," Khottabych explained shyly. "I think this is the only kind of aquarium in keeping with your great dignity."

"Hm, imagine picking up one of those fish. It'll bite your hand off," Volka thought.

"And now, do me the honor of casting a kindly glance at the third palace," Khottabych said.

They entered the portals of the third palace. It glittered so magnificently that Volka gasped.

"Why, it's just like the Metro! It's just like Komsomolskaya Station!"

"You haven't seen it all yet, O blessed one!" Khottabych said quickly.

He led Volka out into the yard. Once again the giants "presented arms," but Khottabych ignored them and pointed to the shining golden plaques adorning the entrances to the palaces. On each the same words were engraved, words that made Volka both hot and cold at the same time:

> These palaces belong to the most noble and glorious of youths of this city, to the most beautiful of the beautiful, the most wise of the wise, to him who is replete with endless qualities and perfections, the unmatched and unsurpassed scholar in geography and other sciences, the first among divers, the best of all swimmers and volleyball players, the unchallenged champion of billiards and ping-pong—to the Royal Young Pioneer Volka ibn Alyosha, may his name as well as the names of his fortunate parents be glorified for ages to come.

"With your permission," Khottabych said, bursting with pride and happiness. "I wish, when you come to live here with your parents, that you assign me a corner too, so that your new residence will not separate us and I may thus have the opportunity at all times to express my deep respect and devotion to you."

"In the first place, these inscriptions aren't very objective," Volka said after a short pause. "But that's not the most important thing in the long run. It's not important, because we have to hang up new signs."

"I understand you and cannot but blame myself for being so shortsighted," the old man said in an embarrassed tone. "Naturally, the inscriptions should have been made in precious stones. You are most worthy of it."

"You misunderstood me, Khottabych. I wanted the inscriptions to read that these palaces belong to the RONO.* You see, in our country all the palaces belong to the RONO, or to the sanatoriums."

"Which RONO?"

Volka misunderstood Khottabych's question.

"It doesn't matter which, but I'd rather it belonged to the Krasnopresnensky RONO. That's the district I was born in, that's where I grew up and learned how to read and write."

"I don't know who that RONO is," Khottabych said bitterly, "and I'm quite ready to believe that he is a worthy person. But did RONO free me from my thousands of years of imprisonment in the vessel? No, it was not RONO, it was you, O wonderful youth, and that is why these palaces will belong to you alone and no one else."

"But don't you see . . ."

"I don't want to! They are yours or no one's!"

Never before had Volka seen Khottabych so angry. His face was purple and his eyes were flashing. The old man was obviously trying hard to keep his temper.

"Does that mean you don't agree, O crystal of my soul?"

"Of course not. What do I need these palaces for? What do you think I am, a clubhouse, or an office, or a kindergarten?"

"Ah-h-h!" Khottabych sighed unhappily and shrugged. "We'll have to try something else then!"

The palaces became hazy, swayed, and dissolved into thin air, like a fog blown by the wind. The giants howled and shot upwards, where they, too, disappeared.

* "RONO" is an acronym for District Department of Education.

A CAMEL IN THE STREET

Instead, the yard suddenly filled with heavily laden elephants, camels, and mules. New caravans kept arriving constantly. The shouts of the dark-skinned drivers, dressed in snow-white robes, blended with the elephants' trumpeting, the camels' snorting, the mules' braying, the stamping of hundreds of hooves, and the melodious tinkling of bells.

A short sunburnt man in rich silk robes climbed down from his elephant, approached the middle of the yard, and tapped the pavement three times with his ivory cane. Suddenly, a huge fountain appeared. Immediately, drivers carrying leather pails formed a long line; soon the yard was filled with the snorting, chomping, and wheezing of the thirsty animals.

"All this is yours, O Volka," Khottabych cried, trying to make himself heard above the din. "Won't you please accept my humble gift?"

"What do you mean by 'all this'?"

"Everything. The elephants, and the camels, and the mules, and all the gold and precious stones they carry, and the people who are accompanying them—everything is yours!"

Things were going from bad to worse. Volka had nearly become the owner of three magnificent but quite useless palaces, and now he was to be the owner of a vast fortune, and owner of elephants, and, to top it all—a slave owner!

His first thought was to beg Khottabych to make all these useless gifts disappear before anyone noticed them. But he immediately recalled how things had gone with the palaces. If he had been smarter, he probably would have been able to talk the old man into letting the city keep them.

He had to stall for time to think and map out a plan of action.

"You know what, Khottabych?" he said, trying to sound nonchalant. "What do you say we go for a ride on a camel while the men take care of the caravan?"

"It would really be a pleasure," answered the unsuspecting old man.

A moment later, a double-humped camel appeared on the street, swaying majestically and looking round with an arrogant air. On its back were an excited Volka and Khottabych, who felt quite at home and was fanning himself lazily with his hat.

"A camel! A camel!" the children shouted excitedly. They had poured out into the street in great numbers, just as if they had all been waiting for the camel to appear.

They surrounded the unruffled animal in a close circle, and it towered over them like a double-decker bus towering over an ice-cream cart. One of the little boys was skipping and shouting:

> They're coming
> On a camel!
> They're coming
> On a camel!

The camel approached the crossing just as the light turned red. Since it was not used to traffic rules, it coolly stepped across the white line with the word "STOP!" written in large letters in front of it. In vain did Volka try to hold it back. The camel continued on its way, straight toward the militiaman who was quickly pulling out his receipt book for fines.

Suddenly a horn blared, brakes screeched, and a light blue car came to a stop right under the steely-nerved camel's nose. The driver jumped out and began yelling at the animal and its two passengers. And true enough, in another second there would have been a terrible accident.

"Kindly pull over to the curb," the militiaman said politely as he walked up to them.

Volka had great difficulty in making the camel obey this fatal order. A crowd gathered immediately, and everyone had an opinion to offer:

"This is the first time I've seen people riding a camel in Moscow."

"Just think, there could have been a terrible accident!"

"What's wrong with a child going for a ride on a camel?"

"No one's allowed to break traffic rules."

"You try and stop a proud animal like that. That's no car, you know!"

"I can't imagine where people get camels in Moscow!"

"It's obviously from the zoo. There are several camels there."

"It makes me shiver to think what could have happened. He's an excellent driver!"

"The militiaman is absolutely right."

Volka felt he was in a jam. He leaned down over the camel's side and began to apologize:

"It'll never happen again! Please let us go! It's time to feed the camel. This is a first offense."

"I'm sorry, but there's nothing I can do about it," the militiaman replied dryly. "They always say it's the first time in cases like this."

Volka was still attempting to soften the stern man's heart when he felt Khottabych tugging at his sleeve.

"O my young master, it makes me sad to see you lower yourself in order to shield me from any unpleasantness. All these people are unworthy of even kissing your heels. You should let them know of the chasm that separates them from you."

Volka waved the old man away impatiently, but all at once he felt as he had during the geography examination: once again he was not the master of his own words.

He wanted to say:

"Please, won't you let us go? I promise never to break any traffic rules as long as I live."

Instead of this humble plea, he suddenly bellowed at the top of his voice:

"How dare you, O despicable guard, detain me during the precious hour of my promenade! On your knees! On your knees immediately, or I'll do something terrible to you! I swear by my beard—I mean, by *his* beard!" And he nodded toward Khottabych.

At these words, Khottabych grinned smugly and fondly stroked his beard.

As for the militiaman and the crowd, the child's insolence was so unexpected that they were more dumbfounded than indignant.

"I am the most outstanding boy in this whole city!" Volka kept on shouting, inwardly wishing he were dead. "You're unworthy of even kissing my heels! I am handsome! I am wise!"

"All right," the militiaman answered darkly. "They'll see just how wise you are down at the station."

"Goodness! What nonsense I'm saying! It's really hooliganism!" Volka thought and shuddered. Nevertheless, he continued:

"Repent, you who have dared to spoil my good spirits! Cease your insolence before it's too late!"

Just then, something distracted Khottabych's attention. He stopped whispering to Volka and for a few moments the boy was once again on his own. As he leaned down over the side of the camel and looked at the crowd pathetically, he began to plead:

"Citizens! Dear people! Don't listen to me. Do you think it's *me* talking? It's *him*, this old man, who's making me talk like this."

But here Khottabych once again picked up the reins, and in the same breath Volka screamed:

"Tremble before me and do not anger me, for I am terrible in my wrath! Oh, how fearsome I am!"

He understood only too well that his words did not frighten anyone; instead, they made some indignant, while others found them simply funny. But there was nothing he could do. Meanwhile, the crowd's feeling of surprise and indignation began to change to one of concern. It was clear that no schoolboy could ever speak so foolishly and rudely if he were normal.

Then a woman shouted, "Look! The child has a fever! Look, he's steaming!"

"What disrespect!" Volka shouted back, but, to his utter horror, he saw large puffs of black smoke escaping his mouth at every word.

People gasped, someone ran to call an ambulance, and Volka whispered to Khottabych, taking advantage of the confusion:

"Hassan Abdurrakhman ibn Khottab! I order you to take this

camel and us as far away as possible. Immediately. Somewhere outside the city limits. Otherwise, we can get in very bad trouble. Do you hear me? Im-me-di-ate-ly!"

"I hear and obey," the old man replied in a whisper.

That very instant, the camel and its riders soared into the air and disappeared, leaving everyone behind in the greatest confusion.

A moment later the camel landed gracefully on the outskirts of the city. There its passengers parted with it forever.

The camel is probably still grazing there. You'll recognize it at once if you see it, for its bridle is studded with diamonds and emeralds.

EXTRA TICKETS

On a bright and sunny summer day, our friends set out to see a football game. During the soccer season the entire population of Moscow is divided into two alien camps. In the one are the football fans; in the other are those strange people who are entirely indifferent to this fascinating sport.

Long before the beginning of the game, the former stream toward the high entrance gates of the Central Stadium from all parts of the city. They look with a feeling of superiority upon those who are heading in the opposite direction. In turn, the latter Muscovites shrug in amazement when they see hundreds of crowded buses and trolley-buses and thousands of cars crawling through the turbulent sea of pedestrian fans.

But the army of fans that appears so unified to an onlooker is actually torn into two camps. This isn't noticeable while the fans are making their way to the stadium. However, as they approach the gates, this division appears in all its ugliness. It suddenly becomes evident that some people have tickets, while others do not. Those possessing tickets pass through the gates confidently; the others dart back and forth excitedly, rushing at new arrivals with the same plaintive plea: "Do you have an extra ticket?" or "You don't have an extra ticket, do you?"

As a rule, there are so few extra tickets and so many people in need of them, that if not for Khottabych, Volka and Zhenya would have certainly been left outside the gates.

"With the greatest of pleasure," Khottabych murmured in reply to Volka's request for tickets. "You'll have as many as you need in a minute."

No sooner were these words out of his mouth than the boy saw him holding a whole sheaf of blue, green, and yellow tickets.

"Will this be enough, O wonderful Volka? If not, I'll . . ."

He waved the tickets. This gesture nearly cost him his life.

"Look, extra tickets!" a man shouted, making a dash for him.

A few seconds later no fewer than a hundred and fifty excited people were pressing Khottabych's back against the concrete fence. The old man would have been as good as dead if not for Volka. He ran aside and shouted at the top of his voice:

"Over here! Who needs an extra ticket? Who needs some extra tickets?"

At these magic words the people who had been closing in on a distraught Khottabych rushed toward Volka, but the boy darted into the crowd and disappeared. A moment later he and his two friends handed the gatekeeper three tickets and passed through the North Gate to the stadium, leaving thousands of inconsolable fans behind.

ICE CREAM AGAIN

No sooner had the friends found their seats than a girl in a white apron carrying a white lacquered box approached them.

"Would you like some ice cream?" she asked, and then gave a shriek. We must be fair. Anyone else in her place would have been just as frightened, for what answer could an ice-cream vendor expect? In the best of cases: "Yes, thank you. Two, please." In the worst of cases: "No, thank you." Now, just imagine that upon hearing the young lady's polite question, a little old man in a straw boater turned as red as a beet, and his eyes growing bloodshot, bristled all over. He leaned over to her and whispered in a fierce voice:

"*A-a-ah!* You want to kill me with your foul ice cream! Well, you won't, despicable thing! The forty-six ice creams that I, old fool that I am, ate in the circus nearly sent me to my grave. They were enough to last me the rest of my life. Tremble, wretch, for I'll turn you into a hideous toad!"

At this, he rose and raised his dry wrinkled arms over his head. Suddenly a boy with sun-bleached eyebrows on his freckled face seized the old man's arms and shouted in a frightened voice, "She's not to blame if you were greedy and stuffed yourself with ice cream! Please sit down, and don't be silly!"

"I hear and I obey," the old man answered obediently. He lowered his arms and resumed his seat. Then he addressed the frightened young lady as follows: "You can go now. I forgive you. Live in peace, grateful to this youth till the end of your days, for he has saved your life."

The young lady did not appear in their section again for the remainder of the afternoon.

HOW MANY FOOTBALLS DO YOU NEED?!

Meanwhile, the stadium was full of that very special festive atmosphere that pervades it during decisive football matches. Loudspeakers blared. A hundred thousand people were heatedly discussing the possible outcome of the game, thus giving rise to a hum of human voices incomparable to anything else. Everyone was impatiently awaiting the umpire's whistle.

Finally, the umpire and the linesmen appeared on the emerald-green field. The umpire was carrying the ball that would be kicked back and forth—thus covering quite a few miles on land and in the air—and, finally, having landed in one goal more times than in the other, would decide which team was the winner that day. He put the ball down in the center of the field. The two teams appeared from their locker rooms and lined up opposite each other. The captains shook hands and drew lots to see which team was to play against the sun. The unfortunate lot fell to the Zubilo team, to the great satisfaction of the Shaiba team and a portion of the fans.

"Will you, O Volka, consider it possible to explain to your unworthy servant what these twenty-two pleasant young men are going to do with the ball?" Khottabych asked respectfully.

Volka waved his hand impatiently and said, "You'll see for yourself in a minute."

At that very moment a Zubilo player smartly kicked the ball, and the game began.

"Do you mean that these twenty-two nice young men will have to run about such a great field, get tired, fall, and shove one another, only to have a chance to kick this plain-looking leather ball around for a few seconds? And all because they gave them just this one ball for all twenty-two of them?" Khottabych asked in a very displeased voice a few minutes later.

Volka was completely engrossed in the game and did not reply. He could not be bothered with Khottabych at a time when the Shaiba's forwards had got possession of the ball and were approaching the Zubilo goal.

"You know what, Volka?" Zhenya whispered. "It's real luck Khottabych doesn't know a thing about football, because he'd surely stick his finger in the pie!"

"I know," Volka agreed. Suddenly, he gasped and jumped to his feet.

At that very moment, the other hundred thousand fans also jumped to their feet and began to shout. The umpire's whistle pierced the air, but the players had already come to a standstill.

Something unheard-of in the history of football had happened, something that could not be explained by any law of nature: twenty-two brightly colored balls dropped from somewhere above in the sky and rolled down the field. They were all made of top-grain morocco leather.

"Outrageous! Hooliganism! Who did this?" the fans shouted.

The culprit should have certainly been taken away and even handed over to the militia, but no one could discover who it was. Only three people of the hundred thousand—Khottabych and his two young friends—knew who was responsible.

"See what you've gone and done?" Volka whispered. "You've stopped the game and prevented the Shaiba team from making a sure point!"

However, Volka was not especially displeased at the team's misfortune, for he was a Zubilo fan.

"I wanted to improve things," Khottabych whispered guiltily. "I thought it would be much better if each player could play with his own ball as much as he wanted, instead of shoving and chasing around like mad on such a great big field."

"Oh, good grief! I don't know what to do with you!" Volka cried in despair and pulled the old man down. He hurriedly explained the basic rules of football to him. "It's a shame that the Zubilo team has to play opposite the sun now, because after they change places in the second half it won't be in anyone's eyes anymore. This way, the Shaiba players have a terrific advantage, and for no good reason at all," he concluded emphatically, hoping Khottabych would bear his words in mind.

"Yes, it really is unfair," the old man agreed. Whereupon the sun immediately disappeared behind a little cloud and stayed there till the end of the game.

Meanwhile, the extra balls had been taken off the field. The umpire totaled up the time wasted, and the game was resumed.

After Volka's explanation, Khottabych began to follow the course of the match with ever-increasing interest. The Shaiba players, who had lost a sure point because of the twenty-two balls, were nervous and were playing badly. The old man felt guilty and was conscience-stricken.

KHOTTABYCH JOINS THE GAME

Thus, the sympathies of Volka Kostylkov and Hassan Abdurrakhman ibn Khottab were fatally divided. When the first beamed with pleasure (and this happened every time a Shaiba player missed the other team's goal), the old man became darker than a cloud. However, when the Zubilo forwards missed the Shaiba goal, the reaction was reversed. Khottabych would burst out in happy laughter and Volka would become terribly angry.

"I don't see what's so funny about it, Khottabych. Why, they nearly scored a point!"

"Nearly doesn't count, my dear boy," Khottabych would answer.

Khottabych, who was seeing a football game for the first time in his life, did not know that there was such a thing as a fan. He had regarded Volka's concern about the sun being in the Zubilo's eyes as the boy's desire for fair play. Neither he nor Volka suspected that he had suddenly become a fan, too. Volka was so engrossed in what was happening on the field that he paid not the slightest attention to anything else—and this oblivion of his caused all the unusual events that took place at the stadium that day.

It all began during a very tense moment, when the Zubilo forwards were approaching the Shaiba goal and Volka bent over to Khottabych's ear, whispering hotly:

"Khottabych, dear, please make the Shaiba goal a little wider when the Zubilo men kick the ball." The old man frowned.

"Of what good will this be to the Shaiba team?"

"Why should you worry about them? It's good for the Zubilo team."

The old man said nothing. Once again the Zubilo players missed. Two or three minutes later a happy Shaiba player kicked the ball into the Zubilo goal, to the approving yells of the Shaiba fans.

"Yegor, please don't laugh, but I'm ready to swear the goalpost's on the Shaiba's side," the Zubilo goalie said to one of the spare players when the game had passed over to the far end of the field.

"Wha-a-at?"

"You see, when they kicked the ball, the right goalpost . . . upon my sacred word of honor . . . the right goalpost . . . moved about half a yard away and let the ball pass. I saw it with my own eyes!"

"Have you taken your temperature?" the spare player asked.

"Why?"

"You sure must have a high fever!"

"Humph!" the goalie spat and stood tensely in the goal.

The Shaiba players were outmaneuvering the defense and were fast approaching the Zubilo goal.

Bam! A second goal in three minutes! And it had not been the Zubilo goalie's fault either time. He was fighting like a tiger. But what could he do? At the moment the ball was hit, the crossbar rose of its own accord, just high enough to let the ball pass through, brushing the tips of the goalie's fingers.

Whom could he complain to? Who would ever believe him? The goalie felt scared and forlorn, just like a little boy who finds himself in the middle of a forest at night.

"See that?" he asked Yegor in a hopeless voice.

"I th-th-th-ink I did," the spare player stuttered. "But you c-c-c-an't tell anyone, n-n-no one will ever b-b-believe you."

"That's just it, no one'll believe me," the goalie agreed sadly.

Just then, a quiet scandal was taking place in the North Section. A moment before the second goal, Volka noticed the old man furtively yank a hair from his beard.

"What did he do that for?" he wondered uneasily, still unaware of the storm gathering over the field. However, even this thought did not come to Volka immediately.

The game was going so badly for the Zubilo team that he had no time to think of the old man.

But soon everything became perfectly clear.

The first half of the game was nearing an end, and it seemed that luck was finally smiling on the Zubilo team. The ball was now on the Shaiba side of the field. The Zubilo men were plowing up the earth, as the saying goes, and soon their best forward kicked the ball with tremendous force into the top corner of the Shaiba goal.

All one hundred thousand fans jumped to their feet. This sure goal was to give the team its first point. Volka and Zhenya, two ardent Zubilo fans, winked happily to each other, but immediately groaned with disappointment: it was a sure goal, but the ball smacked against the crossbar so loudly that the sound echoed all over the stadium.

This sound was echoed by a loud wail from the Shaiba goalie: the lowered crossbar had fouled a goal, but it had also knocked him smartly on the head.

Now Volka understood everything and was terrified.

"Hassan Abdurrakhman ibn Khottab," he said in a shaking voice. "What's this I see? You know both Zhenya and I are Zubilo fans, and here you are, against us! You're a Shaiba fan!"

"Alas, O blessed one, it is so!" the old man replied unhappily.

"Didn't I save you from imprisonment in the clay vessel?" Volka continued bitterly.

"This is as true as the fact that it is now day and there is a great future ahead of you," Khottabych replied in a barely audible voice.

"Then why are you helping the Shaiba team instead of the Zubilo team?"

"Alas, I have no power over my actions," Khottabych answered sadly, as large tears streamed down his wrinkled face. "I want the Shaiba team to win."

THE SITUATION GROWS MORE TENSE

"Just wait, nothing good will come of it!" Volka threatened.

"Be that as it may."

That very moment the Zubilo goalie slipped on an extremely dry spot and let the third ball into the goal.

"Oh, so that's how it is! You won't listen to reason, will you? All right then!" Volka jumped onto the bench and shouted, pointing to Khottabych:

"Listen, everyone! He's been helping the Shaiba team all the time!"

"Who's helping them? The umpire? What do you mean?" people began to shout.

"No, not the umpire! What has he to do with it? It's this old man here who's helping them . . . Leave me alone!"

These last words were addressed to Zhenya, who was nervously tugging at his sleeve. Zhenya realized that no good would come of Volka's quarrel with Khottabych. But Volka would not stop, though no one took his words seriously.

"So you say the old man is shifting goalposts from over here, in the North Section?" People roared with laughter. "*Ha, ha, ha!* He probably has a special gimmick in his pocket to regulate the goals at a distance. Maybe he even tossed all those balls into the field?"

"Sure, it was him," Volka agreed readily, eliciting a new wave of laughter.

"I bet he was also responsible for the earthquake in Chile! *Ho-ho-ho! Ha-ha-ha!*"

"No, he wasn't responsible for that." Volka was an honest boy. "An earthquake is the result of a catastrophic shifting of soil. Especially in Chile. And he was just recently released from a vessel."

A middle-aged man sitting behind Volka entered the conversation. Volka knew him, since they lived in the same house. He was the one who had named his cat Khomych in honor of the famous goalie.

"Keep your shirt on, and don't make a fool of yourself," the man said kindly, when the laughter had died down a bit. "Stop talking nonsense and bothering us. The way things are now, it's bad enough without you adding your bit." (He was also a Zubilo fan.)

And true enough, there were still eleven long minutes left till the end of the first half, but the score was already 14:0 in favor of the Shaiba team.

Strange things kept happening to the Zubilo players. They seemed to have forgotten how to play: their tackling was amazingly feeble and stupid. The men kept falling; it was as if they had just learned how to walk.

And then the defense began to act strangely. Those old football lions began to shy away in fright as soon as they saw the ball approaching, as if it were about to explode.

Oh, how miserable our young friends were! Just think: they had explained the rules of soccer to Khottabych to their own misfortune! What were they to do? How were they to help the unfortunate Zubilo players see justice restored? And what should they do with Khottabych? Even a scandal had proved useless. How could they at least distract the old Genie's attention from the field on which this unique sports tragedy was unfolding?

Zhenya found the answer. He stuck a copy of *Soviet Sports* into Khottabych's hand, saying, "Here, read the paper, and see what a wonderful team you're disgracing in the eyes of the nation!" He pointed toward the heading: "An Up-and-Coming Team." Khottabych read aloud:

"The Zubilo team has improved considerably during the current season. In their last game in Kuibyshev against the local Krylya Sovetov team they demonstrated their . . . That's interesting!" he said and buried his nose in the paper.

The boys grinned at each other. No sooner had Khottabych begun to read, than the Zubilo men came to life. Their forwards immediately proved that the article in *Soviet Sports* had all the facts straight. A great roar coming from the tens of thousands of excited throats accompanied nearly every kick. In a few seconds the game was on the Shaiba half of the field. One kick followed another in quick succession. Those Zubilo players were really good!

A few more moments, and they would finally be able to score.

"Aha!" Volka's neighbor shouted behind his back. "See?! What did I say! They'll show those Shaiba imbeciles a thing or two . . ."

Ah, how much better it would have been for all concerned if he had curbed his joy. He should not have nudged Khottabych in the side with such a triumphant look on his face, as if every man on the Zubilo team were his own favorite son, or at least his favorite pupil!

Khottabych started, tore his eyes from the paper, and took in the field at a glance. He sized up the situation like an expert and handed the paper back to Zhenya, who accepted it with a long face.

"I'll finish reading it later," the old man said. He hurriedly yanked a hair from his beard, and the Zubilo team's inexplicable and disgraceful sufferings began anew.

15:0!—16:0!—18:0!—23:0!

The ball flew into the Zubilo goal on an average of once every forty seconds.

But what had happened to the goalie? Why did he clutch at the goalpost and wail "Mamma!" every time the ball was kicked into the goal? Why did he suddenly walk to the side with a thoughtful expression on his face—and for no apparent reason at all—and this at a most decisive moment, in the middle of a heated tangle right in front of the goal?

"Shame! It's outrageous! What's the matter with you?!" the fans shouted from all sides. But he, the famous goalie, the pride of his country, staggered out of the goal and off to the side every time the opposite team closed in.

"What's the matter with you? Have you gone crazy?" the spare player croaked.

And the goalie moaned in reply:

"I sure have. Someone seems to be pulling me. I try to hold my ground, but something keeps pushing me out of the goal. When I want to turn toward the ball, that same something presses me toward the goalpost so hard that I can't tear myself away."

"Things are really bad!"

"Couldn't be worse!"

The situation was so extraordinary that there was not a person present at the stadium, including the ticket collectors, militiamen, and food vendors, who was not taking the strange events to heart and discussing them loudly.

There was only one fan among the thousands who, though suffering keenly, was remarkably silent. This was an amazingly uncommunicative man of about fifty-five, grey-haired, tall and lanky, with a long, yellowish stony face. His face was equally stony during an unimportant game and during the finals, when a successful kick decides the champion of the year. He was always equally dour, straitlaced, and immobile.

This day he was in his usual seat, which was right in front of Khottabych. As he was a Zubilo fan, one can well imagine the anguish in his sunken, bony chest. However, only the shifting of his eyes and the barely discernible movements of his head indicated that he was far from being indifferent to the events taking place on the field. He apparently had a bad heart, and had to take good care of himself, for any amount of emotion might have produced grave results. However, even as he felt around with a practiced gesture for his box of sugar and his bottle of medicine and dropped the medicine onto a bit of sugar, without ever tearing his eyes from the game, his face remained as immobile as if he were staring into space.

When the score became 23:0 it nearly finished him. He opened his thin pale lips and squeaked in a wooden voice:

"They could at least sell mineral water here!"

Khottabych, whose soul was singing joyfully at the unheard-of success of the Shaiba team, was more willing than ever to do people favors.

Upon hearing the words of his phlegmatic neighbor, he snapped his fingers softly. The man suddenly saw that he was holding a glass of ice-cold mineral water that had appeared from nowhere.

Anyone else in his place would have been astounded, or at any rate would have looked around at the people sitting on all sides of him. But this man merely raised the frosted glass to his lips with the same stony expression. However, he did not even take a sip: the poor Zubilo players were about to get the twenty-fourth ball kicked into their goal. He sat frozen to the spot, his glass raised, and Zhenya, who was still frantically searching for a way to save the disgraced team, snatched the mineral water from him and dashed it onto Khottabych's beard.

"What treachery! What vile treachery!" the old Genie gasped and began feverishly yanking out one hair after another. Instead of the clear crystal tinkling, the boys were happy to hear a dull sound like that of a tightly pulled piece of string.

"And isn't it treachery to help the Shaiba players?" Volka asked acidly. "You'd better keep mum."

Meanwhile, just as had happened after the fourteenth goal, the revived Zubilo players once again tore through the forward defense lines of the Shaiba team and raced the ball toward their goal.

The Shaiba defense had become unhinged from their long idleness and could not collect their wits quickly to ward off the unexpected danger. Their goalie was really something to look at. There he sat on the grass, shelling melon seeds.

Choking, he jumped to his feet, but the Zubilo players had already kicked the ball straight toward the center of the unprotected goal.

Just then, to the great torment of our young friends, they heard a crystal tinkling. Yes, Khottabych had finally been able to find a dry hair in his beard.

Oh, Zhenya, Zhenya! Where were your keen eye and sure hand? Why didn't you take good aim? The Zubilo team was as good as dead now!

"Khottabych! Dear, sweet Khottabych! Let the Zubilo players score at least once!" Volka wailed.

But Khottabych pretended to hear nothing. The ball, which was flying straight at the center of the goal, suddenly swerved to the left and hit the post with such force that it flew back across the whole field, careful to avoid Zubilo players in its way, as though it were alive. Then it rolled softly into the long-suffering Zubilo goal!

"24:0!"

This was an amazing score, considering that the teams were equal.

Volka lost his temper completely.

"I demand—no, I *order* you to stop this mockery immediately!" he hissed. "Otherwise, I'll never be friends with you again! You have your choice: the Shaiba team or me!"

"Why, you're a football fan yourself. Can't you understand my feelings?" the old man pleaded, but he sensed from Volka's expression that this time their friendship might really end. And so, he whispered back, "I await your further orders."

"The Zubilo team isn't to blame that you're a Shaiba fan. You've made them the laughingstock of the country. Make it so that everyone should see they're not to blame for losing."

"I hear and I obey, O young goalie of my soul!"

No sooner had the umpire's whistle died down, announcing the end of the first half, than the entire Zubilo team began to sneeze and cough for all it was worth.

Forming a semblance of a formation, they dragged their feet listlessly to their locker room, sneezing and coughing loudly.

A moment later a doctor was summoned, since all eleven players were feeling ill. The doctor felt each one's pulse in turn, asked them to take off their shirts, then looked in their mouths and finally summoned the umpire. "I'm afraid you'll have to call off the game."

"Why? What do you mean?"

"Because the Zubilo team can't play for at least seven more days. The whole team is sick," the doctor answered dazedly.

"Sick! What's the matter?"

"It's a very strange case. All these eleven grown men have come down with the measles. I would never have believed it if I had not given them a thorough checkup just now."

Thus ended the only football match in history in which a fan had an opportunity to influence the game. As you see, it did not come to any good.

The unusual instance of eleven adult athletes simultaneously contracting the measles for the second time in their lives and waking up the following morning in the pink of health was described in great detail in an article by the famous Professor Hooping Koff and published in the medical journal *Measles and Sneezles.* The article was entitled "That's a Nice How Do You Do!" and is still so popular that one can never get a copy of the magazine in the libraries, as it's always checked out. That is why, dear readers, you might as well not look for it, since you'll only waste your time for nothing.

RECONCILIATION

The little cloud that was covering the sun floated off and disappeared, since it was no longer needed. Once again it became hot. A hundred thousand fans were slowly leaving the stadium through the narrow concrete passages.

No one was in a hurry. Everyone wanted to voice an opinion about the amazing game that had ended so strangely.

These opinions were much more involved than the ones voiced earlier. However, not even the most vivid imagination could think of an explanation that would so much as resemble the true reason for all the strange things they had witnessed.

Only three people took no part in these discussions. They left the North Section in profound silence. They entered a crowded trolleybus in silence and alighted in silence at Okhotny Ryad, where they separated.

"Football is an excellent game," Khottabych finally mustered up the courage to say.

"Mm-m-m," Volka replied.

"I can just imagine how sweet the moment is when you kick the ball into the enemy's goal!" Khottabych continued in a crestfallen voice. "Isn't that so, O Volka?"

"Mm-m-m."

"Are you still angry with me, O goalie of my heart? I'll die if you don't answer me!"

He scurried along beside his angry friend, sighing sadly and cursing the hour he had agreed to go to the game.

"What do *you* think!" Volka snapped, but then continued in a softer tone, "Boy, what a mess! I'll never forget it as long as I live. Just look at this newfound fan! No, sir, we'll never take *you* to a football game again! And we don't need your tickets, either."

"Your every word is my command," Khottabych hurried to assure him, pleased to have got off so easily. "I'll be quite content if you occasionally find the time to tell me of the football matches."

So they continued being as good friends as ever.

1938

THE MALACHITE CASKET

PAVEL BAZHOV

Nastasya, Stepan's widow, inherited a malachite casket with every kind of woman's ornament in it. There were rings and earrings and all sorts of women's baubles. The Mistress of the Copper Mountain herself had given the casket to Stepan before his marriage.

Nastasya had grown up an orphan. She wasn't used to such riches, and she didn't like making a lot of show either. At first, when Stepan was alive, she sometimes used to put on this or that from the casket. But she never felt easy doing so. She'd put on a ring, and it fitted just right, neither too tight nor too loose, but when she'd go to church with it or to visit friends, her finger would start aching as if it were pinched and the end would even turn quite blue. If she put on earrings it was even worse. They'd pull and pull on her ears till the lobes were all swollen. Yet if you picked them up, they didn't seem any heavier than the ones she always wore. The necklace, six or seven strands of it, she tried on only once. It felt like ice round her neck and never got any warmer. And anyway, she was ashamed to let folks see her in a thing like that. "Look at her, all decked out like a tsarina in our own Polevaya," they'd say.

Stepan didn't try to make her wear them, either. Once he even said, "Better put them away, or else there'll be trouble."

So Nastasya put the casket in her bottom chest, where she kept her store of homespun and things of that sort.

When Stepan died he happened to have some precious stones in his hand, and Nastasya was forced to show the casket to various folks. Folks say that the man who knew about all those things, the one who told them what Stepan's stones were, later told Nastasya, "Mind you don't sell that casket for a trifle. It's worth many a thousand."

He had learning, that man, and he was free, too. Once he'd been foreman at the mine, but they let him go. He was too easy on the men. What's more, he also liked his glass of wine. Always in the tavern, he was, though I should speak no ill of the dead. But in all else he was a real good man. He could write a petition, or mark off sections, and he made a proper job of it, not like some. Our folks would always treat him to a glass on the holidays, whoever else might be left out. He lived like that in our village till he died. The people kept him going.

Nastasya had heard from her husband that the foreman was an honest man with a good head on him. His only trouble was drinking. And she heeded what he said.

"So be it," she said, "I'll keep it for a rainy day." And she put the casket back in its old place.

They buried Stepan and mourned forty days, all right and proper. Nastasya was a fine, comely woman, and well-off, so suitors soon started sending around matchmakers. But she had plenty of sense and told all of them one and the same thing:

"A second one, though he be good as gold, would still be a stepfather to the children."

So after a time they let her alone.

Stepan had left his family well-off. They had a solid house, a horse, a cow, everything they needed. Nastasya was a hard worker, the children were obedient, so they had nothing to worry about. They lived like that for a year, and another, and a third. But then they began getting a bit poorer. After all, how could a woman with small children run a farm well?! And they needed a bit of money now and then, too. At least to buy salt and suchlike.

And that's when Stepan's family started pestering Nastasya. "Sell the casket. What do you want with it? What's the point of those jewels just lying around? After all, Tanyushka'll never wear them. Things of that sort! It's only gentry and merchants who buy stuff like that. You can't put them on with our poor clothes. And you could get money for them. It'd give you a boost."

In short, they kept on at her. And buyers flocked like ravens to bones. Merchants, all of them. One offered a hundred rubles, another two hundred.

"We're sorry for your children," they said. "We're doing you a favor, seeing as you're a widow."

They thought they could fool a simple village woman, but they were barking up the wrong tree.

Nastasya minded what the old foreman had told her, not to let the casket go for a trifle. And she was sorry to part with it, too. After all, it was a wedding gift from her dead husband. And moreover, her little girl, the youngest child, begged her in a flood of tears: "Mommy, don't sell it! Don't sell it, Mommy! I'll go out and work if need be, but keep it for Daddy's sake!"

Stepan had left her with three children. Two were boys, just like any others. But the girl, she didn't take after her mother or her father. Even when Stepan was still alive and she was just a baby, folks wondered at her. And not just all the women, but the menfolk, too, would say to Stepan: "Where've you got her from, Stepan?" they'd say. "She don't look like anyone! All dark and pretty, but those green eyes! Not like the other little girls round our way."

Stepan would simply laugh it off. "Naught to wonder at if she's black-haired, with her father working underground since he was a little feller. And green eyes—naught strange there, either, with all the malachite I've brought up for our Master Turchaninov. She's a memento of that work."

So he started calling her Memento. When he wanted her he'd say: "Come here, my little Memento!" And when he bought something for her, it was always green or blue.

Well, the children grew, and everyone took note of her. She was like a bright bead dropped from a colorful necklace—she stood out.

And though she wasn't a child to make friends with folks, they all affectionately called her Tanyushka, Tanyushka. Even envious shrews admired her. A real beauty, she was! Everyone liked to look at her. Only her mother sighed.

"Beauty, aye, but not our kind of beauty. Like a changeling."

The girl took it real hard when Stepan died. She got thin, seemed to waste away till she was nothing but eyes. So one day her mother got the idea of giving her the malachite casket to let her amuse herself with it. Little she might be, but she was still a girl, and even when they're children they like to adorn themselves. So Tanyushka tried on this and that. And it was a wonder—whatever she put on, you'd have thought it was made for her. Her mother didn't even know what some of the things were for, but she seemed to know everything. And that wasn't all. She kept on saying: "Oh, Mommy, it feels so nice in Daddy's presents! They're all warm, it's like sitting in the sun and somebody stroking you softly."

Now, Nastasya had worn them, and she hadn't forgotten how her fingers had got swollen and her ears had hurt and the necklace had been icy cold. And she thought to herself: "There's something funny here. It's uncanny!" And she put the casket away in the chest again. But after that Tanyushka was always at her: "Mommy, let me play with Daddy's presents."

Nastasya wanted to be strict, but she had a mother's soft heart, and would get out the casket, only warning, "See you don't break anything."

When Tanyushka was a bit older she'd get out the casket for herself. Nastasya would take the boys to mow or do some other work and leave Tanyushka to mind the house. First, of course, she'd get through the jobs her mother had left her—wash the dishes, shake out the tablecloth, sweep up, feed the hens, and see to the fire. She'd hurry up and finish, then take out the casket. There was only one chest left now on top of the bottom one, and it had got real light at that. So Tanyushka could easily move it to a stool and get the casket out of the bottom chest. Then she'd take out the trinkets, and start trying them on.

One day a robber came while she was busy with them. Maybe he'd hidden in the garden early, or maybe he'd slipped in some way, for none of the neighbors saw him in the street. He was a stranger, but it looked as if someone had told him everything, when to come and how.

After Nastasya left, Tanyushka did a few bits of work outside, and went into the house to get the casket. She put on the jeweled headdress and the earrings. And that was when the robber slipped in. Tanyushka looked round and there stood a man she'd never seen before, with an ax in his hand. It was their own ax. It had stood in the entry, in the corner. She had just put it there herself when sweeping up. Tanyushka was frightened all right, and just sat there, but the man cried out and dropped his ax and clapped both hands over his eyes as if they burned him. "Oh, I'm blinded! Oh, God, I'm blinded." He cried with a groan and kept rubbing his eyes.

Tanyushka saw something had happened to him, and asked, "What have you come for? Why'd you take the ax?"

But the fellow just kept groaning and rubbing his eyes. Tanyushka began to feel sorry for him; she got a mug of water and wanted to give it to him, but he stumbled to the door and yelled, "Keep off!"

He backed into the entry and stopped there, and held the door so Tanyushka couldn't get out. But she climbed through the window and ran to the neighbors. Well, they came with her and started asking the man who he was and what he wanted. He blinked a bit, and explained he'd been passing and come to ask alms, and then something had happened to his eyes.

"It was like the sun in them, I thought I was blinded. Maybe it was the heat."

Tanyushka hadn't told the neighbors about the ax or the casket. So they said to each other, "It's nothing. Maybe she forgot to fasten the gate and he came in, and then something happened to him. All sorts of things happen."

Still, they kept him there and waited for Nastasya. When she came with the boys the man told her the same as he'd told the neighbors.

Nastasya saw everything in its place, nothing gone, so she didn't try to keep him. The man left, and the neighbors, too.

Then Tanyushka told her mother how it really had been. And Nastasya realized he'd come for the casket, but it seemed it wasn't such an easy thing to steal it. "All the same," she thought, "I should take better care of it."

She said nothing to Tanyushka and the other children, but took the casket into the cellar and buried it.

Again they all went out and left Tanyushka alone. She wanted to get the casket, but it wasn't there. Tanyushka was upset, but suddenly she felt a wave of warmth. What could it be? Where did it come from? She looked round and saw a light coming up through the cracks of the floor. It frightened Tanyushka—was something on fire down there? She looked into the cellar, and saw a light in one corner. She seized a bucket of water to put out the fire, but nothing was burning and there was no smell of smoke. She felt about in the place where the light was coming from and there saw the casket. She opened it and the stones seemed even more beautiful than before. They sparkled with different colors and a light came from them like from the sun. Tanyushka did not take the casket up into the room. She played with the trinkets there in the cellar till she was tired.

So it went on from that day. The mother thought, "I've hidden it well, no one knows where it is," and the daughter, as soon as she was all alone, would spend an hour or so playing with her father's presents. As for selling them, Nastasya wouldn't let their relatives even mention it.

"If it looks like we'll have to go and beg, then I'll do it, but not before."

She had a hard time, but she stuck to it. They struggled through a few years and then things got better. The older children started to earn a bit, and Tanyushka wasn't idle, either. She learned to embroider with silk and beads. And she did it so well that the cleverest embroiderers in the gentry's sewing rooms threw up their hands in amazement— where'd she get the designs, where'd she find the silks?

That, too, came about by chance. A woman knocked at the door one day. About Nastasya's age, she was dark, not tall, with sharp, keen eyes, and there was something in her that took your breath away. She had a homespun bag slung on her back and a cherry-wood staff in her hand, like a pilgrim. She asked Nastasya, "Can I stop and rest a day or two, Mistress? I've a long road ahead and I'm dropping on my feet."

At first Nastasya wondered if it was someone after the casket again, but she let her stay all the same.

"I don't grudge you a rest," she said. "You won't wear a hole in the floor or take it with you. But it's poor fare here. In the morning it's onions and kvass, in the evening kvass and onions, that's all the change there is. If that'll do you, stay as long as you like, and welcome."

But the traveler had already put down her staff and laid her bag on the seat by the stove, and was taking off her boots. Nastasya wasn't too pleased at that. "Pretty free and easy she is! Starts taking off her boots and opening her sack without waiting for a by-your-leave." But she said nothing.

Sure enough, the woman unfastened her sack, then beckoned Tanyushka.

"Come here, child, and look at my handiwork. If it pleases you, I'll teach you to do it too. I can see you've an eye for it."

Tanyushka went up to her, and the woman gave her a strip of cloth with both ends embroidered in silk. And it was such a brilliant pattern, the very room seemed the brighter and warmer for it.

Tanyushka couldn't stop looking at it, and the woman laughed. "So it takes your eye, my work, does it?" she said. "Would you like me to teach it to you?"

"I would."

But Nastasya snapped, "Don't you even think of it! We've no money to buy salt with, and you want to do silk embroidering! Silk costs money."

"Don't fret, Mistress," said the traveler. "If your daughter learns to do it, she'll have the silk. For your kindness I'll leave her enough to last a while. And after that you'll see. Folks pay money for our craft. *We* don't give our work away. We earn our bread."

So Nastasya had to agree.

"If you give her the silk, no reason she can't learn. Why not, if she can do it? And I'll thank you."

So the woman started to teach Tanyushka, and Tanyushka learned it all as quickly as if she'd known it before. And there was another thing. Tanyushka wasn't friendly with strangers, or loving with her family either, but she took to this woman and stuck to her all the time. Nastasya looked askance. "Found herself a new mother," she thought. "Never comes to her own mother, but clings to a tramp!"

And the woman, as if to rub it in, kept calling Tanyushka "Child" and "Daughter," and never once used her Christian name. Tanyushka saw her mother was put out, but she couldn't help herself. She was so taken with the woman that she even told her about the casket!

"We've got a costly memento of Daddy," she said, "a malachite casket. And the stones in it! I could look at them forever and never tire."

"Will you show it to me, Daughter?" asked the woman.

It never entered Tanyushka's head that she shouldn't.

"I'll show it to you," she said, "when none of the family's at home."

As soon as the chance came, Tanyushka took the woman down to the cellar. She took out the casket and showed it; the woman took a quick look, then said, "Put them on. I can see them better that way."

Tanyushka didn't need telling twice. She started putting them on, and the woman began praising them.

"Fine, they look fine, Daughter! But they need just a touch or two."

She drew closer and touched a stone here and a stone there with her finger. And whatever stone she touched sparkled quite differently. Tanyushka could see some of them, some not. Then the woman said, "Stand up straight, Daughter."

Tanyushka stood straight, and the woman started gently stroking her hair and her back. She stroked her all over, then instructed, "When I tell you to turn round, mind you don't look back at me. Look straight ahead, notice all you see and say nothing. Now turn round!"

Tanyushka turned, and there was a great hall in front of her, the like of which she'd never seen in all her life. It looked like a church, and yet not quite the same. The ceiling was very high, supported on columns of pure malachite. The walls were covered with malachite to the height of a man, and there was a pattern of malachite all along the top. And right in front of Tanyushka, as in a mirror, stood a beautiful maiden, the kind you hear of in fairy tales. Her hair was dark as night, her eyes green. She was all decked in precious stones, and her robe was a green velvet that gleamed all shades. It was a robe like the ones worn by tsarinas in pictures. You wonder what keeps them up. Our local folk would die of shame to dress like that, but the green-eyed maid stood there as calm as can be, as if everything was fine and proper. And the hall was full of people, dressed like ladies and gentlemen, all in gold and medals. Some had medals hanging in front, others had them sewn on the back, and some had them all over. It was clear they were the highest authorities. And their women were with them, also with naked arms and naked bosoms, with jewels hung all over them. But none could hold a candle to the green-eyed maid! Not one of them could compare.

At the maid's side stood a tow-headed man. He had a squint and big ears that stuck out. He looked for all the world like a hare. And the clothes he wore—a fair wonder, they were. Gold wasn't enough for him; he had precious stones on his shoes, even. And the kind you'd find once in ten years. You could tell at once he was a mine owner. He kept babbling something to the maid, that hare did, but she didn't so much as twitch an eyebrow, just as if he wasn't there.

Tanyushka looked at the maid, wondered at her, then she suddenly noticed something. "Why, those are Daddy's stones she's wearing!" she cried, and in that moment it all vanished.

The woman just laughed.

"You didn't look long enough, Daughter! Now don't you fret, you'll see it again, all in good time."

Of course, Tanyushka was full of questions—where was that hall she'd seen?

205

"It's in the tsar's palace," said the woman. "It's the hall that's decorated with the malachite your late father used to dig out."

"And who was the maid with Daddy's gems and who was the man who looked like a hare?"

"That I'll not tell you, you'll soon find out for yourself."

When Nastasya came home that day, the woman was getting ready to leave them. She bowed low to the mistress, gave Tanyushka a bundle of silks and beads, then she took out a little button. It might have been made of glass or of crystal cut smooth.

She gave it to Tanyushka with the words:

"Take this, Daughter, as a memento of me. If you forget something in your work, or if you run into trouble, look at the button. You'll find your answer there."

With that she left, vanished in a trice.

From then on Tanyushka became a mistress of her craft. She looked a grown maid, approaching the age for marriage. The local fellows would keep gaping at Nastasya's window, but they didn't dare approach Tanyushka. For she wasn't the friendly or merry sort, and besides, there's no way a free maid would marry a serf. Why'd she want to put her head under a yoke?

In the local lord's house they also heard of Tanyushka's skill at her craft. They started sending messengers to her. They'd pick one of the lackeys, one who was young and handsome, fit him out nicely, hang a watch and chain on him, and send him to Tanyushka with some message or other. They thought a dashing young fellow would catch her fancy. Then they'd have her as a serf. But it did no good. Tanyushka'd reply to the message, but pay no attention to his talk of anything else. And when she tired of it she'd make mock of him, too.

"Go along, my dear, go along! They're waiting for you. They must fear you'll spoil that fine watch and rub the gold off the chain. Can't keep your fingers off it, it's that new to you."

Her words scalded the lackey or any other servant like hot water thrown on a dog. He'd slink off, snarling to himself, "Call that a maid? A stone statue with green eyes! There's plenty better!"

He could snarl all he liked, but he'd still seem bewitched. Everyone they sent was amazed at Tanyushka's beauty. Something drew them back to her, even if only to walk past and eye the window. On feast days all the local young fellows found something to do in that street. They beat a track past the window, but Tanyushka never so much as looked at them.

The neighbors began to reproach Nastasya.

"Who does she think she is, your Tanyushka? She's not made friends with any of the girls and she won't look at the fellows. Is she waiting for the tsarevich, or does she think to be the bride of Christ?"

Nastasya could only sigh at these reproaches.

"Eh, neighbors, I can't make aught of it myself. She always was a strange maid, but since that sorceress was here, she's beyond me. I start talking to her, and she just stares at that witching button of hers and says no word. I'd throw it away, that button, but it helps her in her work. When she needs to change her silks or something, she looks at the button. She showed it to me once, but my eyes must be getting bad for I saw naught there. I could give her a whipping, but she's a right good worker. It's really her craft as keeps us. So I think and think till I start crying. And then she says: 'But Mama, I know my fate is else-where. I don't beguile the fellows, I don't even join the games. Why should I want to plague folks for naught? If I sit by the window it's because I have to, for my work. Why do you scold me? What have I done that's bad?' Now, what can I say to that!"

But with it all, life was better for them. Tanyushka's work got to be the fashion with the gentry. It wasn't only the locals and people in our town who bought it. People in other places who heard about it sent orders, too, and paid well for the work. Many a good man didn't earn as much. But then a disaster happened—a fire. It broke out in the night. The sheds and shelters for the livestock, the horse and cow, the farm tools and other gear—all were lost. They just managed to get out with what they had on them. Except that Nastasya snatched up the casket.

The next day she said, "Seems like we've come to the end. We'll have to sell the casket." And the sons said in unison, "Aye, sell it, Mom. But don't let it go cheap."

Tanyushka looked secretly at the button, and there was the green-eyed maid nodding—aye, sell it. It was a bitter thing for Tanyushka, but what could they do? Besides, sooner or later the memento of her father would go to that green-eyed maid anyway. So she sighed and said, "Aye, sell it if you must." She didn't even take a last look at the gems. Besides, the family had taken shelter with a neighbor, so there was no place to lay them out.

No sooner had they made up their minds to sell than the merchants appeared. Maybe one of them had started the fire himself so as to get hold of the casket. They're that sort—with claws ready to grab what they want! They saw the children were grown now, so they started offering more—some five hundred, and one even went up to a thousand. There was plenty of money about, you could set yourself up quite comfortably. Nastasya, though, asked for two thousand. They kept coming to her, bargaining. They'd raise the price a bit, but hide it from one another, for they never could agree among themselves. It was a tempting bit, that casket, and none of them wanted to lose it. And while they were still at it, a new bailiff came to Polevaya.

There are times when bailiffs stay in their jobs a long while, but in those years they kept changing and changing. The Stinking Goat who was there in Stepan's days maybe got to stink too much even for the old master's stomach. Anyway, he was sent to Krylatovskoye. Then came Roasted Rear—the workers sat him down on a hot ingot one day. After him there was Severyan the Butcher. The Mistress of Copper Mountain settled him, turned him into rock. Then there were two or three more, and finally the last one.

Folks said he was from foreign parts and knew all sorts of languages, all but Russian. That he spoke badly. The one thing he could say well enough was, "Flog him!" He'd draw it out, like, and as if from on high would shout, "Flo-o-o-og him!" And no matter what a man had done, it was always the same, "Flo-o-o-og him!" So the folks called him Flogger.

That Flogger wasn't really so bad, though. He made a lot of noise, but he didn't use the whipping post that much. The tormentors got fat and lazy. They'd nothing to do. Folks had a chance to breathe a bit while Flogger was bailiff.

This is how things were: the old master had grown feeble, he could hardly get about. And he wanted to marry his son to a countess or someone like that. But the young gentleman had a kept woman and he was real attached to her. What could you do? It was awkward. What would the bride's parents say? So the old master began persuading her—his son's kept woman—to marry the music teacher. The old master had hired him to teach the children music and foreign tongues—that's what the gentry do.

"Why go on living with a bad reputation?" he said. "Marry the music teacher. I'll give you a dowry and send your husband to be bailiff in Polevaya. It's all plain and easy there, so long as he's strict with the folks. He should have sense enough to do that, even if he is a musician. And you'll live real well at Polevaya. You'll be the lady of the place, you could say. You'll be respected and honored and all the rest of it. Nothing wrong with that, is there?"

The woman was ready to listen. Maybe she'd quarreled with the young master, or maybe she was just clever.

"It's what I've been wanting a long time," she said, "but I didn't like to ask."

At first the music teacher resisted, of course. "I don't want her," he said. "She's got a bad name. Folks say she's a trollop."

But the old master was sly. That's how he'd got rich. And he turned that music teacher right around. Whether he scared him or flattered him or got him drunk—who knows, but he soon had the wedding arranged, and then the young couple went off to Polevaya. That was how Flogger came to our village. He didn't stay long, but—give him his due—he wasn't so bad. Afterward, when Double Jowl took his place, folks wished him back.

Flogger and his wife came just at the time when the merchants were swarming round Nastasya. Now, that woman of Flogger's was a good-looker, all pink and white—just made for loving. Trust the young master to pick such a fine piece! Well, this wife of Flogger's heard about the casket that was for sale. "I'll have a look at it," she thought. "Maybe it's really worth buying." So she dressed herself up and drove to Nastasya. After all, they had all the estate horses at their disposal!

"Here, my good woman," she said, "show me those stones you're selling."

Nastasya got out the casket and opened it. And the woman's eyes nearly popped out of her head. She'd been raised in Petersburg, and been in countries abroad with the young master too, and she knew something about gems. "What's going on?" she thought. "The tsarina herself doesn't have gems like these, and here they are in Polevaya, owned by folks who've lost everything in a fire! I must see they don't slip through my fingers."

"What do you want for them?" she asked.

"I'm asking two thousand," Nastasya told her.

"Well, my dear, get ready! We'll go to my house with the casket. You'll get your money there."

But Nastasya didn't fall for that.

"Bread doesn't run after a stomach in our parts. Bring the money and the casket's yours."

Well, the lady saw that Nastasya meant it. She hurried home for the money, saying to Nastasya as she left, "See you don't sell to anyone else, my dear."

"Don't you fret," replied Nastasya. "I keep my word. I'll wait till evening, but after that I do as I like."

Off went Flogger's wife, and all the merchants descended on Nastasya. They'd been keeping track.

"So, how did it go?" they asked.

"I've sold them," replied Nastasya.

"For how much?"

"Two thousand, the price I asked."

"Are you crazy or what?" they shouted. "You give them to a stranger and refuse your own folks!" And they started bidding at higher prices. But Nastasya wasn't to be caught.

"Those may be your ways," she said, "say this and promise that and turn it all round, but they're not mine. I've given my word, and that's that!"

Flogger's wife was soon back. She brought the money, handed it over, picked up the casket, and made to go home. And there on the threshold she met Tanyushka. The maid had been away somewhere and the sale was made without her. She saw the lady holding the casket. Tanyushka looked real close at her, but it wasn't the one she'd seen that time. And Flogger's wife stared back.

"What's this sprite? Who is she?" she asked.

"Folks call her my daughter," said Nastasya. "The casket you've bought should have been her inheritance. I'd never have sold it if we hadn't come to the end. Ever since she was a bit of a thing she's always played with those gems. She'd try them on and say they made her feel warm and happy. But what's the good, talking of that now? What falls off the cart's lost and gone!"

"You're wrong there, my dear," said Flogger's wife. "I'll find a place for those gems." But she privately thought, "A good thing this green-eyed girl doesn't know her own power. If she turned up in St. Petersburg she'd turn the heads of tsars. I'd better see that my fool Turchaninov doesn't set eyes on her."

On that they parted.

As soon as Flogger's wife came home she started to brag:

"Well, dear friend, now I don't need to be beholden anymore to you or to Turchaninov either. The first thing that doesn't suit me—off I go! I'll go to St. Petersburg, or maybe better, I'll go abroad, I'll sell the casket and then I'll buy husbands like you by the dozen if I need to."

That's how she bragged, but all the same she badly wanted to show herself in the gems she'd bought. After all, she was a woman! She ran to the mirror and first of all put on the headdress. But—oh, oh, what's this?! It nipped her and pulled at her hair so she couldn't bear it. And she had quite a job taking it off. But she paid no heed. She put on the earrings, but they nearly tore off her lobes. She slipped on a ring and it pressed so tight she could hardly pull it off, even when she soaped it. Her husband sat and kept laughing at her: "Not meant to be worn by the likes of you, looks like!"

"What's going on?" she wondered. "I'll have to go to town, show them to a good craftsman. He'll adjust them so they'll fit. But I must make sure he doesn't change the stones."

No sooner said than done. The next morning off she went. It didn't take long to get to town with three good horses pulling. She found out who was the most reliable craftsman and went to see him. He was an old man, real ancient, and very skilled. He took a look at the casket and asked her where she'd bought it. The lady told him all she knew. The craftsman examined the casket again, but never even glanced at the gems.

"I won't touch them," he said, "no matter what you offer me. This wasn't made by any of our craftsmen. And I'm not about to compete with them."

Of course the lady didn't understand what it was all about. She sniffed and went off to find another craftsman. But it was as if they were all in a plot. One after another they examined the casket, admired it, never so much as glanced at the gems, and refused to have anything to do with it. Then the lady tried cunning. She said she'd bought the casket in St. Petersburg. There were plenty like it there. But the craftsman she served with that tale only laughed at her.

"I know where the casket was made," he said. "And I've heard a lot about the craftsman that made it. There's none of us can try to compete with him. If he's made things to fit one person, no other'll be able to wear them, try as you will."

The lady still didn't understand the whole thing. But she could see one thing—the craftsmen were scared of something. And then she called to mind how Nastasya had said her daughter liked to put on those trinkets.

"Could they have been made for that green-eyed creature? That's really too bad!"

But then she had second thoughts.

"What do I care! I'll sell them to some rich fool—let her worry about them, the money'll be in my pocket!" So back she went to Polevaya.

When she arrived she heard some news. The old master had gone to his eternal rest. He'd been cunning enough, the way he'd fixed it all with Flogger, but death was even more cunning. It went and dealt him a blow. He hadn't had time to get his son married, so now the young man was his own master. And it wasn't long before Flogger's wife got a letter. It told her this and that, and when the spring floods go down, my dear, I'll come and show up at the village and take you back with me. And as for your musician, we'll get rid of him somehow. Flogger found out about it and made a real scene. It made him look bad in folks' eyes. After all, he was the bailiff, and now here was someone taking away his wife. He started drinking hard. With the clerks and suchlike, of course. And they were glad enough so long as he treated them.

One day they were carousing. And one of his boon companions started to brag, "We've got a real beauty in our village, you'd have to go a long way to find another like her."

Flogger asked, "In what family? Where does she live?"

They told him all about it, and reminded him of the casket. "That's the family from which your wife bought it."

"I'd like to take a look at her," said Flogger, and the group of carousers thought of a way to do it.

"We can even go now, see if they've built the new cottage right. They're free, but they live on the village land. If there's a need, you can lean hard on them."

Off they went, two or three of them along with Flogger. They took a chain for measuring, to see if maybe Nastasya had filched a bit of land from the neighbors, and if the boundary posts were the right distance apart. Tried to catch her out, in other words. Then they went into the cottage, and Tanyushka happened to be alone there. Flogger took one look at her and lost his tongue. For he'd never seen such beauty in any land he'd been in. He just stood there like a fool, but as for her—she sat there without a word, as though it was all nothing to her. Then Flogger got his wits back a bit and asked her: "What's that you're doing?"

"It's embroidery folks have ordered," she said, and showed him her work.

"And would you take an order from me?" asked Flogger.

"Why not, if we come to terms."

"Then," said Flogger, "Can you embroider me a portrait of yourself in fine silk?"

Tanyushka looked quietly at her button, and the green-eyed maid made a sign to her—take the order, and then pointed at herself.

"I won't do my own portrait," said Tanyushka, "but I know a woman wearing precious gems, in the robe of a tsarina. I can embroider that. But work like that won't be cheap."

"You needn't fret about that," said Flogger. "I'll pay a hundred rubles or two hundred rubles, if only the woman's like you."

"The face'll be like mine," she said, "but the clothes will be different."

They agreed on a hundred rubles. Tanyushka also set the date—it would be ready in a month. Only Flogger kept on turning up, making as though he wanted to see how it was going, but it was something quite different really. His wits seemed turned, but Tanyushka, she took no notice whatever. She'd say two or three words, and that was all. Flogger's boon companions started to make fun of him.

"You'll get nothing there. Wasting boot leather!"

Well, Tanyushka finished the portrait. Flogger took a look and—God above!—it was her very self, only fitted out in a rich robe and gems! He gave her three hundred rubles, of course, but Tanyushka handed two of them back.

"We don't take gifts," she said. "We work for our bread."

Flogger hurried home. He kept looking at the portrait, but he hid it away from his wife. He didn't carouse so much, and started to take a bit of interest in the village and the mine.

Come springtime, the young master arrived. He drove over to Polevaya. The people were all gathered together, there were prayers in the church, and then all kinds of dancing and prancing in the master's house. A couple of barrels of wine were rolled out for the common folk too, so they could drink to the memory of the old master and the health of the new one. It was like priming a pump—the Turchaninovs were good at that. Add ten bottles of your own to the master's goblet and then it would look like something, but at the end of it all you'd find your last kopek gone and nothing to show for it.

The next day the people went back to work, but there was feasting and drinking again in the master's house. And so it went. They'd sleep a mite and then back to their carousing again. They'd go rowing about in boats, or riding horses in the woods, or playing music—there was everything you could think of. And all this time Flogger was drunk. The master had given the signal to the hardest drinkers—fill him up and keep him that way! Well, of course, they were glad enough to curry favor with the new master.

Flogger was drunk, but he had a good idea of what was coming, all the same. He felt awkward in front of the guests. So when they were all at table he burst out, "What do I care if Master Turchaninov wants to make off with my wife? He can have her, for all I care! I don't want her. Take a look at the maid I've got!" And what does he do but pull that portrait from his pocket. They all gasped, and Flogger's wife, her mouth dropped open and she couldn't get it shut again. The master also stared and stared. And he wanted to know more.

"Who is she?" he asked.

Flogger just laughed. "If you heap the whole table with gold I won't tell you!"

But what was the good of that, when everyone had recognized Tanyushka right away! They all fought to be the first to tell him. But Flogger's wife, she kept arguing and trying to stop them.

"Stuff and nonsense! You don't know what you're talking about! Where'd a village maid get a dress like that, and precious gems too? That portrait, my husband brought it from abroad. He showed it to me before we were married. He's drunk now, doesn't know what he's saying. He soon won't recognize himself. An out-and-out idiot!"

Flogger could see his wife was all agitated, and he started snarling at her: "You're a shameless hussy, that's what you are! Trumping up a cock-and-bull tale to fool the master! When did I ever show you the portrait? I got it here. From the maid they're talking about. About the dress, I won't tell a lie, I know nothing about it. You can put on any dress you want. But the gems, she did have those. And now they're here, locked in your cupboard. You bought them yourself for two thousand, but you couldn't wear them. A Circassian saddle won't go on a cow. The whole village knows how you bought them!"

The master no sooner heard of the gems than he said, "Get them out, show me!"

Now, the young master was a spendthrift, not too bright. Like heirs often are. And he had a real passion for gems. He couldn't boast much of looks, so at least he'd boast of jewels. As soon as he heard of fine gems, he'd be itching to buy them. And he understood about them right enough, though in general he was short on wits.

Flogger's wife saw there was no way out, so she brought the casket. And the moment the master saw the gems he asked, "How much?"

She named a figure beyond all sight or reason. The master started bargaining. They met halfway, and the master signed a paper for the money—he had no money with him. Then he put the casket on the table in front of him and said, "Send for that maid you've been telling about."

So they went off to fetch Tanyushka. She came at once, thinking nothing of it—she expected some big order for work. She came into the room, and it was full of people, and in the middle the very hare she'd seen that time. And in front of the hare stood the casket, her father's gift. Tanyushka guessed at once it was the young master.

"Why'd you call me here?" she asked.

The master couldn't get a word out. He just stared and stared at her. Then at last he found his tongue.

"Are those your gems?" he asked.

"They used to be, but now they're hers," and she pointed to Flogger's wife.

"They're mine now," said Turchaninov.

"That's your affair."

"Would you like me to give them back to you?"

"I've nothing to give for them."

"Well, you won't refuse to try them on? I want to see how they look when they're worn."

"I don't mind doing that," said Tanyushka.

She took the casket, sorted out the trinkets the way she was used to doing, and quickly put them on. The master looked and simply gasped. Gasped and gasped and nothing else. And Tanyushka, she stood there wearing the ornaments and said, "So, now you've seen. Have you looked your fill? I've no time to be standing here. I've work waiting."

But right there, in front of them all, the master said: "Marry me. Will you?"

Tanyushka only laughed.

"It's not fitting for a master to talk that way to someone not his equal." Then she took off the trinkets and left. But the young master couldn't let her alone. The next day he came to her cottage to make his proposal in proper form. He begged and urged Nastasya—give me your daughter.

"I won't force her one way or the other," said Nastasya. "Let it be as she says. But to my mind it's not suitable."

Tanyushka listened and listened, and then said, "Here's what I say. I've heard tell there's a chamber in the tsar's palace decorated with the malachite my father used to mine. If you show me the tsarina in that chamber, then I'll marry you."

The master was ready to agree to anything, of course. He at once

217

started getting ready to go to St. Petersburg, and wanted to take Tanyushka with him—"I'll get you horses," he said. But Tanyushka told him, "It's not our custom for a maid to use a man's horses before she's wed, and we're still nothing to each other. We'll talk of that later on, when you've kept your word."

"When will you come to St. Petersburg, then?" he said.

"I'll be there for sure by Intercession Day," she said. "You can rest easy about that. And now go."

The master left. Of course, he didn't take Flogger's wife with him, didn't even look at her. As soon as he got back to St. Petersburg he told the whole town about the gems and his intended. He showed the casket to many. And folks got real curious to see the bride-to-be. By autumn he'd fitted out an apartment for Tanyushka, bought all kinds of dresses and shoes for her, but she sent word she'd arrived and was living with some widow right on the edge of town.

Of course, the young master went there straight off.

"What are you doing? How can you think of living here? I've got an apartment all ready, you couldn't want a better."

But Tanyushka replied, "I'm quite comfortable where I am."

Talk about the gems and Turchaninov's intended even got to the tsarina.

"Let Turchaninov show me that bride of his," she said. "This non-stop talk about her is beyond belief."

Off went the young master to Tanyushka—she must get herself ready, sew an outfit to wear at court, and put on the gems from the malachite casket.

"About my outfit you needn't concern yourself," she said, "but the gems I'll take as a loan. Only mind you don't think of sending horses for me. I'll come my own way. Wait for me by the entrance to the palace."

Turchaninov wondered where she would get horses from. And an outfit to wear at court? But he didn't dare ask.

All the grand folks gathered at court. They came rolling up in carriages, in their silks and velvets. Turchaninov was early by the door, fidgeting about, waiting for his intended. And there were others curious to see her; they stood about waiting too. But Tanyushka put on the gems, fastened a kerchief round her head village-style, threw on her sheepskin coat, and came along quietly on foot. And the folks who saw her wondered where she'd come from and followed her in huge crowds. She came to the palace but the lackeys wouldn't let her in. "Villagers can't come in here," they said. Turchaninov had seen her when she was a good way off, but he was ashamed to have his bride come on foot and in a country sheepskin, and he went and hid. Tanyushka undid her sheepskin and the lackeys stared. What a robe she had on! Why, the tsarina herself hadn't one like it! They let her in at once. And as soon as Tanyushka took off her kerchief and sheepskin all the people gasped in wonder. "Who is she? Of what land is she a tsarina?"

Turchaninov was there in an instant.

"This is my bride," he said.

But Tanyushka looked at him very sternly.

"That's still to be seen!" she said. "Why didn't you keep your word, why weren't you at the entrance?"

Turchaninov mumbled and stumbled, there'd been a mistake, please forgive him, and so on.

They went into a chamber of the palace, the one where they were told to go. Tanyushka looked round and saw it wasn't the right one.

"What's this, are you trying to fool me?" she asked, more sternly still. "I told you it must be the chamber that's decorated with the malachite my father mined!" And she started walking through the palace just as if she were at home there. And all the senators and generals and the rest followed after her.

"What's going on?" they said. "That must be where we're all to go."

The people crowded in till it was full as could be, and wouldn't take their eyes off Tanyushka. And as for her, she stood close up to the malachite wall and waited. Of course Turchaninov was there right by her. He kept babbling that it wasn't fitting, the tsarina had said they were to wait for her in another chamber. But Tanyushka stood there quietly, didn't even move an eyebrow, just as though he wasn't there at all.

The tsarina went to the chamber where they were to meet. She saw that it was empty. But her informers quickly told her that Turchaninov's bride had led them all to the Malachite Hall. The tsarina grumbled, of course—such high-handed goings on!—and stamped her foot. She was a bit angry. Then she went to the Malachite Hall. Everybody bowed low, but Tanyushka stood there and never moved.

"Now then," cried the tsarina, "show me this high-handed maid, this bride of Turchaninov's!"

When Tanyushka heard that she frowned and said to Turchaninov: "What does this mean? I told you to show me the tsarina, and you've arranged to show me to her. You've lied again! I don't want to see any more of you. Take your gems!"

With those words she leaned against the malachite wall and melted away. All that was left were the gems sparkling on the wall, stuck there in the places where her head, neck, and arms had been.

Of course, all the courtiers were scared and the tsarina fell to the floor in a swoon. There was a great to-do till they set her back on her feet. Then when everything had quieted down a bit, Turchaninov's friends said to him: "Take your gems, at least, before they're stolen! You are in a palace, you know! Folks here know their value!"

So Turchaninov started trying to pick them off the wall. But each one he touched turned into a drop. Some drops were clear, like tears, others yellow, and others thick and red like blood. So he got none of them. He looked down and there on the floor was a button. Just a glass button, plain bottle-glass. A worthless trifle. But in his misery he picked even that up. And as soon as he had it in his hand, the button looked like a big mirror and the green-eyed beauty, wearing a malachite dress and the precious gems, looked out of it, laughing and laughing.

"Eh, you stupid, cross-eyed hare!" she said. "Imagine thinking you could get me! What match for me are you?"

After that the young master lost the last of his wits, but he didn't throw away the button. He'd keep looking in it, and he always saw the same thing—there stood the green-eyed maid and laughed and laughed and mocked him. In his misery he started drinking and got into debt right and left. Our village and mines almost went under the hammer in his time.

As for Flogger, after he lost his job he spent his time making the rounds of the taverns. He drank away all he had, but he still kept that portrait in silk. What happened to it later, nobody knows.

Flogger's wife was left empty-handed too. Try to get your money on a note of hand when all the iron and copper's mortgaged!

From that day on nobody ever heard a word about Tanyushka. It was just as though she'd never been.

Nastasya grieved, of course, but not overmuch. Tanyushka, after all, had always been like a changeling, not like a daughter to her at all. And then, the boys had grown up. They both got married. There were grandchildren. Plenty of folks in the cottage. Plenty to do and think about—watch one, give a slap to another . . . No time to brood!

But the young fellows didn't forget Tanyushka for a long time. They still came around by Nastasya's window. Maybe she'd turn up there some day. But she didn't.

Then, finally, they got married one by one, but time and again they'd remember, "Eh, that was a rare maid used to live in our village! You'll never see another like her."

One other thing happened after that. Talk started going around that the Mistress of Copper Mountain had a double: folks would see two maids together in malachite dresses.

1939

THE FLOWER OF SEVEN COLORS

VALENTIN KATAEV

Once upon a time, there lived a girl called Zhenya. One day, her mother sent her to the store to buy some ring-shaped rolls. Zhenya bought seven rolls: two with caraway seeds for her father, two with poppy seeds for her mother, two sprinkled with sugar for herself, and a small pink glazed one for her little brother, Pavlik. Zhenya took the bunch of rolls and set off home. She walked back, gaping around her, reading the signs on the way, and counting the ravens. Meanwhile, a strange dog appeared behind her and one after another snatched the rolls: it ate her father's with the caraway seeds, then her mother's with the poppy seeds, and then Zhenya's sugar-sprinkled rolls. Suddenly, Zhenya realized that the bag with the rolls had become much too light. She turned, but it was already too late. The empty bag lay dangling as the dog, licking its chops, was finishing the last pink roll bought for Pavlik. "Ah, you beastly dog!" shouted Zhenya, and set off after it.

She ran and ran, yet couldn't catch the dog, and only got lost. She looked around and realized that her surroundings were completely unfamiliar; there were no big houses in sight, only small ones. Zhenya became frightened and began to cry. Suddenly, an old woman appeared out of nowhere.

"Little girl, little girl, why are you crying?"

Zhenya told the old woman everything. The old woman felt sorry for Zhenya, and led her into her little garden.

"Don't cry. I'll help you. It's true I don't have any ring-shaped rolls or money, but, on the other hand, there's a special flower in my garden, a seven-petaled flower of different colors that's capable of anything. I can tell you're a good girl despite your absentmindedness. I'll give you the flower of seven colors, and it'll always look after you."

With these words, the old woman plucked a beautiful flower from the flower bed and handed it to Zhenya. It looked like a daisy. It had seven pellucid petals, each of a different color: yellow, red, green, dark blue, orange, violet, and light blue.

"This is no ordinary flower," said the old woman. "It can fulfill any of your wishes. For this to happen, you need only pluck off one petal, throw it in the air, and say:

> Fly, petal, fly
> From west to east,
> From north to south.
> Return when you've flown all around.
> The second that you touch the ground,
> Make true the wish that left my mouth."

Zhenya thanked the old woman politely, came out of the gate, and then all of a sudden remembered that she didn't know her way home. She wanted to return to the garden and ask the old woman to lead her to the nearest policeman, but neither the little garden nor the old woman was there. What was she supposed to do? Zhenya had already made up her mind to cry, as usual, scrunching up her nose like an accordion, but suddenly remembered her cherished flower of seven colors.

"Well, let's see what our flower of seven colors can do!"

Zhenya somewhat hastily plucked the yellow petal, threw it in the air and said:

> Fly, petal, fly
> From west to east,

From north to south.
Return when you've flown all around.
The second that you touch the ground,
Make true the wish that leaves my mouth.

"Make it possible for me to return home with the rolls!" No sooner had she finished speaking than she found herself at home, and in her hands—the bunch of rolls!

Zhenya handed the rolls to her mother, thinking to herself:

"This is really and truly a remarkable flower and I must place it in the most beautiful vase."

Zhenya was quite a small girl and therefore she needed to climb onto a chair and stretch up high to reach her mother's favorite vase, which stood on the top shelf. At this moment, as if by fate, some crows flew by the window. Zhenya instantly wanted to find out precisely how many crows there were—seven or eight. She opened her mouth and began to count, bending each finger in turn, and then—bang! The vase fell to the floor and shattered into tiny pieces.

"You've broken something again, scatterbrain!" shouted her mother from the kitchen. "Not my favorite vase?"

"No, no, Mommy, I haven't broken anything. It's your hearing!" shouted Zhenya, plucking the red petal with the greatest possible haste, throwing it in the air, and whispering:

Fly, petal, fly
From west to east,
From north to south.
Return when you've flown all around.
The second that you touch the ground,
Make true the wish that leaves my mouth.

"Make Mommy's favorite vase whole again!"

She had no sooner finished speaking than the pieces turned into an unbroken vase once more. Mother ran in from the kitchen, but her favorite vase was in its place, as always. Just in case, Mother shook her finger and sent Zhenya to go for a walk.

When Zhenya went into the yard the boys were playing at great North Pole explorers: they were sitting on old boards, sticking mock flagpoles into the sand.

"Hey, boys, let me play with you!"

"What do you want? Can't you see this is the North Pole? We don't bring girls to the North Pole!"

"What kind of North Pole is this? These are just boards!"

"They're not boards, they're blocks of ice. Don't bother us, leave us alone! We're stuck in the ice."

"You mean I can't."

"No, you can't. Go away!"

"I don't want to, anyway. I'll make my own way to the North Pole without you. Only not like yours, the real one!"

Zhenya walked to the gate, grabbed her cherished flower of seven colors, plucked the dark blue petal, threw it in the air, and said:

> *Fly, petal, fly*
> *From west to east,*
> *From north to south.*
> *Return when you've flown all around.*
> *The second that you touch the ground,*
> *Make true the wish that leaves my mouth.*

"Make it possible for me to appear at the North Pole!"

No sooner had she finished speaking than an almighty blizzard swept down upon her from out of nowhere. The sun vanished and an eerie night appeared, and the earth began to spin like a top under her feet.

Zhenya, dressed in her sundress and with bare feet, found herself all alone at the North Pole, with a hundred degrees of frost.

"Ah, Mommy, I'm freezing!" shouted Zhenya and began to cry, but the tears turned straight into icicles, hanging down from the tip of her nose as if it were a drainpipe.

At that moment, seven bears came from behind the blocks of ice and moved directly toward the little girl, each one scarier than the next: the first bear was nervous; the second—evil; the third wore a beret; the fourth was shabby; the fifth—flabby; the sixth—spotty; and the seventh was the very biggest.

Not knowing what to do out of fear, Zhenya grabbed her flower of seven colors with her little frozen hands, plucked the green petal, and threw it in the air, saying with the greatest possible vigor:

Fly, petal, fly
From west to east,
From north to south.
Return when you've flown all around.
The second that you touch the ground,
Make true the wish that leaves my mouth.

"Make it possible for me to find myself in our yard again!"

And that very moment she found herself in her yard. The boys were looking at her and laughing: "So where's your North Pole?"

"I've just been there."

"We didn't see you there. Prove it to us!"

"Look, there's still an icicle hanging off my nose."

"Those aren't icicles, liar. Stop talking nonsense."

Zhenya took offense and decided not to bother with the boys anymore. She went into the next yard to play with the girls. As she drew near, she saw that the girls had a lot of toys. They had a stroller, a ball, a jump rope, a tricycle, and a big talking doll in a doll's straw hat and doll's mini-galoshes. Zhenya became jealous. Even her eyes grew green with envy, like goat's eyes.

"Right," she thought, "I'll show you who has the real toys!" She took her flower of seven colors, plucked the orange petal, and threw it in the air, saying:

Fly, petal, fly
From west to east,
From north to south.
Return when you've flown all around.
The second that you touch the ground,
Make true the wish that leaves my mouth.

"Make it possible for all the toys in the world to be mine!" And at that very moment, from out of nowhere toys came tumbling down around her from all sides.

First, of course, came dolls, loudly fluttering their eyes and squeaking nonstop: "Mommy—Daddy," "Mommy—Daddy." At first Zhenya was really happy, but the dolls continued to appear in such numbers that they immediately filled the whole yard, the alleys, two streets, and half the square. You couldn't even take a step without treading on a doll. They surrounded her, and can you imagine the clamor five million talking dolls make? And there were no fewer than that. And these were only the dolls from Moscow. What of the dolls from Leningrad, Kharkov, Kiev, Lvov, and other Soviet towns? They'd not had time to run that far and were making a hubbub across all the highways of the Soviet Union. Zhenya actually got a little scared. However, this was only the beginning. Behind the dolls came balls, marbles, scooters, tricycles, tractors, cars, tanks, tankettes, and cannons. Jump ropes slid across the ground like grass snakes, becoming entangled with feet and making the nervous dolls squeak even louder. Through the air flew millions of toy planes, gliders, and blimps. Floating from the sky, like tulips, were tiny parachutes, entangling themselves everywhere in trees and telephone wires. Movement in the town came to a halt. On-duty policemen climbed up lampposts, not knowing what to do next.

"Enough, enough!" Zhenya shouted in horror, clutching at her head. "That'll do! What's the matter with you! I absolutely don't need so many toys. I was joking. I'm scared . . ."

But her words had no effect! Toys continued to tumble down all around. When the Soviet toys ended, the American ones began.

Already the town was full to the brim with toys.

Zhenya fled up the stairs, and the toys followed her. Zhenya fled onto the balcony, and the toys followed her. Zhenya fled into the attic, and the toys followed her. Zhenya leapt onto the roof and hurriedly plucked the violet petal, threw it in the air, and said:

> *Fly, petal, fly*
> *From west to east,*
> *From north to south.*
> *Return when you've flown all around.*
> *The second that you touch the ground,*
> *Make true the wish that leaves my mouth.*

"Make all the toys clear off, back into the shops, as soon as possible." The toys vanished instantly.

Zhenya looked at her flower of seven colors and saw that just one petal remained.

"Some joke! Six petals, it turns out, have been wasted—and I've had no fun from them. All right, fine. In future, I'll be smarter."

She went walking down the street, thinking:

"All the same, what shall I wish for? Perhaps I'll ask for two kilos of chocolate. No, even better, two kilos of lollipops. Or no, I better make it half a kilo of chocolate and half a kilo of lollipops, a hundred grams of halvah, a hundred grams of nuts, and last, a pink glazed ring-shaped roll for Pavlik. But what's the use? Let's say I get and eat all that candy. And then there'll be nothing left. No, better to ask for a tricycle. Though . . . what for? I'll ride around on it a bit, and then what? The boys likely will take it away from me. Maybe they'll even beat me up! No, better to ask for tickets to the movies or circus. That at least would be fun. Or maybe I'd better wish for new sandals? That's no worse than the circus. Though, when you think about it, what's the point of having new sandals?! I can ask for something else much better. The main thing is not to hurry."

Reasoning like this as she walked down the street, Zhenya suddenly

saw a wonderful-looking boy sitting on a bench by the gates. He had big
blue eyes that looked merry but calm. He was extremely attractive and
you could tell immediately that he wasn't a bully, and Zhenya wanted to
make friends with him. Without the slightest fear, Zhenya went up to
him so close that she could see her braids reflected in his pupils.

"Hi, what's your name?"

"Vitya. What's yours?"

"Zhenya. Do you want to play tag?"

"I can't. I'm lame."

Zhenya saw his foot, in a misshapen shoe on a very thick sole.

"What a shame!" said Zhenya. "I like you a lot, and I'd be really glad
to run around with you."

"I like you too and I'd also be really glad to run around with you,
but, unfortunately, I can't. There's nothing to be done. It's for the rest
of my life."

"Ah, what nonsense you're saying!" exclaimed Zhenya, and pulled
the cherished flower of seven colors from her pocket. "Look!"

With these words, the little girl cautiously plucked the last, blue
petal, for a moment pressed it to her eyes, then unclenched her fingers, and sang in a thin voice, trembling with happiness:

Fly, petal, fly
From west to east,
From north to south.
Return when you've flown all around.
The second that you touch the ground,
Make true the wish that leaves my mouth.

"Make Vitya well again!"

And at that very instant, the boy leapt from the bench and began
to play tag with Zhenya, and ran so well that the little girl couldn't
catch him, no matter how hard she tried.

1940

PART

III

Fairy Tales in Critique of Soviet Culture

INTRODUCTION
༝༝

MARK LIPOVETSKY

The communist utopia vitally needed a discourse that would translate its abstract premises into comprehensible and tangible images, accessible both to uneducated adults and to new generations of the Soviet people, including children and even infants. As Katerina Clark in her seminal monograph on the Soviet novel observes, "In Stalinist culture of the thirties there were . . . two orders of reality, ordinary and extraordinary, and correspondingly, two orders of human beings, of time and place and so on. . . . In order to describe *homo extraordinarius*, one needed more fabulous forms, such as fairy tales" (Clark 146–47). Clark's analysis of the master plot of the socialist realist novel, in which she detects deep affinities with the "morphology of the fairy tale," provides one of the most convincing arguments for the profound assimilation of the fairy-tale mentality by Soviet ideological discourse. One can even reasonably claim that fairy-tale archetypes form the anima of Soviet civilization, the core of the Soviet collective unconscious. The fairy-tale paradigm connects the Soviet ideological utopia with the collective unconscious, at the same time selecting those elements of the collective unconscious that already possess utopian potential and therefore can feed and support totalitarian ideology.

The ideological emphasis on the utopian aspect of the fairy-tale tradition in Soviet culture, however, did not eliminate different aspects of "genre memory," to use Mikhail Bakhtin's expression. As a folk genre, the fairy tale appeared on the ruins of mythological beliefs in archaic societies when sacred mythological tales lost their religious meaning and underwent a transformation from symbolic texts to purely fantastic narratives. According to Vladimir Propp's assertion: "When the social order changed and the old, cruel rituals were perceived as meaningless, they started to be targeted against their practitioners . . . In the fairy tale, myth dissociated from ritual becomes a form of protest against its own premises" (Propp 61). This aspect of "genre memory" could explain the fairy tale's ability to disrespectfully mock sacred concepts, as seen, for example, in the "indecent" (*zavetnye*) tales subverting public morality and sexual norms. It also could explain why the early 1920s simultaneously witnessed the first attempts to create utopian, ideologically charged fairy-tale images of the Revolution, and the first examples of fairy-tale satire, which dismantled the newly born Soviet regime and its ideology. Though kindred to the communist utopia, the fairy tale demonstrated its ability to reveal the utopia's dark secrets, and this ability is what serves as a basis for the *anti-totalitarian* vector of the fairy-tale tradition in Soviet culture.

The paradox of fairy-tale discourse within Soviet cultural identity may be defined by its dual function: it simultaneously shapes the luminescent anima and the dark aspects of the Soviet collective unconscious, its *shadow*. In *both* functions it was instrumental in manipulating the deep layers of the popular mentality. In both functions the fairy tale possessed a very powerful language for simplifying the catastrophic and confused reality of the Soviet epoch. This therapeutic function of fairy-tale discourse in Soviet culture is comparable to the role the fairy tale plays in a child's psychological development, as Bruno Bettelheim interprets it: "As he listens to the fairy tale, the child gets ideas about how he may create order out of the chaos which is his inner life" (Bettelheim 75). The only difference between the Soviet fairy tale and the traditional fairy tale for children is the fact that the Soviet fairy tale focuses on *social life* and *social conflicts* rather than on inner life and the mental processes of an individual.

The explosive, anti-totalitarian potential of the fairy-tale genre was first discovered in Soviet literature by Yevgeny Zamyatin (1884–1937), famous as the author of one of the first dystopian novels, *We* (*My*, 1921). In 1922, a year after completing his prophetic novel, Zamyatin wrote and published a cycle of ironic fairy tales under the title *Fairy Tales for Grown-Up Children* (*Bol'shim detiam skazki*). The major targets of his parody and sarcasm were administrative efforts to simplify life according to the utopian project of a happy future for all. The core concept of the cycle was epitomized in the four tales about Fita that also provide a conclusion to the book. In his tales about Fita, Zamyatin shows that the main force propelling the people, supposedly for their own good, to a paradise suspiciously reminiscent either of a military barracks or of the future gulag, is embodied in a bureaucrat. Since a pile of old office files has generated this "homunculus," Fita literally possesses a "bureaucratic soul." His practice of revolutionary reforms is amazingly straightforward: he always chooses the fastest path to achieving happiness for all, a path that inevitably turns out to be the most destructive and degrading one possible. Naturally, it is easier to cancel cholera by official order, to fire all doctors, and to label those sick with cholera as state criminals, than it is to overcome a pandemic in reality. By the same token, Fita "strictly cancels" mass starvation in his region. Even freedom seems to be achievable by means of bureaucratic instructions. Accordingly, Fita orders his people to express "the obligatory freedom to conduct songs and processions in national costumes." And since it is much harder to make everyone be equally smart than to demand that all be equally stupid, "they started living a happy life. There's no one on earth happier than an utter idiot." This is the pessimistic ending of Zamyatin's fairy-tale dystopia and the entire cycle.

All the other tales in this slim volume explain which components of mass consciousness provided the soil for this hideous ideal of total happiness achieved by a violent, bureaucratic simplification of life. Unlike the nineteenth-century satirist Mikhail Saltykov-Shchedrin, whose allegorical fairy tales portray similar bureaucratic monsters, Zamyatin does not perceive his Fita as something contrasting to the masses. On the contrary, Fita *embodies* the people's desire to attain happiness by fairy-tale means, by miracle, with a minimum of effort. The bureaucratic "revolutionary" Fita turns out to be the real protagonist of the people's utopian dream of instant universal happiness. That is why all the subjects of Fita's reforms agree to become fools without any resistance whatsoever.

Traditionally, from the early nineteenth century on, fairy-tale discourse in Russian culture was identified with the artistic representation of the people's perspective on aesthetics, ethics, society, politics, and so forth. Soviet ideology adopted and developed this tendency to an unprecedented degree. Indeed, Lenin stated that fairy tales function as an embodiment of "popular hopes and expectations" (Novikova and Kokorev 48). Zamyatin was one of the first writers who dared to deviate from this authoritative approach. In his *Fairy Tales for Grown-Up Children* he used fairy-tale discourse as a tool for *critical* analysis of the people's mentality, and turned it into a form of *deconstruction* rather than a propagation of "popular hopes and expectations." Beginning with Zamyatin, the Russian satiric fairy tale of the twentieth century developed as perhaps the most consistent exploration of the questions illuminating the *people's* responsibility for totalitarian terror and moral corruption. One can pursue the unfolding of this trend in the satirical novels by Mikhail Bulgakov based on fairy-tale motifs (the magic transformation of an animal into a man in *Heart of a Dog* [1925], the reptiles/dragons' attack in *The Fatal Eggs* [1925]), in Andrey Platonov's parable "Makar, Who Started to Doubt" (1929), and even in his famous *Foundation Pit* (1919–30).[1] But it was Yevgeny Shvarts (1896–1958) who created a new modification of the genre that proved capable of shaping the newly discovered possibilities and submerged intentions of fairy-tale discourse.

Linked by biographical circumstances and in several cases by life-long friendship with writers belonging to the OBERIU circle (Kharms, Oleinikov), as well as to the Serapion Brothers literary group (Zoshchenko, Slonimsky), Shvarts combined sensitivity to the absurdity of reality (inherent for the former) with an explicit orientation toward Western literary traditions (one of the major goals of the latter's "program"). From his early experiments in the genre of fairy-tale plays, Shvarts revisited, in an ironically modernizing vein, famous western European literary tales: Charles Perrault's *Little Red Riding Hood* (1936) and Hans Christian Andersen's *The Naked King* (1934), *The Snow Queen* (1936), and *The Shadow* (1940). In many senses his approach to fairy-tale plots was similar to that of dramatists who from the 1930s to the 1950s recast famous legendary and mythological plots: Jean Giraudoux (*Judith, Electra, Amphitryon 38, The Trojan War Will Not Take Place*), George Bernard Shaw (*Joan of Arc*), Jean Anouilh (*Antigone, The Skylark*), and Jean-Paul Sartre (*The Flies*). But in Shvarts's case, the play with an "alien plot" (as he used to say) already explored by the writers of the past allowed him to dissociate fairy-tale discourse from folk tradition in general and from the tradition of idealized characters representing the people in particular. By the same token, he transformed fairy-tale discourse, enriched by links with romanticism (and many other cultural realms), into an ever-expanding repository of the cultural memory of the Russian intelligentsia, which had grown up with the fairy tales of Perrault, Hoffmann, Andersen, and Hauff, rather than with Russian folklore. Fairy-tale discourse in Shvarts's interpretation preserves archaic "genre memory," with its sensitivity to the archetypes of the collective unconscious, but at the same time it achieves independence from attachment to fairy-tale models engaged in the Soviet masses' process of utopian identification. The fairy tale as created by Shvarts was based on a dialogical structure formed by the interplay between generic archaic elements reflecting the archetypes of the collective unconscious and the tradition of refined and intellectually charged literary models rooted in romanticism and modernism.

The Dragon (*Drakon*, 1943) is undoubtedly the most mature and powerful of Shvarts's fairy-tale plays, in which the heuristic potential of this dialogical structure reaches its fullest realization. Although Shvarts attempted to camouflage his satire with a few superfluous references to Nazism (German names, the Dragon's hatred of gypsies, etc.)—which were particularly visible and recognizable during the Second World War—when the play was finished and performed for the first time, attentive readers had no trouble detecting the play's real subject. For example, the playwright Leonid Malyugin, then literary director of the Big Dramatic Theater of Leningrad, in a private letter to Shvarts, wrote about *The Dragon:*

> This is an angry and sad piece—there is eight times more anger and sadness in it than in any of your other works. The people are so acclimated to trouble, robbery, arbitrariness, violence, and injustice that nothing can surprise or upset them—not even the news of their own death. (Let's agree that this city is located on German territory; it will be easier to take then.) [*Uslovimsia, chto etot gorod nakhoditsia na territorii Germanii—i togda stanet legche.*] (Binevich 227–28)

At the conjunction of the fairy-tale metaphor of a dead kingdom and of social realia instantly recognizable to anyone familiar with Soviet totalitarianism is where Shvarts constructs the Dragon's city, an absurd, isolated world where abnormal is normal and dead is alive. The inhabitants' mundane life in this city demonstrates acclimation to tyranny and a sincere confidence in the axiom: "The only way to get rid of dragons is to have your own." Thus the city archivist, Charlemagne, during his first conversation with Lancelot, a wandering knight, can speak of the Dragon's kindness and greatness without hypocrisy, despite his being forced to give up his beloved daughter Elsa to the monster. Similarly, immediately after her beloved Charlemagne reveals that the Dragon "burned up the suburbs and half the population went berserk from poisonous fumes," Elsa casually invites Lancelot, "Do help yourself to the butter." Fear determines people's actions, but it is an instinctive, subconscious fear unrecognized by the people themselves. This fear blocks memory and magically transforms bad into good, black into white. It is a magic force unknown to the fairy-tale tradition but extremely powerful in totalitarian reality.

The Dragon turns out to be a paradigmatic text about the confrontation of individuals with the *collective shadow*. Jung observed:

> The shadow is the moral problem that challenges the whole ego-personality, for no one can become conscious of the shadow without considerable moral effort. To become conscious of it involves recognizing the dark aspects of the personality as present and real. This act is the essential condition for any kind of self-knowledge, and it therefore, as a rule, meets with considerable resistance. Indeed, self-knowledge as a psychotherapeutic measure frequently requires much painstaking work over a long period. (Jung 91)

Elsa and Lancelot represent the two main stages of confrontation with the shadow: Elsa manifests the first stage in that she consciously sees and admits the existence of the shadow. For Shvarts's purposes it is important that Elsa belongs to the Dragon's people and shares the collective shadow with them. Lancelot epitomizes the second stage, the stage that requires "much painstaking work over a long period." He has to struggle with the Dragon's seed consistently and steadily, yet with a hope that "people in reality, perhaps with some exceptions, are worth careful cultivation."

The transformation of the Dragon into the people's collective shadow provides the paradoxical conclusion to the different levels of the play's plot. As a matter of fact, the fairy-tale "genre memory" enriched by diverse associations with both the past (knight's epic, romanticism) and modern history here becomes self-referential: it discovers a monstrous shadow in the mentality of the people, whose moral values are preserved by the fairy-tale tradition. Shvarts's fairy tale blurs the borderline not only between the father figure and a monster, but also between a tyrant and his victims. It destroys the fairy-tale conviction of easily achieved happiness and redefines personal maturation as the necessity of jettisoning the collective shadow. In short, Shvarts's fairy tale deconstructs all the major premises of the Soviet fairy-tale mentality, while remaining principally within its thematic and structural borders.

Soviet authorities typically appropriated fairy-tale discourse as a means of educating the masses. That is why the fairy tale became a safe form of projecting criticism and satire onto *the other,* who substituted for the real objects of satire. The very discourse of the Soviet fairy tale as a discourse of power's self-justification encouraged this substitution. It is telling that *The Dragon* was not banned by Soviet censorship and was even performed, although only a few times, in spite of its explicitly anti-totalitarian sentiments. Even after the political accusations that caused the ban on theatrical performances of *The Dragon,* Shvarts's literary career suffered no serious problems. He was never arrested and his other works were performed and published. Suspicions as to the political correctness of *The Dragon* remained in place until perestroika (1987–91), although several productions of the play were successfully staged in the 1970s and 1980s at the "studio" level of nonprofessional theaters, such as the student theater of Moscow University (director Mark Zakharov) and the Moscow Theater-Studio South-West (director Vladimir Belyakovich). How does one explain the Soviet authorities' ambiguous attitude toward such an explicitly anti-totalitarian play? Perhaps by the simple fact that *The Dragon* was supposedly a satire on German Nazism, and even the most rigid and suspicious censor would not *dare* to claim that it was about the Soviet totalitarian regime as well, or per se. The Soviet regime pretended not to recognize itself in

Shvarts's parable, and German Nazism played the role of *the other* in the mechanism of shadow projection.

Shvarts's play laid the basis for the development of the satiric fairy tale in Soviet culture. A virtual explosion of this trend occurred in the 1960s and 1970s, when political oppression of the intelligentsia was less harsh than under Stalin, though the pressure of censorship remained heavy. Surprisingly (or not, if we accept the shadow theory), the authorities' attitude toward fairy-tale satires on the Soviet regime was quite ambiguous. Fairy-tale imagery hardly concealed the political meaning of the "Tale of the Troika" ("Skazka o troike," 1968) by Arkady and Boris Strugatsky, "Before the Cock Crows Thrice" ("Do tret'ikh petukhov," 1974) by Vasily Shukshin, or Grigory Gorin's play about Munchausen, *That Very Munchausen* (*Tot samyi Miunkhauzen,* 1976). Yet all these texts were published in Soviet journals or performed in Soviet theaters. Soviet censors were no fools. Their tolerance of such works most likely involved some kind of unannounced etiquette: as long as the writer did not violate the conventional rules of the fairy-tale plot and placed his characters and events outside of the concrete world of Soviet life, he remained under the protection of fantasy. As soon as the author violated this unspoken agreement, he walked a dangerous road. Of the many reasons for this etiquette, the most important is that the authorities, by permitting fairy-tale discourse, hoped to create a "steam valve" for criticism. It was safe enough, since the artistic design of fairy-tale parables had to be rather sophisticated, providing multiple layers for interpretation. Therefore, the readership of these texts was inevitably limited to the well-educated intelligentsia. Such concessions also created a peculiar kind of unwritten agreement that led to trust between the intelligentsia elite and the totalitarian authorities, a trust beneficial for both sides.

In a way, the place of these texts within Soviet culture is similar to that reserved for Shvarts's *Dragon:* they were granted a ghostlike existence, with a short appearance and a long echo. More important, all the satiric fairy tales of the 1960s and 1970s focus on the paradigmatic figures that *The Dragon* interpreted as constructs of the Soviet *shadow* and mirror images of the basic archetypes of the Soviet fairy-tale anima.

The dragon. Shvarts transformed the father figure of the wise leader into the Dragon, and in the fairy tales of the 1960s and 1970s this transformation became the recurring pattern: the three-headed monster was replaced by a crew of senile bureaucrats in "Tale of the Troika," by the sentimental tyrant Zmei Gorynych in Shukshin's "Before the Cock Crows Thrice," and by the double figure of a leader with the cruel face of a Great Python as well as the appearance of a cunning demagogue—the King of Rabbits in Fazil Iskander's *Rabbits and Boa Constrictors.*

The Strugatskys' "Tale of the Troika" is especially illuminating from this point of view. It was written by the Strugatsky brothers as a sequel to their earlier fairy-tale work, *Monday Begins on Saturday* (*Ponedel'nik nachinaetsia v subbotu,* 1964), a cheerful fantasy about a Research Institute of Marvels and Miracles. This early tale presents free-minded scientists of the Thaw generation as magicians enjoying the ultimate freedom of the imagination and intellect. Istvan Csicsery-Ronay accurately interpreted the dominant goal of the Strugatskys' works in the 1960s as an attempt to reinvent the fairy-tale utopia that had been appropriated by socialist realism:

> With the Strugatskys, science . . . became the historical vehicle of a new fairy-tale paradigm, which was more realistically motivated than the old one . . . but was identical in structure. This modification not only allowed the Strugatskys more artistic freedom . . . It also gave them a powerful theme that expressed the hopes of the new Soviet technocracy in the late '50s—the multitude of scientists, engineers, and scientific students who were accorded new respect by the successes in outer space . . . It appeared that they had been empowered to take on the role of

the revolutionary vanguard in a peaceful revolution. (Csicsery-
Ronay 5–6)

During the four years separating "Tale of the Troika" from *Monday,*
the mode of the Strugatskys' fairy-tale fantasy changed drastically:
the fairy-tale utopia of *Monday* was transformed in the later work into
a fairy-tale dystopia. These four years, after all, had witnessed
Khrushchev's replacement by Brezhnev and the beginning of new political purges (the trial of Brodsky in 1965, Sinyavsky and Daniel in
1967). Although the Soviet military invasion of Czechoslovakia (August 1968) that killed all hopes for "socialism with a human face" actually happened after the publication of the Strugatskys' "Tale"
(April–May 1968), it is easy to understand why "Tale of the Troika"
caused a virtual thunderstorm of administrative anger immediately
after the invasion. The very title of this text simultaneously refers to
the dread committees of three that replaced the entire justice system
during the period of the Great Terror, as well as to the three heads of
a dragon (already presented as three different individuals in Shvarts's
Dragon).

The three members of the Strugatskys' committee, plus their
chairman, reflect the different faces of Soviet totalitarianism and its
servants. Lavr Fedotovich Vuniukov smokes Stalin's favorite cigarettes,
but his inability to utter a coherent sentence anticipates Brezhnev's
notorious performances. Farfurkis, a "candidate of the oratorical
sciences," and Vybegallo, stuffing his speeches with senseless French
expressions, represent the new Soviet intelligentsia, "the best pupils"
of the regime, who totally sold out, abandoning their brains and cultivation for the advantages of administrative positions. Khlebovvodov,
on the other hand, is a favorite "positive character" of socialist realism, a man of the masses who has achieved the highest position on a
bureaucratic ladder thanks to "a high degree of tenacity and adaptability, based on his fundamental stupidity and an unwavering desire
to out-orthodox orthodoxy."

Significantly, the two representatives of the scientific intelligentsia sent by the institute on a mission—Sasha Privalov (a narrator in *Monday*) and the qualified magician Eddie Amperian—are, in fact, defeated in their attempts to curb the absurd activity of the Troika. The representatives of the intelligentsia are not immune to the bureaucratic machine that "[goes on] with deadening monotony." At the end of the story, Sasha Privalov's readiness to justify the Troika's absurdity in quasi-Hegelian terms recalls Charlemagne's rationalization of the Dragon's terror: "So what? People live this way too. Everything rational is actual, and everything actual is rational. And as long as it is rational, it must be good. And since it's good, it's probably eternal." A sad prediction of new compromises between the former rebels from the technocratic intelligentsia awakened by the Thaw and the new modifications of totalitarian power may be detected in the ironic finale of the "Tale."

The people. The Soviet cult of the masses as bearers of the banner of historical progress and representatives of every possible good was reinterpreted by Shvarts as the transformation of the people into a collective dragon, the invincible manifestation of totalitarianism. The investigation of the people's responsibility for tyranny was continued by Fazil Iskander (b. 1929) in his *Rabbits and Boa Constrictors* (1980). This fairy tale may be read as a sequel to *The Dragon*, for it poses the question: What happens with the people after they are liberated from totalitarian fear? Iskander's answer is incredibly bitter: without fear, their life turns into chaos; therefore they seek a new fear as a basis for "order" and are not comfortable until they find it. Although the imagery of *Rabbits and Boa Constrictors* recalls the tradition of animal tales and fables, its plot subverts the master plot of the fairy tale, blending it with the master plot of socialist realism.

Every folk fairy tale contains initial family disorder, trials that the characters have to undergo in order to acquire new values and maturity (these trials usually including a temporary death followed by rebirth), and a final family reunion or creation of a new family (through marriage). Such finales signify the restoration of the family cosmos on the basis of newly learned values. Iskander's story includes all these elements too, with a single exception: the family he is talking about is the Big Social Family—the basic archetype of socialist realism. The Big Family portrayed by Iskander is founded on the mutually beneficial symbiosis between victimizers (boa constrictors) and victims (rabbits). The "family" trouble starts when the rabbit named Ponderer makes a great discovery: he comes to the conclusion that the mysterious hypnotic ability of boa constrictors that paralyzes rabbits is nothing but rabbits' fear, and if a rabbit is not afraid, hypnosis does not work! After this discovery, rabbits start mocking boa constrictors and enjoy a freedom that very soon, however, turns into chaos. To restore "family harmony," the rabbits have to endure and pass tests that would reconfirm their "family values." These values are "the submissive reflex," a readiness to betray a fellow rabbit or the one who has liberated all the rabbits, and aspiration toward new forms of control and victimization—something very different from the humanistic interpretation of family values in a folk fairy tale. *Rabbits and Boa Constrictors* not only provides an allegorical analysis of the Russian people's moral corruption during the period of Stagnation, but also contains a deliberately ironic prognosis of a possible finale to the country's postcommunist development (after the 2000 presidential elections in Russia, this prognosis seems to be quite insightful).

A different approach to the same problem was suggested by Vasily Shukshin (1929–74) in his fairy tale "Before the Cock Crows Thrice" (published after the writer's death, in 1975). Probably the most talented representative of "village prose," Shukshin was more inclined to view the people as victims of totalitarian manipulation than as partly responsible for the crimes of the totalitarian regime. The satiric power of Shukshin's fairy tale may be appreciated fully only if one recognizes in its narrative the fairy-tale master plot of the "simple man's" maturation adopted by socialist realist aesthetics. In Shukshin's fairy tale the final goal of this process, the proof of the obligatory transformation from "spontaneity" to "consciousness," is replaced by a parodic requirement: the traditional folk protagonist Ivan the Fool is sent to the Wise Man for a certificate of intelligence. This bureaucratic procedure involves Ivan in a chain of fairy tale–like encounters: with Baba Yaga and her daughter, with the three-headed Zmei Gorynych, with devils that capture a monastery, with the Wise Man, and with the enchanted Princess Neverlaugh. The traditional fairy tale tests Ivan the Fool's moral qualities, just as the socialist realist master plot tests the ideals of the "simple man" and, above all, his devotion to the revolutionary cause.

In Shukshin's fairy tale, however, none of Ivan's counterparts cares about his qualities at all: they either want to use him as a free labor force, or, worse, to entertain themselves at his expense. The latter is the more painful for Ivan because he feels that his opponents intentionally humiliate him by abusing and objectifying his song and dance, something that he values very highly as the manifestations of his soul (or his anima, we might say). Thus, Ivan's "maturation" is absurd, since it constantly requires his humiliation and leads only to a greater degree of humiliation.

An important deviation from the folk paradigm is the finale of Shukshin's tale, which is open-ended, and thus at complete odds with the fairy-tale canon. The inconclusiveness of the fairy tale's quest reflects the writer's disillusionment with the dominant Soviet stereotypes of the people's "truth," as well as his (and the genre's) inability to redefine the people's "righteousness" in new terms.

The protagonist. The intellectual, a man of culture whom socialist realism depicts as the most suspect character and a potential enemy of the people, reappears in Shvarts's fairy tale as Lancelot (and as the Scholar in *The Shadow*), the faithful heir to world culture, whose cultural memory provides the sources for resistance and active struggle against totalitarian magic. In the fairy tales of the 1960s to the 1980s, similar features may be detected in Iskander's Ponderer, who dies for the sake of his fellow rabbits' moral liberation, and especially in Grigory Gorin's protagonist, Munchausen, from his play *That Very Munchausen*.

Rudolf Erich Raspe's (1737–94) version of the folktales about a fa-

mous liar, Baron Munchausen, who concocts stories about his fantastic adventures, is widely known and very popular in Russia, thanks
to a free translation by Korney Chukovsky. These tales belong to the
genre modification of the fairy tale that is called "jest." Jest "is unbelievable because it perverts everyday items and events. In other words,
the more unbelievable a tale, the more closely it must openly border
on reality . . . When the magical world loses its hold, jest flourishes
and mixes with almost every other genre to form new genres," writes
Lutz Röhrich, adding that the jest tale "freely plays with the tradition
of the saints sometimes disrespectfully" (Röhrich 52–54).

Written in 1976, Grigory Gorin's play about Baron Munchausen
perfectly fit the cultural situation of the Stagnation period, when the
"magical world" of totalitarian ideology indeed "lost its hold." Gorin
actualized "genre memory" of the jest by placing a legendary character within a quite realistically depicted setting of political and family
intrigues. In Gorin's play, Munchausen's jest reveals a deeply rooted
fear of freedom as the basis of the social order, although this order is
no longer explicitly totalitarian, but, rather, recalls the corrupt and
cynical Stagnation way of life. Moreover, Gorin developed the folk
jest's potential to play freely with the saintly tradition by writing subversive and ironic neo-romantic versions of hagiographies, wherein
the "jest" becomes the major proof of sainthood. Munchausen's saint-
liness is based on his ability to see unconventional truth and to believe
in it despite misunderstandings and direct pressures. This ability explains his "miracles."

Simultaneously, in accordance with hagiographic tradition, the
baron's paradoxical sainthood is tested by persecution and tempta-
tions, such as his "temporary death" (his suicide at the end of the first
act); his attempt to become an ordinary man—the gardener Miller
(following his failed suicide); and his final decision to prove his identification with the "posthumously" glorified Munchausen by the mortal risk of another flight to the moon (at the play's finale).

As mentioned earlier, the 1930s perceived fairy-tale discourse as the core of an alternative, Soviet religion. Gorin's play presents a paradoxical conclusion to this process, as the implicitly religious image of the anti-Soviet saint, a dissident who questions all societal postulates, is created by means of a fairy-tale jest, epitomized by mockery and parody. This return to the starting point of the fairy-tale formation of the Soviet anima—yet from the opposite side, that of the anti-totalitarian shadow—is very illuminating.

The satiric fairy tales of the 1960s and 1970s turned the entire paradigm of Soviet fairy-tale archetypes upside down. This process demonstrates the natural disintegration of totalitarian magic and the gradual liberation of culture from the archetypes of the totalitarian anima. Each and every significant element of the Soviet anima expressed through fairy-tale images was replaced by corresponding *shadow* images: monsters and impotent rulers instead of the nation's wise fathers; corrupt rabbits instead of victorious, heroic Soviet citizens; dissident saints instead of potential and actual "enemies of the people," the "rotten intelligentsia." The replacement of anima archetypes with the opposite *shadow* archetypes of the Soviet collective unconscious, however, did not destroy the fairy-tale structure of the Soviet imaginative world.

The vacuum left by the dissolution of the Soviet anima during the postcommunist period was filled by a newly emerged combination of totally negative imagery (so-called *chernukha*—dark and grim discourse) with fairy-tale structural patterns. This combination served as the core of post-Soviet political mythology and mass culture, and also infiltrated the realm of refined postmodernist literature and arts. Once again, the fairy-tale paradigm proved its ability to modify its "face" according to changes in the cultural and historical situation. In the 1990s that paradigm survived by giving up its anti-totalitarian powers. These were not amputated, but retreated into the deep layers of "genre memory" in order to surface when needed.

NOTE

1. On the function of the fairy tale's "genre memory" in Platonov's works, see Shubin, and Lipovetskii 78–84.

WORKS CITED

Bettelheim, Bruno. *The Uses of Enchantment: The Meaning and Importance of Fairy Tales.* New York: Alfred A. Knopf, 1976.
Binevich, E., ed. "Iz perepiski Evgeniia Shvartsa." *Voprosy literatury* 6 (1977): 217–32.
Clark, Katerina. *The Soviet Novel: History as Ritual.* Chicago: University of Chicago Press, 1980.
Csicsery-Ronay, Istvan. "Towards the Last Fairy Tale: On the Fairy-Tale Paradigm in the Strugatskys' Science Fiction, 1963–1972." *Science-Fiction Studies* 13, no. 1 (1986): 3–41.
Iskander, Fazil. *Rabbits and Boa Constrictors.* Trans. Ronald E. Peterson. Ann Arbor, Mich.: Ardis, 1989.
Jung, Carl Gustav. *The Essential Jung.* Selected and introduced by Anthony Storr. Princeton, N.J.: Princeton University Press, 1983.
Lipovetskii, Mark. *Poetika literaturnoi skazki (Na materiale russkoi literatury 1920–1980-kh godov).* Sverdlovsk: Izdatel'stvo Ural'skogo universiteta, 1992.
Novikova, A. M., and A. V. Kokorev, eds. *Russkoe narodnoe poeticheskoe tvorchestvo.* Moscow: Vysshaia shkola, 1969.
Propp, Vladimir. *Istoricheskie korni volshebnoi skazki.* Moscow: Labirint, 2000.
Röhrich, Lutz. *Folktales and Reality.* Trans. Peter Tokofsky. Bloomington: Indiana University Press, 1991.
Shubin, Lev. "Skazka ob usomnivshemsia Makare." *Literaturnoe obozrenie* 8 (1987): 46–54.

SUGGESTED READINGS

Aksenov, Vassily. *Surplussed Barrelware.* Ed. and trans. Joel Wilkinson and Slava Yastremski. Ann Arbor, Mich.: Ardis, 1985.
Csicsery-Ronay, Istvan. "Towards the Last Fairy Tale: On the Fairy-Tale Paradigm in the Strugatskys' Science Fiction, 1963–1972." *Science-Fiction Studies* 13, no. 1 (1986): 3–41.
Iskander, Fazil. *Rabbits and Boa Constrictors.* Trans. Ronald E. Peterson. Ann Arbor, Mich.: Ardis, 1989.
Lipovetskii, Mark. *Poetika literaturnoi skazki (Na materiale russkoi literatury 1920–1980-kh godov).* Sverdlovsk: Izdatel'stvo Ural'skogo universiteta, 1992.
Meletinskii, Eleazar. "Mif i skazka," "Skazka-anekdot v sisteme fol'klornykh zhanrov." In *Izbrannye stat'i Vospominaniia.* Moscow: Rossiiskii gosudarstvennyi gumanitarnyi universitet, 1998.

———. *O literaturnykh arkhetipakh*. Moscow: Rossiiskii gosudarstvennyi gumani-tarnyi universitet, 1994.

Oinas, Felix J. "The Political Uses and Themes of Folklore in The Soviet Union." *Journal of the Folklore Institute* 12 (1975): 157–75.

Olesha, Yury. *Complete Short Stories and Three Fat Men*. Trans. Aimee Anderson. Ann Arbor, Mich.: Ardis, 1979.

Propp, Vladimir. *Istoricheskie korni volshebnoi skazki*. Moscow: Labirint, 2000.

Shvarts, Evgeny. *The Naked King, The Shadow, The Dragon*. London: Boyars, 1976.

Strugatsky, Arkady, and Boris Strugatsky. *Monday Begins on Saturday*. New York: Daw Books. 1978.

Tsvetaeva, Marina. "Molodets," "Pereulochki," "Tsar'-devitsa." In *Sobranie sochinenii* v 7 tt., 3:190–340. Ed. Lev Mnukhin and Anna Saakiants. Moscow: Ellis Lak, 1994.

Urban, Michael E., and John McClure. "The Folklore of State Socialism: Semiotics and the Study of the Soviet State." *Soviet Studies* 35, no. 4 (1983): 471–86.

Vaiskopf, Mikhail. "Morfologiia strakha." *Novoe literaturnoe obozrenie* 24 (1997): 53–58.

Voinovich, Vladimir. *The Life and Extraordinary Adventures of Private Ivan Chonkin*. Trans. Richard Lourie. New York: Farrar, Straus and Giroux, 1977.

Von Franz, Marie-Lousie. *The Interpretation of Fairy Tales*. Rev. ed. Boston and London: Shambhala, 1996.

———. *Shadow and Evil in Fairy Tales*. Rev. ed. Boston and London: Shambhala, 1995.

Vysotskii, Vladimir. "Lukomor'ia bol'she net," "Pro dikogo vepria," "O nechisti," "Pro dzhinna," "O neschastnykh skazochnykh personazhakh." Songs for the production of *Alice in Wonderland*. In Vladimir Vysotskii, *Izbrannoe*, ed. N. A. Krymova, 49–56, 308–20, 334–50. Moscow: Sovetskii pisatel', 1988.

FAIRY TALES FOR GROWN-UP CHILDREN
꒰꒱

EXCERPTS

Yevgeny Zamyatin

THE IVANS

And then there was this village called Ivanikha, where all the peasants were named Ivan, but with different nicknames: Ivan Self-Eater (gnawed his own ear off in his sleep), Ivan the Frenzied, Ivan Buttin-sky, Ivan the Salty-Eared, Ivan Off-the-Deep-End, Ivan Out-Spitter: too many to count. Out-Spitter was the main one. Now, some people would plow, or sow, but the Ivans would just lie sprawled, belly-up, and spit at the sky to see who could outspit the others.

"Hey, you! Ivans! Why don't you sow some wheat?"

But the Ivans would just tssst! through their teeth.

"I heard they got some real wheat in the new lands, first-rate stuff, with grains as big as cucumbers. Now that's wheat . . ."

And then they'd go back to seeing who could outspit the others.

They were lying there just like that when good fortune fell on the Ivans from who knows where. They heard hoofbeats on the road and saw a pillar of dust. A rider was galloping through Ivanikha with an announcement: any Ivan who wants to go to the new lands is welcome to do so.

The Ivans crossed themselves, grabbed on to the horse's tail with all their might, and they were off, everything flashing before their eyes: a church, a field, a field, a church.

The rider dropped them off. There were no houses or anything for a hundred versts, just an empty patch with nettles in the middle of it. But what nettles they were: as big around as bottles, and you'd lose your hat looking up at the tops of them. And if you got stung, you'd have blisters the size of fifty-kopek pieces. The Ivans scratched at the earth: it was as black as cobbler's pitch and as rich as cow's butter.

"All right, brothers, drop your packs: it's first-rate, for sure."

They sat in a circle and chewed some hardtack with salt. They wanted a drink before settling in to work, so they started looking all over, but there was no water. So they had to dig a well: what else could they do?

They set to it. The earth was light and crumbly and flew in clumps. Out-Spitter kept stopping and squinting.

"Hey, brothers, the water here must be just as good: sweeter'n anything we're used to . . ."

Right then there was the sound of iron on stone: clink! It was quite a rock. They turned it over and a spring squirted right up. They scooped some and drank: cold and pure, but water just like any other.

Out-Spitter just spat through his teeth: tsst!

"We got as much of this stuff as we want in Ivanikha. Dig deeper: there must be some first-rate water here, not like this . . ."

They dug and dug till long after dark, but there was more of the same. They tossed and turned under the nettles all night, and in the morning went back to digging. The well was getting mighty deep now, and they started to see these filthy worms: pink, naked, and with snouts. They dug and dug some more, stopping sometimes to think. They could barely hear Out-Spitter shouting from above:

"Deeper, brothers! You're nearly there!"

They finally reached some sort of crusty layer, too hard for the shovel, and the water got in the way, lots of water, but still just like in Ivanikha. They banged on the crust with a crowbar and heard a hollow boom, like from a barrel: maybe it was a cave. They banged harder, and suddenly it all came crashing down with a roar: the water, the rubble, the clumps of earth, and all their tools. Blinded by dust and deafened by the noise, they barely managed to grab on to a ledge.

The Ivans wiped their eyes and looked under their feet . . . Good Lord! There was a hole, and in the hole there was blue sky. They looked up and could barely see the blue sky shining in the distance. Good Lord: they had picked their way right through the earth!

They lost their nerve and started to climb up, caps in hand: Self-Eater on Frenzied's shoulders, Frenzied on Buttinsky, Buttinsky on Salty-Ears, Salty-Ears on Off-the-Deep-End, and finally they reached the top.

The first thing they did was to beat up Out-Spitter. Then they put their belongings in their packs and headed back to Ivanikha: what could they do without water or tools? Their only consolation was the clump of earth each took back with him.

They showed their neighbors, but the neighbors weren't buying it: "Tell me another one! If there was earth like that there, why'd you come back?"

But they couldn't tell nobody about how they'd dug right through the earth, or they'd get laughed out of town. So the Ivans got a reputation for being liars, and to this day nobody believes that they've been to the new lands. But they have.

THE ANGEL DORMIDON

There was this foolish angel by the name of Dormidon. Now, everyone knows that angels come from Divine respiration: the Lord takes a breath, and there's an angel, He takes another breath, another angel. But in this case the weather was foul, so He sneezed, and an angel flew out from the force of it. That's why he was so ungainly. Huge mug, eyes that darted back and forth, back and forth, and on his left hand, an amethyst pinky ring. Does that sound like any angel you ever heard of? And the way he acted: he'd do everything in a rush, off the cuff, and then collapse for a snooze. They tolerated him in heaven, mostly out of kindness.

They assigned the foolish angel Dormidon a peasant to look after. The peasant was also a fine one: a rowdy drunk.

So he follows after this peasant of his, Dormidon does, in and out of all the taverns—all to no use.

"Well, if that's how it is," thought Dormidon, "I'll just get you blind drunk and then make you repent right away."

So he whispers in the peasant's ear:

"Go ahead, brother, knock back another! Come on, have one more!"

And the peasant starts running through the village in a state, without his pants, looking for a brawl. He didn't have the strength, but he was holding a chain, so he starts chasing after his own shadow with the chain.

Meanwhile Dormidon was hiding behind a gatepost with the peasant's brother, both of them holding their bellies:

"Ha, ha, ha! Give it to 'im, that's it! Go on, get 'im!"

The peasant ran toward them and his shadow dove through the gate. The peasant went after it:

"You're chuggling at me, huh, you damned thing? Stop right there . . . !"

And he swings the chain with all his might. You can't hurt an angel, but the peasant's brother fell over dead like a stalk of wheat.

The foolish angel flew off with the news: something happened, and so forth. They really chewed him out, as well they should have, but he just stood there and twisted his amethyst ring: like water off a duck's back.

"So, Dormidon," said God, "now go and do whatever you want, walk for twenty years if you have to, but make sure you bring that peasant to me here in heaven."

"Eh, Lord, what gives? D'you think I won't bring him? Me?" And he went back to earth, to his peasant.

It was market day. He and the peasant went to buy planks for his brother's coffin and a rope to lower the coffin into the grave.

The peasant was sober-like and angry as all hell. He barks at Dormidon:

"You're really gettin' under my skin, you burdock on a dog's tail! How long're you gonna follow me?"

Dormidon acted like he hadn't heard, and just twisted his ring. But one thought stuck in his head like a nail: how to ditch the peasant once and for all?

Lo and behold, a gypsy passed by, dragging a pig along by a lasso. The pig was squealing and digging in his heels. The rope was long and white.

Dormidon saw the gypsy with his pig and slapped himself on the forehead: there it is, folks . . . ! And he whispers into the peasant's ear:

"Buy that rope. Go on, buy it. Look at what a fine rope it is, you'll never find another like it."

So the peasant buys it. And as soon as he and Dormidon reach the pasture—you know, the one behind the market—Dormidon grabs the gypsy's lasso, throws it around the peasant's neck, and starts dragging him along.

The peasant yells:

"Hey, fella! Lemme go, good man! My brother's just lying there, all unburied. Where you taking me?"

But Dormidon thinks it's funny. He guffaws and says:

"Are you through? Are you through? Noooooo, you won't get away! I'll drag you straight to heaven!"

The peasant kicked up a fuss for a while, but finally sat down on the ground like a log, just you try and pry him loose.

Dormidon scratched his head and spat on his hands. He had some heft to him, so he held the lasso more tightly and soared upwards with the peasant. He kept moving faster, the wind whistling. He didn't even glance back at the peasant, and the lasso felt heavy, like the peasant had quieted down: all the better.

Dormidon flew into heaven all out of breath and grinning from ear to ear, pleased.

"Twenty years, they said! Here's your peasant. I brought him to heaven."

They took a look: the peasant lay there, limp as could be, all blue with his tongue sticking out. He was finished.

The Lord flew into such a rage—like no one in hell had ever seen before:

"Brought him to heaven? You're an idiot, a complete idiot! Get out of here! Make yourself scarce!"

They clipped Dormidon's wings and banished him to earth. Until, you know, he earns his place with the angels again.

CHOMPER

There was a huge quake—and stars poured down from above like ripe pears. The heavenly firmament emptied out like a yellowed autumn field: the wind whistled bleakly over the yellow stubble, and on the edge, on the far road, two black human gnats crawled along. That was the sun and the moon crawling through the empty sky, as black as the velvet raiment at Good Friday services, black so the Resurrection would shine more brightly.

Right then Chomper set off across the earth. He hobbled on his bearish feet, first the right foot, then the left. His head was a dead boar's head—white, pinched, and bald—but with straight locks down the back to his shoulders, like a pilgrim. And on his belly, a face, like a human's, with squinting eyes, and in the very spot humans have navels, there was a gaping maw.

Old man Kochetyg was plowing a winter field. Coarse cotton trousers, hempen shirt, hair tied back with a string to keep it out of his eyes. The old man looked up at the sky: terrifying. But the plowing had to be done. That's just the way it is.

Chomper ran into the old man from behind: Chomper had eyes, but only for appearances; he couldn't open them to make out where he was going and why.

"Who're you?" he says to the old man. He spoke from his belly, from that gaping maw where humans have navels. "What're you doing in my way?" He opened another maw, the wild-boar one, and Chomp! All that he left above ground was the old man's shoes.

You could barely hear the old man's voice, like it was underground:

"What about the wheat? There won't be any wheat . . ."

And Chomper says through his belly:

"I don't give a damn . . ." And the old man was gone.

The little girl Olenka was picking flowers by a forest cutting, the first spring bluebells. You could see her bare feet flashing white among the bluebells, and she herself was like a golden bell, bursting forth with a song about a mother-in-law and a dashing groom: it tugged at your heart.

Chomper stumbled over Olenka:

"What're you doing in my way?" And then Chomp! Only her heels kicked, all white.

Olenka scarcely managed to cry out from deep within:

"My song . . ."

"I don't give a damn . . ." Chomper belly-bellowed and swallowed the last of her, white heels and all.

Chomper left a void wherever he went, leaving only piles of droppings in his wake.

Well, it would have been the end of humanity on earth if not for this one man, a peddler with an ordinary name, something like Petrov or Sidorov, nothing special about him, just a quick-thinking Yaroslavl man.

The peddler noticed that Chomper never turned around, but just kept moving forward, that he *couldn't* turn around.

So he snuck up behind Chomper with his Yaroslavl smirk. It wasn't very pleasant back there, of course: you couldn't breathe, knee-deep in them piles. But it was for a solid cause.

After the Yaroslavl peddler, others caught on, too: soon they were walking single file behind Chomper like a regular church procession. And only the fools, the utter idiots, didn't rush to hide from Chomper behind Chomper's back.

Chomper made short work of the idiots and then died of starvation, naturally. And the people of Yaroslavl began a life of ease, for the Lord God rewarded them: the earth was rich and bountiful from the droppings. There'll be a fine harvest.

THE FIRST TALE OF FITA

Fita appeared spontaneously in the basement of the police station. Old, closed cases were kept in the basement in stacks, and Officer Ulyan Petrovich listened as someone kept scraping and knocking down there. Ulyan Petrovich opened the door—there was so much dust you'd never quit sneezing—and out stepped Fita, all gray with dust. His sex was predominantly male, and a red wax seal with a number dangled on a string. He was still just a babe, but had the look of a respectable man: bald, with a little paunch, a court counselor through and through. And his face wasn't a face, but . . . in a word, Fita.

Officer Ulyan Petrovich took an immediate liking to Fita: the officer adopted Fita and sat him right in the corner, in the office, and Fita thrived in the corner. He fished old reports and memoranda one after another out of the basement and hung them in frames all over his corner. He lit a candle, bowed, and prayed to them steadily; only that seal kept dangling.

One time Ulyan Petrovich came in and there was Fita, hunched over the inkwell, slurping.

"Hey, Fitka! Whatcha doin' that for, you stinker?"

"The ink," he said, "I drink it. I have my needs, too."

"Go on and drink it, then. It's government ink."

So Fita lived on ink.

And it got to the point—it's silly to say it, even—where Fita'd dunk the pen in his mouth and write, from his own mouth, with actual ink, just like they have in every police station. And all the while Fita kept scrawling out all sorts of reports, memoranda, and orders and hanging them in his corner.

"Hey, Fita," the officer, Fita's adoptive father, said one day, "you oughta be governor."

It was a tough year, what with both the cholera and the famine and all.

Fita didn't waste any time. He rolled into the main town, called the citizens together, and let loose:

"What's this you've got here? Cholera? Famine? I'll show you! What've you been looking at? What've you done?"

The townsfolk scratched their heads:

"Yeah, well, we didn't do anything. The doctors treated the cholera some. We oughta get some more bread from the neighbors up the road . . ."

"I'll give you doctors! I'll give you neighbors!" Fita dunked his pen and wrote:

"Order No. 666. On this date, having properly assumed executive duties, I hereby strictly abolish famine in the province. Citizens are hereby ordered to be full forthwith. Fita."

"Order No. 667. On this date I hereby order an end to cholera, effective immediately. In light of the aforementioned order, all those who without authorization call themselves doctors are hereby dismissed. Those who illegally declare themselves to be sick are subject to corporal punishment under the law. Fita."

The orders were read out in the churches and posted on all the fences. The townsfolk held a prayer service to give thanks, and on the same day erected a monument to Fita in the market square. And Fita—stolid, bald, paunchy Fita—would stroll about his own monument without his hat.

One day passed, and then another. On the third . . . lo and behold, a cholera sufferer showed up right in Fita's office: he stood there writhing in pain—the folk don't know their own worth. Fita ordered him flogged, the punishment required by law. But the cholera patient left and died in a most anti-governmental fashion.

And they kept coming and coming to die, of cholera, of famine, and eventually there weren't enough policemen to deal with the criminals.

The townsfolk put their heads together and decided en masse to bring back the doctors and send for bread from their neighbors. As for Fita, they dragged him out of his office and taught him a lesson in their own peasant way, the way of a dark, uneducated folk.

They say that Fita's end was just as unreal as his beginning: he didn't shout or nothing, just got smaller and smaller as he melted like a blow-up American devil. All that was left of him was an ink spot and that wax seal with the number.

So Fita met his end. But before that he managed to do so many amazing things that you couldn't name them all in one breath.

THE SECOND TALE OF FITA

Fita had abolished cholera by decree. The townsfolk did round dances and prospered. And Fita would go out among the people twice a day to chat with the coachmen and at the same time admire the monument.

"So, my brothers, who's the monument to?"

"Why, it's mister executive Fita, sir!"

"Ah, of course it is. Is there anything you need? I can do anything, in no time at all."

The coachmen's bureau was right near the cathedral. One coachman took a look at the monument, and then at the cathedral, and he spoke to Fita.

"We was talking yesterday, see, about how it's getting awful inconvenient for us to drive around the cathedral. If there was a way to go straight across the square . . ."

Fita's mind was swift as a bullet. He went right to his office, sat at his desk, and it was done:

"The existing municipal cathedral of unknown origin is hereby ordered to be destroyed forthwith. A straight transport road for Messrs. coachmen will be installed on the site of the aforementioned cathedral. In the interest of avoiding prejudices, the work in question will be assigned to Saracens. Signed, Fita."

In the morning the townsfolk were dumbfounded: look at our cathedral, folks! Crawling with Saracens from top to bottom, on all five cupolas, on the cross, and along the walls like flies. All black and naked, with just a rope to gird their loins, kicking up dust with their saws and their awls and their hooks and their battering rams.

And soon the blue cupolas were gone, along with the silver stars painted on top of the blue, and the ancient red brick showed through like blood on the white-breasted walls.

The townsfolk were beside themselves with tears:

"Father Fita, our benefactor, have mercy! It's better that we go around! Good Lord, our cathedral!"

Fita strutted about, steady, with his little paunch, and looked at the Saracens. They were a pleasure to watch as they busily went about their work. Fita stopped in front of the townsfolk, hands in his pockets:

"What odd ducks you are, citizens! I did it for the people, after all. Transport road improvement for the coachmen is an urgent necessity, but what is that cathedral of yours? Just a trifle."

Then the townsfolk remembered that it wasn't so long ago that the Mongol khan Mamai came and threatened the cathedral, and that he had been bought off. Maybe, they thought, we can buy off Fita, too. They sent a tribute to Fita in his storeroom: three of the most beautiful maidens and a gallon of ink.

Fita lit up and stomped in anger at the citizens:

"Get out! And take your Maaaamaaaai with you! Mamai was a muh-mumbling ninny! I gave you my decision. Amen!"

And he waved his hand at the Saracens: keep it up, brothers, fast as you can. It's already getting late.

By sundown all that remained of the cathedral was rubble. Fita chalked out the path of the straight road with his own hand. All night the Saracens kept busy, and toward morning a road lay across the market square, straight and fine to look at.

At the beginning and end of the road they erected posts painted a yellowish black, like police boxes, and wrote an inscription on them: "In such and such a year and date a cathedral of unknown origin was demolished by acting executive Fita. This road, which shortened the route of the coachmen by fifty yards, was also constructed by Fita."

The market square had finally been whipped into proper shape.

THE THIRD TALE OF FITA

The citizens were on especially good behavior, so at five o'clock in the afternoon Fita proclaimed freedom, and dismissed the policemen for good. From five o'clock in the afternoon on, there were free towns-folk standing everywhere: in front of the police department and at every intersection and police box.

The townsfolk crossed themselves:

"Holy Mother of God! What have we come to? Look at the police-man standing there in regular clothes!"

And the main thing was that the freemen in regular clothes knew their trade, like purebred policemen. They dragged people to the sta-tion, and at the station they'd give it to 'em in the snout and in the gut, all proper-like. The townsfolk wept with joy:

"Praise the Lord! It's happened! That's not just anybody beating them in there, it's our folks, the freemen. Hold on, brothers, let me take off my coat: it'll be easier to get my back that way. Go ahead, brothers! That's the way! Praise the Lord!"

The townsfolk tripped all over each other to sit in jail: it was so good in there now, finer than words can describe. They'd search you, and lock you up, and stare at you through the peephole: all of them our folks, the freemen: Praise the Lord . . .

Soon, though, there weren't enough places, and they started let-ting only certain honored citizens into the jail. And the rest of the peo-ple stood outside the entrance all night long to buy tickets to jail from scalpers.

What sort of order is that?! Fita wrote a decree:

"I hereby order all thieves and killers to be driven from the jail in disgrace to the four corners of the earth."

So they drove the thieves and killers to the four corners of the earth, and all citizens who so desired gradually moved into the jail.

The streets were empty: only the freemen in regular clothes were left; something wasn't quite right. Fita issued a new decree:

"Citizens are hereby granted the obligatory freedom to conduct songs and processions in national costumes."

We all know that it's not easy to go with something new. So to make things easier some unknown people gave each citizen (by signed receipt) sample song lyrics. But still the townsfolk were shy, and hid in nooks and crannies: what ignorant folk!

Fita let the freemen in regular clothes loose in the nooks and crannies, and the freemen urged the citizens not to be shy, for there was freedom now; they urged them in the back of the neck and in the ribs, and finally they convinced them.

In the evening it was like Easter . . . No, better than Easter! Specially invited nightingales sang everywhere. The townsfolk marched in platoons in their national costumes, each platoon accompanied by freemen with a cannon. The townsfolk sang jubilantly, in one voice, following the sample song lyrics:

> *Glory, glory to you, our kind tsar.*
> *Fita, our ruler, our gift from God.*

And acting executive Fita would bow from the balcony.

In light of the unprecedented success, the townsfolk right then and there, under Fita's balcony, under the direction of the freemen, with unanimous delight, resolved to introduce daily regimental freedom to sing songs from one to two o'clock.

That night Fita slept peacefully for the first time: the citizens were obviously learning fast.

THE LAST TALE OF FITA

There was also a sage apothecary in the town: he made a person not like us sinners, but in a glass jar. Was there anything he didn't know?

Fita ordered the apothecary to be brought before him.

"Be so kind as to tell me: why do my citizens walk around bored during nonworking hours?"

The sage apothecary peered into windows: some houses had skates, some had roosters, some townsfolk wore pants, some wore skirts.

"It's very simple," he said to Fita. "What kind of order is this? Everything should be the same, all around."

And so. All the townsfolk were marched in formation out of town and into a pasture. Fires were set on all four sides of the empty town, and everything was gutted to cinders, leaving only a black patch with the monument to Fita in the middle.

The saws sawed and the hammers banged all night. By morning it was done: a barracks, like a cholera ward, seven and three-quarter versts in length, with numbered stalls along the sides. Every citizen got a brass plate with a shiny new number on it, and a gray uniform made out of heavy cloth.

Everyone was lined up along the corridor, each in front of his stall, a numbered plate on his belt shining like a firebird, everyone identical, like new coins. It was so fine that even Fita, who was made of iron, felt a tickle in his nose, and there was nothing more to say: he waved his hand and went into his stall, no. 1. Thank the Lord: now he had everything he'd ever wished for, and could die . . .

In the morning, at daybreak, before the first wake-up bell even, someone knocked on the door to no. 1:

"Deputies here to see your honor regarding an urgent matter."

Fita came out: there were four men in uniform, respectable citizens, elderly and bald. They bowed deeply to Fita.

"Who sent you, deputies?"

All four respectable citizens piped in at once: "What's all this, then—it's not right at all, what kind of order is this . . . We represent the baldies. That apothecary's walking around curly-headed, the others have fancy haircuts, but us, we're all bald-headed? Noooo, it's not right at all . . ."

Fita thought and thought: can't make everyone identical by giving them curls, so the only thing to do's to equalize them all with bald heads. So he signaled to the Saracens, and they flew in a flash from every corner of the town. They shaved every head as bare as a knee, both male and female. The sage apothecary looked especially strange, like a cat soaked to the skin.

They hadn't finished shearing everyone when again some deputies came and again demanded to see Fita. Fita came out looking gloomy: what the hell was it now?

And the deputies:

"Guh-guh!" said one, into his sleeve. "Guh-guh!" said another. They were all wet-nosed.

"Who sent you?" Fita growled.

"We, uh, this . . . Guh! We come, Your Honor, from the idiots. Guh! We wants, that, uh, that everybody's . . . equal . . .

Fita went back into no. 1 in a dark mood. He found the apothecary.

"Did you hear, brother?"

"I heard . . ." said the apothecary in a meek little voice. His head was wrapped in a chintz kerchief, since he wasn't used to the cold after his shearing. "What do we do now?"

"What can we do? There's no going back."

The decree was read out to the citizens before morning prayers: starting tomorrow, all citizens without exception will be utter idiots.

The townsfolk sighed, but what can you do: would you go up against the powers-that-be? They sat down hastily to read all the smart books for the last time, and everyone read until the last evening bell. At the bell they went to bed, and in the morning everyone woke up an idiot. And the merriment knew no bounds. They started to elbow one another: "Guh-guh!"—that was the whole conversation.

Now the freemen in regular clothes kept bringing the kasha in troughs, coarse barley kasha.

Fita strolled along the corridor—seven and three-quarter versts—and saw that everyone was happy. What a relief: it was done. He embraced the sage apothecary in his corner:

"Thanks for the advice, brother. I'll never forget it."

And the apothecary to Fita: "Guh!"

So it ended up that Fita was the only one left: one man to think for all the others.

Fita locked himself in stall no. 1 to do just that, to think, when someone was at the door. Not knocking this time, but breaking it down and forcing their way in, yelling something incomprehensible.

"Ehhhh, brother, you won't get off that easy. We may be idiots, but we unnerstand things. You gotta get stupid, too. Or else you'll . . . no way, brother!"

Fita lay down on the bed and cried. But what could he do?

"All right, God save you. Give me till the morrow."

Fita knocked about all day among the idiots, all the while getting stupider and stupider. Toward morning, he was ready: "Guh-guh!"

And they started living a happy life. There's no one on earth happier than an utter idiot.

1922

THE DRAGON:
A SATIRIC FABLE IN THREE ACTS
☙❧

EXCERPTS

Yevgeny Shvarts

Characters

LANCELOT

MR. CAT

CHARLEMAGNE, KEEPER OF RECORDS

ELSA, HIS DAUGHTER

SIR DRAGON

BURGOMASTER

HENRY, HIS SON, ALSO FOOTMAN-
   SECRETARY TO SIR DRAGON

CITIZENS

SENTRY

JAILER

BOY

GUESTS

GARDENER

ELSA'S THREE GIRLFRIENDS

CLERKS

FOOTMEN

WEAVERS

BLACKSMITH

MASTER HATMAKER

MASTER OF MUSICAL
   INSTRUMENTS

ACT 1

[*The scene is laid in a spacious but cozy kitchen. It is very clean. There is a large hearth in the rear. The floor is made of stone and has a brilliant polish to it.* MR. CAT *is dozing in an armchair in front of the hearth. Enter* LANCELOT.]

LANCELOT [*walks in, looks around, and calls out*]: Master Innkeeper! Mistress Innkeeper! Is there anyone here? Not a soul . . . The house is empty, the gates are open, the doors are ajar, the windows unlatched. It's a good thing I'm an honest man or I'd be in a dither right now, looking around for the most valuable thing to grab and then make my getaway as fast as I could. Whereas actually what I really want is to get a little rest.

[*He sits down.*]

I'll wait. Ah, Mr. Cat! Are your masters coming back soon? What? You won't speak?

MR. CAT: No, I won't speak.

LANCELOT: Why not? Will you tell me that?

MR. CAT: When you're in a soft, warm spot it's wiser to doze and keep your mouth shut.

LANCELOT: Yes, of course, but where are your masters?

MR. CAT: They went out, and that suits me perfectly.

LANCELOT: Don't you love them?

MR. CAT: I love them with every hair on my body, with my paws, with my whiskers, but they're threatened with a great disaster. The only time I have any peace of mind is when they leave the premises.

LANCELOT: So, that's how it is. But what threatens them? What kind of threat is it? You won't say?

MR. CAT: That's right, I won't.

LANCELOT: Why?

MR. CAT: When you're in a soft, warm spot, it's better to doze and keep your mouth shut, rather than worry about any unpleasant future. Mee-ow.

LANCELOT: Now you've got me worried. It's so cozy here in the kitchen. I simply can't believe that this nice place, this handsome house, is threatened by any catastrophe. Mr. Cat! What's happened here? Answer me! Come on!

MR. CAT: Don't disturb the peace, Stranger.

LANCELOT: Listen, Mr. Cat. You don't know who I am. I'm a weight-less man, as light as thistledown, and I'm carried all over the world. I love to interfere in other people's affairs. As a result, I've been slightly wounded nineteen times, seriously wounded five times, and thrice I've been mortally wounded. But I'm still alive, and that's because I'm not only as light as thistledown, but also as stubborn as a mule. So, now, tell me, Mr. Cat, what's happened here? It might turn out all of a sudden that I can rescue your masters. That's been done. Well? Come on, now! What's your name?

MR. CAT: Minnie.

LANCELOT: I thought you were—a tom.

MR. CAT: Yes, I am, but people are so unobservant . . . My masters still wonder why I don't have kittens. They say: What's the matter with you, Minnie? But they're sweet, the poor, uninformed creatures! Now I shan't say another word.

LANCELOT: But, please, just tell me—who are your masters?

MR. CAT: He's Charlemagne, Keeper of Records, and she's his only daughter, Elsa, who's got the gentlest little paws and is so sweet and quiet.

LANCELOT: Is she threatened?

MR. CAT: Alas, yes, and so are we all.

LANCELOT: What's she threatened by? Go on . . .

MR. CAT: Mee-ow! You see, it's now four hundred years since a dragon settled in our city.

LANCELOT: A dragon? That's fine!

MR. CAT: He exacts a tribute from us. Every year he chooses a young girl. And we, without a single mee-ow, hand her over to the Dragon. He carries her off to his cave and we never see her again. They say they all die of loathing. F-fpfpt! Skat! F-f-f-t!

LANCELOT: Whom are you speaking to?

MR. CAT: The Dragon. Because he's chosen our Elsa! The damned lizard! F-f-f-t!

LANCELOT: How many heads does he have?

MR. CAT: Three.

LANCELOT: That's a troika. And paws?

MR. CAT: Four.

LANCELOT: I expected as much. What about claws?

MR. CAT: He's got five on each paw.

LANCELOT: Nothing unusual there. Are they sharp?

MR. CAT: As knives.

LANCELOT: And does he breathe fire?

MR. CAT: He certainly does.

LANCELOT: You mean real flames?

MR. CAT: They burn down forests.

LANCELOT: I see. Is he covered with scales?

MR. CAT: He is.

LANCELOT: Thick ones?

MR. CAT: Absolutely.

LANCELOT: How thick?

MR. CAT: You can't scratch them with a diamond. Not that I ever tried.

LANCELOT: How big is he?

MR. CAT: As big as a church.

LANCELOT: Well, I see it all now. Thanks, Mr. Cat.

MR. CAT: Will you fight him?

LANCELOT: I might.

MR. CAT: I implore you to challenge him. Of course, he'll do you in, but before that happens, while we're lying here in front of the hearth, we can dream about a miracle by which somehow or other, this way or that, perhaps, maybe, all of a sudden, it might just turn out that you kill him, after all.

LANCELOT: Thanks, Mr. Cat.

MR. CAT: Pssst, pssst!

LANCELOT: What is it?

MR. CAT: They're coming.

LANCELOT: If only I find her attractive! If only I like her! That would be a great help . . . Ah!

[*He looks out of the window.*]

I do like her! Mr. Cat, she's a fine girl! But, look, Mr. Cat, what's this? She's smiling! She's completely calm! And her father's even got a cheery look on his face. Have you been fooling me?

MR. CAT: No, indeed. That's the saddest part of it all—they smile. Hush. I haven't said a word! . . .

[*Enter* ELSA *and* CHARLEMAGNE.]

LANCELOT: How do you do, sir, and charming lady?

CHARLEMAGNE: How do you do, young man?

ELSA: Good day to you, sir.

LANCELOT: Your home looked so inviting, the gates were open, a fire was burning in the kitchen, so I walked in without any invitation. Please excuse me.

CHARLEMAGNE: No need for that. Our doors are open to all . . .

ELSA: Do sit down. Give me your hat and I'll hang it behind the door. I'll set the table right away . . .

[LANCELOT *looks at her intently.*]

What's the matter?

LANCELOT: Oh, nothing.

ELSA: I rather thought . . . well, you frightened me.

LANCELOT: No, no . . . I always look at people that way.

CHARLEMAGNE: Take a seat, my friend. I love strangers. I suppose it's because my whole life I've never stirred out of this town. Where do you come from?

LANCELOT: From far, far away.

CHARLEMAGNE: And did you have many adventures along the way?

LANCELOT: Alas, yes, more than I liked.

ELSA: You must be tired. Do sit down.

LANCELOT: Thank you.

CHARLEMAGNE: You can have a good rest here. This is a very quiet town. Nothing ever happens here.

LANCELOT: Not ever?

CHARLEMAGNE: Never. Well, to be sure, last week we did have a high wind. The roof was nearly blown off one of the houses. But that's not really much of an event.

ELSA: Supper's on the table. Please take your places. What's the matter?

LANCELOT: You must excuse me, but . . . you say this is a very quiet town?

ELSA: Of course.

LANCELOT: But . . . I've heard tales about . . .

[MR. CAT *turns over.*]

I've read something about a Dragon.

CHARLEMAGNE: Oh, that . . . Well, we're so used to him. He's been living here for four hundred years.

LANCELOT: But . . . they told me . . . that your daughter . . .

ELSA: Sir Stranger . . .

LANCELOT: My name's Lancelot.

ELSA: Sir Lancelot, then, forgive me and believe me I don't mean to give any orders, but I'm asking you not to say a word about that.

LANCELOT: Why not?

ELSA: Because there's nothing to be done about it.

LANCELOT: Is that really so?

CHARLEMAGNE: Yes, there's nothing we can do. We've just been strolling around in the woods and we talked it over in minute detail. Tomorrow, as soon as the Dragon takes her away, I'll die.

ELSA: Papa, don't speak about it.

CHARLEMAGNE: That's all there is to say. That's all . . .

LANCELOT: Excuse me. I've one more question. Has no one ever tried to fight him?

CHARLEMAGNE: Not for the last two hundred years. Before that there were frequent attempts, but he killed all of his attackers. He's an astounding strategist and a great tactician. He attacks his enemy suddenly, showering him with stones from above, then he hurls himself down right onto the head of his opponent's steed, sears him with flames, and completely demoralizes the poor beast. Then he tears the rider to pieces with his claws. So you can understand why finally people have stopped opposing him . . .

LANCELOT: Did the whole city ever attack him?

CHARLEMAGNE: It did.

LANCELOT: What happened?

CHARLEMAGNE: He burned up the suburbs and half the population went berserk from poisonous fumes. He's a great fighter.

ELSA: Do help yourself to the butter.

LANCELOT: Yes, yes, I'll have some. I have to build up my strength. And so—please forgive me for pressing you with questions—no one is even trying to challenge the Dragon anymore? He's grown completely arrogant?

CHARLEMAGNE: Heavens, no! He's very kind.

LANCELOT: *Kind?*

CHARLEMAGNE: I assure you, he is. When our city was threatened with an epidemic of cholera, the municipal physician asked him to breathe fire on the lake. The whole town was saved from the cholera. Everybody had boiled water to drink.

LANCELOT: Was that long ago?

CHARLEMAGNE: Oh, not at all. It was only eighty-two years ago, but a good deed like that isn't forgotten.

LANCELOT: What other good deeds has he ever done for you?

CHARLEMAGNE: Ah . . . let's see . . . well . . . he got rid of the gypsies for us.

LANCELOT: But, gypsies are such nice people.

CHARLEMAGNE: What are you saying?! How terrible! Of course, I've never seen a single gypsy, but I learned at school what dreadful people they are.

LANCELOT: How so?

CHARLEMAGNE: They're vagabonds by nature. It's in their blood. They're enemies of any organized government. Otherwise they'd have settled down and wouldn't be wandering all over the place. Their songs lack virility and their ideas are destructive. They steal children.

ELSA: That's what they say.

CHARLEMAGNE: They infiltrate everywhere. Now we're completely rid of them, yet only a hundred years ago any dark-haired person had to prove that he didn't have any gypsy blood.

ELSA: That's true.

LANCELOT: Who told you all this about the gypsies?

CHARLEMAGNE: Our Dragon. The gypsies quite insolently opposed him from the very first years he was in power.

LANCELOT: Wonderful, intolerant people.

CHARLEMAGNE: You mustn't, you really mustn't talk like that.

LANCELOT: What does your Dragon eat?

CHARLEMAGNE: Our city provides him with a thousand cows, two thousand sheep, five thousand chickens, and eighty pounds of salt a month. Summer and autumn, there are, in addition, ten fields of lettuce, asparagus, and cauliflower.

LANCELOT: He's eating you out of house and home!

CHARLEMAGNE: No, no, you're forbidden to say that! We don't complain, and anyway, how else could we manage? As long as he's here, no other dragon would dare touch us.

LANCELOT: But all the other dragons were destroyed long ago.

CHARLEMAGNE: What if, suddenly, that turned out not to be the case? Really, I assure you, the only way to get rid of dragons is to have your own. But that's enough about him, please. Now you tell us something interesting.

LANCELOT: All right. Do you know what the Book of Wrongs is?

ELSA: No, we don't.

LANCELOT: Then let me tell you. A five years' walk from here in the Black Mountains there's a huge cave. And in this cave lies a book, half-filled with writing. No one ever touches it, yet page after page of writing is added day after day. Who writes in it? The world! The mountains, grass, stones, trees, rivers—they all see what people are doing. They know all the acts of criminals, all the woes of those who suffer unjustly. From branch to branch, from drop to drop, from cloud to cloud, all human wrongs are carried to the cave in the Black Mountains and recorded in the Book, which grows and grows. If there were no such book in the world, the trees would wither from dejection, and the waters would turn bitter. And the people . . .

ELSA: What people?

LANCELOT: Me, for example. I'm an observant fellow. I heard about this book and wasn't too lazy to go and look for it. Once you've read this book, you never have another moment of peace. Oh, what a catalog of wrongs it is! One can't fail to respond to them.

ELSA: How so?

LANCELOT: We involve ourselves in the affairs of others. We help those who must be helped. And we destroy those who must be destroyed. Do you want to be helped?

ELSA: How?

CHARLEMAGNE: In what way could you help us?

MR. CAT: Mee-ow!

LANCELOT: I've been mortally wounded thrice, and in each case by those whom I've forcibly saved. Despite this, and though you don't ask it of me, I'll challenge the Dragon! Do you hear what I'm saying? Elsa?

ELSA: No, no! He'll kill you and that'll poison the last hours of my life.

MR. CAT: Mee-ow!

LANCELOT: I'll challenge the Dragon to battle!

[*An ever louder sound of whistling is heard, then noise, howling, roaring. The windows rattle. Red flashes are visible outside.*]

MR. CAT: Speak of the devil . . .

[*The howling and whistling suddenly stop. There is a loud knock on the door.*]

CHARLEMAGNE: Come in!

[HENRY *enters, richly dressed as a footman.*]

HENRY: Sir Dragon to see you, sir.
CHARLEMAGNE: Have him come right in!

[HENRY *opens the door wide, then departs. Pause. Enter, without haste, a solidly built, middle-aged but youthful-looking, fair-haired man of military bearing. He has a broad smile on his face. His manner, except for a slight coarseness, is not without a suggestion of agreeableness. He is slightly hard of hearing.*]

DRAGON: Greetings, my children! Elsa, pet, how are you doing? Ah, you have a guest. Who is it?
CHARLEMAGNE: A traveler, passing through town.
DRAGON: What's that? Speak up, answer distinctly, like a soldier!
CHARLEMAGNE: He's a traveler!
DRAGON: Not a gypsy?
CHARLEMAGNE: Of course not. He's a very nice man.
DRAGON: What's that?
CHARLEMAGNE: A very nice man.
DRAGON: All right, Mr. Traveler! Why don't you look at me? Why are you peering out of the door?
LANCELOT: I'm waiting for the Dragon to come in.
DRAGON: Ha, ha! I'm the Dragon!
LANCELOT: You? But I was told you have three heads, claws, and are huge!
DRAGON: Oh, well. Today I just dropped in informally, without my regalia.
CHARLEMAGNE: Sir Dragon has been living so long among human beings that he occasionally turns himself into one and drops in, makes a friendly call.
DRAGON: So I do. We're real friends, my dear Charlemagne. Indeed,

I'm more than a friend to every one of you. I'm the friend of your childhood. More than that, I was the friend of your father's childhood, your grandfather's, and your great-grandfather's. I remember your great-great-grandfather in short pants.

[*He wipes his eyes.*]

Dammit! An unwanted tear . . . Ha, ha! Your guest's eyes are popping out! You didn't expect such feelings from me? Well, answer me! He's all embarrassed, the idiot. Well, well, never mind. Ha, ha, Elsa!

ELSA: Yes, Uncle Dragon.

DRAGON: Give me your little paw.

[ELSA *holds out her hand to* DRAGON.]

You cute little kitten! You rascal! What a warm little paw! Hold your little chin up higher! Now smile! That's it. What are you staring at, Stranger? Eh?

LANCELOT: I'm admiring you.

DRAGON: Good boy. You speak up distinctly. Go on admiring. Everything is very straightforward with us, Stranger. Hup, two, three. Soldier fashion. Eat!

LANCELOT: Thank you, I've had enough.

DRAGON: Never mind. Eat! Why've you come here?

LANCELOT: On business.

DRAGON: What business? Well, come on—out with it! Eh? Perhaps I can be of use to you. Why've you come?

LANCELOT: To slay you.

DRAGON: Louder!

ELSA: No, no, he's just joking! Want to hold my hand again, Uncle Dragon?

DRAGON: What for?

LANCELOT: I challenge you to combat. You, do you hear me?

[DRAGON *is silent. His face is flushed.*]

For the third time I'm challenging you to combat. Do you hear?

[*A frightful, ear-splitting triple roar is heard. Despite the volume of the roar, which makes the walls tremble, it is not altogether unmusical. There is nothing human in the roar. It is the roar of the* DRAGON, *who is balling his fists and stamping his feet.*]

DRAGON [*suddenly stopping his roar, he speaks in a quiet tone*]: Well, why are you silent? Are you frightened?

LANCELOT: No.

DRAGON: No?

LANCELOT: No.

DRAGON: Very well, then, watch this!

[*He makes a slight movement with his shoulders and suddenly an astounding change comes over him. A new head appears on his shoulders and the earlier one completely disappears. A serious, self-controlled, narrow-faced, graying blond with a high forehead stands before* LANCELOT.]

MR. CAT: Don't be astonished, my dear Lancelot. He's got three tops and he changes them around as he likes . . . What am I saying?!

[*He hides in a corner.*]

DRAGON [*whose voice is as altered as his face, speaks rather softly but drily*]: Your name is Lancelot?

LANCELOT: Yes.

DRAGON: Are you a descendant of the famous knight-errant called Lancelot?

LANCELOT: He's a distant connection of mine.

DRAGON: I accept your challenge. Knights-errant—they're the same as gypsies. You must be destroyed.

LANCELOT: I won't surrender.

DRAGON: I've already destroyed eight hundred and nine knights, nine hundred and five people of unrecorded professions, one old drunkard, two lunatics, two women—the mother and aunt respectively of girls I'd picked out—one twelve-year-old boy—the brother of another such girl. In addition I've destroyed six armies and five mutinous mobs. Do sit down.

LANCELOT [*sitting down*]: Thanks.

DRAGON: Smoke? Go ahead, don't mind me.

LANCELOT: Thanks.

[*He takes out a pipe and fills it in leisurely fashion.*]

DRAGON: Do you know on what day I made my appearance in the world?

LANCELOT: An unhappy one.

DRAGON: On the day of a great battle. On that day Attila himself suffered defeat. Can you imagine how many warriors' lives it cost to accomplish that feat? The ground was soaked in blood. By midnight the leaves on the trees had turned brown. By dawn huge black mushrooms—they called them cadaver mushrooms—had sprung up under the trees. And after them I crawled up out of the earth. The blood of dead Huns courses through my veins—and it's cold blood. In combat I'm cold, calm, and accurate in my aim.

[*As he says the last words he makes a slight movement with one hand. There is a dry clicking sound. From his index finger emerges a stream of flame. It lights the pipe that* LANCELOT *has been filling.*]

LANCELOT: Thanks.

[*He puffs on his pipe with satisfaction.*]

DRAGON: You're opposing me. Therefore you oppose war?

LANCELOT: Goodness, no! I've been fighting all my life.

DRAGON: You're a stranger here, where the people and I have learned to understand each other. The entire city will look on you with horror and will be delighted to see you dead. You'll meet an inglorious end. Do you realize that?

LANCELOT: No.

DRAGON: You're as determined as ever?

LANCELOT: Even more so.

DRAGON: You're a worthy opponent.

LANCELOT: Thanks.

DRAGON: I shall fight seriously.

LANCELOT: That suits me.

DRAGON: That means that I'll kill you promptly. Right here and now.

LANCELOT: But I'm unarmed!

DRAGON: Do you expect me to give you time to arm yourself? No, no way. I told you I'd put up a serious fight. I'll attack suddenly, right now . . . Elsa, bring a broom!

ELSA: What for?

DRAGON: I'll immediately reduce this fellow to ashes, and you're to sweep him up.

LANCELOT: Are you afraid of me?

DRAGON: I don't even know what fear is.

LANCELOT: Then why are you in such a hurry? Give me until tomorrow. I'll get hold of some arms and we can meet in a field.

DRAGON: Why?

LANCELOT: So that the people will see you're no coward.

DRAGON: The people won't know anything about it. These two will keep their mouths shut. You'll die here and now, quietly, ingloriously.

[*He raises his arm.*]

CHARLEMAGNE: Stop!

DRAGON: What's the matter?

CHARLEMAGNE: You can't kill him.

DRAGON: What?

CHARLEMAGNE: I beg you, don't get mad. I'm completely devoted to you. But, you see, I happen to be the Keeper of Records.

DRAGON: What has your office to do with the present matter?

CHARLEMAGNE: I've a document in my safekeeping that you signed three hundred and eighty-two years ago. This document has never been superseded. You understand, I'm not raising any ob-

jections, but merely reminding you. It bears your signature—
"The Dragon."

DRAGON: So what?

CHARLEMAGNE: After all, this case involves my daughter. And I'd really like to see her live a little longer. That's perfectly natural, you know.

DRAGON: Cut it short.

CHARLEMAGNE: You can't kill him now. Anyone who challenges you is safe until the day of battle—that's written and confirmed by you under oath. And the day of battle is fixed not by you but by the challenger. That's what the document says and it was sworn to. And the entire city is obligated to give aid to whoever challenges you, and no one is to be punished for doing so—that also is sworn to.

DRAGON: When was this document drawn up?

CHARLEMAGNE: Three hundred and eighty-two years ago.

DRAGON: I was very naive in those days, a sentimental, inexperienced boy.

CHARLEMAGNE: But the document has never been superseded.

DRAGON: That makes no difference . . .

CHARLEMAGNE: But the document . . .

DRAGON: That's enough about documents. We're grown-up people.

CHARLEMAGNE: But you yourself signed it . . .

ELSA: I can run and fetch it.

DRAGON: Don't you stir.

CHARLEMAGNE: We've found a man who's trying to save my little girl. Love for one's child—well, that doesn't count for much. That's possible. But there are also laws of hospitality and those are possible too. So why are you looking at me so fiercely?

[*He buries his face in his hands.*]

ELSA: Papa! Papa!

CHARLEMAGNE: I protest!

DRAGON: All right. Now I'll wipe out the whole nest.

LANCELOT: And all the world will learn that you're a coward!

DRAGON: How?

[*With a single leap* MR. CAT *jumps out of the window and hisses from a distance.*]

MR. CAT: I'll tell everyone, everyone everything, absolutely everything, you old lizard.

[*The* DRAGON *again emits a roar. This time it is just as powerful, but it gives evidence of definite hoarseness, sobbing, and spasmodic coughing. It is the roar of a huge, ancient, and evil monster.*]

DRAGON [*suddenly ceasing to roar*]: Very well, then. We'll have our fight tomorrow, as you requested.

[*He leaves abruptly. Immediately there are sounds of whistling, high wind, and great noise outside. The walls tremble, the lamp flickers, then the sound gradually lessens in the distance.*]

CHARLEMAGNE: He's flown away! What have I done?! I'm a damned old fool. Yet I couldn't have acted differently! Elsa, you're not angry with me, are you?

ELSA: No, of course not! I'm proud of you!

CHARLEMAGNE: I suddenly feel very weak. You must excuse me. I'll go lie down. No, no, you don't need to come with me. Stay here with our guest. Entertain him with your conversation—he's been so very nice to us. I must lie down.

[*He goes out. There is a pause.*]

ELSA: Why did you start all this? I'm not reproaching you, but—everything was set. It's not so terrible to die young. Everyone else will grow old.

LANCELOT: Think what you're saying! Even trees sigh when they're cut down.

ELSA: But I'm not complaining.

LANCELOT: Aren't you sorry for your father?

ELSA: But, you know, he'll die just when he wants to. In essence, that's happiness.

LANCELOT: Aren't you sorry to say good-bye to your friends?

ELSA: No, for if I hadn't been chosen, one of them would have been taken.

LANCELOT: And what of your fiancé?

ELSA: How did you know I had one?

LANCELOT: I sensed it. And aren't you sorry to be separated from him?

ELSA: But the Dragon, in order to console Henry, appointed him his personal secretary.

LANCELOT: Ah, that's how it is. In that case it's not too hard to leave him. What about your city, though? Aren't you sorry to leave it?

ELSA: But it's for the sake of my city that I'm going to my death.

LANCELOT: And does it accept your sacrifice so casually?

ELSA: No, no! If I die on Sunday the whole city will be in mourning until Tuesday. For three whole days no one will touch any meat. At tea, they'll serve special little cakes called "Poor Elsas" in memory of me.

LANCELOT: That's all?

ELSA: What else can they do?

LANCELOT: Kill the Dragon.

ELSA: But that's impossible.

LANCELOT: The Dragon has corrupted your soul, poisoned your blood, and dimmed your vision. But we'll set everything to rights.

[MR. CAT *runs in.*]

MR. CAT: Eight of my lady cat friends and forty of my kittens have run around to all the houses and told about the coming fight. Meeow! The Burgomaster's hurrying this way.

LANCELOT: The Burgomaster? That's fine!

[*The* BURGOMASTER *enters, running.*]

BURGOMASTER: How are you doing, Elsa? Where's the stranger?

LANCELOT: Here I am.

BURGOMASTER: First of all, be kind enough to lower your voice, use as few gestures as possible, move quietly, and look me in the face.

LANCELOT: Why?

BURGOMASTER: Because I've all the nervous and psychic diseases there are in the world and on top of them I've three that are still unidentified. Do you think it's a cinch to serve as burgomaster under a Dragon?

LANCELOT: I'll kill the Dragon and you'll feel better.

BURGOMASTER: Better? Ha, ha! Better! Ha, ha! Better!

[*He becomes hysterical. He drinks some water, and grows calmer.*]

The fact that you've dared to challenge the Dragon is a calamity. Everything was running smoothly. The Dragon kept my assistant under his influence—but then, he's a rare scoundrel, and so are all his gang, the merchants and millers. Now everything's all upset. The Dragon will be readying for the battle, he'll neglect matters of civic administration that he has only just begun to grasp.

LANCELOT: Try to get this through your head, you miserable creature: I'm going to save your city!

BURGOMASTER: The city? Ha, ha! *My* city! The city! Ha, ha!

[*He drinks water and calms down again.*]

My son is such a scoundrel that I'd sacrifice two cities if only I could be sure he'd be destroyed. It's better to have five dragons than a snake in the grass like my son. I beg you, go away.

LANCELOT: I'm not going away.

BURGOMASTER: Lucky you—I'm going to have a cataleptic fit.

[*He freezes, with a bitter smile on his face.*]

LANCELOT: But I'm going to save you all! Try to understand!

[*The* BURGOMASTER *does not reply.*]

Do you understand?

[*The* BURGOMASTER *remains silent.* LANCELOT *throws a glass of water in his face.*]

BURGOMASTER: No, I don't understand you. Whoever asked you to fight him?

LANCELOT: The whole city wants me to do it.

BURGOMASTER: Oh, yes? Well, look out of the window. The best people in town have hurried over here to get you to clear out.

LANCELOT: Where are they?

BURGOMASTER: There they are, sticking close to the walls. Come nearer, my friends.

LANCELOT: Why are they walking on tiptoe?

BURGOMASTER: So as not to upset my nerves. Now, my friends, tell Lancelot what you want him to do. All right. One! Two! Three!

CHORUS OF VOICES: Leave town! Hurry, please! This very day!

[LANCELOT *walks away from the window.*]

BURGOMASTER: You see? If you're a humane and civilized person, you'll submit to the will of the people.

LANCELOT: Not for anything!

BURGOMASTER: It's just your luck. I'm about to have a slight attack of madness.

[*He strikes a pose, with one hand pressed to his side and the other in an affected gesture.*]

I'm a teakettle. Boil me!

LANCELOT: I can see why all these people tiptoed when they came here.

BURGOMASTER: Oh, why?

LANCELOT: So that they wouldn't wake up the *real* people. I'll go out and speak to them right away.

[*He rushes out.*]

BURGOMASTER: Boil me! Besides, what can he do? The Dragon will give the order and we'll put him in prison. My dear Elsa, don't get all upset. Any second now, when the appointed time comes, our dear Dragon will take you in his embrace. You can be quite calm.

ELSA: I am calm.

[*There is a knock on the door.*]

Come in!

[HENRY *enters, still dressed as a footman.*]

BURGOMASTER: Hello, Sonny.

HENRY: Hello, Father.

BURGOMASTER: Do you have a message from him? Of course, there'll be no fight! Did you bring an order to slap Lancelot into prison?

HENRY: Sir Dragon sent the following orders: one, schedule the fight for tomorrow; two, equip Lancelot with arms; three, try to use your wits to better purpose.

BURGOMASTER: Congratulations, I'm going right out of my mind! Oh, my mind! Ouch! Help! Go away!

HENRY: I have orders to talk privately with Elsa.

BURGOMASTER: Orders? Oh, yes, of course. I'm going, I'm going, going.

[*He hurries out.*]

HENRY: Hello, Elsa.

ELSA: Hello, Henry.

HENRY: Do you expect that Lancelot will save you?

ELSA: No. What do you think?

HENRY: I don't expect him to, either.

ELSA: What did the Dragon order you to tell me?

HENRY: He ordered me to tell you that you're to kill Lancelot if it becomes necessary.

ELSA [*horrified*]: How?

HENRY: With a knife. Here it is. And it has a poisoned tip . . .

ELSA: But I don't want to!

HENRY: Well, Sir Dragon ordered me to warn you that if you don't obey he'll kill all of your friends.

ELSA: Very well, then. Tell him I'll try.

HENRY: Sir Dragon also ordered me to tell you that any hesitation on your part will be punished as disobedience.

ELSA: I hate you!

HENRY: And Sir Dragon also ordered me to say that he knows how to reward faithful servants.

ELSA: Lancelot will slay your Dragon!

HENRY: To that, Sir Dragon ordered me to say: We'll see!

[*Curtain.*]

[*In Act 2, Lancelot challenges the Dragon to battle, and the battle takes place in front of all the city's inhabitants. After a long struggle, Lancelot finally slays the Dragon, but is himself wounded. He leaves the city, mounting his flying carpet, to a land far away. The fruits of his victory are shamelessly appropriated by the Burgomaster and his son, Henry. The city proclaims the Burgomaster the victorious slayer of the Dragon and the liberator of the people.—Editors*]

ACT 3

[*The setting is a luxuriously furnished apartment in the* BURGOMAS-TER's *palace. On either side of the door at the back of the stage there is a semi-round table laid for supper. In the center stands a medium-sized table. On it lies a thick volume in gold binding. To one side stands a large throne-like chair with a curtain behind it. Opposite it is a window. When the curtain rises an orchestra is playing loudly. A group of citizens, their eyes fixed on one of the doors, is rehearsing a speech.*]

CITIZENS [*in a low voice*]: One, two, three.

[*Loudly*]

Hail to the Conqueror of the Dragon!

[*In a low voice*]

One, two, three.

[*Loudly*]

Hail to our Ruler!

[*In a low voice*]

One, two, three.

[*Loudly*]

Our happiness is so great, it's inconceivable!

[*In a low voice*]

One, two, three.

[*Loudly*]

We hear footsteps!

[*Enter* HENRY.]

[*Loudly but with calculated timing*]

Hurrah! Hurrah! Hurrah!

FIRST CITIZEN: Oh, our Glorious Liberator! Exactly a year ago that cursed, hateful, revolting Dragon was destroyed by you.

CITIZENS: Hurrah! Hurrah! Hurrah!

FIRST CITIZEN: Since then we've been very well-off. We . . .

HENRY: Just a minute, my dear man. Put the accent on "very."

FIRST CITIZEN: Since then we've been vvvvvery well-off.

HENRY: No, no, my dear man. That's not right. You mustn't stress the "v." That makes it sound as though you're hesitating, stuttering. Stress the "r."

FIRST CITIZEN: Since then we've been verrrry well-off.

HENRY: That's it! I approve. You see, you know the Conqueror of the Dragon. He's such a simple, even naive, man. He loves sincerity, heartfelt sentiment. Go on.

FIRST CITIZEN: We don't know what to do with ourselves, we're so happy.

HENRY: Excellent! But wait a minute. Let's put in something there, something like . . . kindness, virtue. The Conqueror of the Dragon loves kindness, virtue.

[*He snaps his fingers.*]

Wait, wait! Just a moment. There! I've got it! Even the birds chirp more cheerily now that evil is banished and good reigns. Cheep-cheep-chirp–hurrah! There, now let's go over it again.

FIRST CITIZEN: Even the little birdies chirp more cheerily. Evil is banished—good reigns, cheep-cheep-chirp—hurrah!

HENRY: Your chirp is too drab, my dear man! See to it that your cheep doesn't become a chop or you'll get it in the neck.

FIRST CITIZEN: Cheep-cheep-chirp! Chirp—hurrah!

HENRY: That's better. Yes, that's good enough. We've already rehearsed the rest, haven't we?

CITIZENS: Yes, Sir Burgomaster, we have.

HENRY: Very good. In a moment the Conqueror of the Dragon, the President of your Free City, will appear before you. Remember, you must all speak in close unison but with warm, humane, democratic feelings. It was the Dragon who insisted on ceremony, whereas we . . .

SENTRY [*from the central door upstage*]: Atten-tion! Eyes on the door! His Excellency the President of the Free City is coming down the corridor.

[*Woodenly, without any expression, in a bass voice*]

Oh, you angel! Oh, you benefactor! Killed the Dragon! Just think of it!

[*There is a blare of music. Enter the* BURGOMASTER.]

HENRY: Your Excellency, Mr. President of the Free City! While I've been on duty there have been no incidents! I have on hand here ten people. Of the ten, all are unbelievably happy . . . In the suburbs . . .

BURGOMASTER: At ease, at ease, gentlemen. How do you do, Burgomaster?

[*He shakes* HENRY's *hand.*]

Who are you? Oh, the Burgomaster?

HENRY: Our fellow citizens were just recalling the fact that exactly a year ago you slew the Dragon. They've hurried here to offer you their congratulations.

BURGOMASTER: You don't say! What a pleasant surprise. Well, well, go ahead.

CITIZENS [*in low tones*]: One, two, three.

[*Loudly*]

Hail to the Conqueror of the Dragon!

[*In low tones*]

One, two, three.

[*Loudly*]

Hail to our Ruler . . .

[*Enter* JAILER.]

BURGOMASTER: Stop! Stop! Good day, Jailer.

JAILER: Good day, Your Excellency.

BURGOMASTER [*to the citizens*]: Thank you, gentlemen. I already know everything you were preparing to say to me. Oh, dammit, an unwanted tear!

[*He wipes his eyes.*]

But, you know, we're having a wedding and I still have a few little things to attend to. So, run along now, and come back for the wedding. We'll have a fun time. The nightmare is over and we can begin to live now. Am I right?

CITIZENS: Hip, hip, hooray!

BURGOMASTER: That's what I like to hear! Slavery is nothing more than a legend. We've been reborn. Do you remember what I was like in the days of the cursed Dragon? I was sick, I was crazy. And now? I'm as sound as a cucumber. I don't even need to speak about you. You're always cheerful and happy as larks. So, now, fly away! Hurray! Henry, show them out!

[CITIZENS *and* HENRY *leave.*]

Now, Jailer, what's going on in the prison?

JAILER: They're locked up.

BURGOMASTER: And how's my former assistant?

JAILER: He's suffering terribly.

BURGOMASTER: Ha, ha! I bet you're lying.

JAILER: No, honestly, he's really suffering terribly.

BURGOMASTER: Come on, how is he?

JAILER: He's climbing the walls.

BURGOMASTER: Ha, ha! Just what he deserves! A revolting personality. There used to be times when I was telling an anecdote, all the others would laugh, but he'd say it was so old it had a beard. So let him rot in prison. Did you show him my portrait?

JAILER: I certainly did.

BURGOMASTER: Which one? The one where I'm all happy smiles?

JAILER: That's the one.

BURGOMASTER: And what did he do?

JAILER: He cried.

BURGOMASTER: I bet you're lying.

JAILER: Honestly, he cried.

BURGOMASTER: Ha, ha! That's nice. What about the weavers who furnished that fellow . . . with the Flying Carpet?

JAILER: They're a pain in the neck, damn them. They're on different floors, but they stick together as one man. Whatever one of them says, so do the others.

BURGOMASTER: But have they at least lost weight?

JAILER: Everyone loses weight in my place!

BURGOMASTER: And the blacksmith?

JAILER: He sawed through his bars again. We had to put bars made of diamonds in the windows of his cell.

BURGOMASTER: Good, good. Don't spare any expense. How's he behaving now?

JAILER: He's puzzled.

BURGOMASTER: Ha, ha! That's nice to hear!

JAILER: The Master Hatmaker has made such pretty caps for the mice that cats don't touch them.

BURGOMASTER: They don't? Why's that?

JAILER: Because they're lost in admiration. As for the musician, he sings. It's very depressing. Whenever I go in to see him I put wax in my ears.

BURGOMASTER: Fine. And what about the city?

JAILER: It's quiet. But people are writing.

BURGOMASTER: Writing what?

JAILER: The letter "L" on the walls. It stands for Lancelot.

BURGOMASTER: Nonsense. The letter "L" stands for "Love the President."

JAILER: I see. So I don't need to arrest those who write it?

BURGOMASTER: No! Why not arrest them? What else do they write?

JAILER: I'm ashamed to tell you. "The President is a beast." "His son is a scoundrel . . . The President . . ."

[*He snickers in a bass voice.*]

No, I don't dare repeat it, not the way they express themselves. But most of all they write the letter "L."

BURGOMASTER: The fools! They were taken in by that Lancelot. By the way, is there still no news of him?

JAILER: He's vanished.

BURGOMASTER: Have you quizzed the birds?

JAILER: Yeah.

BURGOMASTER: All of them?

JAILER: Yeah. The eagle gave me a message from them. Pecked it into my ear.

BURGOMASTER: Well, what did it say?

JAILER: They say they've not seen Lancelot. Only one parrot was affirmative. Whenever you ask him, "Seen him?" he answers, "Seen him." You ask, "Lancelot?" he answers, "Lancelot." But everyone knows what kind of bird a parrot is.

BURGOMASTER: What about the snakes?

JAILER: They'd have crawled into town themselves if they'd heard anything. They're our friends. After all, they're connections of the late lamented. But they haven't been around.

BURGOMASTER: And the fish?

JAILER: Not a word out of them.

BURGOMASTER: Do you think they know anything?

JAILER: No. Learned pisciculturists have looked them straight in the eye and they confirm that they don't know a thing. In short, Lancelot, alias St. George, alias Perseus the Adventurer—he's called something different in every country—hasn't been discovered anywhere.

BURGOMASTER: Well, let him go hang, then.

[HENRY *enters.*]

HENRY: The father of the happy bride has arrived, Charlemagne the Keeper of Records.

BURGOMASTER: Aha! Aha! He's just the man I need to see. Ask him in.

[CHARLEMAGNE *enters.*]

You run along, Jailer. Keep up the good work. I'm pleased with you.

JAILER: We aim to please.

BURGOMASTER: Go on aiming. Charlemagne, are you acquainted with our jailer?

CHARLEMAGNE: Only slightly, Mr. President.

BURGOMASTER: Well, never mind. Perhaps you'll get to know him better.

JAILER: Shall I take him along?

BURGOMASTER: You want to grab everyone right away. No, you go along now. See you soon.

[JAILER *leaves.*]

Well, now, Charlemagne, you no doubt guess why we sent for you? All sorts of government worries and problems have prevented my dropping by to see you myself. But you and Elsa know about the orders that have been put up all over the city and that this is the day of the wedding.

CHARLEMAGNE: Yes, Mr. President, we know about it.

BURGOMASTER: We government people don't have the time to call with a bunch of flowers, make a proposal, or moon around sighing. We don't propose, but merely proclaim our intentions. Ha, ha! It's very convenient. Is Elsa happy?

CHARLEMAGNE: No.

BURGOMASTER: Indeed . . . Of course she's happy. What about you?

CHARLEMAGNE: I'm in despair, Mr. President.

BURGOMASTER: What ingratitude! I slew the Dragon . . .

CHARLEMAGNE: Excuse me, Mr. President, but I can't believe that.

BURGOMASTER: Oh, yes, you can!

CHARLEMAGNE: I give you my word. I can't.

BURGOMASTER: You can, you can. If I can believe it myself, you most certainly can.

CHARLEMAGNE: No.

HENRY: He simply doesn't want to.

BURGOMASTER: But why?

HENRY: He's just raising the ante.

BURGOMASTER: Very well, then. I offer you the post of my first assistant.

CHARLEMAGNE: I don't want it.

BURGOMASTER: Nonsense. You do want it.

CHARLEMAGNE: No.

BURGOMASTER: Stop this bargaining. I have no time for it. You'll have a government house near the park, not far from the market, with a hundred and fifty-three rooms, with all the windows facing south. Your salary will be fabulous. Besides, every time you come to your office you'll get travel expenses, and whenever you go home you'll get a severance allowance. If you dine out you'll do so on an official expense account, but if you stay at home you'll be given an in-residence allowance. You'll be almost as wealthy as I am. That's all. You agree to it?

CHARLEMAGNE: No.

BURGOMASTER: Then what do you want?

CHARLEMAGNE: We want only one thing, Mr. President. Leave us alone.

BURGOMASTER: Now, that's a fine thing—leave you alone! But if I don't choose to? Besides, from the government's point of view the thing has a sound basis. The Conqueror of the Dragon marries the girl he rescued. It sounds so convincing. Can't you see that?

CHARLEMAGNE: Why do you torture us? I've only just learned to think, Mr. President, and that in itself was torture enough, but now there's this wedding. It's enough to make one lose one's mind.

BURGOMASTER: You mustn't, you mustn't! All these mental diseases are sheer psychiatric inventions.

CHARLEMAGNE: Oh, God! How helpless we are! The very fact that our city is as hushed and subservient as it was before—it's so terrifying.

BURGOMASTER: What's all this delirium? What's terrifying? What are you and your daughter trying to do—mutiny?

CHARLEMAGNE: No. While we were out walking in the forest today we talked everything through. Tomorrow as soon as her life ends I'll die too.

BURGOMASTER: What do you mean—as soon as her life ends? What sort of claptrap is this?

CHARLEMAGNE: Do you really think she'll survive this wedding?

BURGOMASTER: Of course I do. It'll be a terrific, cheery holiday. Any other man would be delighted to marry off his daughter to such a wealthy bridegroom.

HENRY: And he's delighted too.

CHARLEMAGNE: No. I'm an elderly, courteous man, and it's difficult for me to say this to your face. But I'll say it anyway. For us this wedding is a calamity.

HENRY: What a tiresome way of bargaining.

BURGOMASTER: Now, listen, my dear man! I'm not going to offer you more than I already have! You, evidently, want shares in our enterprises. But it won't work! Whatever the Dragon accumulated so brazenly is now in the hands of the best people in town. To put it bluntly, in my hands and partly in Henry's. It's all perfectly legal.

CHARLEMAGNE: Of course. You make the laws.

BURGOMASTER: You may go. But remember this: first, at the wedding you'll see to it that you're jolly, full of fun, and witty. Second, there are to be no deaths! Kindly continue to exist as long as I find it convenient for you to do so. Tell your daughter this too. Third, in the future, you'll address me as "Your Excellency." You see this list? There are fifty families on it, all of them your best friends. If you make any trouble, all these fifty hostages will disappear without a trace. Now go along. No, wait. A coach will be sent for you immediately. You'll bring your daughter here to the palace, and no nonsense. Understood?

[CHARLEMAGNE *exits.*]

Now everything will run as smooth as silk.

HENRY: What did the Jailer report?

BURGOMASTER: There's not a cloud in the sky.

HENRY: And what about those "L's"?

BURGOMASTER: Oh, well, weren't there a lot of things scribbled on the walls in the Dragon's time? Let them scribble. It seems to console them and it doesn't do us any harm. Just tell me, is this armchair empty?

HENRY [*feeling the chair*]: Oh, Papa! There isn't anyone in it. Do sit down.

BURGOMASTER: Don't smile. In his Cap of Invisibility he could get in anywhere.

HENRY: Papa, you don't know this man. He's crammed to the gills with prejudices. His knightly courtesy would require him, before entering a house, to remove his cap—and then the guard would seize him.

BURGOMASTER: But in a year's time his character may have deteriorated.

[*He sits down.*]

And now, Sonny, my pet, let's talk about our own affairs. There's the matter of a small debt you owe me, my little ray of sunshine!

HENRY: What debt, Papa?

BURGOMASTER: You bribed my three footmen to spy on me, read my papers, and so on. Isn't that so?

HENRY: Whatever are you talking about, Papa?

BURGOMASTER: Just wait, Sonny, and don't interrupt. I raised their wages five hundred crowns out of my own pocket, to see that they only reported to you what I allowed them to. Therefore you owe me five hundred crowns, you young scamp.

HENRY: No, Papa. When I found out what you'd done I raised them to six hundred.

BURGOMASTER: And I, sensing that, went up to one thousand, you little swine! Therefore the balance is in my favor. So don't raise them any more, my sweet son. On the wages they already receive they've been overeating, getting dissipated, and running wild. If you don't watch out, they'll fall on us. Let's move on to other things. You'll have to extricate my private secretary. It became necessary to send the poor fellow to a psychiatric hospital.

HENRY: You don't say! Why?

BURGOMASTER: You and I bribed and counter-bribed him so many times a day that he now can't tell who's his real master. He was carrying tales about me to me. He was plotting against himself in order to wangle his own job for himself. He's an honest, hardworking fellow, and it's sad to see how he's torturing himself. Let's go and visit him in the hospital tomorrow and straighten him out, at long last, as to whom he's working for. Ah, Sonny! You're my fine boy! And suddenly this desire to fill your Papa's shoes.

HENRY: What on earth do you mean, Papa?

BURGOMASTER: Never mind, little one! Never mind. It's part of everyday life. You know what I want to propose? Let's keep an eye on each other, but let's make it simple, keep it in the family, as father and son, without all these outsiders. We'll save a whale of a lot of money!

HENRY: Ah, Papa, but what's money!

BURGOMASTER: True. You can't take it with you when you die . . .

[*There is a sound of horses' hooves and bells. He rushes to the windows.*]

She's here! Our beauty's arrived! What a coach! A marvel! It's all decorated with dragon's scales! And Elsa herself! The marvel of marvels. All in velvet. Say what you will, power is really something . . .

[*In a whisper*]

Question her!

HENRY: Who?

BURGOMASTER: Elsa. She's been so silent all these last days. Ask her whether she knows where this . . .

[*He looks around.*]

Lancelot is. Question her cautiously. And I'll listen here from behind the curtain.

[*He hides.*]

[*Enter* ELSA *and* CHARLEMAGNE.]

HENRY: Elsa, greetings. You're getting prettier every day—and that's very sweet of you. The President is changing his clothes. He asked me to make his excuses. Have a seat in this armchair, Elsa.

[*He seats her with her back to the curtain hiding* BURGOMASTER.]

And you can wait in the vestibule, Charlemagne.

[CHARLEMAGNE *bows and leaves.*]

Elsa, I'm very pleased that the President is getting into his regalia. I've wanted to have a private chat, a friendly heart-to-heart with you, for a long time. Why don't you say something? Hmm? You don't want to reply? In my own way I'm devoted to you, you know. Speak to me.

ELSA: About what?

HENRY: Anything you like.

ELSA: I don't know . . . I don't want anything.

HENRY: That's not possible. Today's your wedding day . . . Ah, Elsa . . . Once again I've got to give you up. But the Conqueror of the Dragon is the Conqueror, after all. I'm a cynic. I make fun of everything, but I must bow before him. You're not listening?

ELSA: No, I'm not.

HENRY: Ah, Elsa . . . Can I really have become a complete stranger to you? We were such friends as children. Do you remember when you had the measles and I kept coming to your window until I came down with them myself? Then you visited me and wept because I was so sick and listless. Remember?

ELSA: Yes.

HENRY: Can it be that the children we once were have suddenly vanished? Has nothing of them remained in either one of us? Come on, let's talk together as we used to, like brother and sister.

ELSA: Very well, let's talk.

[*The* BURGOMASTER *peeks out from behind the curtain and makes a gesture of applause to* HENRY.]

Do you want to know why I've been silent all this while?

[*The* BURGOMASTER *nods.*]

Because I'm afraid.

HENRY: Of whom?

ELSA: Of people.

HENRY: Is that so? Tell me which people you're afraid of. We'll clap them in jail and you'll immediately feel easier.

[*The* BURGOMASTER *takes out his notebook.*]

Go on, tell me their names.

ELSA: No, Henry, that wouldn't help.

HENRY: I assure you, it would. I've tried it out myself. Your sleep, your appetite, your mood—everything will improve.

ELSA: But, you see . . . I don't know how to explain it to you . . . I'm afraid of everybody.

HENRY: So that's it . . . I understand. I understand very well. Everybody, including me, seems cruel to you? Right? Perhaps you won't believe me, but I myself am afraid of them. I'm afraid of my own father.

[*The* BURGOMASTER *throws up his hands in a gesture of dismay.*]

I'm afraid of our trusted servants. And I pretend to be cruel so as to make them fear me. Alas, we're all caught in our own webs. But, go on, tell me more. I'm listening.

[*The* BURGOMASTER *nods approvingly.*]

ELSA: Well, what else can I tell you . . . First I was angry, then I grieved, and then I became quite indifferent. I'm more submissive now than I ever was. Anything at all can be done with me now.

[*The* BURGOMASTER *snickers out loud, then, alarmed at himself, he hides again behind the curtain.* ELSA *looks around.*]

Who was that?

HENRY: Pay no attention. They're getting ready for the wedding feast in there. My poor, dear little sister. What a pity Lancelot disappeared, disappeared without a single trace. I've only just come to understand him. He was an astonishing man. We were very guilty before him. Is there really no hope of his coming back?

[*The* BURGOMASTER *slips out from behind the curtain. He is all attention.*]

ELSA: He . . . won't return.

HENRY: You mustn't think that. I somehow feel we'll see him again.

ELSA: No.

HENRY: Believe me, Elsa.

ELSA: I like to hear you say that, but . . . Can anyone overhear us?

[*The* BURGOMASTER *leans over the back of* ELSA's *chair.*]

HENRY: Of course not, my dear. Today's a holiday. All the spies are off duty.

ELSA: You see . . . I know about Lancelot.

HENRY: Don't! Don't tell me if it's painful for you.

[*The* BURGOMASTER *shakes a threatening fist at* HENRY.]

ELSA: No, I've been silent so long that now I've the urge to tell you everything. No one except me can understand how sad it is and especially in a city like this one, where I was born. But you're listening so closely to me today . . . Well, in short . . . just a year ago, when the fight ended, Mr. Cat rushed over to the Palace Square. There he saw Lancelot, white, white as a ghost, standing among the Dragon's heads. He was leaning on his sword and smiling so as not to upset Mr. Cat. Mr. Cat then raced over to my house to get help. But the guards were watching me so closely that a fly couldn't get past them to enter the house. They chased the cat away.

HENRY: The brutes!

ELSA: Then he called his friend the donkey. They laid the wounded man on the donkey's back and took him through little side streets out of the city.

HENRY: Why?

ELSA: Alas, Lancelot was so weak that people might easily have killed him. So they took a little trail that led up into the mountains. Mr. Cat remained by his side and kept track of his pulse.

HENRY: It went on beating, I trust?

ELSA: Yes, but more and more faintly. Then Mr. Cat cried, "Halt," and the donkey stopped. Night had fallen. By then they were high, high up in the mountains, and all around it was so very quiet and cold. "You must turn back to the city," said the cat. "People can't harm him anymore. Let Elsa say farewell to him and then we'll bury him."

HENRY: He died, the poor fellow!

ELSA: He did, Henry. But that stubborn donkey said that he refused to turn around. So he went on. But Mr. Cat came back. You see, he's really very devoted to our house. He came back and told me everything, so I have nothing to hope for. Everything's over for me.

BURGOMASTER: Hooray! It's all over.

[*He begins to dance all about the room.*]

It's all over! I'm the complete master over everybody! Now there's no one to fear. Thank you, Elsa! This really is a holiday! Now who'll dare say I didn't slay the Dragon! Well, *who* dares?

ELSA: Did he hear us?

HENRY: Of course.

ELSA: And you knew it?

HENRY: Oh, Elsa, don't play the naive girl. You're getting married today.

ELSA: Father! Father!

[CHARLEMAGNE *rushes in.*]

CHARLEMAGNE: What's the matter with you, my little one?

[*He makes to embrace her.*]

BURGOMASTER: Hands off! You'll stand at attention in the presence of my bride!

CHARLEMAGNE [*drawing himself up at attention*]: There, there, calm yourself. Don't cry. What can you do? You can't do a thing.

[*Music blares forth.*]

BURGOMASTER [*running over to the window*]: How splendid! How neighborly! The guests are arriving for the wedding. The horses are all decked out with ribbons! They've got little lanterns on the shafts! How wonderful it is to be alive and know that no fool can interfere with you. Smile, Elsa. Precisely on the dot at the appointed time the President of the Free City himself will enfold you in his embrace.

[*The doors open wide.*]

Welcome, welcome, my dear guests.

[*The* GUESTS *enter. They come up in pairs past* ELSA *and* BURGOMASTER. *They speak formally, almost in a whisper.*]

FIRST MALE CITIZEN: Our congratulations to the bride and to the groom. Everyone's very happy.

SECOND MALE CITIZEN: All the houses are decorated with lanterns.

FIRST MALE CITIZEN: Outdoors it's as bright as day!

SECOND MALE CITIZEN: All the wine shops are full of crowds.

BOY: They're all cursing and fighting.

GUESTS: Shhhhh!

GARDENER: Allow me to present to you these little bluebells. To be sure, they'll toll rather sadly for you. Never mind. By tomorrow they'll have faded and stopped.

FIRST GIRLFRIEND: Elsa, dear, do try to cheer up. Or you'll make me cry and that would spoil the eyelashes I put on so well today.

SECOND GIRLFRIEND: After all, he's a cut above the Dragon . . . He's got arms, legs, and no scales. After all, even if he is the President, he's a human being. Tell us all about it tomorrow. It'll be so interesting!

THIRD GIRLFRIEND: You'll be able to do so much good for people! For instance, you can ask your husband to discharge my father's boss. Then Papa can have his job and get twice as big a salary, and we'll be so happy!

BURGOMASTER [*counting the guests under his breath*]: One, two, three, four.

[*Then he counts the place settings.*]

One two three . . . So . . . Looks as if there's one guest too many . . . Ah, yes, it's the boy . . . Now, now, don't howl. You can eat from your mother's plate. So, everyone's here. Ladies and gentlemen, be seated. We'll get through the marriage ceremony quickly and informally, and then we'll continue with the wedding feast. I got a fish that was created to be eaten. It smiles with joy when it's being boiled and tells the cook when it's ready. And there's turkey stuffed with its own young. Cozy, family style. And these are roast piglets that were not only fed, but trained especially for our table. They know how to sit up and beg, and to shake hands even when they're roasted . . . Stop whimpering, boy. It's not terrible at all, but amusing. And the wines—you know, they're so old, they're in their second childhood, and are dancing around in their bottles like little kids. The vodka, too, is distilled to such a degree of purity that the carafe seems empty. Let me . . . why, it really is empty. Those damned footmen have cleaned the vodka out completely. Well, never mind, there are a lot more carafes on the sideboard. How pleasant it is to be rich, ladies and gentlemen! Have you all found your places? Excellent. Wait, wait a moment! Don't start eating yet. We're about to marry. Just a minute! Elsa! Give me your little paw!

[ELSA *holds out her hand to the* BURGOMASTER.]

You little rascal! You playful imp, you! What a warm little paw! Hold that little chin higher! Smile! Is everything ready, Henry?

HENRY: Just so, Mr. President.

BURGOMASTER: Proceed.

HENRY: I'm a poor speaker, ladies and gentlemen, and I fear that my speech may be a bit muddled. A year ago a self-assured traveler in these parts challenged the cursed Dragon to mortal combat. A special commission, set up by the Municipal Board for Self-Government, established the following: the late brazen challenger did no more than infuriate the late monster and succeeded in wounding him slightly. Whereupon our former Burgomaster and present President of the Free City heroically attacked the Dragon and, performing various feats of courage, slew him, this time for good.

[*Applause.*]

The thorny growth of shameful slavery was torn up by the roots out of the harvest of our social crop.

[*Applause.*]

The grateful city has reached the following decision: inasmuch as we used to present our best young maidens to the cursed Monster, we can now do no less than accord those simple and natural rights to our dear Liberator!

[*Applause.*]

Therefore, to underscore the greatness of our President, on the one hand, and the subservience and devotion of the city, on the other, as Burgomaster I shall now perform the marriage ceremony. Strike up the organ! The Wedding Hymn!

[*Organ plays fortissimo.*]

Clerks! Open the Book of Fortunate Events.

[CLERKS *enter, carrying huge fountain pens.*]

For four hundred years the names of the unfortunate girls doomed to the Dragon have been entered here. Four hundred pages have been filled. As the first on page four hundred and one, we shall inscribe the name of the lucky girl who'll take as her bridegroom the courageous Slayer of the Monster.

[*Applause.*]

Bridegroom, answer me with a clear conscience. Do you agree to take this maiden to be your wife?

BURGOMASTER: For the good of the city I am prepared to do anything.

[*Applause.*]

HENRY: Clerks, write it down! But be careful! If you make a blot I'll have you lick it up! That's right! Well, that's all. Oh, sorry! There's still one insignificant formality. Bride! You, of course, consent to become the wife of the President of the Free City?

[*A pause.*]

Well, answer, girl, do you consent . . .

ELSA: No.

HENRY: Very good. Clerks, write down that she consents.

ELSA: Don't you dare write that!

[CLERKS *draw back.*]

HENRY: Elsa, don't interfere with our work.

BURGOMASTER: But my dear boy, she's not interfering at all. When a girl says "no" she means "yes." Clerks, go on writing!

ELSA: No! I'll tear out the page from the book and stomp on it!

BURGOMASTER: These charming girlish hesitations, tears, and illusions, and so on. Every girl weeps in her own way before her wedding, then is completely happy afterward. We'll just hold her little hands tight and do what has to be done. Clerks . . .

ELSA: Let me say just one word! Please!

HENRY: Elsa!

BURGOMASTER: Don't shout, Sonny. Everything's going as it should. The bride asks to speak. Let her have her say and that will conclude the formalities. It's all right, we're all friends here.

ELSA: Friends! My friends! Why are you killing me? It's terrifying, like a nightmare. When a robber attacks you with a knife, you can save yourself. Either someone will kill the robber or you'll make your escape . . . But what if the robber's knife comes at you of its own accord? And his rope crawls up to you like a snake so as to bind you hand and foot? If even the curtain at his window, a quiet curtain, suddenly also throws itself at you so as to gag your mouth? What will all of you say then? I always thought that you were simply obedient to the Dragon, the way a knife's obedient to the robber. But you, my friends, all turn out to be dragons yourselves! I don't blame you, you're not aware of it yourselves, but I implore you—come to your senses! Can it be that the dragon didn't die, but, as often happened with him, simply turned into human form? Only this time he turned into many people, and now they're killing me. Don't kill me! Wake up! My God, what misery . . . Tear apart the web in which you've all got entangled. Will no one stand up for me?

BOY: I would, but Mama's holding me back.

BURGOMASTER: So, that's all. The bride has made her speech. Life goes on as before, as if nothing has happened.

BOY: Mama!

BURGOMASTER: Quiet, little one. We'll make merry as if nothing's happened. Enough of this red tape, Henry. Write down: "The marriage ceremony is considered completed"—and let's get on with the eats. I'm awfully hungry.

HENRY: Clerks, write down: The marriage ceremony is considered completed. Well, get a move on! Are you in a trance?

[CLERKS *take up their pens. There is a loud knock on the door.* CLERKS *fall back again.*]

BURGOMASTER: Who's there?

[*Silence.*]

> Hey, you out there! Whoever it is, come back tomorrow, tomorrow during office hours, see the secretary. I have no time now! I'm getting married!

[*Another knock.*]

> Don't open the doors! Clerks, go ahead and write!

[*The door flies open by itself. There is no one outside.*]

> Henry, come here! What does this mean?

HENRY: Oh, Papa, it's the usual story. The plaints of our maiden here have stirred up all the naive inhabitants of the rivers, forests, and lakes. The *domovoi* from the attic, the *vodianoi* from the well. Let them be . . . What harm can they do us? They're as invisible and powerless as a so-called conscience and similar things. Well, so we may have a bad dream or two—big deal.

BURGOMASTER: No, it's he!

HENRY: Who?

BURGOMASTER: Lancelot. He's wearing his Cap of Invisibility. He's standing right beside us. He's listening to what we're saying. His sword is hanging over my head.

HENRY: My dear Papa! If you don't come to your senses I'll take the power into my own hands.

BURGOMASTER: Music! Play! Dear guests! Forgive this little involuntary delay, but I'm so afraid of drafts. A draft opened the doors, that's all. Elsa, my treasure, calm yourself! I'll proclaim our marriage as completed after one last confirmation. What's that? Who's that running?

[*A frightened* FOOTMAN *runs in.*]

FIRST FOOTMAN: Take it back! Take it back!

BURGOMASTER: Take what back?

FOOTMAN: Take back your cursed money! I'm no longer in your service!

BURGOMASTER: Why?

FOOTMAN: He'll kill me for all my vileness.

[*He rushes out.*]

BURGOMASTER: Who'll kill him? Eh? Henry!

[SECOND FOOTMAN *rushes in.*]

SECOND FOOTMAN: He's coming down the corridor! I made a low bow to him, but he paid no attention to me! He doesn't even look at people now. Ow, we're going to get it for everything we've done! Ow, we'll get it!

[*He rushes out.*]

BURGOMASTER: Henry!

HENRY: Behave as if nothing's happened. No matter what happens. That'll save us.

[THIRD FOOTMAN *appears, walking backwards. He shouts into empty space.*]

THIRD FOOTMAN: I'll prove it! My wife can confirm it! I always denounced their behavior! I only took their money because of my nerves. I'll bring documentation!

[*He leaves.*]

BURGOMASTER: As if nothing's happened! For God's sake, as if nothing's happened!

[LANCELOT *enters.*]

BURGOMASTER: Ah, how do you do? You're one person we didn't expect. Nonetheless, we extend you welcome. We don't have enough china to go around, but you can eat from a bowl, and I'll take a plate. I'd order some more dishes brought in, but my footmen, the idiots, have all run away . . . And we're getting married, as it were, he-he-he, a personal, so to speak, intimate matter. So cozy . . . Let me introduce you. Where are the guests? Ah, they've dropped something and are looking for it under the table. Here's my son, Henry. I believe you've already met. So young, and already a burgomaster. He's come far since I . . . since we . . . Well, in a word, after the Dragon was slain. What's the matter? Do come in, please.

HENRY: Why don't you speak?

BURGOMASTER: Indeed, what's the matter? How was the trip here? What's new? Don't you want to rest a bit after your journey? The guard will show you the way.

LANCELOT: Greetings, Elsa!

ELSA: Lancelot!

[*She runs over to him.*]

Sit down. Please, do sit down. Is it really you?

LANCELOT: Yes, Elsa.

ELSA: And your hands are warm. And your hair's grown since we last saw each other. Or does it only seem so to me? But your cloak is the same. Lancelot!

[*She seats him at the small table in the center of the room.*]

Have a little wine. Or, rather, no, don't take anything of theirs. You rest a bit and then we'll leave. Father! He's come! Oh, Father! It's just as it was that evening. It's just as it was then, when we thought that only one thing was left for us—to die quietly. Lancelot!

LANCELOT: Do you mean you love me as before?

ELSA: Father, do you hear? How many times have we dreamed of his coming in and asking: Elsa, do you love me as before? And my answer is: Yes, Lancelot! And then I ask: Where have you been all this time?

LANCELOT: Far, far away, in the Black Mountains.

ELSA: Were you very ill?

LANCELOT: Yes, Elsa. You know, to be mortally wounded is very, very dangerous.

ELSA: Who nursed you?

LANCELOT: The forester's wife. A good, kind woman. Except her feelings were hurt because in my delirium I kept calling her Elsa.

ELSA: You mean you missed me, too?

LANCELOT: I did.

ELSA: And how I suffered! They tormented me here.

BURGOMASTER: Who did? Impossible! Why didn't you complain to us? We'd have taken steps!

LANCELOT: I know everything, Elsa.

ELSA: You do?

LANCELOT: Yes.

ELSA: How so?

LANCELOT: In the Black Mountains, not far from the forester's cottage, there's a huge cave. And in that cave there lies the book I told you about, the Book of Wrongs, full of notations. No one touches it, but page after page is inscribed, with additions made each day. Who writes in it? The world! It records all the crimes of evildoers, all the woes of the innocent victims.

[HENRY *and the* BURGOMASTER *tiptoe toward the door.*]

ELSA: Is that where you read about us?

LANCELOT: Yes, Elsa. Hey, you there! Murderers! Don't stir a step!

BURGOMASTER: Why so harsh?

LANCELOT: Because I'm not the man I was a year ago. I freed you then, and what did you do?

BURGOMASTER: Oh, my God! If you're not satisfied with me, I'll go into retirement.

LANCELOT: You're not going anywhere!

HENRY: Quite right. You can't conceive how he's behaved in your absence. I can furnish you with a complete list of his crimes, which haven't yet made it into the Book of Wrongs, crimes he'd intended to commit.

LANCELOT: Hold your tongue!

HENRY: But, allow me! If you look more closely, I'm not guilty of anything. It's the way I was trained.

LANCELOT: Everyone was trained. But why were you the best pupil, you beast?

HENRY: Let's leave, Papa. He's getting abusive.

LANCELOT: No, you're going nowhere. I've been here for a whole month, Elsa.

ELSA: And you never came to see me!

LANCELOT: Oh, yes, I did, but in my Cap of Invisibility, early in the morning. I kissed you gently, so as not to wake you. Then I roamed through the town. I saw how terrible life was here. It's difficult enough to read about it, but to see it with your own eyes is worse. You there, Miller!

[FIRST MALE CITIZEN *emerges from under the table.*]

I saw you weep with pleasure when you shouted "Hail to the Conqueror of the Dragon" to the Burgomaster.

FIRST MALE CITIZEN: It's perfectly true I cried, but I wasn't pretending, Sir Lancelot.

LANCELOT: Yet you knew that he didn't slay the Dragon.

FIRST MALE CITIZEN: When I was at home, I knew it . . . but in public . . .

[*He spreads his hands.*]

LANCELOT: Gardener!

[*The* GARDENER *emerges from under the table.*]

You were teaching snapdragons to shout: "Hurrah for the President!"?

GARDENER: I was.

LANCELOT: Did they learn to do it?

GARDENER: Yes, except that every time they shouted they'd stick their tongues out at me. I'd expected to get money for new experiments . . . but . . .

LANCELOT: Friedrichsen!

[SECOND MALE CITIZEN *emerges from under the table.*]

When the Burgomaster got angry at you, did he put your only son in the dungeon?

SECOND MALE CITIZEN: Yes, and it was so damp there the boy's still coughing.

LANCELOT: Yet after that you gave the Burgomaster a pipe inscribed with the sentiment "Forever thine"?

SECOND MALE CITIZEN: But how else could I soften his heart?

LANCELOT: What am I to do with all of you?

BURGOMASTER: Let them all go hang. This isn't a job for you. Henry and I can handle them splendidly. That'll be the worst punishment for the scum. You take Elsa by the hand and leave us to live in our own way. That'll be humane, democratic.

LANCELOT: I can't do that. Come in, friends.

[*Enter* WEAVERS, BLACKSMITH, MASTER HATMAKER, *and* MASTER OF MUSICAL INSTRUMENTS.]

You've grievously disappointed me. I thought you'd manage without me. Why did you submit and go to prison? There are so many of you!

WEAVERS: They didn't give us time to collect our wits.

LANCELOT: Take these people away—the Burgomaster and the President.

WEAVERS [*taking hold of* HENRY *and the* BURGOMASTER]: March!

BLACKSMITH: I tested the bars myself. They're strong. March!

MASTER HATMAKER: Here are some fool's caps for you! I used to make magnificent hats, but you made me cruder and crueler in prison. March!

MASTER OF MUSICAL INSTRUMENTS: In my cell I fashioned a violin out of black bread and braided strings out of cobwebs. My violin sounds sad and faint, but you yourselves are the ones to blame for that. So, march to your own music as you go to the place of no return.

HENRY: But this is nonsense, it's not right. Things don't happen this way. A wanderer, penniless, an impractical person—and suddenly . . .

WEAVERS: March!

BURGOMASTER: I protest! It's inhumane!

WEAVERS: March!

[*Gloomy, simple, barely audible music plays.* HENRY *and the* BURGO-MASTER *are taken away.*]

LANCELOT: Elsa, I'm not the person I was before. Can you see that?

ELSA: Yes, but I love you even more.

LANCELOT: We won't be able to leave . . .

ELSA: That doesn't matter. Life can be very cheerful at home, too.

LANCELOT: The work awaiting me is on a micro-scale. It's worse than embroidery. I'll have to kill the dragon in each and every one of them.

BOY: Will it hurt us?

LANCELOT: Not you.

FIRST MALE CITIZEN: And us?

LANCELOT: It'll require a lot of effort on my part.

GARDENER: But be patient, Sir Lancelot. I implore you—be patient. Do some grafting. Light some fires—warmth helps growth. Pull up the weeds carefully, so as not to harm the healthy roots. If you really think about it, people in reality also, perhaps, maybe, all exceptions notwithstanding, are worth careful cultivation.

FIRST GIRLFRIEND: And may a wedding take place today.

SECOND GIRLFRIEND: Because people also become better when they're happy.

LANCELOT: That's true! Hey, music!

[*Music is heard.*]

Elsa, give me your hand. I love all of you, my friends. Otherwise why would I invest so much effort in you? And since I do love you, everything will work out splendidly. And after all this time of worries and torments we'll finally be happy, very happy!

[*Curtain.*]

1943

TALE OF THE TROIKA
꒲꒧

EXCERPTS

ARKADY AND BORIS STRUGATSKY

The story began like this. One day, at the peak of my work rush, as I was sweating over a lost shipment intended for the Kitezhgrad Magicotechnical Plant, my friend Eddie Amperian showed up in my office. Being a polite and well-brought-up person, he did not materialize unceremoniously right in the rickety visitor's chair, or barge in obnoxiously through the wall, or hurtle through the open transom like a catapulted cobblestone. Most of my friends are always in a hurry, late for something, or behind schedule, and they always materialize, or barge in, or hurtle through shamelessly whenever they feel like it, eschewing normal communications. Eddie was not like them: he modestly entered through the door. He even knocked, but came in before I had time to answer.

He stopped in front of me, said hello, and asked, "Do you still need the Black Box?"

"Box?" I muttered, my mind still on the lost goods. "What can I tell you? What box do you mean?"

"I'm disturbing you, aren't I?" polite Eddie said carefully. "I'm sorry, but the boss sent me over. You see, approximately an hour from now the new elevator system will be launched for its first run beyond the thirteenth floor. We've been offered a ride."

My mind was still saturated with the noxious fumes of inventory jargon, and all I could say was, "We were supposed to have lost an elevator at the thirteenth floor of this year?"

316

But then the first few bits of Eddie's information penetrated my gray matter. I laid down my pen and asked him to repeat what he had said. Eddie did so, patiently.

"Really?" I asked in a faint whisper.

"Absolutely," Eddie said.

"Let's go," I said, getting the folder with the requisitions out of my desk.

"Where?"

"What do you mean, where? To the seventy-sixth floor."

"Not just like that," Eddie said, shaking his head. "First we have to drop in to see the boss."

"What for?"

"He asked us to. There's some problem involved with the seventy-sixth floor. The boss wants to brief us."

I shrugged without arguing. I put on my jacket, pulled out the requisition for the Black Box from the folder, and we set off to see Eddie's boss, Fyodor Semyonovich Kivrin, head of the Department of Linear Happiness.

We stopped outside Fyodor Semyonovich's office, and the old house spirit Tikhon, clean and presentable, cheerily opened the door for us. We went in.

Fyodor Semyonovich Kivrin was not alone. Olive-hued Christobal Joséevich Junta was casually draped in the soft armchair behind his large work table, sucking on a smelly Havana cigar. Fyodor Semyonovich himself, his large fingers tucked in his colorful suspenders, was walking up and down the office, his head bowed. He was trying to step along the very edge of the Persian carpet. Crystal vases on the table held the Fruits of Paradise: the large, rosy apples of the Knowledge of Evil and the completely inedible-looking, but nevertheless worm-eaten, apples of the Knowledge of Good. The porcelain dish at Christobal Joséevich's elbow was full of cores and butts.

"And here they are in person," he said without his customary smile. "P-p-please sit down. T-t-time is short. K-K-Kamnoedov is a blowhard, but he'll be through soon. Ch-Christo, why don't you ex-ex-explain the circumstances? It always comes out badly when I try."

We sat down. Christobal Joséevich, his right eye squinting from the smoke, looked at us critically.

"I'll explain, if you wish," he said to Fyodor Semyonovich. "The circumstances are such, young men, that the first people to reach the seventy-sixth floor should be those of us who are experienced and wise. Unfortunately, the administration feels that we are too old and too venerable to go on the first experimental launch. Therefore, you are going, and I warn you right now that this will not be a simple trip, but reconnaissance, and perhaps reconnaissance under fire. You'll need stamina, courage, and the utmost discretion. Personally, I do not observe any of these qualities in you, but I defer to the recommendation of Fyodor Semyonovich. And in any case, you must know that you will most likely be in enemy territory—a merciless, cruel enemy who will stop at nothing."

That preface made me start sweating, but then Christobal Joséevich began explaining how things stood.

The destructive consequences of the invention of the elevator impeded the exploitation of the treasure trove for scientific research. Business correspondence with the administration was extremely difficult and inevitably drawn out: cables lowered with correspondence snapped under their own weight; carrier pigeons refused to fly that high; radio communications were shaky because of the backwardness of Tmuskorpion's technology; and the use of lighter-than-air craft merely led to needless expenditure of the limited supplies of helium. But all that is history now.

Some twenty years ago the berserk elevator dropped off the Inspection Commission of the Solovetsk Committee on Municipal Economy on the seventy-sixth floor. They had come simply to discuss the clogged plumbing in the labs of Professor Vybegallo on the fourth floor. What precisely went on remains unknown. Vybegallo, who was waiting for the commission on the fourth floor, recounts that the elevator rushed up past him with a terrifying roar, the glass door showing a glimpse of distorted faces, and then the horrifying vision passed. Exactly an hour later the elevator car was discovered on the thirteenth floor in a lather, snorting, and still trembling from excitement. The commission was not in the car. A note was glued to the wall, written on the back of a form for reporting unsatisfactory conditions. It said: "Am going out to examine. I see a strange rock. Comrade Farfurkis has been reprimanded for going into the bushes. Chairman of the Commission, L. Vuniukov."

For a long time no one knew on what floor L. Vuniukov and his subordinates had disembarked from the elevator. The police came, and there were many awkward questions. A month later, two sealed packages addressed to the head of the Municipal Economic Committee were found on the roof of the car. One package contained a packet of decrees on cigarette paper that recorded reprimands of Comrade Farfurkis or Comrade Khlebovvodov, mostly for displaying individualism and some inexplicable "Zuboism." The second package contained the materials for a report on the plumbing in Tmuskorpion (the conditions were acknowledged to be unsatisfactory) and an application to Accounting for extra pay for high-altitude duty.

After this, correspondence from above became rather regular. First came the minutes of the meetings of the Inspection Commission of the Municipal Economic Committee, then of the Special Commission on Examining the Situation, then suddenly the Temporary Troika on Examining the Activity of Commandant Zubo of the Colony of Unexplained Phenomena, and finally, after three reports in a row on "criminal negligence," L. Vuniukov signed in as Chairman of the Troika on the Rationalization and Utilization of Unexplained Phenomena. The newly formed triumvirate stopped sending down minutes and began sending instructions and decrees. These documents were terrifying in form and content. They gave incontrovertible evidence that the former commission of the Committee on Municipal Economy had usurped power in Tmuskorpion and that it was incapable of wielding such power rationally.

"The greatest danger," Christobal Joséevich continued in his even voice, sucking on the extinguished cigar, "is the fact that these rascals have the well-known Great Round Seal in their hands. I hope that you realize what this means."

"I understand," Eddie said quietly. "You can't hack it out even with an ax." His clear face clouded over.

"What if we use the humanizer?"

Christobal Joséevich looked at Fyodor Semyonovich.

"You can try, of course," he said, shrugging. "However, I'm afraid that things have gone too far."

"N-n-no, why do you say that?" Fyodor Semyonovich countered. "T-try it, t-try it, Eddie. They're not automatons up there. B-by the way, V-V-Vybegallo is up there, too."

"How come?"

It seemed that three months ago a demand had been sent down for a scientific consultant at a fantastic salary. Nobody believed the salary offer, least of all Professor Vybegallo, who at that time was just finishing up a major project on developing, through reeducation, a worm that would bait itself on a hook. Vybegallo announced to all ears at the academic council his distrust of the offer and ran away that same evening, leaving everything behind. Many saw him, briefcase in his teeth, clambering up the inner wall of the elevator shaft, getting out on floors divisible by five to replenish his strength at the snack bars. A week later a decree was lowered, stating that Professor A. A. Vybegallo had been appointed scientific consultant to the Troika at the promised salary, with bonuses for his knowledge of foreign languages.

"Thanks," said polite Eddie. "That's valuable information. Shall we go?"

"Go, go, my dear friends," Fyodor Semyonovich said, touched to the quick. He peered into the magic crystal. "Yes, it's time. Kamnoedov is g-getting to the end of his s-s-speech. B-be careful up there. It's a c-creepy, terrifying place."

"And no emotions!" Christobal Joséevich insisted. "If they don't give you your bedbugs and boxes—it doesn't matter. You're scouts. We'll maintain one-way telepathic communications with you. We'll follow your every move. Gathering information is your primary goal."

"We understand," said Eddie.

The car stopped, the stranger got out, and Eddie pressed seventy-six one more time. At that very second the elevator rushed up with a ferocity that made us black out. When we came to, the elevator was motionless and the door was open. We were on the seventy-sixth floor. We looked at each other and went out, bearing our requisitions over our heads like white flags. I do not know for sure what it was we expected, but it was bound to be bad.

However, nothing terrible happened. We found ourselves in a round, empty, and very dusty room with a low gray ceiling. A white boulder, looking like an antitank stake placement, grew out of the parquet floor. Old yellowed bones were scattered around the boulder. There was the smell of mice, and it was murky. Suddenly the elevator gate clanged shut. We shuddered and turned around, but all we saw was the roof of the descending car. An evil roar filled the room and died down. We were trapped. I desperately wanted to get back downstairs immediately, but the lost look that crossed Eddie's face gave me strength. I stuck out my jaw, folded my hands behind my back, and headed for the boulder, maintaining an independent and skeptical air. Just as I had expected, the boulder was a road marker, often encountered in fairy tales. The sign over it looked something like this:

NO. 1. IF YOU GO TO THE RIGHT, YOU'LL LOSE YOUR HEAD.

NO. 2. IF YOU GO TO THE LEFT, YOU'LL GET NOWHERE.

NO. 3. IF YOU GO STRAIGHT YOU'LL

"They've scraped off the last part," Eddie explained. "Aha. There's something else written in pencil: 'We are here . . . we consulted the people . . . and the opinion is . . . that we should go straight. Signed: L. Vuniukov.'"

We looked straight ahead. Our eyes had adjusted to the diffused

light, and we saw the doors. There were three of them. The doors leading to what might be considered the right and the left were boarded
shut, and there was a path going around the boulder through the
dust from the elevator to the middle door.

"I don't like any of this," I said with courageous forthrightness.
"These bones . . ."

"I think they're ivory," Eddie said. "But that's not important. We
can't go back, can we?"

"Maybe we could write a note and throw it down the shaft? Otherwise we'll disappear without a trace."

"Alex, don't forget that we're in telepathic communication. It's
embarrassing. Pull yourself together."

I pulled myself together. I stuck out my jaw again and resolutely
strode toward the middle door. Eddie walked next to me.

"The Rubicon is crossed!" I announced and kicked the door. The
effect was wasted. There was a barely noticeable sign on the door that
said "Pull," and the Rubicon had to be crossed a second time, without
the grand gestures and with the humiliating application of force to
the powerful springs.

The door opened, pushed by a powerful hand, and the Troika, that
mighty triumvirate, appeared in the room in full complement—all
four of them.

Lavr Fedotovich Vuniukov, in complete consistency with the description, white, sleek, and strong, moved to his seat without looking
at anyone. He sat down, set his large briefcase in front of himself,
opened it with a flourish, and started arranging on the green baize all
the objects necessary for a successful chairmanship: a blotter trimmed
in alligator leather, a selection of pens in a calfskin holder, a pack of
Herzegovina Flor cigarettes, a lighter in the shape of the Arc de Tri-
omphe, and a pair of prismatic opera glasses.*

Rudolf Arkhipovich Khlebovvodov, shriveled and yellow, sat on

* Herzegovina Flor was Stalin's favorite brand of cigarettes. (Editors).

Lavr Fedotovich's left and immediately began whispering in his ear, letting his eyes roam aimlessly from corner to corner.

Redheaded and baggy Farfurkis did not sit at the table. Democratically, he seated himself on a wooden chair across from the commandant, opened a fat notebook with a tattered cover, and immediately made a notation.

The scientific consultant, Professor Vybegallo, whom we recognized without any description, looked us over indifferently, frowned, and glanced up at the ceiling, as though trying to remember where he had seen us. He may have remembered, maybe not, but he sat at his table and prepared for his important duties. He began setting up the *Small Soviet Encyclopedia*, volume by volume, on his table.

"Harrumph," Lavr Fedotovich said and looked around with a gaze that penetrated walls. Everyone was ready: Khlebovvodov was whispering, Farfurkis made a second notation, the commandant, like a student making last-minute preparations, was hysterically leafing through his papers, and Vybegallo set up volume six. As for the representatives, that is, us, we apparently were of no significance. I looked at Eddie and quickly turned away. Eddie was close to total demoralization—Vybegallo's appearance was the last straw.

There was no evening session. Officially we were informed that Lavr Fedotovich, as well as Comrades Khlebovvodov and Vybegallo, were poisoned at lunch by mushrooms, and that the doctor recommended bed rest all night. However, the ever-meticulous commandant was not satisfied by the official version. He called his friend, the hotel maître d'. It turned out that at lunch Lavr Fedotovich and Professor Vybegallo had ganged up on Comrade Khlebovvodov on the issue of the relative merits of well-done versus rare steak. Striving to determine which of these two states of steak was more beloved by the people, and with the aid and sustenance of cognac and velvety pilsner, each consumed four experimental portions from the chef's stores. Now they were quite ill, flat on their backs, and could not appear in public before morning.

The commandant rejoiced like a kid whose favorite teacher had unexpectedly fallen ill.

We said good-bye to him, bought two ice-cream cones, and went back to our hotel. We spent the evening in our room, discussing our situation. Eddie admitted that Christobal Joséevich had been right: the Troika was a tougher nut to crack than he had expected. The rational part of their psyche turned out to be supernaturally conservative and super-rigid. True, it did yield to the humanizer's powerful hold, but immediately returned to square one as soon as it was removed. I suggested that Eddie leave the field on, but he rejected my suggestion. The Troika's reserves of the rational, good, and eternal were very limited, and Eddie was afraid that lengthy exposure to the humanizer would deplete them. Our business is to teach them to think, said Eddie, not to think for them. But they are not learning. These ex-plumbers have forgotten how. But all is not lost. There is still the emotional side of their psyche. Since we cannot awaken their reason, we must try to awaken their consciences. And that was precisely what Eddie planned to do at the very next session.

We discussed that problem until the excited Gabby burst in on us without knocking. It turned out that he had applied to be seen out of turn by the Troika to weigh a suggestion of his. He had just heard from the commandant that they would, and he wanted to know whether we would be present at the morning meeting, which would be historic. Tomorrow we would understand everything. Tomorrow we would learn just what he was. When grateful humanity carried him on their shoulders, he would not forget us. He shouted and waved his little legs, ran around the walls, and distracted Eddie from his planning. I had to take him by the scruff of his neck and toss him out into the hall. He did not take offense; he was above all that. Tomorrow everything would be clear, he promised, then asked for Khlebovvodov's suite number and disappeared. I went to bed, and Eddie shuffled papers and sat over his dismantled humanizer for several hours.

When the bedbug was called in, he did not enter the meeting room immediately. We could hear him in the reception area squabbling with the commandant, demanding an honor guard. Eddie was getting worried, and I had to go out into the reception area and tell Gabby to stop fooling around or things would go badly for him.

"But all I'm demanding is that he take three steps toward me!" the bedbug said angrily. "Even if there is no honor guard, there has to be some pomp! After all, I'm not asking him to meet me at the door, hat in hand! Let him take three steps in my direction and nod!"

"You jerk!" I shouted. "Do you want them to listen to you? Get in there! You have thirty seconds!"

Gabby gave in. Muttering something about breaking all the rules, he went into the meeting room and obnoxiously lolled on the demonstration table without greeting anyone. Lavr Fedotovich, his eyes puffy and yellow from yesterday's debauch, peered through his opera glasses. Khlebovvodov, suffering from bilious gas, started the session.

"What do we have to listen to him for? Everything is decided already. He's just going to drive us crazy."

"Just a minute," Farfurkis said, bright and cheery as usual. "Citizen Gabby," he addressed the bedbug, "the Troika deemed it possible to receive you out of turn and hear what you described as your very important announcement. The Troika suggests that you be as brief as possible and not take up too much of its valuable work time. What do you wish to announce? We are listening."

Gabby maintained a rhetorical silence for a few seconds. Then he gathered himself up noisily, struck a haughty pose, and, puffing up his cheeks, began.

"The history of the human race," he said, "contains many shameful incidents of barbarism and stupidity. A rough ignorant soldier bumped off Archimedes. Lousy priests burned Giordano Bruno. Rabid fanatics attacked Charles Darwin and Galileo Galilei. The history of bedbugs also contains references to victims of ignorance and obscurantism. Everyone remembers the unbearable sufferings of the great encyclopedist bedbug Sapukol, who showed our ancestors, the grass and tree bugs, the path of true progress and prosperity. Imperutor, the creator of the theory of blood types, died a forgotten and impoverished bedbug, as did Rexophobe, who solved the problem of fertility, and Nudin, who discovered anabiosis.

"The barbarism and ignorance of both our races could not avoid leaving its mark on their interrelationship. In vain have the ideas of the great utopian bedbug Platun been preserved. He preached the idea of a symbiotic relationship between man and bedbug, no longer based on the age-old parasitism of the bedbug's bright and shining future of friendship and mutual assistance. We know of instances when man proffered peace, protection, and patronage to the bedbug, under the slogan: 'We are of one blood, you and I,' but the greedy, always-hungry bedbug masses ignored this call, repeating over and over: 'We drank, we drink, and we will drink.' "

Gabby gulped down a glass of water, wiped his lips, and continued, increasing in tempo and volume. "Now for the first time in the history of our two races we face a situation where the bedbug offers humanity peace, protection, and patronage, demanding only one thing in return: acknowledgment. For the first time, the bedbug has found a common tongue with man. For the first time, the bedbug communicates with man not in bed but across a conference table. For the first time, the bedbug seeks not material wealth but spiritual communication.

"Now at the crossroads of history, standing at the turn that may lead both races to undreamed-of heights, dare we waste time through indecision, follow once more the road of ignorance and hostility, rejecting the obvious and refusing to acknowledge the miracle that has taken place? I, Gabby Bedbug, the only talking bedbug in the universe, the only link between our races, say to you in the name of millions upon millions: come to your senses! Throw away your prejudices. Throw off the shackles of stagnation, muster all that is good and reasonable in you and look with open and clear eyes into the eyes of a great truth: Gabby Bedbug is an exceptional individual, an unexplained phenomenon, and perhaps an inexplicable one!"

Yes, the vanity of that insect was enough to stun the most jaded imagination. I felt that this would come to no good and nudged Eddie with my elbow. There was a chance that the digestive prostration that afflicted the larger, and better, part of the Troika would preclude any show of passion. Another hopeful factor was the absence of the dissipated Vybegallo, who was still bedridden. Lavr Fedotovich was not well, he was pale and sweating profusely. Farfurkis did not know what course of action to take and kept looking over at him uncertainly. I thought that perhaps it would pass, when suddenly Khlebovvodov spoke up.

" 'We drank, we drink, and we will drink!' Who do you think they're talking about? Us! He's talking about us, the bugger! Our blood! Hah!" He looked around wildly. "I'll squash him right now, I will! Get no sleep at night from them, and now they torture us in the daytime too! Torturers!" And he set about scratching furiously.

Gabby was frightened but continued to carry himself with dignity. However, he was eyeing a convenient corner in case it came to that. The odor of very strong cognac spread through the room.

"Bloodsuckers!" Khlebovvodov rasped, as he jumped up and lunged forward. My heart stopped. Eddie grabbed my hand—he was frightened too. Gabby just squatted in horror. But Khlebovvodov, clutching his stomach, raced past the demonstration table, opened the door, and ran out. We could hear his footsteps on the stairs. Gabby wiped the cold sweat from his brow and dispiritedly lowered his antennae.

"Allow me," said Farfurkis. I realized the machine was starting up. "Citizen Gabby's announcement has created a unique impression on me. I am sincerely and categorically incensed. And not only because Citizen Gabby is giving a perverted history of the human race as the history of the suffering of exceptional individuals. I am also willing to leave the orator's totally unself-critical pronouncements as to his own person to his conscience. But his idea, his offer of union— even the idea of such a union sounds, to me, both insulting and blasphemous. Just what do you take us for, Citizen Gabby? Or perhaps the insult was intentional? Personally, I am inclined to classify it as intentional. And on top of that, I looked through the minutes of the earlier meeting on the case of Citizen Gabby and noted with chagrin that, as far as I am concerned, there is a total lack of the necessary interlocutory decree for the case. This, comrades, is our mistake, our oversight, which we must correct with all due speed. What do I mean? I mean that in the person of Citizen Gabby we are confronted by nothing more than a typical talking parasite—in other words, a sponging loafer with means of support that can only be classified as illegal."

At that moment the exhausted Khlebovvodov appeared in the doorway. As he walked past Gabby he brandished his fist at him and muttered, "You tailless, six-legged cur!" Gabby ducked his head. He finally understood that things were bad. "Alex," Eddie whispered to me in a panic. "Alex, think of something." I feverishly looked for a way out, while Farfurkis droned on.

"Insulting humanity, insulting an authoritative body. This is typical parasitism, which belongs behind bars. Is this not a little much, comrades? Are we not displaying spinelessness, toothlessness, bourgeois liberalism, and abstract humanism? I don't know the feelings of my respected colleagues in this matter, and I don't know what decision will be reached in this case; however, as a man who is not malicious by nature but who is principled, I permit myself to address you, Citizen Gabby, with a word of warning. The fact that you, Citizen Gabby, have learned to speak, or rather to gab, in Russian, may be a temporizing factor in our attitude toward you. But beware! Don't pull the string too tight!"

"Squash the parasite!" rasped Khlebovvodov. "Here, I've got a matchstick." He started patting his pockets.

Gabby's face was blank. So was Eddie's. He was feverishly tinkering with the humanizer. And I still had not come up with a way out.

"No, no, Comrade Khlebovvodov," said Farfurkis, grimacing in disgust, "I am against illegal acts. Why this lynch law? We're not in America, you know. Everything must be done according to the law. First of all, if Lavr Fedotovich has no objections, we must rationalize

Citizen Gabby as an unexplained phenomenon, which will therefore put him in our competence."

Gabby, the fool, cheered up at those words. Ah, vanity!

"Then," continued Farfurkis, "we will classify the rationalized unexplained phenomenon as a dangerous one, and therefore one that can be expunged during the utilization procedure. The rest is ridiculously simple. We will write the decree along these lines: the decree on expunging the talking bedbug, hereafter referred to as Gabby."

"Excuse me!" Farfurkis was on the attack. "What do you mean arbitrary? We are expunging you in accordance with paragraph 75 of the Appendix on Expunging Social Vestiges, where it most clearly states . . ."

"Hold on," I said. "Lavr Fedotovich! I beg you to intervene! This is squandering your cadres!"

Lavr Fedotovich barely managed his "Harrumph." He was so sick that he didn't care.

"Do you hear that?" I asked Farfurkis. "And Lavr Fedotovich is absolutely right! You must pay less attention to form and look more closely at content. Our injured feelings have nothing to do with the best interests of the people's resources. Why this administrative sentimentality? Is this a boarding school for young princesses? Or courses for improving qualifications? Yes, Citizen Gabby is rude and impertinent and uses questionable parallels. Yes, Citizen Gabby is far from perfect. But does that mean that we should expunge him as being unnecessary? What are you thinking of, Comrade Farfurkis? Or are you perhaps prepared to pull out another talking bedbug from your pocket? Maybe your circle of acquaintances includes a talking bedbug? 'Why this lèse-majesté?' 'I don't like the talking bedbug, let's write off the talking bedbug.' And you, Comrade Khlebovvodov? Yes, I can see that you are a man who has suffered deeply from bedbugs. I sympathize deeply with your sufferings, but I ask you: perhaps you have already found a means of combating these bloodsucking parasites? These pirates of the bed, these gangsters of the people's dreams, these vampires of run-down hotels?"

"That's just what I'm saying," said Khlebovvodov. "Just squash him without any to-do. All these decrees and nonsense."

"Oh, no, Comrade Khlebovvodov! We forbid it! We will not allow you to take advantage of the scientific consultant's sickness to introduce and apply crude administrative methods instead of scientific administrative methods. We will not allow voluntarism and subjectivism to reign once more! Don't you understand that Citizen Gabby here is the only opportunity we have so far to begin a reeducation program among these frenzied parasites? In the past, some homegrown talent turned peaceful vegetarian bugs to their present disgusting modus vivendi. Don't you think that our contemporary, educated bedbug, enriched with the full power of theory and practice, is capable of doing the reverse? Armed with carefully composed instructions and the latest techniques of pedagogy, knowing that all of humanity supports him, he could become the Archimedean lever with whose help we will turn the tide of bedbug history back to the forests and fields, to Nature's bosom, to a pure, simple, and innocent existence. I beg the commission to take all these thoughts into consideration and carefully examine them."

I sat down. Eddie, pale with joy, gave me a thumbs-up sign. Gabby was on his knees, fervently praying. As for the Troika, it was dumbstruck by my oratorical power. Farfurkis stared at me with joyous amazement. I could tell that he thought my idea was a stroke of genius and that he was feverishly examining the best way to take over the command of this new undertaking. He was picturing how he would write a wide-ranging, detailed instruction manual; he could see the paragraphs, chapters, appendixes, and footnotes in his mind's eye; in his imagination he was consulting with the bedbug, organizing courses in Russian for gifted bedbugs, being named head of the State Committee on Propaganda for Vegetarianism among Bloodsuckers, whose expanding sphere of activity would also include mosquitoes and gnats, midges and leeches.

"Grass bugs are no joy either, let me tell you," grumbled the conservative Khlebovvodov. He had already capitulated, but he did not want to admit it, so he was picking on minor points. I shrugged expressively.

"Comrade Khlebovvodov is thinking along rigid, narrow lines," countered Farfurkis, pulling ahead by half a length.

"They're not narrow at all," said Khlebovvodov weakly. "They're quite broad, those . . . whatchamacallits. Boy, do they stink! But I realize that can be fixed up in the process, too. I mean, do you think we can trust this upstart? He just doesn't seem serious—and he has no good record of anything."

"I have a motion," said Eddie. "Perhaps a subcommittee should be set up, headed by Comrade Farfurkis, to study this matter. I would suggest Comrade Privalov, a man who is impartial, as a scientific consultant pro tem."

Lavr Fedotovich stood up. Anyone could see that he had been seriously impaired by yesterday's lunch. Ordinary human weakness shone through his usually stony countenance. Yes, there was a crack in the granite, the bastion was breached, but despite all that he stood firm and powerful.

"The people," began the bastion, rolling his eyes in pain. "The people do not like being locked within four walls. The people need room. The people need fields and rivers. The people need the wind and the sun."

"And the moon," added Khlebovvodov, loyally looking up at the bastion.

"And the moon," Lavr Fedotovich confirmed. "The health of the people must be safeguarded, it belongs to the people. The people need work in the great outdoors. The people cannot breathe without the open air."

We didn't understand. Even Khlebovvodov was still trying to figure it out, but the perceptive Farfurkis had already gathered his papers, packed up his notebook, and was whispering to the commandant. The commandant nodded and inquired respectfully:

"Do the people like to walk or drive?"

"The people," announced Lavr Fedotovich, "prefer to ride in a convertible. Expressing the consensus, I move that we postpone the present session and hold at once the field session scheduled for this evening. Comrade Zubo, take care of the details." With those words Lavr Fedotovich fell back heavily into his chair.

Everyone started bustling. The commandant ordered the car, Khlebovvodov plied Lavr Fedotovich with mineral water, and Farfurkis dug around for the necessary documents. I took advantage of the bustle, grabbed Gabby by the leg, and threw him out. Gabby did not protest: this experience had shaken him profoundly and changed him for a long time to come.

The car arrived. Lavr Fedotovich was led out by both arms and seated in the front. Khlebovvodov, Farfurkis, and the commandant, fighting and scratching, shared the back seat with the safe containing the Great Round Seal.

"The car seats five," Eddie said worriedly. "They won't take us." I replied that that was fine with me, I had talked enough to last me a month. It was all a waste of time. We wouldn't change them in a hundred years. We saved the stupid bedbug, fine, let's go for a swim. However, Eddie said that he would not go swimming. He would follow in invisible form and try one more session—in the open air. Maybe that would be more effective.

I started the engine, and the car sped merrily toward the mountain. The odometer clicked off the miles, the wheels whirred in the grass. [. . .] We drove on this way for twenty minutes. When the odometer showed eight miles, Khlebovvodov gasped.

"But what's happening?" he said. "We're moving all right, but the mountain is just where it was."

"We'll never get to the mountain," the commandant said meekly. "It's enchanted. You can't drive there, you can't walk there. We're just wasting gas."

Everyone stopped talking after that, and the odometer racked up another four miles. The mountain was not even a foot closer. The cows, attracted by the sound of the engine, looked in our direction for a while, then lost interest and went back to their grazing. Indignation mounted in the back seat. Khlebovvodov and Farfurkis exchanged several remarks that were maliciously businesslike. "Sabotage," said Khlebovvodov. "Sabotage," said Farfurkis. "Premeditated sabotage."

"Difficulties?" inquired Lavr Fedotovich. "Get rid of them, Comrade Khlebovvodov."

We had been rid of the difficulties for quite some time. I had to go get Khlebovvodov, who lay some thirty yards back on the road, ragged, in torn trousers, and very surprised. It turned out that he had suspected the commandant and me of conspiring to set the car on blocks and to run up the mileage for our own benefit. Impelled by a sense of duty, he decided to get out and reveal our plot by looking under the wheels. The commandant and I dragged him back to the car and laid him down so that he could see for himself. Then we went to help Farfurkis, who was looking for his glasses and upper dentures in the car. The commandant found them on the road.

The confusion was done away with completely, Khlebovvodov's arguments turned out to be rather superficial, and Lavr Fedotovich, who finally realized that there would never be any milk, ever, moved that we not waste gas, which belongs to the people, and get on with our primary responsibilities.

"Comrade Zubov," he said. "Read the report."

Case 29, as was to be expected, had no surname, name, or patronymic. It was provisionally called "Enchantings." The date of birth was lost in the mists of time, but the place of birth was given with extremely precise coordinates. Enchantings's nationality was Russian, it had no education, spoke no foreign languages, its profession was being a hill, and its place of work was again given by the same coordinates. Enchantings had never been abroad, its closest relative was Mother Earth, and its place of permanent residence was again those same coordinates. As for the brief summary of its unexplainability, Vybegallo had wasted no words: "First of all, you can't drive there, and second of all, you can't walk there."

The commandant glowed. The case was definitely proceeding to rationalization. Khlebovvodov was pleased with the application form. Farfurkis was enjoying the self-evident unexplainable factor that did not threaten the people in any way, and it looked as if Lavr Fedotovich had no objections. In any case, he confided to us that the people need mountains, as well as dales, ravines, gullies, Elbrus Mountains, and Kazbek Ranges.

But then the door to the shack opened, and an old man dressed in a long shirt tied at the waist came out onto the porch, leaning on a stick. He stood on the porch, looked at the sun, shielding his eyes, shook his stick at the goat to get it off the roof, and finally sat on the steps.

"So he's a witness," the commandant said sadly. "Isn't everything clear? If you have questions, I can . . ."

"No!" said Farfurkis, peering at him suspiciously. "Why shouldn't we call him? Remember, you don't live here. He's a local."

"Ah!" exclaimed the commandant, throwing his hat on the ground. The case was falling apart before his very eyes. "If he could come here, do you think he'd be sitting over there? He's a prisoner, you see. He can't get out! He's stuck there, and there he'll stay!"

In total despair, under the suspicious scrutiny of the Troika, anticipating new difficulties and therefore becoming very talkative, the commandant told us the Kitezhgrad legend about the forester Feofil. How he had lived peacefully with his wife, how he was still young and hearty then, how green lightning struck the mountain and horrible things started to happen. His wife was in town at the time, and when she came back she couldn't get up the mountain to the house. And Feofil tried to get to her. He ran nonstop for two days—to no avail. And so he stayed there. Him up there, and her in town. Then of course, he got used to it in time. You have to go on living. And so he did. He got used to it.

Having heard this horrible tale and having posed several tricky questions, Khlebovvodov suddenly made a discovery. Feofil had avoided the census takers, had never been subjected to any educational activity, and for all we knew could still be an exploiter, a kulak.

"He has two cows," Khlebovvodov said, "and look, a calf. And a goat. And he doesn't pay taxes." His eyes lit up. "If he's got a calf, he must have a bull, too, hidden away somewhere!"

"He has a bull, that's right," the commandant admitted glumly. "It must be grazing on the other side."

"Well, brother, you really run things well here," Khlebovvodov said. "I knew you were a phony, but I didn't expect something like this, even from you. That you would be a kulak's henchman, that you would cover up for a kulak."

The commandant took a deep breath and waded. "Holy Mother of God. In the name of the twelve original Apostles."

Feofil the forester suddenly looked up and, shading his eyes from the sun, gazed in our direction. Then he tossed his stick aside and started walking down the hill slowly, slipping and sliding in the tall grass. The dirty white goat trailed after him like a puppy. Feofil came up to us, sat down, and rubbed his chin with his bony brown hand in puzzlement. The she-goat sat next to him and stared at us with her yellow devilish eyes.

"You're regular people," Feofil said. "Amazing."

The goat looked over and settled on Khlebovvodov.

"This here is Khlebovvodov," she said. "Rudolf Arkhipovich. Born in 1910 in Khokhloma. His parents got the name out of a romantic novel. Education, seventh grade. He is ashamed of his parents' background, studied many foreign languages, speaks none."

"*Oui*," Khlebovvodov confirmed, giggling with embarrassment. "*Naturalichjawohl!*"

"Has no profession as such. At the present time is a public administrator. Traveled abroad to Italy, France, both Germanies, Hungary, England, and so on—a total of forty-four countries. Has bragged and lied everywhere. His distinguishing character trait is a high degree of tenacity and adaptability, based on his fundamental stupidity and an unwavering desire to out-orthodox orthodoxy."

"Well," said Feofil. "Is there anything you could add to that, Rudolf Arkhipovich?"

"No way!" Khlebovvodov said gleefully. "Except maybe that ortho-ortho-doro-orthxy, it isn't quite clear!"

"To be more orthodox than orthodoxy is sort of like this," explained the goat. "If the authorities are displeased by some scientists, you declare yourself to be an enemy of science in general. If the authorities are displeased by some foreigner, you are ready to declare war on everyone on the other side of the border. Understand?"

"Absolutely," said Khlebovvodov. "How else could it be? Our education is awfully limited. Otherwise, I might make a mistake."

"Does he steal?" asked Feofil casually.

"No," said the goat. "He picks up things that fall off the gravy train."

"Murder?"

"Don't be silly," laughed the goat. "Personally, never."

"Say something," Feofil asked Khlebovvodov.

"There have been mistakes," Khlebovvodov said quickly. "People are not angels. Anyone can make a mistake. Horses have four legs and still they stumble. He who makes no mistakes does not exist, that is, does not work."

"I understand," said Feofil. "Are you going to go on making mistakes?"

"Never!" Khlebovvodov said firmly.

"Thank you," said Feofil. He looked at Farfurkis.

"And this kind gentleman?"

"That's Farfurkis," said the goat. "No one has ever used his name and patronymic. Born in 1916 in Taganrog, higher education in law, reads English with a dictionary. Profession, lecturer. Candidate of oratorical sciences. Has never been abroad. Outstanding character trait is perspicacity and caution. Sometimes he risks incurring the wrath of his superiors, but his actions are always calculated to lead eventually to their gratitude."

"That's not quite right," Farfurkis said softly. "You're mixing your terms a bit. Caution and perspicacity are part of my character whether

I deal with my superiors or not. They're in my chromosomes. As for my superiors, well, that's my job, pointing out the legal parameters of their competence."

"And if they go outside the parameters?" asked Feofil.

"You see," said Farfurkis. "I can tell you're not a lawyer. There is nothing more flexible than a legal parameter. You can delineate one, but you can't overstep one."

"How do you feel about perjury?" asked Feofil.

"I'm afraid that that's a rather old-fashioned term," Farfurkis said. "We don't use it anymore."

"How's he on perjury?" Feofil asked the goat.

"Never," she replied. "He always believes every word he says . . ."

"Tricky," said Feofil. "Very neat. Of course, Farfurkis's philosophy will remain after him?"

"No," said the goat with a laugh. "I mean, the philosophy will remain, but Farfurkis had nothing to do with it. He didn't invent it. He hasn't invented anything at all, except his dissertation, which will be his only legacy, a model of such works."

Feofil was thinking.

"Do I understand correctly?" asked Farfurkis. "Is everything finished? Can we continue our work?"

"Not yet," Feofil replied, awakening from his meditations. "I would like to ask a few questions of this citizen."

"The people . . ." said Lavr Fedotovich, gazing into the distance through his opera glasses.

"Question Lavr Fedotovich?" muttered Farfurkis in shock.

"Yes," the goat said. "Lavr Fedotovich Vuniukov, born in . . ."

"That's it," said Eddie. "I've run out of energy. That Lavr is a bottomless barrel."

"What's this?" shouted Farfurkis in dismay. "Comrades!! What's going on? It's improper!"

"That's right," said Khlebovvodov. "It's not our concern. Let the police take care of it."

"Harrumph," said Lavr Fedotovich. "Are there any other motions? Questions to the speaker? Expressing the consensus, I move that Case 29 be rationalized as an unexplained phenomenon that should be of interest to the Ministry of the Food Industry and the Treasury. As part of preliminary utilization Case 29, known as Enchantings, should be turned over to the district attorney's office of the Tmuskorpion Region."

I looked toward the top of the mountain. Feofil the forester leaned heavily on his stick, standing on his porch, and peered into the sunlight, shading his eyes. The goat wandered in the garden. I waved my beret at him in farewell. Eddie's bitter sigh sounded in my ear simultaneously with the thud of the Great Round Seal.

EPILOGUE

The next morning, before I was fully awake, I immediately sensed how bitter and hopeless it all was. Eddie was sitting at the table in his shorts, his disheveled head in his hands. The shiny parts of the humanizer were spread out before him on a sheet of newspaper. I could tell that Eddie was also depressed and without hope.

I threw off my blanket, put my feet on the floor, and reached over to get cigarettes from my jacket pocket. I lit up. Under other circumstances this unhealthy action would have gotten an immediate reaction from Eddie, who could not stand moral weakness or air pollution. Under other circumstances I would not have tried to smoke in front of Eddie. But today we did not care. We were destroyed, we were hanging over an abyss.

First of all, we hadn't had enough sleep. That was point one, as Modest Matveyevich would have put it. We had glumly tossed and turned until three a.m., toting up the bitter sum of our experiences, opening windows, closing windows, drinking water. I had even chewed my pillow.

It was bad enough that we found ourselves helpless before those plumbers. We could have lived with that. After all, no one had taught us how to deal with them. We were too weak, and, I guess, too green.

It was bad enough that our hopes of at least getting out the Black Box and our Talking Bedbug were completely shattered after the historic conversation in front of the hotel. After all, the enemy was armed with the Great Round Seal, and we couldn't counter that.

But now it was a question of our own future.

The historic conversation in front of the hotel had gone something like this. No sooner had I driven the dusty car up to the hotel, than Eddie appeared on the steps out of nowhere. He was grumpy.

EDDIE: Excuse me, Lavr Fedotovich. Could you spare me a few minutes?

[LAVR FEDOTOVICH *breathes heavily, licks mosquito bites on his arm, waits for the car door to be opened for him.*]

KHLEBOVVODOV [*peevishly*]: The session is over.

EDDIE [*frowning*]: I would like to know when our requisitions will be complied with.

LAVR FEDOTOVICH [*to* FARFURKIS]: Beer is good to drink.

KHLEBOVVODOV [*jealously*]: That's right! The people love beer.

[*Exeunt all from car.*]

COMMANDANT [*to* EDDIE]: Don't you worry, we'll look into your requisitions the very next year.

EDDIE [*suddenly satanic*]: I demand an end to this red tape!

[*He stands in the doorway, blocking the path.*]

LAVR FEDOTOVICH: Harrumph. Difficulties? Comrade Khlebovvodov, get rid of them.

EDDIE [*exploding*]: I demand immediate consideration of our requisitions!

ME [*gloomily*]: Drop it. It's hopeless.

COMMANDANT [*frightened*]: Jesus Christ, in the name of Our Lady of Tmuskorpion, I beg you.

[*Tumultuous scene.* KHLEBOVVODOV *stops in front of* EDDIE *and mea-*

sures him from head to toe with his eyes. EDDIE *quickly releases his excess rage in the form of small bolts of lightning. A gathering of curiosity-seekers. Shout from an open window: "Let 'im have it! What are you staring at? Right in his ugly mug!"* FARFURKIS *whispers to* LAVR FEDOTOVICH.]

LAVR FEDOTOVICH: Harrumph. There is an opinion that our talented young people should be promoted. The motion is to establish Comrade Privalov as chauffeur to the Troika and to name Comrade Amperian as official replacement for our ailing Comrade Vybegallo, with the salary difference paid in full. Comrade Farfurkis, please write a draft of the decree. A copy goes below.

[*Walks straight at* EDDIE. EDDIE's *innate politeness wins out. He lets the older man pass and even holds the door for him. I am stunned, can barely see or hear.*]

COMMANDANT [*joyously shaking my hand*]: Congratulations on your promotion, Comrade Privalov! See, everything is working out.

LAVR FEDOTOVICH: Comrade Zubo!

COMMANDANT: Yes sir!

LAVR FEDOTOVICH [*joking*]: You sweated it out today, Comrade Zubo, so why don't you go down to the steambaths?

[*Horrible laughter of exiting Troika. Curtain.*]

Remembering that scene and remembering that from now on I was fated to be the Troika's chauffeur, I stubbed my cigarette and rasped:

"We have to beat it."

"We can't," Eddie said. "It would be disgraceful."

"And staying isn't?"

"That's disgraceful, too," Eddie agreed. "But we're scouts. No one has relieved us of our duties. We have to bear the unbearable. We must, Alex! We have to go to the session."

I groaned but could not think of a rejoinder.

We washed, we dressed, we even had breakfast. We went out into the city, where everyone was busy with useful and necessary work. We bore our pain stoically. We were pitiful.

As we entered the meeting room, the commandant was reading aloud, and the plumbers and Vybegallo were listening and nodding. We sat down quietly, got a grip on ourselves, and started listening, too. For some time we didn't understand a thing and didn't even try to, but we finally gathered that they were looking into the complaints, applications, and declarations received from the populace. Fedya had told us that they did this once a week.

It befell us to listen to several letters.

The schoolchildren of the village of Vuniukhino reported the local hag Zoia. Everybody says that she is a witch, that she causes crop failures, and that she turned her grandson, a former straight-A student, Vasily Kormilitsyn, into a juvenile delinquent and a dropout just because he took her leg down to the refuse heap. The schoolchildren asked them to investigate this witch, in which they did not believe, being good Pioneers, and have the scientists explain how she ruined crops and turned good students into bad, and couldn't they change her faults into strengths, so that she could change failing students into top ones.

A group of tourists had seen a green scorpion the size of a cow around Lopukhi. The scorpion's mysterious rays put the guards to sleep, and he made off into the woods with a month's supply of groceries. The tourists offered their services in catching the monster, as long as their travel expenses were taken care of.

An inhabitant of Tmuskorpion, P. P. Zaiadlyi, expressed his unhappiness with the fact that the municipal park was littered with all kinds of monsters that made a simple walk impossible. It was all the fault of Commandant Zubo, who used the leftovers from the colony kitchen to feed three personal pigs and his parasitic no-good brother-in-law.

A country doctor from the village of Bubnovo wrote to tell them that during a stomach operation on Citizen Pantsermanov, age fifteen years, he discovered an ancient Sogdian coin in his appendix. The physician called their attention to the fact that the late Pantsermanov had never been to Middle Asia and had never seen the discovered coin before. The remaining forty-two pages of the letter revealed the highly erudite doctor's views on telepathy, telekinesis, and the fourth dimension. He appended tables, graphs, and full-scale photographs of the coin, obverse and reverse.

Action was taken thoughtfully and leisurely. After the reading of each letter, there was a long pause, filled with profound interjections. Then Lavr Fedotovich would take a Herzegovina Flor, turn his gaze to Vybegallo, and ask the comrade scientific consultant to draft an answer for the Troika. Vybegallo would smile broadly with his red lips, smooth his beard with both hands, and, asking permission not to rise, would give the reply. He did not spoil the correspondents with variety. He had a standard reply: "Dear Sir (Madam, Sirs): We have received and read your interesting letter. The facts you relate are well known to science and are of no interest to it. Nevertheless, we thank you warmly for your alertness and wish you success in your work and personal life." Signature. That was it. In my opinion it was Vybegallo's best invention. One could not help but experience great satisfaction in sending that letter in reply to a declaration that "Mr. Shchin has drilled a hole in my wall and is sending poisonous gases through it."

The machine went on with deadening monotony. The commandant droned on nasally. Lavr Fedotovich burped. Vybegallo smacked his lips. A deadly apathy overpowered me. I knew that this was decay, that I was falling into a quagmire of spiritual entropy, but I did not want to struggle any longer. "All right," I thought. "So what? People live this way too. Everything rational is actual, and everything actual is rational. And as long as it is rational, it must be good. And since it's good, it's probably eternal."

"And really, what difference is there between Lavr Fedotovich and Fyodor Semyonovich Kivrin? They're both immortal, and they're both omnipotent. So why argue? I don't understand. What does man need? Mysteries? I don't need them. Knowledge? Why know things when the salary is so high anyway? Lavr Fedotovich even has his good points. He does no thinking himself and doesn't let others do it either. He doesn't allow his fellow workers to strain themselves. He is a good man, and an attentive one. And it will be easy to get ahead under him. It'll be easy to get rid of Farfurkis and Khlebovvodov. After all, they're fools, they only undermine the authority of the leadership. And authority must be supported. If God did not give the leader a brain, he must at least be allowed to have authority. You give him authority, and he gives you everything else. The important thing is to become useful to him, his right hand, or at least his left."

And I would have perished, poisoned by the horrible emanations from the Great Round Seal and the band of plumbers, and at best I would have ended my life as an exhibit in our institute's vivarium. Eddie too would have perished. He was still moving, he was still striking poses, but it was all a show. Actually, as he later confessed to me, he was trying to figure out how to get rid of Vybegallo and get a piece of land in the suburbs to build on. Yes, we surely would have perished. They would have trampled us, taking advantage of our despair and depression.

But at that moment silent thunder shook our universe. We came to our senses. The door opened, and Fyodor Semyonovich and Christobal Joséevich stood before us.

Their rage was indescribable. They were terrible to behold. Their gaze made walls smoke and windows melt. The poster about the people and sensationalism went up in flames. The house shook and shuddered, the parquet floor buckled, and the chairs squatted on their terror-weakened legs. It was impossible for even the Troika to endure it.

Khlebovvodov and Farfurkis, pointing at each other with trembling fingers, howled in unison: "It wasn't me! It's all his fault!" and turned into yellow smoke and disappeared without a trace.

Professor Vybegallo yelped "*Mon Dieu!*" and dove under his table. Pulling out his large briefcase, he handed it over to the thunder gods: "*C'est,* all the materials, that is, I have the goods on these scoundrels, all here!"

The commandant tore at his collar and fell on his knees.

As for Lavr Fedotovich, he sensed some discomfiture around him. Turning his head anxiously, he rose, leaning on the green baize.

Fyodor Semyonovich approached us, put his arms around us, and hugged us to his ample stomach. "There, there," he said as we fell against him, bumping our heads, "It's all r-r-right, b-b-boys. You held out for th-th-three d-d-days. M-m-marvelous." Through my tears, I saw Christobal Joséevich, brandishing his cane, approach Lavr Fedotovich and address him through clenched teeth:

"Get out."

Lavr Fedotovich slowly registered surprise.

"The people . . ." he said.

"OUT!!!"

They eyeballed each other for a second. Something human flickered across Lavr Fedotovich's face—maybe shame, maybe fear, maybe anger. He slowly put his accoutrements of chairmanship into his briefcase.

"There is a motion: in view of special circumstances the session of the Troika will be postponed for an indefinite period."

"Forever," said Christobal Joséevich, laying his cane on the table.

"Harrumph," said Lavr Fedotovich doubtfully.

He majestically circled the table without looking at anyone, and went to the door. Before leaving, he announced:

"There is an opinion that we shall meet again in another place and at another time."

"I doubt it," said Junta with disdain, biting off the end of his cigar.

We really did run into Lavr Fedotovich in another place and at another time.

But, of course, that's another story.

1968

BEFORE THE COCK CROWS THRICE

EXCERPTS

VASILY SHUKSHIN

A TALE ABOUT IVAN THE FOOL, HOW HE TRAVELED BEYOND THE THRICE-NINTH KINGDOM TO ACQUIRE SOME WITS AND WISDOM

Once upon a time, in a certain library, at about six o'clock in the evening, some characters in Russian classical literature started arguing. While the librarian was still at her desk, they watched her from their shelves with interest—and waited. Toward closing time, she had a telephone conversation with somebody. The characters listened, but, to their surprise, they couldn't understand what she was talking about.

"Well, no," said the librarian, "I think that's a load of hogwash. He's an ass . . . Why don't we go dancing instead? Eh? No! I told you he was an ass. So we'll go dancing? Afterward we'll call on Vladi . . . Yes I know he's a mule but he's got a Grundig—we can sit down for a bit . . . The walrus will be there and who else? Oh, yes, the owl . . . yes, I know they're all asses, but we've got to pass the time somehow! Yes, I'm listening."

"I don't understand a word," said a man in a top hat—either Onegin or Chatsky—to his neighbor, a heavily built landowner who looked like Oblomov. The latter smiled.

"They must be going to the zoo."

"Why are there so many asses?"

"I suppose it's some sort of private joke. She's pretty, eh?"

The man in the top hat frowned.

"Rather vulgar."

"I know you prefer French women," said Oblomov disapprovingly, "but she looks good to me. See how much of her legs she's showing. Not a bad idea, eh?"

A man of threadbare appearance, obviously a Chekhov character, joined in the conversation. "But there's no need for her to wear her skirt as short as that, is there?"

Oblomov laughed softly.

"You don't have to look down there if you don't want to."

The Chekhov character was embarrassed. "I didn't mean . . . There's no need to worry . . . Only why did they begin with the legs?"

"Begin what?" asked Oblomov, puzzled.

"To change the fashions."

"It seems the natural place to start. Begin at the bottom and work upwards."

"You don't change," observed the battered man with hidden contempt.

Oblomov laughed again quietly.

"Tammy! Tammy! Listen!" the librarian shouted into the receiver. "Listen! He's an ass, then! Who's got a car? He has? No, seriously?" She listened in silence for a long time. "Really! A PhD? What in?" she asked softly. "Really? That makes me an ass."

She was very upset. She replaced the receiver, sat still for a while, then got up and went out, locking the door behind her.

The characters jumped down from their shelves and arranged the chairs.

"Quickly, quickly!" cried a bald, bureaucratic type. "Let's get on with it. Who else wants to speak about Ivan the Fool? But, please, don't repeat yourself. And make it short. We must make a decision today. Who's first?"

"Can I speak?" asked Poor Liza.

"Go ahead, Liza," said the bald man.

"I'm a peasant too," began Poor Liza. "You all know how poor I am . . ."

"We know, we know!" everybody groaned. "Keep it short!"

"I'm ashamed to live on the same shelf as Ivan the Fool," Liza went on angrily. "How much longer are we going to be degraded by his company?"

"Expel him!" they shouted.

"Quiet!" said the bureaucrat sternly. "What do you propose, Liza?"

"He must get a certificate of intelligence," said Liza.

Everybody made noises of approval. "Good idea!"

"If he doesn't get a certificate, he can clear off!"

"You're being much too hasty," said big Ilya Muromets. He was still sitting on his shelf—he couldn't stand up. "It's all very well to shout, but where's he going to get it from?"

"I propose we send Ivan the Fool to the Wise Man for a certificate," said Liza clearly and convincingly. "If he doesn't bring it before the cock crows thrice, he can—I don't know—he can leave us."

"Where would he go?" asked Ilya gloomily.

"He can go to a secondhand bookseller!" cried Liza harshly.

"That's a bit tough, isn't it?" somebody demurred. "Not at all," said the chairman, also very harshly. "It's perfectly fair. Ivan . . ."

"Ay-ay-ay-!" exclaimed Ivan. He stood up, [. . .] went to the middle of the library, bowed low to everybody, pulled his cap down tighter, and headed for the door. "If I fail, don't think too badly of me," he said from the doorway.

"If you come back with the certificate, Ivan," said Liza enthusiastically, "I'll marry you." "I wouldn't marry you," said Ivan rudely. "I'd much rather marry a princess."

"I shouldn't, Ivan," Ilya shrugged. "None of them are any better than she is. Mind you, I don't know why you want him to get a certificate," he said to Liza. "You're making a terrible fuss about it, sending the lad off at this time of night! What if this Wise Man of yours won't give him a certificate?"

"He's got to have a certificate, Uncle Ilya," said Liza firmly. "As for you, Ivan, I shan't forget that you refused me."

"Off you go, then," said the chairman. "It's getting late. You'll have to hurry." "Good-bye," said Ivan. And off he went, following his nose.

He walked a long, long way.

It was dark. He walked and walked until he came to a wood. And he had no idea where to go next, so he sat down on a tree stump and gave way to lamentation.

"Oh, woe is me!" he said. "Where is this Wise Man? If only there were someone to help." But nobody helped him.

He sat for a little longer, then went on. He walked and walked; then he saw a light. He went nearer and saw a little cottage standing on chicken legs, as in the old tales. Piled up all round it were joists and breeze blocks and roofing-felt.

"Is anybody there?" shouted Ivan.

Baba Yaga came out onto the porch. She looked at Ivan and asked: "Who are you? And where are you going?"

"I'm Ivan the Fool. I'm going to the Wise Man for a certificate," answered Ivan. "But I don't know where to find him."

"Why do you need a certificate?"

"I don't know; I was just told to get one."

"Ah!" said Baba Yaga. "Well, come in, come in. Have a rest from your travels. I expect you'd like something to eat?"

"I wouldn't say no."

"Come in."

Ivan went inside the cottage.

Just an ordinary cottage—nothing special. A big stove, a table, and two beds.

"Who else lives here?" asked Ivan.

"My daughter. Look, Ivan," began Yaga, "how foolish *are* you? Are you a complete fool?"

"How do you mean?"

"I mean, are you a complete fool or did they call you a fool on the spur of the moment? Sometimes people get cross and shout: 'You fool!' I sometimes say that to my daughter. 'You're a foolish girl,' I say. But she's not really foolish. She's ever so intelligent. Perhaps the same thing happened to you. People got so used to calling you a fool and yet you're not a fool at all—just guileless. Eh?"

"I don't know what you're driving at."

"Well, I can see with my own eyes that you're not a fool. As soon as I saw you, I thought: there's a talented lad! Surely you don't think you're foolish, do you?"

"I've never thought it!" said Ivan angrily. "How could I think I was a fool?"

"So why should I think it? Were you ever in the building trade?"

"How do you mean? I helped my father and brothers knock up a few palaces. Why d'you ask?"

"Well, you see, I want to build myself a little bungalow. I've got all the materials together but I've got nobody to build it. Would you take it on?"

"I've got to get my certificate."

"But what do you need it for?" exclaimed Baba Yaga. "If you build the bungalow, people will see it—all kinds of people come and visit me—and when they see it, they'll want to know who built it. And it'll be Ivan who did it. You see? Your fame will spread through the entire forest."

"But what about the certificate?" Ivan asked again. "They won't have me back without the certificate."

"What of it?"

"Where would I go?"

"You can be the boiler-house attendant at the bungalow. When you build it, plan yourself a room in the basement. It'll be warm and quiet— no worries. When the guests upstairs are bored, they'll go and see you and listen to your stories. You can tell them some of your adventures and make up a few. And I'll look after you! I'll call you Ivanushka."

"You old hag!" said Ivan. "So that's what you're up to! You'll call me Ivanushka, will you? And I'll be your slave, eh? Not bloody likely, Grandma!"

"A-a-a!" screamed Baba Yaga. "Now I know who I'm dealing with. You sham, you rogue, you monster. We know how to deal with the likes of you—we roast them. Hey, who's there?" Baba Yaga clapped her hands three times. "Guard! Take this fool and tie him up. We'll give him a bit of a roasting."

Four hearty-looking bodyguards seized Ivan, bound him, and laid him on a bench.

"I ask you for the last time," Baba Yaga tried once more. "Will you build my bungalow?"

"Go to hell!" said Ivan proudly. "Scarecrow! You've got hair growing out of your nostrils!"

"Into the stove," yelled Yaga. She stamped her feet. "Monster! Hooligan!"

"Hooliganess!" Ivan yelled back. "Witch! You've got hair growing from your tongue as well as your nostrils! Bloodsucker!"

"Into the fire!" Yaga was beside herself. "Into the fire!"

They began to shovel Ivan into the stove. Then Ivan began to sing:

> *I shaved you in the garden, among the hollyhocks,*
> *And in return you gave to me a pair of shoes and socks.*
> *Toora-loora-loora, toora-loora-lay.*
> *Fire doesn't burn me, so I needn't be afraid!*

No sooner had Ivan been bundled into the stove than there was the ringing of sleigh bells and the neighing of horses outside.

"My daughter's come!" rejoiced Baba Yaga, looking through the window. "She's brought her fiancé with her, too! We've got a nice feast for them."

The bodyguards also rejoiced, jumping up and down and clapping their hands.

"Gorynych the Dragon has come! Gorynych the Dragon has come!" they cried. "We can have a party! We can get drunk!"

Baba Yaga's daughter came into the cottage. She was as hideous as her mother and had a mustache.

"Fee Fi Fo Fum," she said. "I smell the blood of a Russian man! Who is it?"

"Supper," said Baba Yaga. She gave a coarse laugh.

"What's the matter with you, cackling away like that?! Tell me— who is it?"

"We're roasting Ivan!"

"Really!" the daughter was pleasantly surprised.

"Can you imagine? He didn't want our forest to be beautiful. He wouldn't build us a bungalow. The lazy devil!"

The daughter glanced into the stove and heard what sounded halfway between sobs and laughter.

"I can't stand it!" groaned Ivan. "I won't die of burning, but I'll certainly die laughing!"

"What did you say?" asked Baba Yaga's daughter. Yaga also approached the stove.

"What's going on?"

"Is he laughing?"

"What's the matter?"

"Oh dear, I'll die laughing!" shouted Ivan. "I can't stand it!"

"He's crazy!" said the daughter. "What's the matter with you?"

"That mustache! That incredible mustache! Dear God, I've never seen anything like it! How are you going to sleep with your husband when you get married?"

"Like everyone else. What are you talking about?" The daughter didn't understand, but she was alarmed.

"I'm talking about your mustache."

"What about it? It's no problem. On the contrary, it improves my sense of smell."

"It may not be a problem to you, but what about your husband? When you get married—"

"My husband! What are you driving at, you fool? Why should you be bothered about my husband?" Now the daughter was very worried.

"I'll tell you. He'll kiss you in the dark and he'll think: 'Hell and damnation! Have I married a man or a woman?' And he won't love you anymore. I mean, you can't love a woman with a mustache! Good God, you witches don't understand a damn thing. I tell you, he won't live with you if you've got a mustache. He might decide to bite your head off in his temper. I know these Gorynyches."

Baba Yaga and her daughter thought for a moment.

"Come out, then," ordered the daughter.

Ivan the Fool quickly climbed out and shook himself.

"Nice and warm in there—"

"So, what do you advise?" asked Baba Yaga. "About the mustache?"

"Well, you'll have to get rid of it if you want a successful family."

"And how can she get rid of it?"

"If I tell you, you'll throw me back in the stove."

"No, we won't, Vanyushka," said Baba Yaga's daughter affectionately. "We'll let you go whenever you want, if only you'll tell me how to get rid of my mustache."

Ivan decided to prolong negotiations and make bargains, like our present-day plumbers and mechanics.

"It's not so simple. I'll have to make up the prescription."

"Well, get on with it, then!"

"That's all very well, but when am I going to see the Wise Man? I've got to get back before the cock crows thrice."

"I'll tell you what we'll do," said Baba Yaga excitedly. "Listen! You get rid of the mustache and I'll give you my broomstick and you'll be with the Wise Man in a trice."

Ivan thought for a moment.

"Hurry up!" urged the bewhiskered daughter. "Gorynych'll be here in a minute."

It was Ivan's turn to be alarmed.

"He's coming here?"

"Yes."

"He may eat me up as soon as he comes in."

"He may," agreed the daughter. "What shall we tell him?"

"I'll say you're my nephew," Baba Yaga suggested. "Agreed?"

"All right," agreed Ivan. "By the way, my prescription doesn't work immediately."

"Why not?" The daughter was on her guard.

"We'll make up the prescription and put the mask on your face. Then you can lie down for a bit while I'm flying to the Wise Man on the broomstick."

"What if he lets us down?" The daughter was suspicious.

"Let him try," said Baba Yaga. "If he gets up to any tricks, I'll get him back from the other end of the world and that'll be the end of him."

"You stupid bitches!" Ivan was alarmed again. (In fact, he had been planning to trick them.) "Why are you so suspicious? Do you want to get rid of the mustache or not? It makes no difference to me! I make you a fair offer and you start . . . Do you trust me or not?"

"What's trust got to do with it? Stick to the point."

"I can't," Ivan went babbling on. "You don't trust me. Well, keep your mustache! Keep it! You'll have to manage as best you can. Not a woman, but a major general. Phew! And what about the children? Your baby son will stretch out his hand and say, 'Mom, what's this you've got?' And what about when he grows up? The kids in the street will start teasing him. 'Your mom's got a mustache! Your mom's got a mustache!' Do you think it'll be easy for the child? Will he enjoy hearing that sort of talk? Nobody else's mother's got a mustache, but his mom's got one. How's he going to answer? He won't know what to say. Tears'll stream down his face and he'll run home to his hairy mother . . ."

"Stop!" said Baba Yaga's daughter. "Get your mixture ready. What do you need?"

"A handful of chicken droppings, a handful of warm cow's dung, and a handful of warm clay. Then we'll make a mask for your face . . ."

"The whole of my face? How am I going to breathe?"

"You still don't trust me!" Ivan complained bitterly. "I can't do anything if you . . ."

"All right," barked the daughter. "Can't I ask a simple question?"

"No, you can't," Ivan barked back. "When the maestro's thinking, you mustn't ask any questions! I repeat: droppings, dung, and clay. The mask will have an opening for you to breathe through. Simple!"

"Did you hear?" said Baba Yaga to the bodyguards. "To the barn. As fast as you can."

The bodyguards ran to get the droppings, the dung, and the clay.

Suddenly the three heads of Gorynych the Dragon burst through the window and began to stare at Ivan. Everyone in the cottage stood stock-still. Gorynych looked at Ivan for a long time. Then he asked:

"Who's this?"

"It's my nephew, Ivanushka," said Yaga. "Ivanushka, say hello to Uncle Gorynych."

"Hello, Uncle Gorynych!" said Ivan. "How're things?" Gorynych took a long, hard look at Ivan—so long and so hard that Ivan began to get nervous.

"Well, what's up with you? I'm her nephew, didn't you hear? I've come to visit Auntie Yaga. I'm her guest. So you eat guests, do you? And when you've raised a family, I suppose you'll eat them too. Fine daddy you'll make!"

Gorynych's heads began to debate among themselves. The first said: "I think he's a lout."

After a moment's thought, the second said:

"I think he's a fool. He's nervous, too."

"He'll make nice chopped meat," said the third.

"I'll show you how to make chopped meat!" Ivan exploded in terror. "You watch out! Aunt, where's my magic sword?" He jumped from the bench and ran round the cottage, pretending to look for it. "Aren't you tired of carrying three heads?! Well, I'll soon put that right!" Ivan was shouting at Gorynych but without looking at him. He was still too scared to look at those three motionless heads.

"He's very vulgar," repeated the first head.

"He's very nervous," observed the second. "And afraid." The third didn't manage to say anything because Ivan was now standing in front of Gorynych and staring at him.

"Reptile!" said Ivan. "I'm going to eat you." [. . .]

Thereupon Ivan sat down on the bench, took out his flute, and began to play. "Go on then, eat me," he said, breaking off from his flute-playing. "If you want to eat me, eat me. Skunk! Then kiss your bride's mustache. Then you can produce children with mustaches and march them up and down. You think you can frighten me! Well, you bloody well can't!" With that he began to play his flute again.

"Ignore him, Gorynych," said the daughter. "Don't be insulted."

"He's a boor," retorted the first head. "What a way to talk!"

"He's desperate. He doesn't know what he's doing."

"Oh yes, I do," interjected Ivan. "I know exactly what I'm doing. I'm composing a march for you. For the future battalion—"

"Vanyushka," began Baba Yaga gently. "Don't be rude, my dear. Why are you behaving like this?"

"To prove that he can't frighten me. Look at the way he's rolling his eyes! You can roll your eyes when you've got a battalion of musta-chioed monsters, but not now!"

"He's extremely rude!" said the first head, almost in tears. "Isn't he?"

"Cry away," said Ivan harshly. "While the rest of us laugh. Into our mustaches."

"We're wasting time," said the second head.

"Yes, stop wasting time," agreed Ivan. "Why are we wasting time?"

"Oh!" said the third voice in surprise. "Who's talking?"

"Aha!" Ivan answered meaninglessly. "Vanka's a fine fellow! Let's sing!" And Vanka began to sing:

I shaved you in the garden, among the hollyhocks,
And in return you gave to me a pair of shoes and socks.

"Sing the chorus, Gorynych! 'Toora-loora-loora, toora-loora-lay,'" concluded Vanka.

There was a very long silence.

"Do you know any ballads?" asked Gorynych.

"What sort of ballads?"

"Old ones."

"As many as you like. You like ballads? All right, sir. I'll sing as many as you like. Romantic ballads by the score. For instance:

> *In his humble cottage*
> *Sits Has-Bulat the Bold.*
> *I should like to give him*
> *A palace made of gold.*

"How d'you like my ballad, eh?" Detecting a change in Gorynych, Vanya went up and slapped one of his six cheeks. "You grumpy old thing."

"Behave yourself," said Gorynych. "Or I'll bite your hand off." Vanya withdrew his hand.

"Now, now," he said gently. "You mustn't talk to the skilled workers like that. If you're not careful, I won't sing."

"Yes, you will," said the head that Ivan had slapped. "Or I'll bite your head off."

The other two heads laughed. Ivan also laughed a short, bitter laugh.

"If you do that, I won't sing at all. I won't have anything to sing with."

"Meatballs," remarked the head that had earlier said "chopped meat." This was the stupidest head.

Ivan got angry with it. "You want to eat everything! Everything! You're a real glutton."

"Vanyushka, don't be awkward," said Baba Yaga. "Sing."

The daughter also wanted him to sing. "You've done enough talking. We're all listening, so sing."

"Sing," said the first head. "And you two must sing, too."

"Who?" asked Baba Yaga. "Us?"

"Yes, you."

"I'd rather sing on my own," rasped the daughter. She didn't relish the idea of accompanying Ivan. "I'm sorry, but singing with a man, you know . . ."

"Three, four," said Gorynych softly. "Begin." Ivan began:

> *I'll give you a saddle,*
> *I'll give you a horse,*

Baba Yaga and her daughter joined in:

> *I'll give you my pistol,*
> *And you in return*
> *Must give me your wife.*
> *You're already old,*
> *You're already gray.*
> *She's better without you.*
> *The moment she saw you*
> *Her ruin began.*

Gorynych's round, expressionless eyes became moist. Like every tyrant, he was sentimental. "More," he whispered.

Ivan continued:

> *Under the plane-tree,*
> *Together we sat,*
> *The moon swam with gold;*
> *Not a sound could be heard.*

Ivan repeated the last bit with feeling:

> *The moon swam with gold;*
> *Not a sound could be heard.*

Gorynych was greatly moved. "What's your home like, Ivan?" he asked.

"What do you mean?"

"Nice cottage?"

"I live in a library with a lot of other people."

"Would you like a detached cottage?"

"No. Why should I?"

"Carry on singing."

> She let me make love to her
> Day after day—

"Cut that out," said Gorynych.

"What do you mean?"

"Cut it out."

"Gorynych, you can't leave words out of songs," Ivan smiled. There was another long and ominous pause, during which Gorynych stared at Ivan.

"If you cut that out, there's no song!" said Ivan nervously. "Don't you see? No song!"

"Yes, there is," said Gorynych.

"How can there be?"

"It's better like that—laconic."

"You see what they're doing?" Ivan slapped his thighs in amazement. "They think they can do what they like! You can't cut out the whole point of the song! I won't sing a more laconic version!"

"Don't be obstinate, Vanyushka," said Baba Yaga.

"Go to hell!" Ivan was very angry now. "Sing on your own. I won't! Damn the lot of you! I'll eat you all up! Mustache and all. And as for the three pumpkins . . . I'll roast them until . . ."

"Lord give me patience," sighed the first head. "The effort, the nervous energy we waste on teaching people like this. No education. No upbringing."

The second head said: "When he talks of 'roasting' he's talking sense, eh?"

"What mustache are you referring to?" asked the third head. "I keep hearing about this mustache. Whose mustache?"

Through his flaxen mustache
The young man smiled,

sang the first head jokingly. "How does the song about Has-Bulat go on?"

"She let me make love to her," said Ivan succinctly. Another silence.

"That's coarse, Ivan," said the first head. "It's bad aesthetics. How could you? You, who live in a library. You've got such fine characters there. Where did you acquire this sexuality? Poor Liza's there, I know—a lovely girl. I knew her father. Is she your fiancée?"

"Liza? Certainly not!"

"Why not? I expect she's waiting for you."

"Let her wait!"

"Mmmm—a fruit," said the third head. And the head that was always bent downward, chewing something, responded:

"No, not fruit," it said seriously. "How could he be fruit? No, I still think chopped meat. Or possibly a kebab."

"What happened to Has-Bulat after that?" asked the first head.

"He was killed," said Ivan meekly.

"Who was?"

"Has-Bulat."

"Who killed him?"

"Mmmm—" Ivan frowned painfully. "The young lover killed him. The song ends like this: 'The old man's head went rolling down the hill . . .'"

"You can cut that out as well," said the head. "That's too violent."

"How should it go, then?"

The head thought for a moment. "They made peace. Has-Bulat gave him a horse and saddle and they went home." [. . .]

"Do you know how to dance?" asked the intelligent head.

"Yes, but I'm not going to."

"I think he knows how to build bungalows," interjected Baba Yaga. "But when I suggested—"

"Quiet!" barked all three heads. "We didn't authorize anybody to speak."

"Heavens above!" whispered Baba Yaga. "I'm not allowed to speak now."

"No, you're not," barked the daughter. "What d'you think this is? A cattle market?"

"Give us a dance, Vanya," said the intelligent head in his most ingratiating voice.

"No, I won't," persisted Ivan.

The head thought for a moment.

"So you're going for a certificate?"

"That's right."

"And the certificate will say: 'This certificate is given to Ivan in recognition of his intelligence.' Is that right? With a rubber stamp?"

"I suppose so."

"You won't get there." The intelligent head gazed thoughtfully at Ivan. "You'll never get your certificate."

"Why won't I get there? I've got this far."

"I tell you, you won't." The head kept looking at Ivan. "You won't get there. You won't even leave here."

After a few minutes of agonizing indecision, Ivan raised his hand and mournfully announced: "The porch!"

"Three, four," said the head. "Let's go." [. . .]

Ivan danced round and round, clicking his heels. But instead of putting his hands on his hips, he let them hang down at his sides. He didn't toss his head in the air and he neglected the traditional "falcon stare."

"Why aren't you staring like a falcon?" asked the head.

"I *am*," Ivan answered.

"You're looking at the floor."

"A falcon can have a think."

"What about?"

"The future. How he's going to bring up his little falcons. Have pity on me, Gorynych," implored Ivan. "How much more? I've had enough . . ."

"Ah!" said the intelligent head, "now you're being more sensible. You'd better go for your certificate. Otherwise you'll be getting too big for your boots. Just because you can clap your hands and whistle, I suppose you think that makes you a star?"

Ivan said nothing.

"Stand facing the door," ordered Gorynych. Ivan said nothing.

"Stand facing the door," ordered Gorynych. Ivan obeyed.

"At my command, you'll fly from here at the speed of sound."

"The speed of sound—that's too fast, Gorynych," objected Ivan. "I can't manage that."

"Well, do your best. Get ready . . . Three, four!"

Ivan flew out of the cottage.

Baba Yaga, her daughter, and all of Gorynych's three heads roared with laughter.

"Come here," Gorynych summoned his fiancée. "Let me cuddle you."

Ivan came to some gates and a high wall. There was a notice on the gates: "Devils not admitted."

Before the gates stood a large sentry, holding a lance and peering in front of him.

It was a chaotic scene—the aftermath of an orgy. Some of the devils, their hands thrust into the pockets of their narrow trousers, were doing a lazy tap dance. Some were browsing through illustrated magazines. Some were shuffling cards. One was juggling with skulls. A couple in a corner were learning how to stand on their heads. A group of devils had spread newspapers on the ground and were consuming brandy and hors d'oeuvres, and a quartet, three guitarists, and a girl singer were giving a beautiful performance of "Dark Eyes." The girl was very pretty, with lovely shoes and trousers. Yet the sentry didn't seem in the least concerned. He just watched her calmly and smiled condescendingly into his mustache.

"Can I join you?" said Ivan, approaching the drinkers. They looked him up and down and turned away.

"Is this what you call hospitality?" asked Ivan sharply. They looked at him again.

"Who do you think you are, a prince?" asked one of them, a fat man with big horns.

"Yes, and if you're not careful I'll drag you across that bumpy ground over there and your flesh will come away in lumps. Stand up!"

The devils were astonished. They looked at Ivan. "Did you hear me?" Ivan kicked the bottles. "Get up!!!" The fat one jumped up and was about to attack Ivan, but his colleagues grabbed him and dragged him aside. An elegant, middle-aged, bespectacled person appeared before Ivan.

"What's the matter, my friend?" he asked, taking Ivan by the arm. "Why all the fuss? Mmm? Have we hurt ourselves? Or are we in a bad mood? What do you want?"

"I want a certificate," said Ivan defiantly.

More devils came up. A circle was formed, with Ivan in the middle.

"Carry on," shouted the elegant one to the musicians and the girl. "What sort of certificate do you want, Ivan?"

"That I'm intelligent . . ."

The devils exchanged glances. They had a hurried consultation.

"A schizo," said one of them. "Or a con man."

"I don't think so," replied another. "I expect he's applying for a job. Do you want just the one certificate?"

"Yes."

"But what sort, Ivan? There are various sorts. There are character references, affirmations . . . 'in the absence of,' 'in the presence of,' 'inasmuch as,' 'because of the fact that,' 'in view of the fact that,' 'in conjunction with,'—various sorts, you see. Which sort exactly did they tell you to get?"

"That I'm intelligent."

362

"I don't understand. Do you want a degree?"

"No, a certificate."

"But there are hundreds of certificates! There's 'in connection with' and 'notwithstanding.' "

"There's—"

"I'll drag you over the bumpy ground until you're sick! Or I'll recite the Lord's Prayer."

"Calm down, Vanya. Calm down," said the elegant devil nervously. "Why are you making such a commotion? We can provide any certificate, as long as we understand what sort you want. We can provide—"

"O-ho!"

"He's not satisfied with a fake certificate. He's incorruptible! A real Angelo!"

"He must be a cardinal! He's going to recite the Lord's Prayer. Will you sing: 'I'd live on bread and water'?"

"Listen, devils! I'd like to know how he's going to drag us across the bumpy ground. Is he pulling our legs? I think it's just a leg-pull. How could a country bumpkin like this drag us anywhere?"

More devils came up. Ivan was surrounded on all sides. They all stared at him and gesticulated.

"He's been knocking back the brandy!"

"He's ill-mannered! What does he mean by 'dragging us across the bumpy ground'? Is it blackmail?"

"Give him a dose of his own medicine!"

"Punch him! Punch him!"

Things were not looking too good. Ivan was being hemmed in. "Listen, devils," he shouted, raising his hand. "Listen, I have a proposal."

"Listen, brothers," said the elegant one. "He has a proposal. Let's hear his proposal." Ivan, the elegant devil, and several other devils went aside and began to parley. Ivan spoke softly and his head was turned toward the sentry. The others were looking in the same direction.

The girl and the musicians were still performing in front of the sentry. The girl was singing an ironic song, "You're no man!" She danced as she sang.

"I'm not sure," said the elegant devil. "What do you think?"

"We shall have to do some checking," the others said. "But it seems to make sense." "Yes, we shall have to check. But it makes sense."

"We'll check it," said the elegant devil to his assistant. "There's some sense in it. If the idea works, we'll send one of our devils with Ivan and he'll arrange for the Wise Man to receive them. It's very difficult to reach him."

"But no deception!" said Ivan. "If the Wise Man doesn't receive me, I'll take the devil by the throat . . ."

"Now listen, Ivan," said the elegant devil. "Don't get carried away. Everything will be comme il faut. What do we need, maestro?" he asked his assistant.

"We need some data about the sentry," replied the latter. "Where he was born, who his parents are. And one more consultation with Ivan."

"Consult the card index," said the elegant one succinctly. Two devils ran off somewhere and the elegant one embraced Ivan and began to walk up and down with him, whispering.

They brought up the data. One reported:

"From Siberia. Parents were peasants."

The elegant devil, Ivan, and the maestro had a short conference.

"Really?" asked the elegant one.

"Absolutely correct," replied Ivan. "Cross my heart."

"Maestro?"

"In two and a half minutes," answered the maestro, looking at his watch.

"Get on with it, then," said the elegant one.

The maestro and six other devils—three males and three females— sat a little way off with their instruments and had a short rehearsal. When they were satisfied, the maestro nodded and the six began to chant:

In Zabaikal the miners
Dig for gold all day.
Cursing fate, a beggar
Winds his weary way.

Here we must break off from the story and consider the power of song. It was a beautiful song, soulful and sad. The music was soft yet powerful and clear, and it struck into the very heart. The devils no longer seemed to be taking part in a witches' sabbath. All of them, but particularly the ones who were singing, became beautiful, intelligent, and kind. Suddenly it seemed that the real purpose of their existence was not orgies and wantonness but something quite different—love and sympathy.

The beggar finds a fishing boat
Upon Lake Baikal's sand.
He launches it and sings a song
About his native land.

How they sang! The sentry leaned his lance against the gates and stood motionless, listening to the song. His eyes filled with tears. He was carried away. Perhaps he even forgot where he was and why.

The beggar crossed Lake Baikal
And reached his native shore;
He asked about his father,
But his father was no more.

The sentry went up to the singers, sat down, buried his head in his hands, and began to rock backwards and forwards.
"M-mmm," he said.
And the devils went through the unguarded gates.
The song poured forth, tearing at the heartstrings, drowning the

bustle and pettiness of life—a declaration of freedom. And the devils kept going through the gates.

They brought the sentry an enormous goblet. He drank it without thinking, banged the goblet on the ground, buried his head in his hands again, and repeated, "M-mmm."

> *Your father's in his coffin,*
> *Released from earthly pains;*
> *Your brother's in Siberia,*
> *A-rattling his chains.*

The sentry beat his knee with his fist. He raised his head and there were tears in his eyes.

> *Your brother's in Siberia,*
> *A-rattling his chains.*

His voice was full of suffering. "My beloved childhood. Was it real or was it a dream? Sing 'Kamarinsky'! To hell with everything! Let's have a good cry! More wine!"

"I shouldn't, old chap," said the wily maestro. "You'll get drunk and forget everything."

"Who do you think you are?" the sentry yelled. He prodded the maestro in the chest. "You think you can teach me, you goat? I'll tie you up in knots, you skunk! I'll drag you over the bumpy ground!"

"Why are they so keen on the bumpy ground?" the elegant devil wondered. "First one, then the other. Which bumpy ground have you in mind, my dear sir?" he asked the sentry.

"Shut up!" said the sentry. " 'Kamarinsky'!"

" 'Kamarinsky,' " the elegant one ordered the musicians.

"Wine!" yelled the sentry.

"Wine," the elegant one repeated obediently.

"Perhaps he'd better not," argued the hypocritical maestro. "It'll make him bad."

"Of course it won't," the elegant devil raised his voice. "It'll do him good!"

"Friend!" roared the sentry. "Let me embrace you! Come here!"

"I'm coming," said the elegant devil. "Let's get drunk, the two of us! We'll drag them all across the bumpy ground. Everybody!"

Ivan watched in amazement as the devils whirled round the sentry. The elegant one was particularly amazing. "Are you going mad?" he asked him.

"Shut up," rasped the elegant one. "Or I'll drag you so fast you'll—"

"What?" Ivan challenged him. He got up. "Who are you going to drag? Say that again."

"Who do you think you're threatening?" the tall sentry asked Ivan menacingly. "My friend? I'll make chopped meat out of you!"

"Not chopped meat again," said Ivan, halting. "I thought we'd finished with that!"

" 'Kamarinsky,' " said the elegant devil mischievously. "Ivan will dance for us. 'Kamarinsky'!"

"Come on, Ivan."

"Go to hell!" said Ivan angrily. "Dance yourself. With your friend. Leave me alone!"

"I won't send a devil with you," said the elegant devil. He glared at Ivan. "Do you understand? Do you think you'll get to the Wise Man by yourself? You won't get near him."

"You heathen scum!" Ivan choked with rage. "What's the meaning of this? How can you behave like this? Have you no shame? We had an agreement. When I showed you how to get through the gates, I was committing mortal sin."

"I ask you for the last time. Will you dance?"

"Damnation!" groaned Ivan. "Why do I have to submit to so much torture?"

" 'Kamarinsky'!" ordered the elegant devil. " 'The trials and tribulations of a country bumpkin.' "

The musicians struck up "Kamarinsky." And Ivan danced, with his hand on the floor, danced round himself, tapping his heels. He danced and wept. He wept and danced.

"Oh, my little certificate!" he exclaimed angrily and bitterly. "You've cost me dearly! I can't describe how dearly!"

Behold—a block of offices! Like so many blocks of offices. Ivan would have got completely lost if it hadn't been for the devil. The devil was as helpful as could be. For a long time they wandered through corridors and up stairs until they found the Wise Man's reception room.

"Just a minute," said the devil. "You wait here. I won't be long." And he dashed off.

In the reception room sat a young secretary—like the librarian, but with different-colored hair. She was called Milka instead of Galka. Milka was typing and talking on two telephones all at once.

"That's a load of hogwash," she said into one telephone, smiling. "Do you remember her at the Morgunova? She had a bright yellow dress on. I suppose it symbolized a haystack. But why make such a fuss? I ask you!"

Then into the other phone, sternly: "He's not here. I don't—. Don't talk to me like that. I've told you five times already—he's not here . . . I don't know.

"What time did you get there? Eleven? Just the two of you? Interesting . . . So she was on her own? Did she try to get off with you?

"Listen, I'll . . . Don't talk to me like that. I don't know."

Ivan remembered that when the librarian wanted to ask her friend on the phone whether her boss was in, she asked, "Is the big chief in?" So he asked Milka, "When will the big chief be in?" He suddenly got rather cross with Milka.

Milka glanced at him. "What do you want?" she asked.

"I need a certificate—"

"Mondays and Wednesdays from nine till eleven."

"But I—" Ivan was about to say that he needed the certificate before the cock crowed thrice.

Milka banged her desk and repeated,

"Mondays and Wednesdays from nine till eleven. Are you stupid?"

"That's a load of hogwash," said Ivan. He got up and walked non-chalantly around the room. "Or strawberry jam. It might even be that. As our Galka puts it, 'If you want a hell of a good time, you need two things—a goat and a Grundig.' Tell me, are you looking for a husband? I'll answer for you. Of course you are. Just as Galka is." Ivan was getting more and more excited. "But you haven't got nice pink cheeks, so how do you expect to find a husband? Now, I'm a con-firmed bachelor. So ask me whether I'd like to marry you. Go on—ask me!"

"Would you like to marry me?"

"No," said Ivan firmly.

Milka laughed and clapped her hands.

"Encore, encore," she cried.

"What do you mean?"

"Let's have some more. Please!"

"I see. You think I'm a brainless idiot. That I go about in clogs. You called me stupid. You may as well know that I'm cleverer than all of you. I'm deeper, more of a folk hero. I radiate hope. What do you ra-diate? Not a damn thing! You're like magpies. You're as empty as . . . I'm the essence of the Russian soul and you're nothing. All you think about is dancing. It's impossible to have a serious conversation with you. I'll get angry in a minute. I'll pick up a club and—"

Milka again laughed loudly.

"Ah, fascinating! Let's have more, eh!"

"You'll be sorry!" shouted Ivan. "You shouldn't make me angry, you really shouldn't." At this point the devil flew into the reception room and heard Ivan yelling at the girl. "Tut, tut," clucked the frightened devil, hustling Ivan into a corner. "What's going on here? Who said you could behave like this? I can't leave you alone for a minute. He's been reading too many prefaces," he said to the girl in explanation of Ivan's behavior. "Sit still. They'll receive us shortly. I've arranged for them to see us first."

No sooner had the devil spoken than a little white-haired man burst into the room like a whirlwind. Ivan realized that it was the Wise Man himself.

"Nonsense, nonsense, nonsense," he muttered as he came in. "Vasilisa was never on the Don."

The devil nodded respectfully.

"Come along in," said the Wise Man to nobody in particular and disappeared into his office.

"Go on." The devil gave Ivan a push. "Let's not hear any more prefaces. Just agree with everything."

Ivan fell on his knees before the Wise Man.

"Father," he prayed. "I've committed a sin. I told the devils how to get into the monastery."

"So what? Get up—I don't like this sort of thing. Get up," ordered the Wise Man.

Ivan got up.

"Well? How did you teach them?" asked the old man with a smile.

"I suggested that they should sing a song of the sentry's own country. They were buzzing about in front of him and he wasn't taking any notice, so I said: 'Sing him a song of his own country.' So they began to sing."

"What did they sing?"

" 'The Wild Steppes of Zabaikal.' "

The old man laughed.

"The rascals!" he exclaimed. "Did they sing it well?"

"They sang it so sweetly that it brought a lump to my throat."

"And can *you* sing?" asked the Wise Man quickly.

"A little."

"And dance?"

"Why do you ask?" Ivan was on his guard.

"Well," said the old man enthusiastically, "how about this? I'll take you to see a great friend of mine. I'm so tired, Vanya, so tired. I'm afraid I shall fall down one day and not get up again. Not from strain, you understand, but from thinking. [. . .] I'm tired, Vanya my friend," continued the old man as if there had been no interruption. "So tired that I sometimes think: 'That's it. I can't make any more decisions.' But then the moment comes and I carry on making them, seven or eight hundred decisions a day. That's why I sometimes feel like . . ." The old man laughed mischievously and delicately, "like plucking flowers or munching grass. So when I've made decision number eight hundred and one, I shall call a break. There's a certain Princess Neverlaugh living nearby; we'll call round and see her."

Milka, the secretary, came in again.

"Tishka, the Siamese cat, has jumped from the eighth floor."

"Is he smashed to pieces?"

"Yes."

"Take this down," he ordered. "Tishka the cat couldn't stand it any longer."

"Is that all?" asked the secretary.

"That's all. How many decisions have I made today?"

"Seven hundred and forty-eight."

"Time for a break."

Milka nodded and went out.

"Let's go and see the Princess, shall we?" exclaimed the old man. "Cheer her up, Vanya, shall we? Amuse her. What's the matter? I suppose you don't approve. Think it's wrong, eh?"

"It's not that. But shall we have time before the cock crows thrice? I've still got a long way to go."

"Plenty of time. Wrong, you say? Of course, of course it's wrong. Not allowed, eh? Sinful perhaps?"

"I was thinking about a different sort of sin. Letting the devils into the monastery—that's what I call sinful."

The old man became pensive.

"The devils? Yes, yes," he mumbled. "It's not so easy as all that, my boy. Not so easy at all. And what about the cat, eh? The Siamese. From the eighth floor! Let's go!"

Neverlaugh was going mad with boredom. At first she just lay perfectly still. Then suddenly she began to howl.

"I'm going to hang myself!" she announced.

She was attended by a number of young men and women who were just as bored as she. They lay in swimming costumes among the rubber plants beneath infrared lamps. They were acquiring a suntan and they were very fed up.

"I shall hang myself!" yelled Neverlaugh. "I can't stand it anymore!"

The young people turned their transistors off.

"Carry on, then," said one of them.

"Bring a rope," she requested.

Nobody moved. Then one of them got up.

"After that I suppose you'll need a stepladder and then a hook," he said. "It'd be far easier to beat her up."

"No, don't do that," said the others. "Let her hang herself. It might be interesting."

A girl got up and fetched a rope. A boy brought a stepladder and placed it under the hook, which supported the chandelier.

"Better remove the chandelier," somebody said. "We can put it back later."

"Remove it yourself!" growled the boy.

The chandelier was taken down by the youth who had suggested it and everything was gradually made ready.

"We must put some soap on the rope."

"Yes, that's usual. Where's the soap?" They went to find some soap.

"Did you find any?"

"Only household soap. Will that do?"

"What's the difference? Take hold of the rope. It won't break, will it?"

"How much do you weigh, Alka?" That was Neverlaugh's first name.

"About seventy-five kilos."

"It'll hold. Soap it!"

They smeared the rope with soap, made a noose, tied the other end to the hook, and climbed down from the stepladder.

"Come on then, Alka."

Alka Neverlaugh got up lazily, yawned, and climbed the stepladder.

"Say your last words," somebody suggested. "No, no, don't do that!" the others protested.

"Don't bother, Alka. Don't say anything."

"That's the last thing we want!"

"Please, Alka! No speeches. Why don't you sing instead?"

"I won't sing and I won't make a speech either," said Alka.

"Sensible girl! Get on with it, then."

Alka put her head in the noose and waited. "Push the stepladder away with your foot." But Alka suddenly sat down on the step and started to whine again.

"This is boring, too!" She was half-sobbing, half-chanting. "It's not amusing."

They agreed with her.

"True."

"It's not new. It's been done before."

"Moreover, it's an unhealthy deviation."

"Naturalism."

The Wise Man and Ivan arrived on the scene.

"Look at them." The old man was giggling and rubbing his hands together. "They're going mad with boredom. They've tried *everything*, but they can't escape. That's right, isn't it, Neverlaugh?"

"Last time you promised to think of something," said Neverlaugh petulantly from the stepladder.

"I *have* thought of something!" exclaimed the old man cheerfully. "I've kept my promise. My dear friends, in your search for so-called pleasure, you've completely forgotten about the people. The people were never bored, you know! The people laughed! They knew how to. There have been moments in history when the people have driven whole regiments from their land—and always with a laugh. The castle walk would be completely surrounded by the enemy when suddenly a gale of laughter would burst forth from within. The enemy would be disconcerted and flee. You should study history, my friends.

We're all very witty, very intellectual, but we don't know our own history. Eh, Neverlaugh?"

"What have you thought of?" asked Neverlaugh.

"What have I thought of? I've decided to go back to the people!" said the old man emotionally. "Back to the people. What shall we sing, Vanya?"

"I feel a little uncomfortable; they're all naked," said Ivan. "Can't they put some clothes on?"

The young people maintained a scornful silence and the old man giggled condescendingly, indicating that he was not in sympathy with Ivan's old-fashioned ideas of propriety.

"Vanya, if you don't mind my saying so, that's none of our business. Our job is to sing and dance. True? Bring a balalaika!"

A balalaika was brought.

Ivan took it. He strummed and he trilled and gradually built up a great volume of sound. Then he went outside. Suddenly he burst back into the room with a whoop, a whistle, and a ditty:

> *O my darling,*
> *O my dear,*
> *What a beauty . . .*

"O-o-o-o-o!" groaned the young people and Neverlaugh. "Please, stop, Ivan. Do stop. We can't stand it!"

"Very well," said the old man. "In the language of the door-to-door salesman, you haven't seen anything yet. Bring up the reserves. Dance, Ivan!"

"Go to hell!" Ivan was very angry. "Who do you think I am—Petrushka? You can see they're not amused and neither am I!"

"And the certificate?" asked the old man maliciously. "You've got to earn it, you know."

"So now you're trying to wriggle out of it. It's not fair, Granddad."

"But that's what we agreed on."

"But they're not amused. I wouldn't mind if it amused them, but, as it is, it's embarrassing."

"Don't torment him," said Neverlaugh.

"Give me the certificate," Ivan was getting desperate. "We've wasted too much time already. I won't make it. The first cocks have already crowed! The second lot'll be crowing any moment and I've got to get back before the third. And I've got an awful long way to go."

Unfortunately, the old man was still determined to cheer them all up, so he sank to a very shameful trick. He decided to make Ivan a laughingstock. The old reprobate was very annoyed by his failure to amuse these bored creatures.

"Certificate?" he asked with idiotic perplexity. "What sort of certificate?"

"For God's sake!" exclaimed Ivan. "I told you—"

"I've forgotten. Tell me again."

"That I'm intelligent."

"Ah!" remembered the old man, who was trying hard to involve the young people in his wicked game. "You need a certificate that you're intelligent? I remember now. But how can I give you a certificate like that? Eh?"

"You've got a rubber stamp . . ."

"Oh, yes, I've got that. But I don't know whether you're intelligent or not. Suppose I give you a certificate stating that you're intelligent when you're a complete idiot. What would be the point of that? It'd be a lie and I couldn't agree to that. So I'll have to ask you three questions. If you get them right, I'll give you the certificate. If not, you mustn't be upset."

"All right," said Ivan reluctantly. "All the prefaces say that I'm not a fool at all."

"The prefaces? Do you know who writes the prefaces?"

"Is that the first question?"

"No, no. That's not a question. That's just by the way. Here's the first question. What did Adam say when God removed one of his ribs and created Eve?" The old man gave the princess and the other young-sters a crafty sidelong glance. He was curious to know what they thought of the first question. He was rather pleased with it himself. "Well, what did Adam say?"

"That's not funny," said Neverlaugh. "It's stupid. Banal."

"Very amateurish," agreed the others.

"Idiotic. I know what he said: 'You created her, so you live with her.'"

The old man laughed obsequiously and pointed at the young man who had answered so wittily.

"Very near! Very!"

"I can be even wittier than that."

"Just a minute! Just a minute!" fussed the old man. "We're trying to find out what Ivan's answer is. Vanya, what did Adam say?"

"May I ask a question of my own?" asked Ivan in turn. "Then . . ."

"No, answer first. What did . . ."

"No, let him ask," said Neverlaugh mischievously. "Ask away, Vanya."

"What can he possibly ask? What's the price of a hundredweight of oats?"

"Go on, Vanya, ask. Ask away, Vanya. Vanya, do ask. Ask, Vanya!"

"This is puerile," the old man said crossly. "All right, Vanya, ask."

"Why have you got an extra rib?" said Ivan, imitating the old man by pointing a finger at him.

"I didn't know I had." He was taken aback.

"I didn't know either," said Neverlaugh. "Why wasn't I informed about this?"

"Very curious," the others were equally curious. "A spare rib? That's most unusual!"

"So that's where he gets all his wisdom!"

"How interesting!"

"Show us, please. Please!"

The young people began to surround the old man.

"Now, now, now," the old man was scared. "What's all this about? What sort of a joke is this? You liked the fool's little idea, did you?"

They pressed closer and closer to the old man. One of them grabbed his jacket. Another tugged at his trousers. They'd every intention of undressing him, and no mistake.

"We must have a look at this. Why should he have more ribs than anybody else?"

"Hold his jacket, hold his jacket! I can't feel a thing, he's so fat."

"Stop!" shouted the old man. He was struggling furiously, but this only spurred them on the more.

"Stop this indecent behavior immediately! It's not funny, do you understand? It's no joke. It's no joke! The fool was joking, and they . . . Ivan, tell them you were joking!"

"I believe I can just feel them, but his shirt's in the way!" said a hefty youth excitedly. "He's got another shirt on underneath. No, it's thermal underwear! Synthetic. Medicinal. Get hold of his shirt."

They removed the Wise Man's jacket and trousers. They removed his shirt. The old man stood in his thermal underwear.

"This is disgraceful!" he shouted. "This is no basis for humor! What is comedy? It's when the intention, the means, and the end are all distorted! When there's a deviation from the norm!"

The hefty youth delicately slapped the old man's rotund stomach.

"And what about this? Isn't this a deviation?"

"Take your hands off!" the old man yelled. "Idiots! Fools! You've no idea of comedy! Cretins! Good-for-nothings!"

By now they were tickling him where he was most ticklish and he began roaring with laughter, trying to escape, but he was completely surrounded by his youthful tormentors.

"Why didn't you tell us about your spare rib?"

"What rib? Ha-ha-ha-! Where? Ha-ha-ha-! I can't . . . This is . . . Ha-ha-ha! This is . . . Ha-ha-ha!"

"Let him speak."

"This is primitive! This is the humor of the Stone Age! It's all stupid. I haven't got an extra rib. You seem determined to—O-o-o!" Here the old man farted, rather quietly, as old men do. He was very frightened, his heart was beating very fast, and he seemed to have shrunk. The young people were in hysterics. It was their turn to laugh. They rolled on the ground, spluttering. Neverlaugh was rocking dangerously on the stepladder. She tried to climb down but couldn't move, she was laughing so much. Ivan climbed up and carried her down. He put her down, still laughing, next to the others. Then he searched the old man's trousers and found the rubber stamp in one of the pockets. He put it in his own pocket.

"Carry on, everybody," he said. "I must be off."

"Why do you want the rubber stamp?" asked the Wise Man pitifully. "Give it back to me. I'll let you have the certificate."

"I'll be able to issue my own certificates now. To all and sundry." Ivan made for the door. "Good-bye."

"This is treachery, Ivan," said the Wise Man. "Using force."

"Nothing of the sort," Ivan said smugly. "Force is when people knock each other's teeth out."

"I shall pass a resolution!" declared the Wise Man threateningly. "I'll make you dance! I'll pass . . ."

"Careful what you pass, Dad!" the youngsters cried.

"My darling one!" Neverlaugh put her hands together in prayer. "Pass some more! Shake the atmosphere!"

"Decisions!" announced the Wise Man solemnly. "I declare the aforementioned humor of the aforementioned bunch of idiots to be uncontemporary and beastly. Consequently it forfeits its right to find expression in the phenomenon referred to as laughter. Full stop. My so-called extraordinary resolution is hereby rendered inoperative."

In the library Ivan and the Cossack were greeted with joy and enthusiasm.

"Thank God, you're alive and well."

"How you frightened us, Ivan! How you frightened us!"

"Ivan!" called Poor Liza. "O, Ivan!"

Ilya stopped her. "Stop drooling, girl. Let's find out what happened. Did you get the certificate?"

"I got the rubber stamp. Here it is." Ivan handed it over. They looked at it for a long time in amazement, turning it this way and that. They handed it round. The last one to touch it was Ilya. He kept turning it over and over with his enormous fingers. Then he asked them all: "What are we going to do with it?"

Nobody knew.

"And why was it necessary to send the man such a distance?" Ilya asked.

Nobody knew this either now. Only Poor Liza, keen as ever, was eager to answer the question:

"Uncle Ilya, I don't know why you're asking . . ."

"Why shouldn't I ask?" Muromets interrupted her sharply. "I say why was it necessary to send the man such a distance? All right, we've got the rubber stamp. What next?"

Even Poor Liza couldn't answer that.

"Sit in your place and stay there, Vanka," commanded Ilya. "The cocks will now be crowing."

"We spend far too much time sitting down." Ivan suddenly boiled over. "It's bad for us!"

"What's got into you?" asked Ilya in surprise. "In that case you can dance." Ilya laughed and looked at Ivan attentively. "You've certainly changed."

"Yes, I have." Ivan still hadn't calmed down. "But I still get the blame for everything. Sit here, indeed!"

"Just sit down for a little and think," said Ilya calmly.

"Attack!" exclaimed the Cossack. He pulled his hat off and hurled it on the floor. "Why should we sit down?! Chop off their—"

He was interrupted by the trumpet-like voice of the cock. The third cock crow. All of them jumped onto their shelves.

"My hat!" shouted the Cossack. "I left my hat on the floor."

"Quiet!" ordered Ilya. "Don't move! We'll pick it up later. We can't now."

At this moment the key scraped in the keyhole. Aunt Masha the cleaner came in and started to clear up.

"Looks like a hat," she said. She picked it up. "Funny sort of hat, though." She looked at the bookshelves. "Who does it belong to?"

The characters sat in silence, motionless. The Cossack gave no indication that it was his hat.

Aunt Masha put the hat on the table and went on clearing up. There'll be another night, no doubt. Perhaps there'll be further adventures. But that'll be another story. This one is finished.

1975

THAT VERY MUNCHAUSEN

༇༇

Comical Fantasy in Two Parts about the Life and Death
of the Famous Baron Karl Friedrich Hieronymus von Munchausen,
Who Has Become a Hero of Many Entertaining Books and Legends

EXCERPTS

GRIGORY GORIN

Characters

KARL FRIEDRICH VON MUNCHAUSEN,
    THE BARON

MARTHA, HIS WIFE

JAKOBINE VON MUNCHAUSEN, HIS
    ESTRANGED WIFE, THE BARONESS

THEOPHILUS VON MUNCHAUSEN,
    HIS SON

THOMAS, FAITHFUL SERVANT OF
    THE BARON

BURGOMASTER

RAMKOPF, THE LAWYER

JUDGE

REVEREND

SERGEANT

MUSICIAN

The action takes place in one of the numerous German principalities of the eighteenth century.

SCENE 1

[*The spacious living room in the house of* BARON MUNCHAUSEN. *The walls are adorned with numerous paintings that depict the* BARON *in the midst of his famous travels and exploits. Beside them hang the heads*

381

and antlers of the wild beasts shot by the BARON. *A big fireplace occupies the middle of the living room. Next to it there are bookshelves filled with books in expensive bindings. A harpsichord stands in the right-hand corner of the living room. Stairs in the back lead to the* BARON'S *study. At the bottom of the stairs, there is a huge clock with a pendulum. The servant,* THOMAS, *leads in the* REVEREND.]

THOMAS: Please come in, Father. His Excellency will be down in a minute.
REVEREND: Thank you, I'll wait.

[THOMAS *makes an attempt to leave. The* REVEREND *stops him.*]

Listen, is your master that very Munchausen?
THOMAS: Yes, Father. That very man.
REVEREND [pointing to the antlers and stuffed animals]: And these would be his hunting trophies?
THOMAS: Yes, they are.
REVEREND: And that bear?

[*He points to the stuffed animal.*]

THOMAS: Yes, Father. His Excellency caught him last winter.
REVEREND: Caught him?
THOMAS: Yes! His Excellency was hunting in the woods and there he met with this bear. The bear attacked him, and since His Excellency was without his gun . . .
REVEREND: Why without his gun?
THOMAS: As I said, he was hunting . . .
REVEREND [*perplexed*]: Huh? All right, all right . . . Go on.
THOMAS: And when the bear attacked him, His Excellency seized him by his front paws, squeezed him, and gripped him until he died.
REVEREND: What did he die from?
THOMAS: From hunger . . . As we know, in winter the bear feeds on whatever he can get his hands on, but since His Excellency deprived him of that possibility . . .

REVEREND [*with a smirk*]: And you believe this?

THOMAS: Of course, Father. [*Pointing to the bear*] You can see how thin he is.

REVEREND: All right, you can go . . .

[THOMAS *leaves. The* REVEREND *looks around the living room with curiosity, intently examining the books. The wall clock gives off a quiet hiss, then strikes three times. Immediately in the* BARON's *study two pistol shots ring out. The* REVEREND *jumps, pressing himself against the wall in fear.* THOMAS *and* MARTHA *enter quickly.*]

THOMAS: Frau Martha, I didn't hear—what time is it?

MARTHA: The clock struck three. His Excellency two . . . It was five altogether.

THOMAS: Then I'll begin roasting the duck.

MARTHA: Yes, it's time.

[MUNCHAUSEN *runs from his study down the stairs. He looks about fifty, but is vigorous and energetic, with a dashing mustache and white wig with a braid. There is a pistol in his belt.*]

MUNCHAUSEN: So, my dears, it's six o'clock! Time to eat!

MARTHA: Don't confuse us, Karl. You shot twice.

MUNCHAUSEN [*looking at the clock*]: What time is it according to this snail? Ah, damn it, I thought that it had already crept as far as four . . . well, let's add an hour or so . . . [*reaching for the pistol in his belt*].

MARTHA [*seizing his hand*]: Karl, there's no need. It might as well be five! Thomas hasn't prepared dinner yet.

MUNCHAUSEN: But I'm hungry! [*He shoots. The pistol misfires.*] Well, damn it, look what's happened. It's half past six . . . All right!

[*To* THOMAS] Hurry! You've got half an hour!

[THOMAS *goes out. The trembling* REVEREND *comes out from his hiding place.*]

MARTHA [*having noticed the* REVEREND]: We have a guest, Karl.

MUNCHAUSEN: Ah, dear Father! I'm delighted to see you in our home.

REVEREND [*still in complete shock*]: I'm delighted to see you, too, Your Excellency. I came because I received a letter from you, in which . . .

MUNCHAUSEN: I know, I know . . . After all, I wrote the letter. And so, you received the letter and came. Very kind of you. How was your journey here?

REVEREND: Fine, thank you.

MUNCHAUSEN: You've come from Hanover, haven't you?

REVEREND: Absolutely right.

MUNCHAUSEN: You weren't caught in the rain, were you?

REVEREND: No. Storm clouds began to gather, but then . . .

MUNCHAUSEN: Yes, yes, I dispersed them . . . Do sit down!

[*The* REVEREND *sits down.*]

But no, first I'd like to introduce my wife.

[*The* REVEREND *stands up.*]

This is Martha.

REVEREND: Nice to meet you, Baroness.

MUNCHAUSEN: Unfortunately, she's not the Baroness yet. She's simply my wife.

REVEREND: Excuse me . . .

MUNCHAUSEN: We're not married. That's the reason I asked you here. Would you agree to perform the holy ceremony for us?

REVEREND: It would be a great honor for me . . . But . . .

MUNCHAUSEN: What?

REVEREND: I'd like to ask . . . I'm interested to know why you chose me? Surely there's a parish priest in town?

MUNCHAUSEN: There is, but he refused to marry us.

REVEREND: Why?

MUNCHAUSEN: Because he's a fool!

MARTHA [*interrupting*]: Karl, why are you starting off like this?!

[*To the* REVEREND] We'll explain all, but later. For now, let's eat!

MUNCHAUSEN: Yes, yes, of course! [*Looks at the clock.*] It's an amazingly slow mechanism, Father, isn't it? How it manages to count off the centuries, I simply don't understand . . . Where's Thomas?

MARTHA: He's only just put in the duck to roast.

MUNCHAUSEN: My dear, please go down and speed him up. Tell him we have a guest!

MARTHA: Very well, my dear! [*Leaves.*]

MUNCHAUSEN: Would you like to see my library, Father?

REVEREND: With pleasure! I've already had a look at it. You have rare books.

MUNCHAUSEN: Yes! And many of them are autographed . . .

REVEREND: How nice.

MUNCHAUSEN [*taking a volume from the shelf*]: Here, for example, Sophocles.

REVEREND: Who?!

MUNCHAUSEN: Sophocles. This is his greatest tragedy, *King Oedipus.* It's signed by the author.

REVEREND: For whom?

MUNCHAUSEN: For me, of course.

REVEREND [*categorically*]: Excuse me, Your Excellency . . . I've heard so much about you . . . about your, let's say, eccentricities. But allow me to say, for all that, it's simply impossible.

MUNCHAUSEN [*handing him the book*]: Look here, it says, "To dearest Karl Munchausen from an affectionate . . ." Do you read classical Greek? Look! . . .

REVEREND: No, I won't!

MUNCHAUSEN: But why not?

REVEREND: Because it's simply impossible! He couldn't have written it to you!

MUNCHAUSEN: But why, damn it?! You're confusing him with Homer.

Homer really was blind, but Sophocles read and wrote wonderfully.

REVEREND: He couldn't have written it to you because he lived in ancient Greece.

MUNCHAUSEN: And I also lived in ancient Greece.

REVEREND [*indignantly*]: But, you know . . .

MUNCHAUSEN: Let me tell you a secret, Father: you, too, quite possibly, lived in ancient Greece. You simply don't remember, but I do.

REVEREND: Nonsense! Prove it!

MUNCHAUSEN: Oh Lord, I *am* proving it to you . . . [*Hands him a book again.*] These doubts of yours are unsubstantiated. And I have the document in my hand!

[THOMAS *enters with a tray.* MARTHA *accompanies him.*]

MARTHA: Dinner is served! I hope that you've not been bored here, Father.

MUNCHAUSEN: No, we've had a good chat. I've been showing the Reverend this papyrus.

MARTHA: The one Sophocles gave you?

MUNCHAUSEN: Yes, *King Oedipus.*

MARTHA [*sadly*]: Poor Oedipus. How they pursued him—blind, decrepit . . . in the pouring rain . . .

MUNCHAUSEN: Now, now . . . Let's not recall it! I asked you not to look.

REVEREND [*gazing at* MARTHA *in fear*]: Lord, where have I landed?

MUNCHAUSEN: You've landed in good hands, Father. It's fun here! And, besides, the food's good. [*He checks the contents of the tray.*] Greens, ham, fish . . . And where's the duck, Thomas?

THOMAS: It's not ready yet, Your Excellency.

MUNCHAUSEN [*indignantly*]: Still?! How so? Nobody here can ever do what they're told to. I have to do everything myself . . . [*Takes his gun from the wall.*] Have a look, Thomas, are they flying?

THOMAS [*glancing out the window*]: They are, Baron. As always, there's a flock over the house.

MUNCHAUSEN: Charge! [*Seizes a dish from the table, runs to the fireplace, and thrusts his gun up it.*]

THOMAS: Attention! Fire!

[MUNCHAUSEN *shoots. There's the sound of a falling bird. He holds out the dish and takes a roasted duck from the fireplace.*]

MUNCHAUSEN [*pinching off a small piece of it*]: Ah! Delicious. It's well done, Father.

REVEREND [*ironically*]: I see, Your Excellency. It seems to have got covered with sauce on the way.

MUNCHAUSEN: Really? That's extremely kind of it. Let's sit down and eat!

REVEREND: No, dear Baron, I seem to have lost my appetite. Besides, I'm in a hurry . . . Would you please tell me the gist of your request?

MUNCHAUSEN: The request is simple: I want to get married to the woman I love. To my dear Martha. The most beautiful, most clever, most tender . . . Lord, I don't need to explain—you can see for yourself!

REVEREND: All the same, why did your local priest refuse?

MUNCHAUSEN: He says I'm already married.

REVEREND: Already married?!

MUNCHAUSEN: Precisely! And because of such nonsense he won't unite me with Martha! . . . Can you imagine?! Real swinishness, isn't it?

MARTHA: Wait, Karl . . . [*To the* REVEREND] The fact of the matter is that the Baron had a wife but she left him.

MUNCHAUSEN: She ran away from me two years ago.

REVEREND: To tell the truth, I'd do the same.

MUNCHAUSEN: That's why I'm not marrying you, but Martha!

REVEREND: Unfortunately, Your Excellency, I cannot help you!

MUNCHAUSEN: Why's that?

REVEREND: If your wife's alive, you can't marry a second time!

MUNCHAUSEN [*in amazement*]: Are you suggesting I kill her?!

REVEREND: Heaven forbid! [*To* MARTHA, *despairingly*] Madam, you're a more reasonable person. Explain to the Baron that this request cannot be carried out.

MARTHA [*sadly*]: We thought there'd be some way out. Maybe you could help the Baron divorce his former wife?

REVEREND: The church is strictly against divorce!

MARTHA: You permit kings to divorce!

REVEREND: That's by way of an exception. In certain circumstances . . . say, when it's necessary for the continuation of the family line . . .

MUNCHAUSEN: For the continuation of the family line, one needs something different!

REVEREND [*decisively*]: Allow me to take my leave now!

MUNCHAUSEN [*taking the* REVEREND *by the arm and glancing into his eyes*]: Listen, Father, the people who advised me to turn to you said you were an intelligent and educated priest. Surely you must understand that due to these foolish conventions, two good people are suffering. The church should bless love!

REVEREND: If it's lawful!

MARTHA: Any love's lawful if it's true love.

REVEREND: Allow me to disagree with that!

MARTHA [*to the* REVEREND]: What advice do you give us?

REVEREND: What can I advise, Madam? . . . Live how you will, but under the people's and church's laws, you cannot consider yourself the Baron's wife if you're not!

MUNCHAUSEN: What nonsense! . . . And so, you, a servant of the church, are suggesting we live in deceit?!

REVEREND [*smiling ironically*]: It's strange that that scares you . . . I thought that falsity was your natural element!

MUNCHAUSEN: I always speak the truth . . .

REVEREND [*angrily*]: Stop it, Your Excellency! . . . You're playing the fool! You're up to your neck in lies, swimming in them as in a puddle . . . It's a sin! . . . I read your book in my spare time . . . Oh Lord! What nonsense you wrote there!

MUNCHAUSEN: I read your book and it's no better.

REVEREND: Which one?

MUNCHAUSEN: The Bible. There are many questionable things there, too . . . The creation of Eve from a rib . . . Noah's ark . . .

REVEREND: God performed those miracles!!!

MUNCHAUSEN: And how am I any worse? God, as we know, created man in his own likeness and image.

REVEREND: Not everyone!!!

MUNCHAUSEN: I can see that. In creating you, he got distracted from his intentions.

REVEREND [*enraged*]: You . . . you . . . monster! I curse you! And I take nothing you say seriously . . . You hear me? . . . Nothing! . . . All of this [*gesturing*] is a lie! Your books, and your ducks, and these antlers, the heads—it's all fraud! None of it happened! You hear me? . . . It's all . . . lies!

[MUNCHAUSEN *looks intently at the* REVEREND, *then silently takes a hammer from the shelf, and proceeds to hammer a nail into the wall.*]

MARTHA: Karl, don't!

MUNCHAUSEN: No, no . . . I'll have his head here, or else I'll be accused of lying again!

REVEREND: Good-bye, Madam! Thank you for your hospitality!

[*The* REVEREND *hurriedly runs out.* MARTHA *goes up to the harpsichord, bows her head.* MUNCHAUSEN *comes to her side, and with one finger begins to play a cheerful tune.* MARTHA *weeps.*]

MUNCHAUSEN: Now, that's foolish! Shedding tears over every priest is extremely wasteful.

MARTHA: He was the fourth, Karl.

MUNCHAUSEN: We'll call a fifth, sixth . . . a twentieth.

MARTHA: The twentieth will be coming to my funeral. No one will ever marry us.

MUNCHAUSEN: Is that really so important to you?!

MARTHA: Not to me, Karl . . . But there are people. They whisper behind my back. They point their fingers: 'There goes that kept woman of the mad Baron!' Our priest said that he won't let me enter the church.

MUNCHAUSEN: The scoundrel! God won't let him enter paradise for that! It's all the worse for him!

MARTHA: Forgive me, Karl. I know you don't like the opinion of others . . . But maybe you're doing something not quite right?! Don't you think? Maybe you should have handled this conversation with the Reverend in some other way?

MUNCHAUSEN: Hold on, why should I change because of what every idiot says?!

MARTHA: Not for keeps! . . . Temporarily! Pretend! Be like everybody . . .

MUNCHAUSEN: Like everybody?! What are you saying . . . ? Like everybody . . . Not to tamper with time, not to live in the past and present, not to fly on cannonballs, not to hunt for mammoths? . . . Never! What am I—abnormal?

MARTHA: But for my sake . . .

MUNCHAUSEN: Precisely for your sake! If I become like everybody else, you'll fall out of love with me!

MARTHA [*uncertainly*]: I don't know . . .

MUNCHAUSEN: Oh, yes, you do! Enough of this . . . Dinner's on the table.

MARTHA: No, my dear, I don't feel like it. I'm tired. I'll go and lie down.

MUNCHAUSEN: Very well, dear. Take a nap. I'll make it nighttime now. [*The* BARON *goes to the clock, rearranges the hands so as to make it twelve o'clock.*] Like this, right?

MARTHA: Yes. Thank you, my dear. [*Leaves.*]

[MUNCHAUSEN *sits down at the harpsichord, pensively jingling the keys.* THOMAS *enters with a tray.*]

THOMAS [*loudly*]: Baron, Sir . . .

MUNCHAUSEN: Shhh! . . . Why are you yelling at night?

THOMAS [*in a whisper*]: I wanted to say—the duck's ready.

MUNCHAUSEN [*in a whisper*]: Set it free! Let it fly! . . .

THOMAS: Yes, sir! [*He goes to the window and throws out the bird.*]

[*One can hear the flapping of wings. The clock strikes twelve and darkness falls.*]

SCENE 2

[*The house of* BARONESS JAKOBINE VON MUNCHAUSEN. *Expensive furnishings. On the walls hang numerous portraits of ancestors. The last of the portraits is covered by a black veil. Sitting in an armchair, the* BARONESS *listens to a tale by Mr. von Ramkopf, a middle-aged man, in a wig and with a bandaged forehead. Her son,* THEOPHILUS VON MUNCHAUSEN, *a young man clad in a cornet's uniform, walks nervously about the room.*]

RAMKOPF [*finishing his story*]: . . . And that's what he said, "Set it free, let it fly."

BARONESS: And then?

RAMKOPF: And then it grew dark and someone poured meat stew onto my head.

THEOPHILUS: Terrible! Terrible! What have we come to if noblemen eavesdrop beneath windows?

RAMKOPF: First, I wasn't eavesdropping, but heard this story by pure chance. Second, Baroness, you yourself asked . . .

BARONESS: Of course. [*To her son*] Theo, apologize immediately! Mr. Ramkopf took a risk for our sakes, even suffered . . . [*She kisses* RAMKOPF *on the forehead and frowns.*] You must replace this bandage, Henry—it smells of onions . . .

THEOPHILUS [*approaching* RAMKOPF]: Excuse me, Mr. Ramkopf! [*He holds out his hand, which* RAMKOPF *shakes reluctantly.*] I don't understand what I'm saying . . . Nerves! Oh Lord, when will this nightmare come to an end?! Is there really nothing that can be done?

BARONESS: The Burgomaster will soon return and tell us what they decided in Hanover.

THEOPHILUS: What can officials decide, Mama? While we seek protection from the law, he, in the end, will marry this broad. We must take action! Immediately! Mr. Ramkopf, you're a family friend. You take our affairs to heart, touchingly so. Please do one more thing for us.

RAMKOPF: I'll do everything I can!

THEOPHILUS: Challenge him to a duel!

RAMKOPF [*in fright*]: No! Not under any circumstances . . . First, he'll kill me, second . . .

BARONESS [*interrupting*]: That's enough! [*To her son*] For God's sake, Theo! It's your father we're talking about, after all.

THEOPHILUS: Don't remind me, Mama, please! . . . That's the sole cause of all my unhappiness. I'm already nineteen, but I'm only a cornet, with no prospects . . . They didn't even include me in the maneuvers . . . The Colonel declared that he refused to take reports from Baron Munchausen . . . When they shout out my name at roll call, the soldiers bite their lips so as not to burst out laughing!

BARONESS: Poor boy! Still, you can bear your family name with pride. It's one of the most ancient in Germany. [*Pointing to the portraits.*] These are your ancestors: Knights of the Crusade, His Majesty the Court Marshal . . .

THEOPHILUS: And, finally, him! [*He walks up to the last portrait and tears off the veil. The portrait reveals a smiling* MUNCHAUSEN, *pulling himself from a bog by his hair.*] Why don't you throw away this daub?

BARONESS: What about it bothers you?

THEOPHILUS: It drives me mad! [*He seizes his sword.*] I'd like to chop it to pieces!

BARONESS [*in fear*]: Don't you dare! . . . He claims it's Rembrandt's work.

THEOPHILUS: What utter rot!

BARONESS: Of course! . . . But the auctioneers offered ten thousand for it.

RAMKOPF: So, sell it.

BARONESS: To sell it would mean to admit it's true. [*Covers the painting with the veil.*] Calm down, Theo!

[*The* BURGOMASTER *enters. He's dressed in traveling clothes, having only just arrived from Hanover.*]

BURGOMASTER: Good evening, ladies and gentlemen! [*He kisses the* BARONESS's *hand.*] You are charming as ever, Baroness! [*He shakes* RAMKOPF's *hand.*] I've seen your new carriage, Ramkopf: mahogany, blue velvet—the ultimate in taste. [*He nods to* THEO.] How are you, young Cornet? . . . You look well!

BARONESS [*gloomily*]: Judging by the abundance of compliments, you've returned with bad news.

BURGOMASTER: But why do you say that? . . . All is not bad, ladies and gentlemen, all is not bad . . . I had a long conversation with the judge in Hanover, followed by a long conversation with the Bishop, and then a brief conversation with someone very important . . .

THEOPHILUS [*gloomily*]: With God, no doubt?

BARONESS [*angrily*]: Theo!

BURGOMASTER: Yes, my friend, perhaps, perhaps!

RAMKOPF: And what did they all decide?

BURGOMASTER: Unfortunately, the judge believes that there are insufficient grounds for the confiscation of the Baron's estate and its placement under the guardianship of his heir.

RAMKOPF: Insufficient grounds! The man destroyed a family and drove a wife and child out of their home!

BURGOMASTER: As far as I know, they left of their own accord.

BARONESS: Yes! But who could live with such a man?

BURGOMASTER: As you see, Frau Martha can . . .

RAMKOPF: But she's a mistress! Gentlemen, let's call a spade a spade!

If you have a mistress, that's fine! Everyone has a mistress. But that doesn't mean you should be allowed to marry one. It's amoral!

BURGOMASTER: Here's the saddest part of my report: His Majesty the Duke has approved the Baron's petition for a divorce.

BARONESS [*in a tone of dismay*]: That's impossible!

BURGOMASTER: Unfortunately, yes! Last week, His Majesty found himself in some confrontation with Her Majesty . . . They say she caught him with the maid of honor and it was something terrible . . . [*He makes a significant gesture.*] In his agitation, the Duke approved various petitions for divorce with the words: "Be free! All of you, be free!" Now, if the spiritual consistory confirms this decision, the Baron can marry a second time . . .

THEOPHILUS: So! That's what we've come to! [*To* RAMKOPF] You still refuse to fight a duel?

RAMKOPF: Just wait a moment, Theo!

THEOPHILUS: We can't wait any longer! If you refuse, then I'll challenge him myself. You can be my second.

RAMKOPF: Not under any circumstances!

THEOPHILUS: Why?

RAMKOPF: First, he'll kill the second too, and, second . . .

BARONESS [*imperiously*]: Stop it! [*To* BURGOMASTER] He doesn't have the right to marry! Madmen cannot marry! It's against the law! And you as Burgomaster must forbid it!

BURGOMASTER: Baroness, I understand your anger, but what can I do? To declare a man insane is rather difficult! There must be weighty evidence!

RAMKOPF: Fine! Let me read you a document, and you honestly tell me whether it was written by a man of sound mind or not. [*He takes a document from his pocket.*] I pinched it from the Baron's house . . .

THEOPHILUS: That's terrible! What's the world coming to, noblemen pinching documents.

RAMKOPF [*nervously*]: Will you be quiet, for God's sake! What impatience . . . Spitting image of your father! . . . And so! . . . [*He reads.*] "The day's routine of Karl Friedrich Hieronymus von Munchausen on the 30th of May, 1776 . . ."

BURGOMASTER: Interesting!

RAMKOPF: It certainly is! . . . [*He reads.*] "Arise at six o'clock in the morning!" [*A significant glance in the* BURGOMASTER's *direction.*]

BURGOMASTER: That's not punishable!

RAMKOPF: But, you know . . .

BURGOMASTER: No, I agree that rising at such an early hour is unnatural for people in our social circle, but . . .

BARONESS: Read on, Henry!

RAMKOPF [*reading*]: "Seven in the morning—disperse the clouds, ensure good weather . . ." What do you have to say to that?

BURGOMASTER: Let me see . . . [*He takes the document.*] That's what it says—"disperse the clouds" . . . [*He glances out of the window.*] As fate would have it, today the sky is clear . . .

THEOPHILUS: Are you trying to say that that's his work?

BURGOMASTER: I'm not trying to say anything, Theo! I'm simply noting that today is indeed a splendid day. I've no grounds to assert that he dispersed the clouds himself, nor can I say that he *didn't* disperse them—that would be a contradiction of what we can see.

BARONESS: Are you making fun of us?

BURGOMASTER: What do you mean, Baroness?! I'm completely on your side. I simply think that such expropriation from the Baron will hardly be successful . . . A man with his service record, his noble deeds for his country's sake . . . I don't think His Majesty would agree to it! . . . That's why it's perhaps better not to create a scandal and agree to a divorce.

BARONESS: Never!

BURGOMASTER: The property and dowry will remain yours . . . You'll be free. You'll be able to live with the man you love.

BARONESS: I can live with the man I love without a divorce. But the Baron belongs either in the hospital or in prison! Read on, Henry!

RAMKOPF [*reading*]: "From eight until ten—a heroic deed!"

BURGOMASTER: How am I to understand that?

BARONESS: That means that from eight until ten in the morning, he has a heroic deed planned . . . What can you say about people who daily plan a heroic deed, as if it were part of their professional work?!

BURGOMASTER: I myself work, Madam. Every day, before nine, I have to go to the magistrate . . . I don't call these acts heroic deeds per se, but there's generally something heroic in them.

BARONESS: That's enough! You're ridiculing us!

BURGOMASTER: Nothing of the sort! I'm simply trying to understand the matter objectively.

THEOPHILUS: To hell with your objectivity!

RAMKOPF: Wait, ladies and gentlemen! Stay calm . . . Now, we've arrived at an interesting point . . . Let's see what you have to say to this, Mr. Burgomaster . . . [*He reads.*] "At four p.m. exactly— WAR WITH ENGLAND!"

BURGOMASTER [*mournfully*]: Oh Lord, what did the English do to him?

BARONESS: One man declares war on a whole state! . . . Is that normal?!

BURGOMASTER: No. That's really something! . . . That could be considered a breach in the social order.

THEOPHILUS: Finally!

BURGOMASTER: As I say, I'm trying to remain objective! What's punishable is punishable . . . [*He walks to the window and calls out.*] Sergeant!

[*The* SERGEANT *enters.*]

Sergeant, find the Baron immediately and bring him here! If he resists, use force!

SERGEANT: Yes, sir! [*Exits.*]

BURGOMASTER [*excitedly*]: I was appointed the Burgomaster so that there'd be order in town, and there will be order! War is no joke! War is war! I promise you this: if this is what's happened, then the Baron will be severely punished!

BARONESS: Thank the Lord! Even your nerves snapped!

BURGOMASTER [*to* RAMKOPF]: Henry, as a lawyer, tell me, what's he
   likely to get?
RAMKOPF: Frankly, I have no idea . . . The code makes no provisions
   for such a case.
BARONESS: Twenty years in prison! I demand it be twenty years! That's
   as long as I was married to him.
THEOPHILUS: Even this doesn't mean salvation for me . . . Prison, hospital . . . Either way there'll be scandal, gossip—and I'll remain a
   cornet my whole life! . . . Mr. Burgomaster, I've wanted to ask you
   for a long time now: can I change my surname?
BURGOMASTER: Of course. Marry and take your wife's surname!
THEOPHILUS: It's easy to say—marry! But who'll marry a Munchausen?!
BURGOMASTER: Then take your mother's maiden name. Theophilus
   von Dutten—beautiful!
BARONESS: Forget it, Theo! . . . Everybody will still say: "That's von
   Dutten, formerly a Munchausen!" It'll only be an additional excuse for jokes!
THEOPHILUS [*in despair*]: Does this mean there's no way out? No! A
   duel, only a duel!

[*The* SERGEANT *enters. His wig is awry, and he has an enormous black
   eye.*]

SERGEANT: He's coming, Mr. Burgomaster.
BURGOMASTER: What's wrong with you?
SERGEANT: You ordered me to use force.
BURGOMASTER: You, not him! . . . Where did you find him?
SERGEANT: He was sitting in a tavern.
RAMKOPF [*with a smirk*]: A strange place for conducting war.

[MUNCHAUSEN *enters. He's in uniform, with a sword.*]

MUNCHAUSEN [*cheerfully*]: Good day, gentlemen! . . . [*To his wife*]
   Hallo, Jakobine.

[*She turns away.*]

Mr. Ramkopf!

Hallo, son!

[*In a rage* THEOPHILUS *runs into a corner.*]

Did you summon me so that we could all be silent?

BURGOMASTER: I'm the one who summoned you, dear Karl . . . Strange news has been reported to me here . . . I don't quite know how to say it. Well, it would seem you . . . you've declared war . . . on England . . .

MUNCHAUSEN [*taking out his watch*]: Not quite yet. War will begin at four o'clock if England cannot satisfy the conditions of the ultimatum.

BURGOMASTER: Ultimatum?

MUNCHAUSEN: Yes! I dispatched an ultimatum to them a week ago!

BURGOMASTER [*nervously*]: Who's "them"? Be clearer!

MUNCHAUSEN: To King George and his Parliament. I demanded that they cease their senseless war with the North American colonies and recognize their independence. The ultimatum expires today at exactly sixteen o'clock. If my conditions are not met, I will wage war!

RAMKOPF: Interesting how this will look. Will you start shooting your gun from here or engage in hand-to-hand combat?

MUNCHAUSEN: Methods of conducting a campaign are a military secret! I can't divulge them, especially in the presence of civilians!

BURGOMASTER [*decisively*]: So! . . . Baron, I don't think there's any point in continuing this fruitless conversation. In sending the ultimatum, you have gone too far! [*He shouts.*] War is not a game of poker! You cannot declare it when you feel like it! You are under arrest, Baron! Sergeant, take the Baron's sword!

SERGEANT [*indecisively*]: If he'll give it up . . .

MUNCHAUSEN: Mr. Burgomaster, don't act foolish. I know you're a decent man. In your soul, you're also against England . . .

BURGOMASTER: That's nobody's business!

MUNCHAUSEN: My war's also only between England and myself.

BURGOMASTER: Baron! As your superior, I order you to surrender your sword!

THEOPHILUS [*approaching his father with determination*]: Baron, I challenge you to a duel!

BURGOMASTER [*nervously*]: Wait, Theophilus! [*To* MUNCHAUSEN] Surrender your sword!

THEOPHILUS [*unsheathing his sword*]: Defend yourself!

MUNCHAUSEN [*angrily*]: Can't you sort it out between yourselves?

[THOMAS *runs in.*]

THOMAS: Your Excellency, you asked for the evening paper!

MUNCHAUSEN: Well? [*He takes the newspaper, glances through it, and hands it to the* BURGOMASTER *in silence.*]

[*The* BURGOMASTER *peruses the paper.*]

THEOPHILUS: What now?

BURGOMASTER [*in a dismayed voice*]: England has recognized America's independence.

MUNCHAUSEN [*glancing at his watch*]: Ten till four! . . . They did it in time! Lucky for them! [*To everyone*] Your servant! [*Exits, accompanied by* THOMAS.]

RAMKOPF: Inconceivable!

BARONESS [*To the* BURGOMASTER]: You let him go!

BURGOMASTER: What could I do?

RAMKOPF: But it's simply a monstrous coincidence.

BARONESS: You're not a Burgomaster, but a dishrag!

BURGOMASTER: Madam, what do you want from me? England surrendered . . .

[*Curtain.*]

SCENE 3

[*A spacious room at the town court. There is an armchair in the middle of the room, occupied by the* JUDGE *of Hanover, an elderly gentleman in a robe and luxurious wig. Sitting next to him are the* BURGOMASTER *and the* REVEREND. *Just in front of them are the* BARONESS, RAMKOPF, *and* THEOPHILUS. *On the other side is* MUNCHAUSEN. *In the back of the room is a* MUSICIAN *seated at a harpsichord.*]

JUDGE: I declare the legal case regarding the divorce of Baron Karl Friedrich Hieronymus von Munchausen and Baroness Jakobine von Munchausen open.

[*The* MUSICIAN *plays the hymn of the dukedom of Hanover. Everyone stands until it finishes.*]

JUDGE: Mr. Burgomaster, please begin!

BURGOMASTER [*turning to the audience*]: Ladies and gentlemen! I begin my speech with great excitement. The case we're about to hear may be deemed unusual and even unique, for while people get married in every town in Germany, divorce is not permitted in every town. For this very reason our magistrate will first give a word of thanks to Duke George, whose all-merciful signature has allowed us to become witnesses to this celebration of freedom and democracy!

[*Applause.*]

Ladies and gentlemen! We happen to have the good fortune to live in the eighteenth century, the century of Enlightenment, having forever shed the tatters of the Middle Ages that concealed spiritual ignorance and obscurantist inquisitions. How many tragedies has our history recorded, how many cries of despair have reached our ears from ancient times! These are the cries of spouses lacking the possibility of separation! Let us remember the story of the English King Henry VIII, who was forced to send his wife Anne Boleyn to the block so as to sever his matrimonial ties with the executioner's axe. Let us also remember the Neapolitan

Joanna I, who out of love for another man hanged her husband
by a silk cord that she herself had woven . . .

No, ladies and gentlemen, we are not Catholics, whose chronic
hypocrisy does not allow spouses to separate even when their
feelings have died. Nor are we, thank God, like Muslims, whose
spiritual ignorance permits several wives when one is enough. We
are Lutherans, and the teaching bequeathed to us by Luther says:
"May what is false be destroyed, and what is true be decreed!"
[*He sits down.*]

JUDGE [*to the* REVEREND]: Your Reverence, do you wish to speak?

REVEREND [*rising*]: I have listened to the Burgomaster's speech with
great interest and thank him for his words directed at the spiritual
consistory. However, the actions of the church cannot be defined
as humane unless, in blessing the end of matrimony, it did not at
first endeavor to restore it. Therefore, now, appealing from the
high chair, I want to say the following: My children! Listen to your
spiritual leader. Reveal to us the reasons that have prompted you
to sunder the union blessed by God. Do not be disturbed by these
walls and robes—this is no court, but a confession, and repen-
tance is a blessing! [*He sits down.*]

RAMKOPF [*rising*]: Your Honor, may I?

[*The* JUDGE *nods his consent.*]

RAMKOPF: Ladies and gentlemen! I appear as the Baroness's lawyer
and would like to state the essence of the matter briefly, omit-
ting, naturally, those unsavory details that would put my client
in an uncomfortable position. So, twenty years ago in Hanover,
the young Baron Karl von Munchausen and Baroness Jakobine
von Dutten met by chance. He was twenty-five years old, and she
even younger. The Baron was a noncommissioned officer, she was
very pretty, and they seemed to have been made for each other . . .
They were married in Hanover Cathedral and soon after, as a result of the unsavory details that I promised not to mention, gave

birth to a boy, Theophilus, our young cornet, now the son of our plaintiff and defendant.

THEOPHILUS [*with displeasure*]: What's my being a cornet got to do with it?

JUDGE: Sir, I ask you not to interrupt!

RAMKOPF: To continue . . . Did they love each other? Absolutely! But their life together, nonetheless, did not flow in calm tranquillity. The strange character of Mr. Munchausen, his tendency to exaggeration and ludicrous fantasies, often cast a shadow over matrimonial happiness. I direct the attention of the court to the fact that these fantasies of the Baron flared up exactly when he had an interest on the side. As soon as Munchausen had a fleeting passion, he immediately began to hunt tigers, fly on cannonballs, and the like . . . Ladies and gentlemen! Every husband returning home after a week's absence tries to deceive his wife, but not everyone would think of maintaining that he'd been on the moon . . . Yet my gentle, defenseless client tried to close her eyes to this. She would extinguish the flames of indignation in the name of their domestic well-being. However, last year, when Baron Munchausen came across a certain unmarried lady by the name of Martha, the daughter of a chemist, his eccentricities reached a climax. He began to go off the deep end, conversing with Socrates and corresponding with Shakespeare. Now, that's something no normal person can stand! And the Baroness left the castle. And that's the whole story! You, respected judges, must decide who is guilty of befouling the bonds of Hymen! As to you, Mr. Munchausen, the Baroness charged me with saying the following words: "Karl! Even now I'm ready to forgive everything! See reason, repent, humble yourself, and I will take you to my bosom once again!" [*He sits down, satisfied with his speech.*]

JUDGE: I thank you, Mr. Ramkopf! Your Excellency, please rise.

MUNCHAUSEN [*leaping to his feet*]: Ladies and gentlemen! I am profoundly amazed by Mr. Ramkopf's words, especially by his last offer. However, I am compelled to reject it, for almost everything said by the defendant, unfortunately, doesn't correspond to the truth. Our marriage, strange as it may seem, began long before our birth: the Munchausen family long ago dreamed of uniting with the von Duttens through marriage, which is why when a daughter was born to them, I in turn was born not only as a boy but also as a husband. We met while still in the cradle and I instantly found my wife unappealing, which I proclaimed upon learning how to speak. Unfortunately, they didn't heed my words, and hardly had we come of age when they escorted us to church. In the church, to the question of whether I was ready to take Jakobine von Dutten as my wife, I honestly responded: "No!" And they married us on the spot. After the ceremony, we went on our honeymoon: I—to Turkey, she—to Switzerland, and for three years we lived there in love and harmony. Then, having relocated to Germany, I was invited by the Count of Brandenburg to a masquerade ball, where I danced with a charming lady in a Spanish mask. There, I enticed her into the summer house, seduced her, and only after she took off her mask did I see that she was in fact my own wife. So, if I've cheated, then above all I've cheated myself. Having discovered my mistake, I immediately wanted a divorce, but it transpired that we were expecting someone to be born. As a decent man, I couldn't leave my wife until the child came of age. I returned to serve in the regiment, took several world tours, took part in three wars, where I received a head wound. That's probably why I got the absurd idea that I could live out the rest of my days in the family circle. I returned home, spent three days in the company of my wife and son, after which I immediately went to the chemist to buy poison. And there—a miracle took place! I saw Martha . . . the most wonderful, most honorable, most beautiful . . . Ladies and gentlemen, why am I telling you all this?—you all know her! Life acquired meaning! I fell in love for the first, and, most probably, the last time in my life, and I'm happy! I hope that Jakobine will understand everything and finally will rejoice with me . . . And, long live divorce, ladies and gentlemen! It destroys falsehood, which I hate so much!! [*He sits down.*]

JUDGE: Baroness, do you wish to add anything relevant to the case?

BARONESS [*rising*]: . . . It's difficult to speak when so many sympathetic eyes are looking at you. Divorce is disgusting, certainly, not because spouses become separated, but because people start to consider the man "free" and the woman "abandoned." No! Don't humiliate me with pity, ladies and gentlemen! Better pity yourselves! My husband is a dangerous man, ladies and gentlemen! I married him not out of love but out of a sense of obligation to our country . . . For twenty years I restrained him and held him safely within the boundaries of family life, thereby saving all of society from him! Now you'll sunder those ties . . . Well! Blame only yourselves for the consequences . . . What's frightening is not that I'm alone, what's frightening is that he's free!!

[*Applause.*]

JUDGE: I thank you. [*To everybody*] And so, ladies and gentlemen, the spouses have stated their views on the matter. However, there's a third participant in the family drama present . . . Theophilus von Munchausen, would you like to make a statement?

THEOPHILUS: Yes, Your Honor!

BARONESS [*to her son*]: Theo, restrain yourself . . . I implore you!

THEOPHILUS: Don't worry, Mama . . . [*He rises.*] Respected court! I will be brief, as befits a soldier. You'd like to know my opinion? Here it is! [*He draws a pistol and points it at* MUNCHAUSEN.]

[*Everyone jumps up in fright.* THEOPHILUS *pulls the trigger, and there's a click.*]

THEOPHILUS: Don't worry, ladies and gentlemen! I didn't put any bullets in it . . . I loaded it instead with bitterness and contempt . . . [*He sits down.*]

MUNCHAUSEN: Lord, how vulgar!

BURGOMASTER [*jumping up*]: Ladies and gentlemen, stay calm . . . Your Honor, I think there's no sense in fanning passions. If such respected people have not found a means of achieving peace in twenty years, it's foolish to hope that they'll do so at the last minute . . . And what is your opinion, Your Eminence?

REVEREND: I agree with you.

JUDGE: Good! So . . . Baron, Baroness, would you please approach me and familiarize yourselves with the divorce papers.

[MUNCHAUSEN *and the* BARONESS *approach the* JUDGE, *take the papers, and read them.*]

MUNCHAUSEN: "I, Karl Friedrich von Munchausen, being of sound mind and clear judgment, voluntarily sunder conjugal ties with Jakobine von Munchausen and declare her free."

BARONESS: "I, Jakobine von Munchausen, born von Dutten, being of sound mind and clear judgment, voluntarily sunder conjugal ties with Karl von Munchausen and declare him free."

JUDGE: Authenticate these divorce papers with your signatures . . . Date them. Give the documents to each other . . .

[MUNCHAUSEN *and the* BARONESS *sign and exchange the documents.*]

Reverend, I ask you to complete the dissolution of the conjugal ties . . .

REVEREND: I fulfill my mission with a heavy heart, ladies and gentlemen. But such is the fate of every priest: he presides not only at confirmations but also at funerals. In the name of God he joins hearts and in the name of God he must also separate devastated ones . . . But let this bitter moment instill in your souls not only grief but also hope for future joys . . . Approach me! Stand together!

[MUNCHAUSEN *and the* BARONESS *approach him.*]

Take off your rings!

[*They remove their rings and hand them to the* REVEREND.]

In the name of the holy spiritual consistory, I pronounce you free from each other! [*He separates them with the sides of his palms.*]

RAMKOPF: Stop, Father!

[*Confusion ensues.*]

JUDGE: What's the meaning of this?

RAMKOPF [*waving the divorce papers*]: Excuse me, Your Honor! Excuse me, Reverend, for interfering with your sacred rites, but it's better to do this now than later, when we'll be persuaded that our court has turned into a shameful farce!

JUDGE: Mr. Ramkopf, mind what you say!

RAMKOPF [*raising his voice*]: A shameful farce! Yes! Shameful . . . I'm ready to use even stronger language . . . Your Honor, please read Baron Munchausen's divorce papers carefully.

JUDGE: [*He takes the paper and reads it.*] "I, Karl Friedrich Hieronymus . . ."

RAMKOPF: The date! Read the date!

JUDGE: "1776. The 32nd of May." What?! [*To* MUNCHAUSEN] You made a mistake, Baron.

MUNCHAUSEN: Why? I put down the exact date.

RAMKOPF: There is no such date!

MUNCHAUSEN: Come on, what do you mean there isn't? . . . Don't give me that!

BURGOMASTER: If yesterday was the thirty-first of May, what is the date today?

MUNCHAUSEN: The thirty-second. You needn't worry, ladies and gentlemen. I'll explain it all . . . This is my discovery.

BARONESS [*hysterically*]: Buffoon! Madman!

THEOPHILUS: *En garde!* Immediately! At two paces! . . .

MUNCHAUSEN: Just wait a minute! I'll explain . . .

JUDGE: A signed document with such a date is invalid!

REVEREND [*to* MUNCHAUSEN]: Damn you! [*He throws the rings on the floor.*] Damn anyone who even touches you!

BURGOMASTER [*in despair*]: Wait, Reverend . . . Ladies and gentlemen . . . What have you done, Baron? What have you done?
MUNCHAUSEN [*trying to be heard above the noise*]: Ladies and gentlemen, let me speak! Why won't you listen to me?
JUDGE: This is an affront to the court! This session is closed!

[*Following these words the* MUSICIAN *strikes the keys. The hymn rings
out. All fall silent and express their indignation only by outraged glances
and facial expressions. Lights out.*]

SCENE 4

[*Once again the living room of* MUNCHAUSEN'S *house. Standing on a
ladder,* THOMAS *is wiping a picture with a dustcloth.* MARTHA *is sitting
at the harpsichord, playing a tune with one finger.*]

THOMAS [*addressing a portrait*]: You're a great man, Baron Munchausen, yet the dust settles on you, too.
MARTHA [*Sharply slamming down the lid of the harpsichord, she looks
at the clock.*]: Already six o'clock! Lord, why are they taking so
long? It's unbearable! It should be five o'clock! [*She goes up to the
clock and moves the hands.*]
THOMAS [*addressing the portrait*]: You can conquer whole armies, but
to overcome dust—not a chance . . . Neither cannonballs nor
buckshot does the job . . . Only Thomas with a dustcloth. If I
don't wipe your heroic deeds, who'll see them?
MARTHA [*praying quietly*]: Great God, make it all go well! Don't be
angry with Karl, Lord! You're older and wiser, you must yield to
him . . .
THOMAS: Or take this thing . . . [*He takes down a spyglass.*] A long-
distance telescope for surveying the Universe . . . But without
Thomas, it would be two dirty lenses soiled by flies . . . If you
clean it and wipe it with a felt cloth—it'll become a long-distance
telescope again . . . [*He peers into the telescope and focuses it on
the window.*] They're coming back, Frau Martha.

MARTHA [*in fear*]: Who's "they"?

THOMAS: The Baron . . . the Burgomaster . . . and some small boys.

MARTHA: Small boys? What small boys? . . . Ah yes . . . of course . . . If the Baron's coming, inevitably little boys will run after him.

THOMAS: And they're shouting.

MARTHA: Of course, of course they're shouting. What? What are they shouting, Thomas?

THOMAS: I don't know. I can only see them, but not hear . . . Probably the usual: "Crazy Baron! Crazy Baron!"

MARTHA: The usual! . . . Why do I have a horrible premonition? Lord! . . . And what of the Burgomaster?

THOMAS: The Burgomaster is saying something to the Baron and waving his arms.

MARTHA: And Karl?

THOMAS: His Excellency is walking . . . And the Burgomaster is waving . . . No, no. Now the Baron is stopping and has also started waving his arms . . . The Burgomaster has grabbed his head and run off . . . And the little boys have stopped shouting! . . .

MARTHA [*in dismayed tones*]: It means something has happened.

THOMAS: No. His Excellency has caught up with him and is now leading him to the house. Don't worry, Frau Martha, he's holding firmly onto him . . . There's no way he can get free!

MARTHA: I'm going to change my clothes. If Karl asks for me—I'm changing. [*Quickly goes to her room.*]

[MUNCHAUSEN *and the* BURGOMASTER *enter noisily.*]

BURGOMASTER [*freeing his arm*]: Leave me in peace! Everyone's patience has a limit!

MUNCHAUSEN: No, listen! It's impossible for one clever man not to understand another. [*To* THOMAS] Where's Martha?

THOMAS: Frau Martha is changing, Your Excellency.

MUNCHAUSEN: Changing? . . . What for? . . . Ah, yes, I told her to put on her wedding dress. We were planning to go to the church.

BURGOMASTER: Right away?!

MUNCHAUSEN: Why wait?

BURGOMASTER: Divorce and marriage in one day?!

MUNCHAUSEN: Of course! Why postpone it? . . . And besides, what a day—the thirty-second!

BURGOMASTER [*plaintively*]: Your Excellency, for God's sake, allow me to leave . . . I have a weak heart . . . I won't be able to endure this explanation . . .

MUNCHAUSEN: Martha's an intelligent woman. She'll understand everything.

BURGOMASTER: That means I'm an idiot. I can't and don't want to understand . . . Lord, how will you able to tell her? . . . Well, invent something. Let's say that the court session was adjourned . . .

MUNCHAUSEN: No! We'll tell her the truth. No one's ever practiced deceit in this household!

[MARTHA *appears. She is in a dark cloak and has a traveling case in her hand.*]

MUNCHAUSEN: And here's Martha! [*To the* BURGOMASTER] Well? . . . As I said, she'll understand everything immediately.

MARTHA [*calmly*]: Absolutely, Karl . . . Good day, Mr. Burgomaster.

BURGOMASTER: Good day, Frau Martha. As always, you're charming . . . That cloak suits you so nicely . . .

MUNCHAUSEN [*interrupting*]: Rubbish! It doesn't suit you at all . . . And the traveling case does not match. Sit down, stay calm, and let's discuss our state of affairs.

MARTHA: Fine. And in the meantime, Thomas, go and have them prepare the carriage . . .

BURGOMASTER [*to* MARTHA]: You already know what's happened?

MARTHA: No. But I gather that the divorce papers have not been signed.

BURGOMASTER: The problem is precisely that they were signed! . . . Everything was going ideally. Our Baron was self-controlled as never before. He wasn't rude, didn't fire shots into the air . . . And then, suddenly this absurd fantasy of the thirty-second of May! [*To* MUNCHAUSEN] So, tell me, where the hell did it come from?

MUNCHAUSEN: I've been trying to explain to you for a long time.

MARTHA: The thirty-second? That's something I didn't know about.

MUNCHAUSEN: That's right! I wanted to surprise you.

BURGOMASTER: Don't despair—you succeeded!

MUNCHAUSEN: Will you listen or not? Martha! Thomas! Burgomaster! I discovered a new day. This is one of the greatest discoveries ever, and perhaps the very greatest . . . I was moving toward it for years, meditating and observing . . . Then it came—the thirty-second!

BURGOMASTER [*grinning*]: That we already heard. I'm asking: where did it come from?

MUNCHAUSEN: Tell me, how many days are there in a year?

BURGOMASTER: I don't know. And anyway, who's asking the questions, you or I?

MUNCHAUSEN: Fine! I'll ask the questions and answer them myself. You just follow the train of thought . . . How many days are there in a year? . . . Three hundred and sixty-five! . . . Exactly? . . . No, not exactly . . . In a year there are three hundred and sixty-five days and six hours. These hours add up, and then every fourth year becomes a leap year . . . But I was thinking: are there exactly three hundred and sixty-five days and six hours in a year?! As it turns out, no! In a regular year there are three hundred and sixty-five days, six hours, and three seconds . . . Any astronomer will confirm as much, and not even a particularly authoritative one, such as me. All you need to do is to reach the stars with a chronometer and from there trace the Earth's rotation. I've done this more than once. Martha can confirm this! So, there are three seconds of time unaccounted for. Over the years, these seconds add up to minutes and over centuries they turn into hours. In short, my dears, in the course of our town's existence, we've gained a day! The thirty-second of May! [*He gazes at everyone with a triumphant look.*]

BURGOMASTER [*wearily*]: Is that all?

MUNCHAUSEN: That's it!

BURGOMASTER: And you couldn't think of anything more clever than to announce this in court?

MUNCHAUSEN: What's the court got to do with it? . . . I had to tell everyone about it, which I did.

BURGOMASTER: And you hoped they'd believe you?

MUNCHAUSEN: How can one hide from facts?! We're not such idiots as to give up an extra day of life! Thomas, aren't you happy that we have the thirty-second?

THOMAS: Not very, Your Excellency! . . . I get my salary on the first . . .

MUNCHAUSEN: What's that got to do with it?! You don't understand . . . Go and get dinner ready.

[THOMAS *exits.*]

BURGOMASTER: There's no reason to get angry with the servant. He's absolutely right. Even if your date of the thirty-second exists, no one needs it. Try to understand, Baron, that there exists a certain order in the world: one day replaces another; Monday follows Tuesday . . . You cannot simply in the heat of the moment violate life's rhythms. It's inadmissible! Chaos will ensue. People won't know when it's Christmas, and when it's Easter . . . You must have seen how infuriated the Reverend was!

MUNCHAUSEN: Which Reverend? What's the Reverend got to do with it? We decide the fate of the universe . . . Martha, tell him. You understand that I'm right, don't you?

MARTHA: Excuse me, Karl . . . Everything's got muddled in my head . . . You're probably right, as always . . . I don't understand calculations and I believe you . . . But they're not willing to marry us! That I've understood! . . . And I'm leaving. Don't be angry, my dear. I'm tired . . .

BURGOMASTER: Baron, you shouldn't make mock of the woman who loves you! For her sake, for your family's sake, can't you acknowledge that today is a regular day—the one that's in the calendar?!

MUNCHAUSEN: But how can I do that? Anything you want, except lies! I'll agree to anything, but I'll never say white is black and the thirty-second is the first.

BURGOMASTER: That means you don't love Frau Martha!

MUNCHAUSEN: That's not true!

MARTHA: Of course, Karl . . . You love me—I know that . . . But at the same time you won't forgo anything for my sake . . . Do you remember when we met Shakespeare and he said: "All lovers swear to fulfill more than they can, but they don't fulfill even that which is possible . . ."?

MUNCHAUSEN: He said that in the heat of the moment. In any case, do you remember, he then added: "Obstacles to love only intensify it!"?

MARTHA: We have too many obstacles! I can't deal with them. Lord! Why didn't you marry Joan of Arc? She'd have agreed.

MUNCHAUSEN: I knew that I'd meet Martha.

MARTHA: What if you mistook her for someone else? . . . What if your Martha is somewhere far away or not yet born? . . . Don't demand from me more than I'm capable of . . . Do you know what I dream about?

MUNCHAUSEN: Of course. We always do it together.

MARTHA: No! Now, I sometimes dream alone . . . I dream that there might be a day when nothing happens.

MUNCHAUSEN: That's terrible!

MARTHA: Probably! . . . But I dream of such a day . . . I'm not suited for the thirty-second! [*Suddenly she shouts.*] I don't want it!

MUNCHAUSEN: You don't want it?! You don't want another day of spring? The very last day? . . . The whole sunrise and sunset . . . an extra noon . . . thousands of new seconds . . . You don't want all of that?!

MARTHA: No. And that's why I'm leaving . . . [*She picks up her traveling case.*]

MUNCHAUSEN: Wait! What the hell's going on? . . . You can't just suddenly leave like this!

BURGOMASTER: You yourself are to blame for this, Baron. You simply cannot violate the order of things . . .

MUNCHAUSEN: A fine order! I asked to get a divorce from Jakobine and I get separated from Martha.

BURGOMASTER: Your yourself are to blame . . .

MUNCHAUSEN: But I only spoke the truth!

BURGOMASTER: To hell with the truth! . . . Sometimes you can tell lies. My God, to think I have to explain such simple things to Munchausen. One could lose one's mind!

MUNCHAUSEN [*to* MARTHA]: Is that what you think too?

[MARTHA *is silent.*]

No, no, don't say anything . . . I'll understand everything myself . . . [*He goes up to her and looks into her eyes.*] So . . . All right! Let it be as you wish. What must I do, Mr. Burgomaster?

BURGOMASTER: I don't know whether it's possible to set things right now.

MUNCHAUSEN: Come on . . . There's always a way to extricate oneself . . . You have so much experience . . .

BURGOMASTER: We can try, of course . . . But above all you must acknowledge that today is the first of June.

MUNCHAUSEN [*indifferently*]: Even the tenth . . .

BURGOMASTER [*indignantly*]: Not the tenth, but the first! Please don't do me any favors! . . . Furthermore, we'll have to persuade the Reverend to repeat the ceremony . . . That will be the hardest thing. I tried to talk with him after the hearing, but he was seething with indignation . . .

MUNCHAUSEN: The old hypocrite!

BURGOMASTER [*severely*]: Calm down! . . . After long exhortation, I did manage to convince him of a few things . . . In short, he might agree to repeat the divorce ceremony if you renounce everything . . .

MUNCHAUSEN: Everything?

BURGOMASTER: *Everything!* . . . All your blasphemous fantasies. Don't scowl at me—that was his expression . . . You'll have to acknowledge that it's all falsehood . . . Like an unsuccessful joke. Moreover, you'll need to do this in writing.

MUNCHAUSEN: In writing!

BURGOMASTER: Of course! You lied in writing, and now you must renounce your words in writing . . .

MUNCHAUSEN: I won't be able to write a second book. I spent my whole life on this one.

BURGOMASTER: No one's asking you to write a book. Everything should be written in the form of an official document: "I, Baron von Munchausen, declare that I am an ordinary man, I did not travel to the moon, I did not ride on cannonballs, did not pull myself out of a swamp by my hair . . ." And so on, addressing all points.

MUNCHAUSEN [*to Martha*]: Do you also believe this?

MARTHA: I don't know . . . Perhaps, it'll be better if I leave?

MUNCHAUSEN [*pensively*]: No, no, without you I'd be worse off than without myself . . . I'll write it all, Mr. Burgomaster! . . . How did you put it: "I, Baron von Munchausen, declare that I am an ordinary man . . ." It sounds like the beginning of a romance . . . Nothing terrible about it.

BURGOMASTER: Well, of course, my dear man. What's so special about it? Galileo also renounced his position!

MUNCHAUSEN: And that's why I love Giordano Bruno more . . . But one can't compare, for there everything was more significant and terrible . . . I remember the flames at the stake well . . . Here it's all simpler . . . "I, Baron von Munchausen, an ordinary man, did not travel to the Moon . . ." Ah, how beautiful the moon is, Mr. Burgomaster. If only you could see it . . . White mountains and red rocks in the setting sun . . . I didn't fly to it! . . . And I didn't ride on cannonballs during that terrible fight with the Turks, when half of my regiment perished and they drove us into that devil's swamp, but we stood our ground and hit them from the flank, and at that moment my horse stumbled and started to sink, and it was when the vile green slush started to flow into my mouth and I was choking that I seized my own hair and yanked . . . And then soared over the sedge! I'd demonstrate this for you right now, Mr. Burgomaster, but my hand is already weak and there's nothing to pull at . . . [*He removes his wig.*] I'll write it all, ladies and gentlemen! If no one needs the thirty-second, then that's that . . . On such a day it's difficult to live, but easy to die . . . In five minutes there'll no longer be a Baron Munchausen. You may stand up to honor his memory! . . . [*He heads for his study.*]

BURGOMASTER: Now, now, well, my dear sir. There's no need to be so tragic. In any case, the whole town will stop laughing at you.

MUNCHAUSEN: Not laughing, but making fun of. These are two different things! [*Enters his study.*]

BURGOMASTER [*with a sigh of relief*]: Phew! . . . Looks as if we made him change his mind . . . I simply can't believe it . . . Honestly, I'm all in a sweat!

[MARTHA, *not listening to him, quickly approaches the study.*]

Don't distract him, Frau Martha, let him write . . .

MARTHA [*rattling the door handle, which turns out to be locked*]: Karl, let me in! You hear me? . . . Open up!

BURGOMASTER [*in fear*]: Why has he locked himself in? [*Rushes over to the door.*] Baron, do you hear me? Your Excellency! Open up immediately! I order you! . . . As a superior in rank . . . Baron!

MARTHA [*weeping, on her knees by the door*]: Karl! Don't! . . . I implore you!

BURGOMASTER [*pounding on the door*]: Your Excellency! What are you doing in there?!

[*From behind the door a loud shot is heard.* MARTHA *faints.* THOMAS *appears with a tray.*]

THOMAS: Frau Martha, I didn't hear—what time is it?

End of Part One

1976

TRANSLATORS AND SOURCES

All tales in part 1 except "The Magic Mirror" and "The Magic Ring" were translated by Helena Goscilo from A. N. Afanas'ev, *Narodnye russkie skazki A. N. Afanas'eva v 3-kh tomakh* (Moscow: Gosudarstvennoe izdatel'stvo khudozhestvennoi literatury, 1957).

"The Magic Mirror" was translated by Seth Graham from A. N. Afanas'ev, "Volshebnoe zerkal'tse," in *Narodnye russkie skazki A. N. Afanas'eva v 3-kh tomakh* (Moscow: Gosudarstvennoe izdatel'stvo khudozhestvennoi literatury, 1957), 2:126–33.

"The Magic Ring" was translated by Helena Goscilo from A. N. Afanas'ev, "Volshebnoe kol'tso," in *Narodnye russkie skazki ne dlia pechati, zavetnye poslovitsy i pogovorki, sobrannye i obrabotannye A. N. Afanas'evym 1857–1862*, ed. O. B. Alekseeva et al. (Moscow: Ladomir, 1997): 77–83.

"Tale of the Military Secret, Malchish-Kibalchish and His Solemn Word" was translated by Helena Goscilo from Arkadii Gaidar, "Skazka o voennoi taine, o Mal'chishe i ego tverdom slove," in his *Sobranie sochinenii v 4-kh tomakh* (Moscow: Gosudarstvennoe izdatel'stvo detskoi literatury, 1959), 2:180–92.

The Golden Key, or The Adventures of Buratino (excerpts) was adapted from Aleksey Tolstoy, *The Golden Key, or The Adventures of Buratino*, trans. Eric Hartley (London: Hutchinson's Books for Young People, 1947). The Russian text is Aleksei Tolstoi, "Zolotoi kliuchik, ili prikliucheniia Buratino," in his *Sobranie sochinenii v 10-ti tomakh* (Moscow: Khudozhestvennaia literatura, 1960), 8:180–259.

The Old Genie Khottabych (excerpts) was adapted from L. I. Lagin, *The Old Genie Hottabych*, trans. Faina Solasko (Moscow: Foreign Language Publishing House, 1973). The Russian text appears in Lazar' Lagin, *Starik Khottabych. Povest'-skazka* (Moscow: Gosudarstvennoe izdatel'stvo detskoi literatury, 1970).

"The Malachite Casket" was adapted from P. P. Bazhov, *Malachite Casket: Tales from the Urals*, trans. Eve Manning (Moscow: Foreign Language Publishing House, 1949). The Russian text appears in P. Bazhov, *Malakhitovaia shkatulka* (Moscow: Khudozhestvennaia literatura, 1961).

"The Flower of Seven Colors" was translated by Christopher Hunter and Larissa Rudova from Valentin Kataev, "Tsevetik-semitsvetik," in his *Sobranie sochinenii v 9-i tomakh* (Moscow: Khudozhestvennaia literatura, 1968), 1:573–79.

Fairy Tales for Grown-Up Children (excerpts) was translated by Seth Graham from Evgenii Zamiatin, *Bol'shim detiam skazki* (St. Petersburg and Berlin: Izdatel'stvo Z. I. Grzhebina, 1922).

The Dragon (excerpts) was adapted from Eugene Schwarz, *The Dragon*, trans. Elizabeth Reynolds Hapgood (New York: Theatre Arts Books, 1963). The Russian text, *Drakon*, appears in Evgenii Shvarts, *Drakon. Klad. Ten'. Dva klena. Obyknovennoe chudo, i drugie proizvedeniia* (Moscow: Gud'ial, 1998), 269–339.

"Tale of the Troika" (excerpts) was adapted from Arkady Strugatsky and Boris Strugatsky, *Roadside Picnic, Tale of the Troika*, trans. Antonina W. Bouis (New York and London: Macmillan, 1977). The Russian text, "Skazka o troike," appears in Arkadii Strugatskii and Boris Strugatskii, *Ponedel'nik nachinaetsia v subbotu. Skazka o troike* (Moscow: Tekst, 1992).

"Before the Cock Crows Thrice" (excerpts) was adapted from Vasily Shukshin, *Roubles in Words, Kopeks in Figures, and Other Stories,* trans. Natasha Ward and David Iliffe (London and New York: Marion Boyars, 1985), 108–62. The Russian text, "Do tret'ikh petukhov," appears in Vasilii Shukshin, *Sobranie sochinenii v 3-kh tomakh* (Moscow: Molodaia gvardiia, 1985), 3:496–544.

That Very Munchausen (part 1) was translated by Christopher Hunter and Larissa Rudova from Grigorii Gorin, *Tot samyi Miunkhausen,* in his *Komicheskaia fantaziia* (Moscow: Sovetskii pisatel', 1986).